SARAH MORGAN

Holiday in the Hamptons

HQN™

ISBN-13: 978-0-373-80399-6

Recycling programs
for this product may
not exist in your area.

Holiday in the Hamptons

www.HQNBooks.com

Printed in U.S.A.

Dear Reader,

I love writing about friendship, especially friendship between sisters. My heroine in *Holiday in the Hamptons*, Fliss, is a twin, but she couldn't be more different from her sister, Harriet. What could be more interesting than two people who are identical on the outside and yet totally different on the inside? Fliss is a fighter and protective of her sister, but deep down she has her own vulnerabilities. When her ex-husband appears on the scene, she's forced to confront issues she thought she'd left behind. But Fliss isn't the same person she was at eighteen (are any of us?) and she is about to learn just how much time, and life, alter things.

This book explores how relationships change—not just romantic relationships, but the relationship between grandmother and granddaughter, sister and sister (and woman and dog!), all against the backdrop of the ocean and sand dunes.

My first glimpse of the Hamptons was from a plane, and I was captivated by the long stretches of sandy beaches, dunes and the yachts studding the sparkling ocean. It's a favorite place for New Yorkers looking to escape the madness of the city, and it seemed like the perfect place to set a summer book.

Wherever you are this summer, I hope this book gives you the perfect escape.

Love,

Sarah

xxxx

To Flo, with love and thanks for all the insight into life as a twin. You're the best.

"The human heart has hidden treasures,
In secret kept, in silence sealed;
The thoughts, the hopes, the dreams, the pleasures,
Whose charms were broken if revealed."
—Charlotte Brontë

PROLOGUE

AS EIGHTEENTH BIRTHDAYS WENT, it had to be the worst ever.

Fliss ran through the overgrown garden that wrapped itself around three sides of the beach house. She didn't feel the sharp sting of nettles or the whip of the long grass against her bare calves because she was already feeling too many other things. Bigger things.

The old rusty gate scraped her hip as she pushed her way through it. Misery fueled every stride as she took the grassy path that ran through the dunes to the beach. No one could catch her now. She'd find a place away from everyone. Away from *him*. And she wasn't returning home until he'd left. The birthday cake would stay uneaten, the candles unlit, the plates untouched. There would be no singing, no salutations, no celebration. What was there to celebrate?

Fury licked around the edges of her misery, and underneath anger and misery was hurt. A hurt she worked hard never to show. *Never let a bully see you're afraid. Never let yourself be vulnerable.* Wasn't that what her brother had taught her? And her father, she'd worked out long before, was a bully.

If she'd had to find one word to describe him it would be *angry*. And she'd never understood it. She got mad from time to time, so did her brother, but there was always a cause. With her father, there was no cause for the anger. It was as if he rose in the morning and bathed in it.

Words pounded in her head, matching the rhythm of her strides. *Hate him, hate him, hate him...*

Her feet hit the sand. The wind lifted her hair. She gulped in another breath and tasted sea and salt air. Squeezing her eyes against the tears, she tried to replace the sound of her father's voice with the familiar soundtrack of seagulls and surf.

It should have been a perfect summer's day, but her father had a way of sucking the sunshine out of the sunniest day, and no day was exempt. Not even the day you turned eighteen. He always knew how to make her feel bad.

She tried to outrun her feelings, her breath tearing in her chest and her heart pounding like fists on a punching bag.

You're nothing but trouble. Useless, no good, worthless, stupid—

If she was as worthless as he believed then she should probably run into the ocean, but he'd be pleased to be free of her, and she was damned if she was going to do a single thing that might please him.

Lately she'd made it her life's focus to live down to the low opinion he had of her, not because she wanted to make trouble but because his rules just didn't make sense and pleasing him was impossible.

The cruelest part was that he wasn't even supposed to be here.

The summer months were their oasis of time away from him. Time spent with her siblings, her mother and her grandmother while her father stayed in the city and took his anger to work every day.

She'd grown to love those precious weeks when sunlight burst through the darkness and all she trailed into the house was sand and laughter. They stayed up late and woke in the mornings feeling lighter and happier. Some days they carried their breakfast to the beach and ate it there right by the ocean. This morning's choice, her birthday breakfast, had been a basket of ripe peaches. She'd been wiping the juice from her chin when she'd heard the wheels of her father's car crunch on the gravel of the beach house.

Her twin sister had turned pale. Her peach had slid slowly from her fingers and thudded onto the sand, the fruit instantly transformed from smooth to gritty. *Like life*, Fliss had thought, hiding her dismay.

Her mother had panicked, thrusting her feet into her shoes while trying to tame wind-blown hair with a hand that shook like the branch of a tree in a storm. During the summer she was a different woman. An outsider might have thought the changes were a result of the relaxed pace of beach life, but Fliss knew it was due to being away from their father.

And now he was here. Intruding on their blissful beach idyll.

Her brother, calm as always, had taken control. It was probably just a delivery, he'd said. A neighbor.

But they all knew it wasn't a delivery or a neighbor. Their father drove the same way he did everything, angrily, revving the engine and sending small stones flying. *Angry* was his calling card.

Fliss knew it was him, and the sweet-tasting peach turned bitter in her mouth. She was used to her father ruining every part of her life, but now he was ruining summer, too?

The cloudless blue sky seemed hazed with gloom, and she knew that until he left again she was going to be dragging her bad mood around like a ball and chain.

She was determined to see him as little as possible, which was why she'd chosen the beach over her bedroom.

Her flip-flops hampered her pace, so she slowed and kicked them off. This time when she ran her feet were silent, the sand cool and smooth under her soles. In the distance she could see the white mist of surf erupting over rock, and she could hear the crash and hiss of waves advancing and retreating.

Somewhere in the far distance someone called her name, and she quickened her pace.

She didn't want to see anyone. Not like this, when she was raw and vulnerable. She always kept her feelings inside, but right now there didn't seem to be room for them all. They filled the space around her heart, made her head ache and her eyes sting. She wasn't going to cry. She never cried. She wouldn't give him the satisfaction. If her eyes were watering, it was because of the wind.

"Fliss!"

She heard her name again and almost missed her stride because this time she recognized the voice. Seth Carlyle. Oldest son of Matthew and Catherine Carlyle. Old money. Wealthy, successful, smart and decent. Classy. No skeletons in *that* family. No raised voices or kids quivering in fear. She was willing to bet Catherine Carlyle didn't virtually crawl around the walls in order to prevent herself drawing the attention of her husband, and she could never in a million years imagine Matthew Carlyle raising his voice. In the Carlyle house, plates would be a vessel for food, not a weapon for throwing. And she was sure Seth had never made his father feel ashamed or disgusted. He was the golden boy.

He was also her brother's friend. If he knew she was upset, he'd tell her brother and Daniel would once again step between her and their father. His protective instincts had put him in the firing line on more occasions than Fliss wanted to count. She didn't mind him doing it for her twin because when Harriet was stressed her stammer got so bad she couldn't always speak for herself, but Fliss didn't want him to do it for her. She could fight her own battles, and right now she felt like fighting to the death.

Ignoring Seth's voice, she kept running. He wouldn't follow her. He'd return to the group and join them in a game of beach volleyball, or maybe they'd surf or swim. Things she'd planned to do today, before her father had arrived unexpectedly for the weekend and ruined it all.

She ran until she reached the rocks. She clambered over jagged edges without pausing, ignored the sharp sting in the palm of her hand and landed on the smooth sand on the other side.

She'd been visiting this part of the Hamptons since she was born, and the summers that she, her twin and her brother had spent with their grandmother had given her the only happy memories of her childhood.

"Fliss?" It was Seth again, and this time his voice was deeper, lower, *closer.*

Damn. "Leave me alone, Seth."

He didn't. Instead, he vaulted down from the rocks, lithe and athletic, his shoulders blocking out the sun. He was wearing nothing but board shorts. His chest was bare and glistened with droplets of water. He was on the swim team at college, and the four summers he'd spent as a lifeguard had given him muscles in all the right places. Everyone on the island knew about the time Seth Carlyle had risked his own life to save two young kids who had ignored the warnings and stupidly taken an inflatable out onto the ocean. That was the kind of guy Seth was. He did the right thing.

She only ever did the wrong thing.

Fliss had spent the summer listening to the other girls lusting after Seth, and it wasn't hard to understand what they saw in him. He was smart and good-humored, self-assured without being cocky. And sexy. Insanely sexy, with that lean, powerful body and skin that turned golden at the first touch of the sun. His hair and his eyes were dark as jet, a legacy from his grandfather's side of the family, who were Italian. He was the same age as her brother, which made him too old for her. Her father would freak at the five-year age gap. *Girls your age should date boys, not men.*

As she watched Seth stroll toward her, she felt her muscles clench. Clearly her libido hadn't gotten the memo. Either that, or sexual attraction was no respecter of ages.

Or maybe she wanted him *because* she knew her father would freak.

He planted himself in front of her. "What's wrong?"

How could he tell that something was wrong? She'd had years of practice at hiding her feelings, but Seth always seemed to see through the layers of protection that blinded everyone else to the truth.

She'd joked to Harriet that he was like an X-ray machine, or an MRI scanner, but the truth was he was just scarily perceptive. Or perhaps what she should really say was that he was perceptive, and she was scared.

If she'd wanted people to know how bad she felt most of the time, she would have told them.

"Nothing is wrong." She didn't mention the fight with her father. She never talked about it with anyone. She didn't want people to know. She didn't want sympathy. She didn't want pity. Most of all she didn't want people knowing how bad those fights with her father made her feel, not just because she'd learned to hide her feelings, but because part of her was afraid that saying the words aloud might give them credence. She didn't want to give voice to the niggling thought that maybe her father was right. That she might actually be as worthless and useless as he believed her to be.

But Seth wasn't so easily deflected. "Are you sure? Because you don't look like a woman celebrating her eighteenth birthday."

Woman.

He'd called her a woman.

It made her giddy. Right there and then, she felt the age gap evaporate. Poise and power replaced doubt and insecurity. "I wanted time to myself."

"On your birthday? That doesn't sound right to me. No one should spend their birthday alone, especially not an eighteenth birthday."

She'd known Seth for years, but they'd grown closer than ever this summer. Unlike her father, Seth never seemed outraged by her antics. When she'd gone skinny-dipping in the ocean late at night, her twin, Harriet, had begged her not to go, but Seth had simply laughed. He hadn't joined her, but he'd waited on the rocks until she returned safely. *Because Seth Carlyle always does the right thing.*

Still, he hadn't judged or lectured, simply handed her a towel and sprang down onto the sand as if his job was done. He never touched her, and she'd wished a million times that he would, even though she knew he was watching over her because he was Daniel's friend and a responsible person.

She found herself wishing it again now. Which proved she was anything but a responsible person.

To be sure she didn't give in to temptation and fling her arms around him, she wrapped them around herself.

His gaze dropped. "You've cut your hand. You should be more careful on these rocks. Does it hurt?"

"No." She snatched her hands behind her back, one half of her hoping he'd leave while the other half hoped he'd stay.

"If it doesn't hurt, why are you crying?"

Was she crying? She brushed her cheek with the heel of her hand and discovered that they were wet. "I kicked sand in my eyes when I was running."

He thought she was upset because of the wounds he could see.

He had no idea about the wounds she kept hidden.

"Why were you running?" He closed his hands over her arms and drew them gently in front of her. Then he turned her hands over so he could examine them. His fingers were broad and strong, and her hand looked small in his. Delicate.

She didn't ever want to be delicate. Her mother was delicate. Watching her navigate her stormy marriage was like watching a single daisy struggling to stay upright in a hurricane. Fliss wanted to be hardy, like a thornbush. The sort of plant people treated with respect and care. And she was fiercely determined to earn a good living so that she would never, ever find herself trapped in the situation her mother had found herself in.

If I leave your father, I'll lose you. He'd make sure I don't get custody, and I don't have the money or influence to fight that.

Seth bent his head, and she watched as strands of dark hair flopped over his forehead. She itched to touch it, to slide her fingers through it, to feel its softness under her hands. And she wanted to touch the thick muscles of his shoulders, even though she already knew they wouldn't be soft. They were everything hard and powerful. She knew that for sure because last summer someone had tossed her in the water and it had been Seth who had hauled her out. Being held by him was something that no woman would forget in a hurry.

Unsettled, she dragged her gaze to his face. His nose had a slight bump in it thanks to a football injury the summer before, and he had a scar on his chin where he'd head-butted a surfboard and needed fourteen stitches.

Fliss didn't care. To her, Seth Carlyle was pretty much the most perfect thing she'd ever laid eyes on.

There was something that set him apart from the others. It wasn't just that he was older, more that he was so *sure*. He knew what he wanted. He was focused. He made doing the right thing sexy. He was studying to be a vet, and she knew he'd be good at it. He was going to make his father proud.

Unlike her.

She'd made her father disdainful, exasperated and angry but never proud.

And she didn't want to drag Seth down with her.

She snatched her hand away from his and curled her fingers into her palm to stop herself from touching him. "You should join the others. You're wasting a perfect beach day."

"I'm not wasting anything. I'm exactly where I want to be." His gaze was focused exclusively on her. And then he gave her that wide, easy smile that made her feel as if she was the only woman on the planet. She didn't know which got to her most—the way his mouth curved, or the way those sleepy dark eyes crinkled slightly at the corners.

Her stomach flipped. After being made to feel unwanted, it was a change to feel the opposite.

What would happen if she put her arms around his neck and kissed him? Would he get carried away and do the wrong thing for the first time in his life? Maybe he'd take her virginity right here on the sand. That would really give her father something to complain about.

The thought made her frown. Not even by virtue of a thought did she want her father to tarnish her relationship with Seth.

"You really shouldn't be here. With me." She leaned her back against the rock and gave him a fierce stare designed to repel, but it didn't work with Seth.

"I saw a car outside your house. Was it your father? He doesn't usually join you in the summer, does he?"

She felt as if she'd plunged naked into the Atlantic. "He arrived this morning. Decided to surprise us."

Seth's gaze didn't shift. "To celebrate your birthday or ruin it?"

He knew.

She squirmed with horror and embarrassment. Why

couldn't she have a normal family like everyone else? "I didn't hang around to find out."

"Maybe he wanted to deliver his gift in person."

"That's your father, not mine." The words blurted out of her mouth before she could stop them. "Mine didn't bring a gift."

"No? Then it's a good thing I did." He braced one arm on the rock behind her and reached into the pocket of his board shorts with the other. "Hope you like it."

She dragged her gaze from the swell of his biceps and stared at the cream velvet pouch in his palm. "You bought me a gift?"

"It's not every day a woman turns eighteen."

There it was again, that word. *Woman*. And he'd bought her a gift. Actually *chosen* her something. He wouldn't have done that if he didn't care, would he?

Her parched self-esteem sucked up the much-needed affirmation. She felt dizzy and light-headed, even more so than she had the time she'd smuggled a bottle of vodka to the beach.

"What is it?"

"Open it and see."

She took the bag from him, recognizing the shell logo picked out in silver. She knew that whatever was inside it wouldn't have come cheap. She and Harriet had walked past the exclusive jewelry store when they had occasion to be in town, but the prices had stopped them even staring in through the window. Of course, price wasn't an issue if your name was Carlyle.

She tipped it out of the bag onto her palm, and for a moment she forgot to breathe because she'd never seen anything so pretty. It was a necklace, a silver shell on a silver chain. It was the shiniest, most perfect gift she'd ever been given.

Forgetting about keeping her distance, she flung her arms around him. He smelled of sunshine, sea salt and man. Hot, sexy man. Too late she remembered that she was wearing only her tiny shorts and a tank top. She might as well have been wearing nothing for all the barrier it created. Her skin slid against his and her fingers closed on those shoulders. Under the silken, sun-bronzed skin she felt the dip and swell of hard muscle and the dangerously delicious pressure of his body.

She knew she should let him go. Her father would freak if he could see her. He hated her hanging out with boys.

But Seth wasn't a boy, was he? Seth was a man. A man who recognized that she was a woman. The first person to see her that way, and she decided that just might be the greatest birthday gift of all time.

Her father made her feel like nothing, but Seth—Seth made her feel like something. Everything.

"Fliss—" His voice was husky and his hands slid to her hips, holding her still. "We shouldn't—you're upset—"

"Not anymore." Before he could say anything else, she pressed her mouth to his. She felt the coolness of his lips and his sudden start of shock, and she thought to herself that if he pulled away she'd die of embarrassment right here on the sand.

But he didn't pull away. Instead he tugged her against him with purposeful hands, trapping her against the solid length of his body. Behind her she could hear the rush of the ocean, but here in the privacy of the dunes there was only Seth and the indescribable magic of that first kiss.

As he angled his head and kissed her back, she thought that her eighteenth birthday had gone from being the worse day of her life to the best. Melting under the erotic slide of his tongue and the intimate stroke of his hands, she stopped thinking about her father. All she could think about was the way Seth's mouth made her feel. Who would have thought it? Who would have thought that good-boy Seth had such a bad-boy side? Where had he learned to kiss like this?

She told herself that she deserved romance on her eighteenth birthday. She deserved *this*.

Never before had anyone, or anything, made her feel this way.

And never before had doing the wrong thing ever felt so right.

CHAPTER ONE

Ten years later...

"I'VE DECIDED WE should expand the business." Fliss kicked off her shoes and left them in the middle of the floor as she walked barefoot to the kitchen. "Have you looked at our schedule for the next month? We don't have a single available slot. Our referrals have doubled, and bookings are through the roof. Time to capitalize on success and think about growth." Onward and upward, she thought. It felt good.

Her sister, busy feeding a puppy she was fostering, was less enthusiastic. "We already cover the whole of the east side of Manhattan."

"I know, and I'm not suggesting we expand the dog-walking part of the business." She'd thought it over, studied the competition and run the numbers. Her head was filled with possibilities. "I think we should branch out into an area that has a better profit margin. Offer additional services."

"Like what?" Harriet pulled the puppy closer. "We're a dog-walking business. The Bark Rangers. You're thinking of branching into cats? The Meow Movers?"

"We already feed and care for cats if the owner requests it. I'm talking about pet sitting. Overnight stays. Holiday cover." That part got her sister's attention.

"You want me to stay overnight in a stranger's home? Forget it."

"*Obviously* the stranger won't be there. If the owner is in residence they're not going to need pet sitting."

"I still don't like the sound of it." Harriet wrinkled her nose. "I like my own home. And if I do that, how do I foster?"

"I haven't worked that part out yet." And she knew better than to suggest her sister reduce her fostering commitment. There was no way Harriet would ever turn her back on an animal in trouble.

And she didn't want her sister unhappy.

She'd grown up protecting Harriet. First from her father, and then from anyone and everything that threatened her twin.

It was protecting Harriet that had given her the idea of starting the business in the first place, and if she was going to expand then she needed to introduce the idea gradually.

She checked her phone for new bookings. "All I'm saying is that I'd like to look at the business more broadly. You don't need to worry."

"I'm not worried, exactly. But I don't understand where this is coming from. Have we had a complaint about one of our dog walkers or something?"

"No. Our dog walkers are the best on the planet. Mostly because you have an uncanny instinct for sensing when someone doesn't really like animals. Our screening process is excellent, and our attrition rate is close to zero."

"So why the sudden change?"

"It's not sudden. When you're running your own business it's important to evolve. There's a lot of competition out there." She'd seen just how much competition, but she didn't share that with Harriet. No sense in worrying her.

"But you've said yourself that plenty of people who set up as dog walkers are unreliable. People are not going to trust their beloved pets with an unreliable walker. We've never lost a client. Never. Clients trust us."

"And they will trust us in their homes, too, which is why I think we should extend the service we're offering. I'm considering running obedience classes, too. I can think of a few dogs who might benefit."

Harriet grinned. "Who was it this time? Dog or owner?"

"Dog. Name of Angel."

"The poodle? Belongs to that magazine editor?"

"That's the one." The thought of it had Fliss rolling her eyes. She didn't share Harriet's tolerance when it came to misbehaving dogs. "If ever a dog was misnamed, it's that one. He may be an angel on the outside, but on the inside he's all devil."

"I agree, but I don't see why one badly behaved canine would make you question our entire business. Our business is fine, Fliss. You've done well."

"*We've* done well." Fliss emphasized the *we* and saw Harriet flush.

"Mostly you."

"That's rubbish. Do you really think I would have come this far without you?"

"You bring in all the business. You handle the finances and all the difficult phone calls."

"And you make the animals so happy, and their owners so happy, that our word-of-mouth recommendations are through the roof. It's *our* business, Harry. We're a team. We've done well, but now I intend to do better."

Harriet sighed. "Why? What are you trying to prove?"

"I'm not trying to prove anything. Is it wrong to want to grow the business?"

"No, if that's what you really want, but I'd like taking the time to enjoy my job. I don't always want to be rushing to the next thing. And if we expand, we'd have to find premises."

"Way ahead of you. I thought we could look for something that also has space for an office. Then our apartment might not be flooded with paperwork and I might actually be able to find my bed. And the coffee machine." She glanced from her phone to the stack of papers on the countertop. It seemed to grow every day. "There used to be a coffee machine hidden somewhere here. With luck I might find it before I die of caffeine withdrawal."

"I moved it. I had to put it out of Sunny's reach. He's chewing everything he can find." With the puppy still tucked under one arm, Harriet stood up. She pushed Fliss's shoes to the side of the room and then walked to the kitchen and scooped up the papers. "There's a message on the machine. I didn't get to it in time. New business call."

"I'll call them back. I know you hate talking to strangers on the phone." Fliss grabbed an energy bar from the cupboard and saw her twin frown. "Don't look at me like that. At least I'm eating."

"You could eat something wholesome."

"This is wholesome." She flicked the button on the coffee machine. "So going back to my plan—"

"I don't want to spend the night in someone else's apartment. I like my own bed. We'd have to recruit, and that would be expensive. Could we even afford it?"

"If you'd been paying attention at our last company meeting, you wouldn't be asking me that question."

"Was that the 'meeting' where we had take-out pizza and I had to bottle-feed those kittens?"

"Same one."

"Then I don't think I gave you my full attention. Just give me the top line."

"It's the bottom line that should interest you, and the bottom line is looking good." Fliss poured coffee into two mugs, her head buzzing. With each new success, the buzz seemed to grow. "Better than our wildest dreams." She eyed her sister. "Not that you're the wild-dream type."

"Hey, I have wild dreams!"

"Are you naked in them and writhing on silk sheets with a hot, naked guy?"

Harriet turned pink. "No."

"Then trust me, your dreams aren't wild." Fliss took a mouthful of coffee and felt the caffeine bounce through her system.

"My dreams are no less valid than yours just because the content is different." Harriet settled the puppy in his basket. "Dreams are to do with wanting and needing."

"As I said—naked, silk sheets, hot guy."

"There are other types of wanting and needing. I'm not interested in a single night of sex."

"Hey, if he was hot enough I'd be willing to stretch it out a few days, at least until we're both dying of thirst or starvation."

"How are you ever my twin?"

"I ask myself the same question frequently." About as frequently as she counted her blessings. How did people survive without a twin? If her childhood had felt like being trapped in a windowless room, Harriet had been the oxygen. Together they'd discovered a problem really did seem smaller if it was shared, as if they could carry half each and make it weigh less. And if Fliss knew, deep down, that her sister shared more than she did, she comforted herself with the knowledge that she was protecting Harriet. It was something she'd done all her life. "It's because I'm your twin that I know your dreams as well as I do my own. Yours would be a white clapboard beach house, picket fence, a sexy doctor who adores you and a menagerie of animals. Forget it. If you want that kind of relationship, you're going to need to read about it in a book. And now back to business. I think the Bark Rangers could legitimately offer pet sitting and even possibly dog grooming and obedience training. Think of it as an extension of what we do. We can offer packages where we—"

"Wait a minute." Harriet frowned. "Are you saying you think romance only exists in books?"

"The type of romance *you* want only exists in books."

"You only have to look at our brother to know that isn't true."

"Daniel fell in love with Molly. There's only one Molly. And they're basically together because their dogs are best friends." She caught her twin's eye and shrugged. "All right, they seem happy, but they're the exception, and it's probably because Molly is a relationship expert. That gives her an unfair advantage over the rest of us."

"Maybe instead of expanding the business, you could

take more time for yourself. You've been working at top speed since we started this business. It's been five years, and you've hardly paused to breathe."

"Six years." Fliss grabbed a yogurt out of the fridge. "And why would I want time to myself? I love being busy. Busy is my drug of choice. And I love our business. We have freedom. Choices." She nudged the door shut with her bare foot and saw Harriet wince.

"I love our business, too, but I also like the parts of my life that have nothing to do with the business. You've made a huge success of it, Fliss." She hesitated. "You don't have anything to prove."

"I'm not proving anything." The lie slid off her tongue while the voice inside her head shouted more loudly than usual. *Useless, worthless, never make anything of yourself...*

"Don't you ever want more out of life?"

"More?" Fliss thrust a spoon into the yogurt, deciding it was time she shifted the conversation. This was starting to feel uncomfortable. "I'm young, free, single and living in New York City. What more is there? I have the world at my feet. Life is perfect. I mean, seriously, could life *be* any more perfect?"

Harriet looked at her steadily. "You didn't do it, did you?"

Fliss's heart started to pound. Her appetite vanished.

This, she thought, was one of the disadvantages of having a twin. She could hide the way she was feeling from everyone else in the world, but not from her sister.

She put her yogurt down and decided she needed to work harder at it. She didn't want Harriet to know that she was terrified. It would make her anxious. "I was going to, I really was. I had the building in sight and I'd memorized what I was going to say—"

"But?"

"My feet wouldn't go that way. They were glued to the spot. Then they turned around and walked in the opposite direction. I tried arguing with them. I said, *'Feet, what do you think you're doing?'* But did they listen? No." And since when had she been so pathetic? She gave what she hoped passed for a careless shrug. "Please don't say what I know you're about to say."

"What was I about to say?"

"You were going to gently point out that it's been three weeks since Daniel bumped into him—"

"Seth," Harriet said. "At least say his name. That would be a start."

The start of what? She didn't want to start something she'd worked hard to put behind her.

And she couldn't blame her sister for pushing because she hadn't been honest, had she? She hadn't told Harriet how she felt.

"Seth—" His name stuck in her throat. "It's been three weeks since Daniel bumped into him—*Seth*—at the vet practice. The plan was that I'd take control of the situation and go and see him in order to avoid an awkward encounter in the street."

"You've changed the plan?"

"Not officially. It's more that the plan isn't working out. It's awkward." It was okay to admit that much, wasn't it? Finding something awkward wasn't as bad as finding it terrifying. "And I don't think an encounter in the street could be any more uncomfortable than a face-to-face in the clinic."

"I can imagine it feels a little awkward, but—"

"A little awkward? That's like calling a hurricane a light breeze. This isn't a little awkward, it's mega awkward, it's—" She floundered for a description and gave up. "Forget it. No word has been invented that correctly reflects this situation." And even if it had, she wouldn't be using it. She didn't want Harriet to know how bad she felt.

"'This situation' being bumping into your ex."

"You manage to make a highly complex and delicate situation sound simple."

"That's probably the best way to look at it. Don't overthink it." Harriet lowered the puppy to the floor and stood up. "It's been ten years, Fliss. I know it was a traumatic time."

"No need to dramatize it." Why was her mouth so dry? She took a glass from the cabinet and poured herself some water. "It was fine."

"It wasn't fine. But everything that happened is all in the past. You have a whole new life, and so does he."

"I never think about it." The lie came easily even though a day rarely passed when she *didn't* think about it. She also thought about what Seth's life might have looked like if he hadn't met her and occasionally, when she was indulging herself, what her life with Seth Carlyle could have looked like if the circumstances had been different.

Harriet studied her with a mixture of concern and exasperation. "Are you sure? Because it was a big deal."

"As you say, it's been ten years."

"And you haven't been seriously involved with a man since."

"Haven't met anyone who interested me." Anyone who measured up. Anyone who made her feel the way

Seth had made her feel. There were days when she wondered if what she'd felt had been real, or if her teenage brain had augmented those feelings.

"It upsets me when you don't share your feelings with me. I can understand why you hid everything from Dad, and even from Daniel, but this is *me*."

"I'm not hiding anything."

"Fliss—"

"All right, maybe I hide some things, but there's nothing I can do about that. It's the way I am."

"No. It's the way you learned to be. And we both know why." Weary, Harriet stooped to remove Fliss's shoe from the puppy's mouth.

Fliss stared at her sister, the urge to confide momentarily eclipsing her quest for privacy. "I—I think about it sometimes. About him." Why had she said that? If she opened the door a crack, her emotions were likely to come pouring out and drown everyone around her.

Harriet straightened slowly. "Which part do you think about most?"

That fateful birthday. The kiss on the beach. His mouth and hands. The laughter, the sunshine, the smell of the ocean. Passion and promise.

She could still remember it vividly. Almost as vividly as she remembered everything that had followed.

"Forget it. I don't really think about it."

"Fliss!"

"All *right*! I think about it. All of it. But I was dealing with it pretty well, until Daniel told me he'd seen Seth here in New York." You were supposed to be able to leave your past behind. What were you supposed to do when it followed you? "Do you think he knew I was living here?"

New York was a city of eight million people. Eight million busy people, all running around doing their thing. It was a city of possibilities, but one of those possibilities was to live here anonymously, blending in. It had been perfect, until the day Seth Carlyle had taken a job in the vet practice they used regularly.

"In New York? I don't know. I doubt he knew he'd be this close to you. It's not as if you've been in touch."

"No. Never been in touch." It was the only way she'd been able to cope. Put it behind her. Move on. Don't look back.

He hadn't been in touch with her either, so presumably he'd been taking the same approach.

Harriet lifted the puppy back into his basket. "I know it feels difficult, but you've built a whole new life, and he has, too."

"I know, but I wish he hadn't chosen to move his life onto *my* patch. I should be able to walk the few blocks around our apartment without having to peer around street corners like a fugitive."

"You're doing that?" The shock in her twin's eyes made her wish she'd kept that information to herself.

"I was talking hypothetically."

"If you'd done what you planned to do and just walked in there and said, 'Hi, good to see you again,' you would have cleared the air and you wouldn't be glancing over your shoulder. Things will feel easier when you've actually seen him."

"I have seen him," Fliss muttered. "He was standing in Reception when I made my first attempt to approach the building last week." It was his hair that had caught her eye first, and then the way he'd angled his head to listen to something the receptionist was saying to him.

He'd always been a good listener. It had been ten years since she'd touched him or stood close to him, but everything about him was achingly familiar.

Harriet was gaping at her. "You *saw* him? Why didn't you tell me?"

"Nothing to tell. And don't worry, he didn't see me."

"How do you know?"

"Because I dropped to the ground like a navy SEAL on a secret mission. I didn't move until I was sure he'd gone. I had to stop a passerby calling 911, which was both annoying and reassuring because usually New Yorkers are too busy doing their own thing to pay much attention to a body on the ground. Why are you gaping at me?"

"You dropped to the ground. And you're trying to pretend you're fine with this?"

"No pretense necessary." She ground her teeth. Didn't her sister have a dog to walk or something? "You're right. I have to do this. I have to meet him and get it over with." The thought of it made her heart and pulse thunder a protest. It was a fight-or-flight response, and her body seemed to be choosing flight.

"Do you want me to come with you?"

"What I really want is for you to pretend to be me so that I don't have to do it at all." She saw Harriet's eyes cloud with worry and cursed herself for saying too much. "I was joking!"

"Were you?"

"Of course. If I let you do that I'd lose the last shred of my self-respect. I have to do this by myself."

"Remember what Molly said. You should control the meeting. Make an appointment for one of the animals. That way you have a reason to be there and something

else to talk about. If it's awkward you can keep it professional."

"If?"

"Memorize one line. 'Hi, Seth, good to see you. How
are you doing?' I can't believe I'm saying this to you.
You're the one who is great with people. I'm the one
who is tongue-tied and awkward."

"You're right. It should be easy. So why isn't it?"

"Probably because you left so much unresolved."

"We're divorced. How much more resolved than that
can you get?"

"You were in love with him, Fliss."

"What? Don't be crazy. It was a teenage crush, that's
all. Sex on a beach that got a bit more hot and heavy
than we'd planned—" Her voice tailed off as she met
Harriet's unwavering gaze.

"You're doing it again. Hiding your feelings from
me."

"Believe me, you don't want a dose of my feelings."
She stiffened as Harriet stepped forward and gave her
a hug. "Oh. What's that for?" She felt her sister's arms
tighten around her.

"I hate seeing you hurt."

Which was why she never let her twin see the true
extent of her hurt. "Of course you do. You're the good
twin. I'm the bad twin."

"I hate it when you call yourself that. I would love
to have your qualities."

"You don't have room for any more qualities. You're
already loaded with them."

"I hate it when you call me 'good.' I'm not good,
and one of these days I'm going to do something really
bad to prove it."

"You couldn't be bad if you tried, although if you ever decide to give it a try I hope you'll call me. I'd like to see it. You're strangling me, Harry. I can't handle affection before I've had at least two cups of coffee." And because she didn't trust herself not to say more than she wanted to say. Harriet's affection was like a key, unlocking a part of herself she preferred to keep secured.

"You're not bad, Fliss."

"Try telling that to Seth and the rest of the Carlyle family." And to her father. "He had a glowing future until I came along." She poured herself another glass of water.

"He's a vet. His future looks just fine from where I'm standing. And why do you take all the responsibility for what happened? He made a choice, Fliss."

Had he? Remembering the details, Fliss felt color flood her cheeks. There were things she hadn't even told her twin. Things she hadn't told anyone. "Maybe. That's enough talking for one day." She felt unsettled, like a snow globe that had been shaken, leaving her previously settled feelings to swirl madly around inside. How could she still have so many feelings after so long? Weren't they ever going to fade? It was annoying and unfair. "If Seth is going to be living here, maybe I should leave New York. That would be a solution."

"That's not a solution, that's avoidance. Your business is here. Your life is here. You love New York. Why would you leave?"

"Because now he's here I'm not sure I love it anymore."

"Where would you go?"

"I've heard Hawaii is pretty."

"You're not going to Hawaii. You're going to channel your inner warrior and go see him. You're going to say, 'Hi, Seth, how's the family?' And then you're going to let him talk. And when he's finished talking you're going to notice the time and leave. Done. How do you know he won't be pleased to see you?"

"Our relationship didn't exactly end in a good way."

"But it was a long time ago. He will have moved on, as you have. He's probably married."

The glass slipped through Fliss's nerveless fingers but fortunately didn't break. "He's married?"

Why did she even care whether he was married or not? What relevance did it have? What was *wrong* with her?

"I don't *know* he's married. I was just putting it out there, but clearly I shouldn't have." Ever practical, Harriet retrieved the glass and started mopping up water.

"You see? I can't possibly talk to him because I'm not in charge of my emotions. But you are. You should definitely pretend to be me. That way you could have this conversation and get it over with and you won't feel awkward."

Harriet straightened. "I haven't pretended to be you since I was twelve."

"Fourteen. You're forgetting that time when I pretended to be you in biology."

"Because that sleazy creep wouldn't stop tormenting me about my stammer. Johnny Hill. You punched him. How could I have forgotten that?"

"I don't know. It was a great day."

"Are you kidding? You had to have eight stitches in your head. You still have the scar."

"But he never touched you again, did he? And neither did anyone else." Fliss grinned and rubbed her fingers along the scar hidden under her hair. "You got a reputation for being scary. So you owe me. Go and see Seth. Be me. It's easy. Just do and say everything you'd never do or say and you'll be convincing."

Harriet gave a wry smile. "You're not such a bad girl, Felicity Knight."

"I used to be. And Seth paid the price."

"Stop it." Harriet's voice was firm. "Stop saying that. Stop thinking it."

"How? It's the truth." But she'd paid it, too, and it seemed as if those payments never stopped. "If I could find a way to avoid seeing him, I would. I have no idea what to say to a man whose life I ruined."

FOUR BLOCKS AWAY Seth Carlyle had his hands full of moody cocker spaniel.

"How long has he been like this?"

"Like what? Angry?"

"I meant, how long has he been limping?"

"Oh." The woman frowned. "About a week."

Seth examined the dog thoroughly. The dog snarled, and he eased the pressure of his fingers. "Sorry. Didn't mean to hurt you. Just need to take a good look and see what's going on here." He kept his voice and his touch gentle and felt the animal relax under his hands.

"He likes you." The woman looked at him with surprise and dawning respect. "Dr. Steve says you're helping him out. Said you were a big-shot vet who worked in some animal hospital in California."

"I don't know about the first part, but the second part is true."

"So why leave California? Tired of all that sunshine and blue skies?"

"Something like that." Seth smiled and turned his attention back to the dog. "I'm going to run some tests and see if those will give us the answers we want."

"Do you think it's serious?"

"I suspect it's a soft-tissue injury, but there are a few other conditions I need to rule out." He gave some instructions to the vet technician, ran some tests and checked the X-ray. "We should limit his exercise."

"How am I supposed to do that?"

"Make sure you keep him in a small space."

"No more walks in Central Park?"

"Not for the time being. And give him some time in his crate."

Once he'd completed the notes, he walked to Reception.

"Meredith?"

"Hi, Dr. Carlyle." Her face turned pink, and she dropped the magazine she'd been reading under the desk. "Is there something I can do for you? Coffee? Bagel? Anything at all? You just need to ask. We're so grateful to you for stepping in and helping out." It was clear from the look in her eyes that *anything* wasn't an exaggeration, but Seth ignored the unspoken invitation and the hopeful look in her eyes.

"I'm good, thanks. Did I miss any calls while I was in the clinic?"

"Yes." She checked the notepad in front of her. "Mrs. Cook called to tell you Buster's wound is looking better. One of the vet techs took the call. And Geoff Hammond called about his pooch. I put him through to Steve."

"That's it?" He felt a stab of disappointment, and Meredith checked again, desperate to please.

"Yeah, that's it." She glanced up. "Why? Were you expecting someone in particular?"

My ex-wife.

"No." His reason for asking wasn't something he intended to share.

He'd been waiting for her to come to him. Thinking about it, he realized he was treating Fliss much the same way he'd treat an injured, frightened animal. With patience. No sudden moves.

He couldn't even pretend that perhaps she didn't know he was here. He'd run into her brother, Daniel, on his second night in Manhattan. It had been an uncomfortable encounter, and it had been obvious from the tension heating the air that the animosity Daniel Knight felt toward him hadn't diminished over time. Daniel would have told Fliss that Seth was in Manhattan. The Knight siblings were so close they might as well have been sutured together. He suspected that part of the reason for that was their stormy family life. Growing up they'd formed a bond. Seth didn't blame Daniel for being protective of Fliss. Someone had to be, and it hadn't been her father.

He'd met her when she'd been a leggy fourteen years old. She'd been part of the group who hung out together on the beach during those long, blissful summers in the Hamptons. At first glance she was indistinguishable from her twin, but anyone who spent a few minutes in their company would have known which twin they were talking to. Harriet was reserved and thoughtful. Fliss was wild and impulsive and attacked life as if she was leading an army into battle. She was first into the water and last out, swimming or surfing until the final rays of the sun had burned out over the ocean. She was bold, brave, loyal and fiercely protective of her quieter sister. She was also a daredevil, but he'd sensed a level of desperation to her actions, almost as if she wanted someone to challenge her. He'd had the feeling sometimes that she was living life just a little too hard, determined to prove something.

He'd known nothing about her family life that first summer. Her grandmother had owned the beach house on the bay for decades and was well-known in the area. Her daughter and children visited every summer, but unlike his own mother, who was actively involved in the local community both at the beach and back in their home in upstate New York, Fliss's mother was virtually invisible.

And then one day the rumors had started. They'd trickled along the narrow lanes and into the village stores. A couple of people passing had heard raised voices and then the sound of a car driving too fast along the narrow island roads toward the main highway. The rumors spread from person to person, whispers and questions, until finally Seth heard them. *Marriage problems. Family problems.*

Seth had rarely seen her father. Almost all his impressions of the man had come from Fliss and Harriet's reaction to him.

"Dr. Carlyle?" Meredith's voice brought him back to the present, reminding him that his reason for being here was to move forward, not backward.

Since he'd arrived in New York he'd seen Fliss twice. The first time had been in Central Park on his first day in Manhattan. She'd been walking two dogs, an exuberant Dalmatian and a misbehaving German shepherd who had seemed determined to challenge her skills.

She'd been too far in the distance for him to engineer a meeting, so he'd simply watched as she'd strode away from him, noticing the changes.

Her hair was the same smooth buttermilk blond, pinned haphazardly at the top of her head in a style that could have been named "afterthought." Lean and athletic, she walked with purpose and a touch of impatience. It had been her attitude that had convinced him he was looking at Fliss and not Harriet.

She'd grown into a confident woman, but that didn't surprise him. She'd never been short of fight.

He was desperate to see her face, to look into those eyes and see the flare of recognition, but she was too far away and didn't turn her head.

The second time he'd seen her had been outside the office. The fact that she was hovering indecisively convinced him again that this was Fliss and not her sister. He guessed she'd been trying to summon up courage to confront him, and for a moment he'd believed maybe they were finally on their way to having the conversation they should have had a decade before. He'd also witnessed the exact moment she'd lost her nerve and fled.

He'd felt a burst of exasperation and frustration, followed by an increased determination that this time they were going to talk.

The last time they'd seen each other the atmosphere had been full of emotion. It had filled the air like thick smoke from a fire, choking everything. Maybe, if she'd been different, more willing to talk, they could have stumbled their way through it, but Fliss, as always, had refused to reveal her feelings, and although he had more than enough feelings for both of them, he'd not known how to reach her. The brief intimacy that had connected them had vanished.

He refused to believe that connection had been purely physical, but it had been the physical that had devoured their attention.

If he could have wound time backward he would have done it all differently, but the past was gone and there was only the present.

They'd had no contact for ten years, so this was always going to be an awkward meeting for both of them, but it was a meeting that was long overdue, and if she wasn't going to come to him, then he was left with only one option.

He'd go to her.

He'd tried leaving it alone. He'd tried pushing it into his past. Neither had worked, and he'd come to the conclusion that tackling it head-on was the only way forward.

He wanted the conversation they should have had a decade before. He wanted answers to the questions that had lain dormant in his head. Most of all, he wanted closure.

Maybe then he could move on.

CHAPTER TWO

HARRIET'S PHONE RANG just after 5:30 a.m., and Fliss was already halfway through the door. She'd been woken early by one of their dog walkers who'd picked up stomach flu after a night out and couldn't crawl out of her bed let alone walk an energetic dog. Thoughts of Barney the bulldog waiting patiently in his owner's apartment in Tribeca for someone who wasn't going to turn up drove Fliss from the comfort of her bed a full hour before she would normally have forced herself upright.

At least it was walking a dog.

She liked the simplicity of dealing with animals. Animals never tried to force you to talk about things you didn't want to talk about.

"Harry? Someone is calling you." She yelled her sister's name and then cursed as she heard the shower running.

Knowing there was no way her sister was going to hear the phone through the sound of running water, she eyed the device, torn between the need to leave and do battle with the subway, and the almost irresistible lure of possible new business.

They'd call back.

But Harriet might not answer it because she hated talking to strangers on the phone. And then they'd lose business.

Damn. She closed the front door, checked the number and frowned as she answered.

"Grams?"

"Harriet? Oh, I'm so glad I've reached you, honey."

"I'm—" Felicity was about to say that she wasn't Harriet, but her grandmother was still speaking.

"I don't want to worry you, but I had a fall."

"A fall? How? Where? How bad?"

"I tripped in the garden. So silly of me. I was trying to do something about the fact it's so overgrown. And the gate is so rusty it will hardly open. You remember how it always made a noise?"

"Yes." Fliss stared through the window of her apartment. She'd poured oil on the gate to try to stop its creaking when she'd sneaked out in the night to meet Seth. "Are you hurt? Where are you now?"

"I'm in the hospital. Would you believe I'm in the same room they put me in when I had my gallbladder removed ten years ago?"

"What?" She shouldn't be thinking about Seth. "Grams, that's awful!"

"It's perfect. This room has a beautiful view of the garden. I'm very pleased to be here, and they're taking very good care of me."

"I meant awful that you're in the hospital, not awful about having a nice room."

"Well, it's not so awful while I'm here. The awful part will be when they send me home. And they won't do that until I assure them I have someone there to keep an eye on me for a while. I think it's a fuss about nothing, but I'm a little bruised and apparently I was unconscious for a while." There was a pause. "I was wondering—I hate to ask since I know the two of you are so busy with your business, but is there any chance you could come just for a few weeks? Just until I'm back on my feet? I'm too far from town to be able to manage easily, and if I can't drive I'm going to struggle. Would Fliss be able to manage without you? It would mean leaving New York, but you always used to love the summers here."

It would mean leaving New York.

They were the best words she'd heard in a while.

Fliss tightened her grip on the phone. "Leave New York?" Her mind raced ahead. "You want me to spend the summer with you?"

"A few weeks should be enough. I'll need help with the shopping and cooking, and simple things around the house. Just until I'm back on my feet and mobile. And then there's Charlie, of course. I don't know how I'm going to walk him, and he does need exercise."

Fliss winced. Charlie was her grandmother's beagle. He was stubborn and single-minded. He also bayed a lot, which meant Fliss invariably resorted to headache tablets whenever she visited.

Biting back her natural response, she reminded herself that she was pretending to be Harriet.

"How is darling Charlie?" She almost choked on the words. How did her sister manage it? How was she so unfailingly kind and generous?

"Too energetic for me to handle for a while, and you're so lovely with him. I shouldn't have got another dog at my age, but he brings me so much joy. Sadly I can't cope with him if I'm resting."

"Of course you can't." Fliss glanced up as Harriet emerged from the bathroom wrapped in a towel. "I'll come."

"You will? Oh, you're such a good girl. You always were."

No, she wasn't. She'd never been a good girl. That was the problem. And even now she was doing the right thing for the wrong reasons. But she was doing it, so that was what counted, wasn't it? Did it really matter if she had her own reasons for wanting to escape the city?

"When are you able to come home, Grams?"

"The day after tomorrow if you're able to pick me up from the hospital. You'll need to rent a car—"

"No problem. I'll handle that." She felt a rush of relief. The cloud that had dampened her mood for the past few weeks lifted. Here was the perfect solution to her problem, right under her nose. She didn't have to fly to Hawaii. She didn't even have to leave the state of New York. "Take care, Grams. I'll give your love to Fliss." She ended the call, and Harriet raised her eyebrows.

"Why are you giving love to yourself?"

"She thought I was you."

"And saying, 'I'm Fliss, not Harry,' didn't enter your head?"

"I was about to say that, but then my genius plan came into my head instead."

"Suddenly I'm nervous."

"You know I mentioned going to Hawaii? Turns out I don't need to. I'm going to spend the summer in the Hamptons."

"Summer in the Hamptons?"

Fliss grinned. "Yeah, you remember the place. Beaches, villages, sand and surf, ice cream dripping on your fingers, traffic and tourists—"

"I know all about the Hamptons. I also know you usually avoid it."

"I avoid it because I'm afraid I might bump into Seth, but Seth is in Manhattan. If I go to the Hamptons I can walk instead of skulking. And Grams needs me."

"I thought it was me she needed."

"We're interchangeable."

"Why does she need you? Has something happened?"

"She had a fall. She's in the hospital but they're letting her go home as long as someone is there for her."

"Oh no! Poor Grams." Harriet looked horrified. "Why didn't you tell her it was you on the phone?"

"Because then she would have asked to speak to you. She wanted you, not me. She probably doesn't think I'll be a good nurse." She wondered, just for a moment, what it would be like to be the one everyone wanted around. "And she's probably right."

Harriet sighed. "Fliss—"

"What? We both know I'm not the nurturing type, but I swear if you agree to let me go and stay here instead, I'll take really good care of her. I'll do anything. I'll bathe her. I'll be sympathetic. I'll walk Charlie."

"You don't even like Charlie."

"I take exception to his selective deafness, that's all. I hate the way he has to smell absolutely everything we pass. He almost pulled my arm out of its socket last time I walked him."

"He's a beagle. Beagles are hunting dogs."

"He shouldn't be hunting when I'm walking him."

"He's the perfect dog for Grams. She can't walk as fast these days, but that just gives Charlie more sniffing time. I think beagles are incredible. They're basically a nose on four legs."

"You think all dogs are incredible. And Charlie is

not so incredible when he's baying. But I'll handle it. I'll handle everything. I'll even hug him if that's what it takes. And I'll tell you everything that is happening and I'll do anything you ask. I'll even make your chocolate chip cookies."

"No!" Harriet looked alarmed. "Don't do that. You'll set the house on fire."

"All right, no chocolate chip cookies." Fliss flopped down onto the chair. The sheer relief at the prospect of a reprieve made her realize how stressed she'd been. "Please, Harry. I really need to get out of Manhattan. It's driving me crazy. I can't relax, I'm not sleeping, and when I don't sleep I'm in a continually rotten mood—"

"I'd noticed. Fine, go." Harriet rubbed the ends of her hair with the towel. "But you'll have to tell Grams the truth. You can't pretend to be me. That crosses a line."

Fliss didn't comment.

She'd crossed so many lines in her life she no longer knew which side of the line she stood on.

"I can't tell her before I go. She might tell me she doesn't want me." There was an ache in the pit of her stomach. The truth was everyone wanted Harriet. Harriet was kind and generous. She was warm-natured and even-tempered. Harriet had never gone skinny-dipping. She'd never lied to a man and had wild sex on a beach. "I'll tell her the moment I arrive and pick her up from the hospital."

"Are you sure this is going to help? Sooner or later you're going to have to come back and meet Seth. You're postponing the inevitable, that's all."

"Postponing the inevitable looks good from where I'm standing. Never do today what you can put off until next week."

Harriet folded the towel neatly. "All right. But the moment you pick Grams up from the hospital, you explain everything."

"Absolutely."

"You tell her what's happened and you tell her you're Fliss."

"I will. That's what I'm going to do."

"No skinny-dipping."

"Hey—" Fliss spread her hands "—I'm a reformed character."

"No stealing tomatoes."

"They were good tomatoes. And the family were away for the summer, or so I thought at the time." Fliss grinned and then caught Harriet's eye and stopped grinning. "But just to be safe I'll buy tomatoes on one of the roadside stands, I promise. No taking produce that doesn't belong to me, even if it is perfectly ripe and no one is picking it and I know it's going to go to waste. No way would I do that."

Harriet gave her a long look. "And what am I supposed to say if I bump into Seth?"

"You're sure you couldn't pretend to be me?"

"No."

"Because you're so honest."

"Well, there's that, but also I'm a terrible actor. And what if he kissed me thinking I was you?"

You'd be the luckiest woman on the planet.

Her stomach gave a lurch. "That wouldn't happen. You're not going to bump into him, but if you do then you smile and say hello. I suppose." She shrugged. "If I knew what to say, I'd be saying it myself. I don't think you're going to run into him."

"It's because you're afraid of running into him that

you're leaving." Harriet gave her a pointed look. "And I use that vet practice all the time."

"Then maybe you will run into him. But you'll be fine. So will you hold the fort while I go to the Hamptons? I promise I'll still do all the paperwork, handle the accounts and make any phone call that makes you feel nauseous."

"All right." Harriet walked toward the bedroom and paused in the doorway. "But don't burn the house down."

"No cooking. I promise."

She'd promise anything. Anything. She couldn't live here with Seth working just a few blocks away, knowing that she could bump into him at any moment.

She needed to get out of town.

"MOM WANTS TO know if you'll be joining us in Vermont for the Fourth." Vanessa's voice held a trace of irritation.

Seth knew his younger sister well enough to know it was best ignored. She was an organizer, and no one else ever did things to her satisfaction. If she'd been an animal she would have been a sheepdog, rounding everyone up the way she wanted them. "I can't get away. I'm working."

"On the holiday weekend?"

"This may surprise you, Vanessa, but pets don't always get sick according to a schedule."

"You're not the only vet in the state of New York. Can't you switch with someone? We need to plan. We've rented two cabins at Snow Crystal Resort and Spa, right by the lake. It will be idyllic. And so good for Mom. This is all new. Nothing we've ever done before. It's the land of maple syrup, applesauce and great hiking. The place has the best restaurant for miles around. I keep reading about the chef. She's French. You know how much Mom loves everything French. And, best of all, there will be no reminders of Dad."

Seth felt a wrench in his gut. His father's sudden death was recent enough that he saw reminders everywhere. He wasn't sure if they were painful or precious, but one thing he did know was that traveling to Vermont wouldn't make the loss any easier to bear.

"Plan without me."

"I'm planning with you, that's why I'm calling." There was a pause. "I thought you could invite Naomi."

It was Seth's turn to feel irritation. "Why would I do that?"

"Because she's still in love with you! You dated her for almost a year, Seth."

"And we broke up ten months ago."

"Dad died and it was a terrible time. None of us were ourselves."

It was more than that. So much more. "Drop it, Vanessa."

"I will not."

Families, he thought. "Why are you bringing this up now?"

"Because I don't understand what's going on with you. You meet the perfect woman and then you break up with her?"

"This isn't your business, Vanessa. You don't need to understand. It's my relationship. My life."

"What relationship? That's the point, Seth, you don't have a relationship! You had a dream relationship, the perfect relationship, and you crashed it. And I just don't get you. I love Naomi. Mom *loves* Naomi."

"Yeah, well, this may come as another surprise to you, but it's not enough that my family loves the woman I'm dating. I have to love her, too."

"How could you not? Naomi is the sweetest person on the planet. What is wrong with her?"

"There's nothing wrong with her. And you're right, she's a sweet person."

"Finally we agree on something. So the question I should probably be asking is what is wrong with *you*?"

The problem was that he didn't have a sweet tooth. He liked something with a kick. Bite. Tooth-rotting sweetness didn't hold much appeal, but he had no intention of sharing that detail with his older sister. His youngest sister, Bryony, would never in a million years have dreamed of interfering.

"You need to leave this alone, Vanessa."

"I can't leave it alone. You're my brother, and Naomi is my friend."

And for Vanessa, that was enough. She wanted things to be the way she'd wanted them.

"*Seth won't play my game*," had been her constant whine as a child. Remembering brought a wry smile to his lips. He hadn't played her game then, and he certainly wasn't playing it now.

"If you truly care about Naomi then you'll step back from this one. If you interfere, you'll make things worse. It's not fair to her."

"I thought, maybe, if you spend some time together in Vermont the two of you might—"

"It's over, Vanessa. And if you hint at anything else to her, if you imply that if we got together for the Fourth then there might be a big reconciliation, then you'll be the one hurting her. It's the wrong thing to do."

"Is it wrong to want to see you settled and married one day?"

"I've been married."

There was a tense pause. "That one didn't count. It wasn't real."

He'd counted it. Every hour. And it felt as real now as it had then. "Are you done?"

"Now I've annoyed you, but it was Vegas, Seth. *Vegas!* Who gets married in Vegas? I can only assume you did it because you had some misguided notion about taking her away from her father. Protecting her. You've spent your life rescuing things, but she didn't need protecting. You're such a gentleman, and she took advantage of you."

Seth decided it was a good thing his sister couldn't see him smiling. "Maybe I'm not such a gentleman. Maybe you don't know me as well as you think you do."

"I know you never would have married her unless she'd forced you."

"You think she handcuffed me to the door of the Elvis Chapel?"

"So if it was a real wedding, why didn't you invite us?"

"Because it's impossible to invite you without your opinions coming along for the ride."

"You hurt Mom's feelings."

He tensed, knowing it was true and knowing also that his sister knew exactly how to wound. "I need to go, Vanessa. I have patients to see." *An ex-wife to track down.*

"Maybe I'm crossing a line—"

"You always do."

"—but that happens every time we talk about *her*.

You've seen her, haven't you? That was why you took the job in New York."

He didn't need to ask whom she meant. He contemplated not answering but decided that would prolong the conversation. "I haven't seen her yet."

"'Yet'? That means you're intending to. What are you *thinking*? Or maybe you're not thinking and it's testosterone affecting your brain." She sighed. "I'm sorry. I want you to be happy, that's all. Maybe you should meet her. Maybe if you actually came face-to-face with her again, you would get her out of your system." She made Fliss sound like a drug overdose; something that could be overcome with the right antidote.

"There's nothing wrong with my system, but thank you for granting your permission."

"I hate sarcasm."

"And I hate your need to control other people's lives as well as your own."

"You drive me crazy, do you know that?"

"It's a brother's duty to drive his sister crazy."

"Not this crazy." Vanessa sighed. "On second thoughts, I take it back. I don't think you should see her. You don't make good decisions when you're around her. She ripped your heart out, Seth, and then she used it as a football."

"'She' has a name."

"Felicity. Fliss—" Vanessa almost choked "—and you're talking in your quiet voice, which I know means you're mad at me—messes with your head, Seth, and she always did. She's a—a minx."

Minx? Only his sister would have come up with a word like that. Seth thought about Fliss, remembering the wicked gleam in her catlike eyes and the teasing curve of her mouth. Maybe *minx* suited her. Maybe he had a minx addiction.

Maybe he was in as much trouble as his sister thought he was.

"Are you done?"

"Don't cut me off! I don't want you to be hurt again, that's all. I care about you."

"You don't have to worry about me. I know what I'm doing."

"Are you sure?" His sister's voice was thickened. "You were the one who held it all together when Dad died. You were there for everyone. Our rock. You've got broad shoulders, Seth, but who do you lean on? If you don't want to get back together with Naomi, you should find someone else. I don't want you to be alone for the rest of your life."

"We're not populating Noah's Ark, Vanessa. We don't all have to be in twos."

"I'm not going to mention it again. You're old enough to make your own decisions, you're right. Let's talk about the house, instead. Mom wants to sell it."

His gut twisted. "It's too soon to make that decision."

"I know you don't want to sell it, but she can't stand the thought of going back there."

"She might feel differently in a while."

"And she might not. Why does it matter to you, Seth? You're building your own place near the water. Once that is finished, you won't need Ocean View."

He thought of the big house that had been part of his life for as long as he could remember. Maybe Vanessa was right. Maybe he was holding on to it for himself, not for his mother. "I'll speak to a Realtor as soon as I have a chance. Get a valuation."

"Good. I can leave that with you, then?"

"Yes." He could almost hear her mentally ticking it off her list. Vanessa survived by lists. If something wasn't on her list, it didn't get done. He could imagine her, pencil in hand, ready to tick off *find Seth a wife*. She'd inherited her organizational tendencies from their mother, who was a warm and generous hostess. No one arriving at the Carlyle home would ever feel anything other than welcome. Summer at the Hamptons had been an endless round of entertaining both friends and family. No one would ever be fed the same thing twice. His mother had a file. People's likes and dislikes, marriages, divorces, affairs—everything carefully recorded so that there were no awkward moments. And she had a team of people to help her.

Vanessa was the same, except she was more drill sergeant than congenial host.

"And you'll think about the Fourth?"

"I don't need to think. I know I'm working."

"In that case I'll visit you soon. We'll have lunch. And, Seth—"

"What?"

"Whether you see her or not—whatever you do, don't let her hurt you again."

CHAPTER THREE

SHE RENTED A CONVERTIBLE, because if you were going to drive to the beach on a hot summer's day, you might as well enjoy the ride. The insurance alone should have been enough to make a grown woman cry. Fortunately she'd never been much of a crier. Her business was going well. She was young, free and single. She intended to enjoy every minute of it. She was leaving her troubles—or should that be *trouble* in the singular?—behind in Manhattan.

Feeling pleased with herself, she took the Long Island Expressway out of the city and then hit Route 27. As usual it was clogged with traffic, cars idling bumper to bumper. She sat in it, inched forward, then stopped, inched forward again, working hard on her patience, drumming her fingers on the steering wheel as she stared moodily ahead of her. Too many people going nowhere. It was almost as bad as the traffic in Manhattan, except that she had more sense than to drive in Manhattan.

Calm, she thought. *Breathe.*

Harriet always told her she should try meditation or mindfulness, but Fliss didn't know what to do with all the energy burning up inside her. She wasn't a mellow person. She wasn't calm either. Harriet practiced yoga and Pilates, but Fliss preferred kickboxing and karate. There was nothing quite so satisfying as landing a punch or smacking someone hard with a well-placed turning kick. Restful and calm she certainly wasn't, but hey, she could pretend. With a touch of her finger, she changed the playlist, switching from pounding rock that had perfectly matched the pounding beat of New York City, to something more mellow and laid-back.

Instead of thinking about Seth, she tried to think about her plans for the business. Harriet was all for keeping it small. Fliss wanted expansion. She'd need to convince her sister it was the right thing to do, remembering that they each loved the business for different reasons. Harriet loved it because it allowed her to work with animals, which kept her well within her comfort zone. Fliss loved it because she fed on the adrenaline rush of building something and watching it grow. Each new client was another brick in the wall of financial security she was building around herself.

No one would ever be able to control her or dictate to her.

She earned her own money. She made the decisions about her life.

Useless? Worthless? Not so much.

She tried to focus on the business, tried to think about everything and anything but Seth. So why was it that trying to not think seemed to make her think of him more? Maybe it was because she was going back to the beach. Back to the place where she'd spent the happiest days of her childhood. The place where the land met the water.

Back to the place where they'd met.

At the mouth of the Peconic River, at the eastern end of Long Island, the land split into two forks at a place

SARAH MORGAN   59

the Native Americans called Paumanok. Fliss took the
south fork leading to the coveted side of the island. She
waited until she hit an open stretch and then floored
it. Too fast, but who cared? She finally had the road to
herself, and after idling in traffic she wanted the speed.

As the road narrowed slightly, she slowed and made
a right turn, inching through the tiny hamlets that led
down to the water's edge. This was where the elite chose
to spend their summers. People who had made it, and
people who wanted to pretend they'd made it by hir-
ing out a beach house for a few weeks each summer.

She spotted a farm stand overflowing with produce
and on impulse pulled over and grabbed her purse. She
didn't know what food her grandmother would have
in the house. If she shopped now at least she wouldn't
starve, and even she couldn't burn salad.

She was wearing cutoffs and a T-shirt, but after a
couple of hours idling in the car under a baking-hot
sun she couldn't wait to strip them off and dive into the
ocean. Naked? She grinned, remembering her promise
to her twin. This visit she was going to try her hard-
est to keep all her clothes on. Which was going to be
tough, because it was the type of heat that fried brains
and sharpened tempers.

She pulled on a baseball cap and tugged the bill
down. Not that she was likely to see anyone she knew,
but she wasn't in the mood for polite conversation. She
waited, head dipped, foot tapping, while the family in
front of her chose fruit for their lunch—*make up your
minds already*—and then stepped forward to make her
choice. There were plump juicy peaches, local strawber-
ries, fresh-picked lettuces and a dome of shiny, jewel-

like tomatoes. She bought a selection, then she took a photo and sent it to her sister.

Proof I'm not borrowing from people's gardens.

Next to the farm stand was a food truck. They served macchiato, and Fliss sipped the coffee thinking that as far as exiles went, this wasn't so bad. The availability of good coffee in this comparatively small spit of land was disproportionate to the number of inhabitants.

She'd forgotten how it felt to be standing with the sun heating your skin with the scent of the ocean clinging to the air. It took her back to her childhood, to those delicious first moments when they'd arrived at the beach with the long, lazy weeks of summer stretching ahead.

They'd loaded the car early in the morning so they could make the drive before the worst of the heat. She could still remember the painful tension of those early-morning departures. She could picture her father's thunderous expression, and hear her mother soothing and placating. It was like spreading honey on burned toast. Didn't matter how much you tried to sweeten it, the toast was still burned.

They'd learned to gauge his mood. When her brother arrived at the breakfast table and muttered "stormy today," or "dark clouds and a little threatening," they all knew he wasn't talking about the weather.

On the day they left for the summer, they all hoped and prayed that the weather would be in their favor.

Harriet had slid into the back of the car and tried to make herself invisible, while Fliss had helped her brother load, pushing the bags in randomly in her haste to get away. *Just do this. Let's go.*

Right up until the moment they drove away there was always the chance that they wouldn't leave. That her father would find some way to stop them.

She remembered the catch of fear in her throat. If he refused to let them go, the summer would be ruined. And she remembered that delicious feeling of freedom when they pulled away and realized they'd done it. It was like bursting out from a dark, oppressive forest into a patch of bright sunlight. Freedom had stretched ahead like a wide-open road.

She'd watched, bathed in relief, as her mother's death grip on the wheel lessened, the blood finally returning to her knuckles.

Her brother, claiming seniority and therefore the front seat, had covered their mother's hand with his. *"It's all right, Mom."*

They all knew it wasn't all right but were willing to believe it was, to pretend, and the more miles they put between themselves and the house, the more her mother changed.

They all did, Fliss included. She'd left her old life and her bad mood back in Manhattan, like a snake shedding its skin.

She glanced around, wondering how being here could still make her feel that way and wondering why it had taken a crisis in her life to bring her back here. Apart from brief visits to her grandmother, she hadn't spent a significant block of time here since her teenage years.

Coffee finished, she continued on her way. This part of the island had some of the most coveted real estate in the whole of the Hamptons. She drove past curving driveways, high hedges and cedar-clad mansions topped with high gables and worn by the wind and the weather to shimmering silver gray. Some were inhabited year-round, some were rented by "summer people," visitors who clogged the roads and the stores and drove the locals mad. Most belonged to the seriously rich.

Her grandmother's house lacked the square footage and sophisticated security of some of its nearest neighbors, but what it lacked in grandeur, it made up for in charm. Unlike some of the newer mansions that surrounded them, Sea Breeze had been standing for decades. It had a pitched shingle roof and wide windows facing the ocean, but its real benefit was its proximity to the ocean. Developers hungry for any opportunity to exploit the most coveted piece of land in the area had offered her grandmother eye-watering sums of money to purchase the property, but her grandmother had steadfastly refused to sell.

The local community knew the story of how Fliss's grandfather had bought the beach house for her grandmother on the day of their marriage. Her grandmother had once told her that selling it would have felt like giving away a wedding ring, or breaking a vow.

Marriage, she'd told Fliss, was forever.

Fliss felt pain in her hands and realized she was gripping the wheel so tightly she'd almost cut off the blood supply.

Her marriage hadn't been forever.

She and Seth hadn't even hit the three-month mark. And that was her fault, of course. She wore the guilt of that, and it made for uncomfortable clothing.

For a split second she lost concentration, and in that moment a dog shot into the road. He appeared without warning, a blur of golden brown.

Fliss slammed on the brakes, sending dust and her pulse rate flying.

"Dammit." She sat there, fighting the shock, her heart almost bursting out of her chest. Her hands shook as she groped for the door and opened it. Had she hit it? No. She hadn't felt a bump or heard anything, but the dog lay in the road, eyes closed. She must have hit it.

"Oh God, *no*–" She dashed to its side and dropped to her knees. Along with her other crimes she was now a destroyer of innocent creatures. "I'm sorry! I didn't see you. Please be okay, please be okay," she was muttering under her breath when she heard a voice behind her.

"She's fine. It's a trick of hers."

The voice punched the air from her lungs. She wanted it to be a mistake, but the recognition was visceral, and she wondered dimly how it was that a voice could be so individual, like a fingerprint. It could have belonged to only one person. She'd known that voice measured, teasing, commanding, amused. She'd known it hard with anger and soft with love. She'd been hearing that voice in her dreams for the past ten years, and she knew there was no mistake even though it made no sense.

Seth was in Manhattan. He was the reason she was here. If it hadn't been for Seth, she wouldn't even have *been* on this road at this time, and if she hadn't been thinking about him she would have been concentrating and maybe spotted the dog before it appeared without warning from behind the sand dunes.

"Are you all right?" Now the voice was deep and calm, as if he was used to soothing the ragged edges of a person's anxiety. "You seem pretty shaken up. I promise you the dog really is fine. She used to work in the movies and they trained her to play dead."

Fliss closed her eyes and wondered if she should do the same thing.

She could lie down in the road, hold her breath and hope he stepped over her and moved on.

She was relieved about the dog, of course, but she wasn't ready to talk to Seth. Not yet. And not like this. How could this have happened? After all her careful planning, how had she found herself in this situation?

There was no justice. Or maybe this *was* justice. Maybe this was her punishment. Being made to suffer now for all the sins of her past.

The dog opened its eyes and sprang to its feet, tail wagging. Fliss had no choice but to stand up, too. She did so slowly, reluctantly, brushing the dust from her knees, postponing the moment when she was going to come face-to-face with him.

"Maybe you should sit down."

Maybe I should make a run for it.

She forced herself to turn.

Her gaze locked with his, and instantly she was sucked back in time. She was eighteen years old, lying on the sand naked, lazily warm and content, her limbs entwined with his, their faces so close they were almost touching. She'd always liked being physically close, as if proximity lessened the chance that she would ever lose him. *Touch me, Seth, hold me.*

He'd touched her, held her, and she'd lost him anyway.

And clearly he was surprised to have found her again.

Shock flickered across his face, followed by confusion. He reached out and pushed her hat back, taking a closer look at her face. "Fliss?"

She was confused, too. She'd assumed time would have diluted the effect he had on her. Neutralized her feelings. Instead it seemed as if it had concentrated everything. She hadn't seen his face for almost ten years, and yet everything about it was painfully familiar. The crinkles at the corners of his eyes, the few wayward strands of hair that insisted on flopping over his forehead, those thick lashes that framed eyes as dark as a pirate's heart. Sexual awareness punched through her with shocking force. The magnetic pull was so powerful the force of it almost jerked her forward. If she'd been in the car, the air bag would have deployed.

She was baking hot and sweaty, which made her all the more resentful that he managed to look so cool. He was wearing a white button-down shirt and khakis. He'd always been strikingly handsome, and the extra years had stripped away the last of the boy and shaped the man. He had the same athletic physique, but his shoulders were wider, his body stronger and more powerful.

Once, she'd believed that maybe happy endings really weren't just for books and movies. Her feelings for him had filled her until there was no room for anything else, until she hadn't known how to contain them. Fortunately all those years with her father had provided advanced training in how to hide them, which was just as well because Seth looked insanely good and she looked—

She didn't want to think how she looked.

It was definitely karma. Punishment for her past sins, which were too many to count.

She was trapped by that gaze, and her brain and her

tongue knotted at the same time. So she did what she always did when she found herself in a tight corner. She acted on impulse.

"I'm not Fliss," she said. "I'm Harriet."

CHAPTER FOUR

HARRIET.

Until she'd said that, he'd been about to kiss her. Right there on the road and to hell with anyone who happened to be passing. The knowledge unsettled him. Fliss had always brought out a side of him he rarely accessed, and it seemed not much had changed.

Except that this was Harriet, not Fliss. And kissing her would have brought on more than mutual embarrassment. His objective had been to douse old flames, not rekindle fires.

Vanessa was right. He was in trouble.

He stepped back, almost treading on Lulu. The dog yelped and jumped out of the way, sending him a reproachful look. Her day wasn't going well. His wasn't much better.

"I didn't expect to see you here." There was a time when the Knight twins had spent every summer with their grandmother, but that time was long past. Most of the group of kids who had hung out together during those long hot summers had gone their separate ways. The only friend he still saw from those days was Chase Adams, who had taken over the running of his father's construction company based in Manhattan. Since his marriage, he'd been spending more time at his beach house.

"Didn't expect to see you either." She pulled the brim of her hat down, virtually concealing the top half of her face. "I heard you were in Manhattan. Daniel mentioned that he ran into you—" Her tone was casual, but there was something else there that he couldn't identify. Nerves? Since when had he made Harriet nervous?

"That was temporary. I was doing a favor for a friend of mine."

"Steven?"

"Yes. We were at college together. He was short-handed and he asked me to help out."

"So that's it? You're done? No more Manhattan?"

"For now." He wondered why she was asking so many detailed questions about his whereabouts. Maybe Fliss was thinking of visiting her grandmother and her twin was going to deliver a warning. You didn't have to be a genius to figure out that she was avoiding him.

"So you're here for the rest of the summer? Staying with your family?"

"Just me." How much did she know? They'd had no contact since that summer ten years before, but these days there were a myriad ways to find out information. Did Fliss ever talk about him? He had a million questions, but he reined them in. What was the point in asking them? He didn't need answers from Harriet. He needed them from Fliss. "And you? What are you doing here?" It was unsettling looking at her because she could so easily have been Fliss. Outwardly the twins were identical. Same blue eyes, same buttermilk-blond hair.

Inwardly they were as different as the sun and the moon.

"Grams fell. She's in the hospital."

"I hadn't heard." And that surprised him because wherever he went on this patch of land someone, somewhere, was always keen to fill him in on local gossip. "How bad is it? When did it happen?"

"A couple of days ago. I'm not sure how bad it is, but they won't let her go home unless someone is there with her. She was knocked unconscious, I believe, and she says she's a little bruised. I'm off to the hospital as soon as I've unpacked."

"Is there anything I can do?"

"No, but thanks. I'll be picking her up tomorrow." She gestured vaguely to the car, a showy red convertible that gleamed in the sunshine.

He glanced at it, thinking that it didn't seem like something Harriet would drive. On the other hand it had been ten years and a lot changed in ten years, including the fact that she no longer seemed to be shy with him. There was no sign of the stammer that had plagued her teenage years. Fliss had confided in him how difficult it was for her sister, how the moment their father had started shouting, Harriet had been unable to push a single word out of her mouth.

For her sake he was pleased that had changed.

It was partly because he didn't want to be the one to bring her stammer back that he didn't question her about Fliss.

"How did she fall?"

"In the garden. It needs work."

"So you're here to take care of her. That's lucky for her. She doesn't need to worry about being well fed." He smiled at her. "I still remember those chocolate chip cookies you used to make. If you ever have any spare that need eating, I'm right next door."

"Cookies?" A look of alarm flickered across her face, and he wondered what he'd said to trigger that reaction.

"You don't cook anymore?"

"I—yes, of course I cook. But proper food." She stumbled. "Nutritious—er—things. Are your parents here this summer?"

The question knocked him off balance.

So she didn't know.

Sadness washed over him. It came and went like the tide over the sand.

The years opened up like a gulf. So many changes. So many life events he and Fliss should have shared and weathered together. Instead they'd done it apart.

"My father died. Ten months ago. Heart attack. No warning. It was very sudden."

"Oh, Seth—" Her reaction was as spontaneous as it was genuine. Her hand came out and she touched his arm for a few seconds before snatching it back. "I'm truly sorry."

"Yeah, it's been tough. We're selling Ocean View." And he was still getting his head around that, trying to untangle his own wishes from those of his mother. Trying to work out what his father would have wanted him to do. And in a way that was easy. His father would have wanted him to do whatever made his mother happiest.

Which meant he was selling the house.

"That's why you're here? Because you need to sell the house?"

"No. I'm here because this is my home." So that was something else she didn't know. "I live here."

"But you said—"

"I bought a house close to Sag Harbor. It's near the

beach and the nature preserve. It needed some work, but it's nearly finished."

"You're saying you're here permanently?"

Was he imagining it or did he see panic? He had to be imagining it. "Yes. I run Coastal Vets, on the edge of town."

"Oh. Well, that's great." Her tone told him it was anything but great.

He studied her face intently, searching for answers. "How are things with you, Harriet?"

"Good! Fliss and I run a dog-walking business in Manhattan. The Bark Rangers. We're doing well. A bit too well. Fliss wants to expand—you know what she's like."

He didn't know. Not anymore. But he wanted to. Had she changed? Was she still impulsive? Did she still kick her shoes off at every opportunity? *Did she still hide her feelings?*

He had an urge to ask a million questions but held himself back.

He was pleased, but not at all surprised, that Fliss had set up and was running a successful business.

"So if your grandmother has fallen, you're going to be here for a while. How will Fliss manage the business without you?"

"We have an army of reliable dog walkers, and I'm sure she'll be fine."

"So we're going to be neighbors. I'd like to help in any way I can."

The look of panic was back. "That's not necessary! I'm sure we'll be fine, and I wouldn't want to bother you."

"It's no bother. Everyone in my family is fond of

your grandmother, myself included. She brings Charlie to the clinic for checks, as do all her friends. And she has many. She's been part of this community as long as any of us can remember. My mother would never forgive me if I didn't help out." He looked at her for a long moment and decided to test a theory. "How is Fliss?"

"Fliss? She's so happy. Doing really well. She's built the business up from nothing, and now she's so busy she barely has time to breathe. It's an exciting time. All good."

It didn't tell him anything he wanted to know, but that was because he hadn't asked the right questions, of course. Is she seeing someone? Is she married? Why did she get as far as the door of the vet clinic and then turn around? Why is she avoiding me?

Those were the questions he'd wanted to ask.

But he'd got one thing cleared up.

An important thing.

"I'd better go. The clinic opens in an hour and there's always a crowd at this time of year." He whistled to Lulu. "We'll be seeing you around, Harriet."

"Looking forward to it." Her tone told him she wasn't looking forward to it at all.

He loaded the dog into his truck and drove back toward his house. It was within easy driving distance to the clinic, down a road that was little more than a rough track.

He'd found the house two years before and fallen in love with the location. The property itself had been a little harder to love, and it had taken every day of those two years to transform it into the home he wanted.

With the help of Chase, who had pulled together a team to help both with the design and the construction, he'd knocked down the single-story building and replaced it with a two-story structure with a double-height dining and living area and a wall of glass opening onto the pool.

The house nestled behind dunes that were part of a bird sanctuary, and in the evenings during the renovation he'd often sat on the deck, nursing a beer, watching the gentle sway of the sea grass and listening to the plaintive call of the gulls.

A short drive and he was on the edge of town, but here there was only the whisper of the wind and the rhythmic crash of the ocean. People had been listening to the same sound for centuries, and there was a simplicity to it, a soporific blend of nature that soothed the senses.

His house lacked the palatial feel of his childhood home, and in his opinion, it was all the better for that.

There were no ghosts here, and no memories.

He let Lulu out of the car and stood for a moment, admiring the lines of his new home.

"Got yourself something good here." The voice came from behind him, and he turned with a smile.

"Chase! I didn't notice your car."

"I was right behind you, but you were obviously thinking about something else."

Not something, *someone*.

"I wasn't expecting to see you this week. I thought you were in Manhattan, wheeling and dealing." He eyed his friend's board shorts. "You don't look much like a CEO of a major corporation."

"What can I say? I've discovered the joys of the weekend."

"It's Wednesday."

Chase grinned. "So the weekend has started early."

"This from a guy who didn't used to know what the weekend was. Who are you and what have you done with my friend? On second thoughts, don't answer that. I like this version of you better. I guess that's what being married has done to you." Seth closed the car door. "How's Matilda?"

"Uncomfortable. The heat is bothering her. The baby's due in four weeks, and I'm working down here from now until it arrives." He raked his fingers through his hair, looking uncharacteristically nervous. "I'm going to be a dad. CEO of a family. Toughest job yet."

"Funny, because I would have said Matilda was CEO of your family. You're just staff."

"You could be right about that." Chase narrowed his eyes as he studied Seth's house. "It's coming along."

"Yes."

"Are you going to admit I was right about the deck?"

They'd argued about the details by email and in person. "You were right. And I owe you."

"You're welcome. And you can pay me in babysitting."

Seth felt a stab of pain under his ribs. "Not my area of expertise. But if Hero ever needs a vet, I'm your guy."

"He's bound to need a vet. That dog has no clue about personal safety, and I can tell you he is no one's idea of a hero. I keep suggesting Matilda rename him—Liability was my suggestion—but she refuses. He's too big and strong for her to walk at the moment." Chase frowned. "I don't suppose you know of any dog-walking companies around here you can vouch for?"

Seth shook his head and then thought for a moment. "Have you heard of the Bark Rangers?"

"Yes, but they're in Manhattan. It's run by the Knight twins, but I'm guessing you already know that. We use them when we're in town, although I've never dared confess that to you before. Not sure if it's sensitive." Chase looked at him cautiously. "The name *Knight* doesn't exactly come up in conversation these days. Is this a topic we should be avoiding?"

"No. And it so happens I just ran into Harriet." He paused, wondering how much to say. "Her grandmother fell, so she's here for a while. I'll see if she can help you."

"Matilda is friendly with Harriet, but I haven't seen either of the twins for ten years. Not since—"

"Not since you were best man at my wedding. You don't have to tiptoe around, Chase. As you say, it was ten years ago." Plenty of time to adjust and put it in his rearview mirror. People had dismissed it at the time— *too young, too fast*—so he hadn't had to deal with shock or surprise. There had been more than a few knowing nods from folks who thought you could judge a relationship from the outside, as if you could get the measure of a house by peeping in through one window.

"I didn't know you were still in touch."

"We're not."

"This is the first time you've seen Harriet since you broke up? That must have been weird."

"Yes." *Weird* wasn't the word he would have chosen, but he went with it.

"Maybe it's easier that it's just Harriet."

"Maybe." Seth didn't expand on that. "Anyway, she'll be walking her grandmother's dog, so I'll ask her if she'll walk yours, too."

"Thanks. I appreciate that." Chase changed the subject. "So when are you moving in? And, more importantly, when's the housewarming? Are you here for the Fourth or are you going away?"

"I'm here. Working and on call over the holiday weekend."

"That's tough."

"Honestly? Not really." Seth rescued Lulu, who had managed to wedge her head in a hedge. "The rest of the family are spending it in Vermont."

"Having a change." Chase nodded, understanding. "How's your mom doing?"

"Considering everything, she's doing okay. But she wants to sell Ocean View."

"And how do you feel about that?"

Seth looked at his new home, at the smooth lines, the deck, his view of the dunes. He wouldn't swap it for anything. So why wasn't he more motivated to sell the house? "I think it's the right thing to do, although I'm not sure about the timing."

"The timing is perfect. It's summer, the house will show at its best. Trust me on that. I may not know a thing about babies, but I do know about real estate."

"I wasn't talking about the timing for the market, more the timing for my mother. I'm worried it's too soon and that she'll regret the decision."

Chase put his hand on Seth's shoulder and squeezed. "I'll ask you again—how do *you* feel about it?"

As always Chase was observant. And sensitive. It was one of the reasons they'd been friends for so long.

"Conflicted."

"I can imagine." Chase sighed. "For what it's worth, I don't think hanging on to things necessarily eases the pain. Maybe it even makes it worse."

"Intellectually I know that. Emotionally, I seem to be having trouble with it. We spent every summer there from the year I was born. It feels as if I'm not just selling a house, I'm selling memories. And Mom always loved it here." He paused as Chase's phone rang. "You should get that. It might be Matilda."

"It is Matilda. Damn—" His friend fumbled with the phone and almost dropped it. "What's wrong, honey? Is it happening? Is it now? What do I need to do? Who do I call?"

Seth watched, amused, as his friend went from calm to agitated. He waited for him to end the call and raised an eyebrow. "Well? Do we need to put the midwife on alert?"

"No. She wanted me to buy peaches from the farm stand. Peaches! Look at me. I'm a wreck. What the hell is wrong with me?" Chase pocketed his phone and shook his head. "I run a successful corporation—"

"—which has nothing to do with delivering babies."

"True. I'm not good with that stuff. I prefer my problems numerical. If it can't be analyzed or put on a spreadsheet, I'm clueless."

"We both know that's not true. There's not a job in your company you can't do."

"Maybe, but being able to caulk a window isn't going to help me if the baby comes early. If that happens, I'm going to be calling on you."

"I'm a vet," Seth said mildly. "I've delivered puppies, kittens, foals and even a camel—"

"A camel?"

"Don't ask. I've never delivered a human, but don't worry. This baby is not going to come early. First babies never do."

"You'd better be right about that or I'll sue you. And then I'll bring the baby to our poker nights."

Seth gestured toward the house. "Do you need something to calm your nerves? I haven't stocked the fridge yet, but I might be able to find a beer."

"That is tempting, but my pregnant wife wants peaches, so I guess I'd better find her peaches." He flashed Seth a smile and strolled to his car. "One day this is going to happen to you, Seth Carlyle, and that will wipe that grin off your face. In the meantime, if you could ask Harriet about walking Hero, I'd be grateful."

Holding his smile in place, Seth bent to give Lulu a belly rub, watching as Chase reversed the car and headed down the lane toward the main road.

Lulu whined and licked his hand, understanding that something wasn't right.

It was lucky for him Chase wasn't so perceptive.

And lucky for him Chase needed help with a dog.

He told himself that offering to ask Harriet about dog walking had everything to do with helping his friend, and nothing to do with creating another opportunity to talk to Harriet.

CHAPTER FIVE

Sea Breeze.

Fliss parked and stared at the house. It hadn't changed. Same weathered clapboard, same gravel drive that had skinned her knees so many times. Juniper and cypress lined the driveway, and clusters of *Rosa rugosa* bushes erupted with delicate pink blossoms.

Right now she didn't feel as if she'd changed much either.

What had happened to her confidence? The grit and drive that had propelled her this far?

She couldn't stop shaking. Not because of the dog, but because of Seth.

She'd been prepared for everything except bumping into him.

She'd told herself that she'd built it up in her head, but in the end seeing him in person had been worse than she'd imagined. She hadn't anticipated the powerful jolt of chemistry or the sudden frantic fluttering inside her. It seemed that time could heal a lot of things, but not the strange, indescribable pull that drew her to Seth Carlyle. It would have been easy to dismiss it as sexual attraction. Easy, and incorrect.

None of which explained why she'd been stupid enough to pretend to be Harriet.

Frustrated with herself, she grabbed her small suitcase, retrieved the key from under the flowerpot and let herself in.

Calm descended like a comforting blanket. Apart from the odd occasion when their father had joined them unexpectedly, this was the place she'd always been happiest.

She stood for a moment, drinking in familiarity. The large seascape on the wall had been painted by her grandfather. The basket on the floor, stuffed with boots and flip-flops, had been there forever. There were towels, neatly folded, ready to mop sand and mud from overeager dogs because here, at the beach, there had always been dogs.

It had been a place of noise, chaos, chatter and laughter.

No one had to tiptoe. No one had needed to watch what was said.

Summer in the Hamptons.

She stepped forward, and the planks creaked under her tread. How many times had her grandmother scolded her for running into the house with sandy feet?

She pressed down harder, feeling the wood give a little beneath the pressure. Right there. That was where she and Harriet had hidden their "treasure." Fliss knew about the loose floorboard because she'd been careful to tiptoe around it whenever she'd sneaked out to meet Seth. Harriet had returned from one of her many trips to the beach, her pockets stuffed with shells and stones rubbed smooth by the ocean. She'd wanted to take them back to the city, as a memory, but they both knew their father would throw them out, so Fliss had found a box and tucked them out of sight under the floorboards.

They were probably still there.

She stared down at the floor, lost in memories of happy times. And, despite everything, there had been happy times. And perhaps those times had been all the happier, even more precious, because of the tough times that surrounded them. The good moments shone brighter because of the dark.

She strolled through the house, and the years fell away. She remembered the camps they'd built, the games of hide-and-seek they'd played, the hours spent splashing in the waves and digging in the sand. In this place, Fliss had seen her twin sister blossom. The tortured, tongue-tied silence that punctuated their days in New York had been replaced by conversation. Reluctant at first. Tentative. A trickle of words. And then the trickle became a steady stream and the stream became a torrent, like a surge of water escaping past an unwanted obstruction. Harriet's stammer had reappeared only on those rare occasions their father visited.

That was all in the past now.

These days there were no unexpected visits. He stayed out of all their lives.

Pushing aside that thought, Fliss shoved the door closed and walked into the kitchen.

It had all the signs that the occupant had left in a hurry.

A pan lay unwashed on the stove, a carton of milk on the countertop.

Fliss threw the milk away and washed the pan.

Domesticated? She could do that if she had to. And maybe she'd even ask her grandmother for a cooking lesson while she was here. That would surprise Harriet.

She moved through the rest of the house, checking everything. The back door was locked, so presumably whoever had helped her grandmother from the garden had taken the time to secure the house. She went upstairs and checked her grandmother's bedroom. The window was secure, the bed made.

She wandered past the room her brother, Daniel, had occupied whenever they'd stayed and took the stairs up to the attic room she'd shared with her sister. Instinctively she stepped over the fourth step with its telltale creak, and then realized what she'd done and smiled. She knew a hundred ways to sneak out of this house undetected. She knew which stair would betray her, which window would stick and which door would creak.

She pushed open the door of the bedroom, remembering how she'd oiled the hinges.

Her mother slept like the dead, but had her grandmother known she was sneaking out?

Harriet had known, but she'd never said anything. She'd pretended to be asleep so she wouldn't have to lie if questioned.

Fliss glanced around the room.

Not much had changed. Two beds were tucked under the slope in the roof so that you had to duck your head before you stood up in the morning. She strolled to the window and gazed down into the garden, noting the offending apple tree with its curved branches and thick trunk. The roots were visible on the surface, as if it was trying to remove itself from ground it had occupied for so long.

And there, beyond the apple tree, was the gate.

She'd oiled that, too, turning it from an alarm to an ally.

From her vantage point high in the house she could see that the path to the beach was overgrown. It didn't surprise her. No one used the path except the inhabitants of Sea Breeze, and she doubted her grandmother was in the habit of taking the rough sandy trail that led through the sand dunes to the beach.

For a moment she was tempted to kick off her shoes and run down that path as she had as a child, eagerly anticipating the moment when she crested the dunes and saw the rolling waves of the Atlantic Ocean.

Her feet were halfway out of her shoes before she stopped herself.

She needed to stop giving in to impulse and behave responsibly.

She slid her feet back into her shoes and instead rose on tiptoe and leaned her forehead on the cool glass, trying to see past the knotted vegetation that obscured the path to the dunes beyond. She knew every dip and curve of that path.

People said that memories faded in time, but hers hadn't faded at all.

She could still remember that warm summer night in minute detail, every sound, every color, every touch.

She moved away from the window. What was the point of torturing herself? It was behind her. She should be moving on. And she would have been doing exactly that if she'd just told Seth the truth when she'd met him earlier. A few words, that was all she'd needed to say. Instead she'd pretended to be Harriet.

Why had she done that? Of all the stupid, impulsive—

And she wished she'd known about his father. If she had, she wouldn't have asked that tactless question about his family. She'd probably hurt him, and she'd already hurt him enough.

And by pretending to be Harriet she hadn't been able

to offer anything more than conventional platitudes. Her twin wouldn't have understood how close they were, or how much he had admired his father. Fliss understood that. For a fleeting second before he'd hidden it she'd seen the raw pain in his eyes, and she'd ached for him. She'd wanted to wrap him in her arms and offer whatever comfort she could. She wanted to tell him that she understood.

Instead she'd uttered a few meaningless words. And in pretending to be Harriet, all she had done was postpone the moment when she came face-to-face with him as herself.

Now what was she going to do?

The question wasn't whether she would bump into him again, but when.

Which left her with only two options. Either she carried on pretending to be Harriet, or she confessed all and told him she was Fliss.

That would be both awkward and embarrassing. He'd want to know why she'd pretended to be her sister, and he'd read too much into it.

No, until she could work out a way to extract herself from the lie she'd spun, she'd have to continue the pretense. Which raised the question of what she was going to do about her grandmother.

She'd promised Harriet that she'd tell their grandmother she was Fliss.

And she would. She just had to hope Seth and her grandmother didn't meet until after she had untangled the mess she'd made.

Why did everything she touched get so complicated?

Frustrated with herself, she flung open windows, letting in the smell of the ocean.

Then she went back downstairs into the kitchen and unloaded the food she'd bought at the roadside stand.

She piled fruit into a bowl and placed it in the center of the table. The long cedar table had a few more scratches than she remembered, but other than that it looked the same as ever. Some of her earliest memories were of staying here, and she was glad nothing significant had changed, as if by finding things the same, a certain level of happiness was guaranteed.

How many meals had they eaten here, the three of them, wriggling impatiently on their chairs, waiting for the moment they could return to the beach? Because summers had been all about the beach. The beach and freedom.

The beach and Seth.

And that was the problem, of course. Seth was part of almost every memory she had of this place. Which meant that somehow she had to fill her head with something else.

Fliss returned to the entryway and picked up her suitcase. She'd unpack and then drive straight to the hospital.

She'd tell her grandmother the truth, and then try to work out a way to unpick the lie she'd told Seth.

SETH FINISHED EXAMINING the dog. "Chester is doing well, Angela."

"Good. I need him fit for the Fourth of July."

"You're doing something special for the holiday weekend?"

Angela lifted Chester down from the examination table. "No. We're staying home. That's why I need him fit. He hates loud noises. He was so scared last year I almost called you and asked for a tranquilizer."

"That's always a possibility, but there are other methods I prefer to try first."

"Such as?"

"Back in 2002 there was a study by an animal behaviorist and psychologist that showed that classical music had a soothing effect on dogs in shelters." Seth washed his hands. "And a few years after that another study by a veterinary neurologist showed that slower tempos, single instruments were more calming than busy, noisier music."

"So you're saying I should be playing Beethoven instead of Beyoncé?"

Seth tugged paper towel from the dispenser and dried his hands. "That's your choice. There are other things you can do, of course. Close doors, windows and curtains so that you block out the noise as much as possible." At this time of year he delivered an endless stream of advice about keeping pets away from fireworks and checking the yard for debris.

"I'm dreading it. Chester hates fireworks, and our neighbors love them." Angela stroked the dog's head. "The moment they start he tries to escape."

"Take him for a long walk during the day," Seth suggested. "It will tire him out and he's more likely to relax. As for the noise, have you tried turning up the TV?"

"No, but it's a good idea."

"And make sure your yard is secure. This is the busiest time of year for the animal shelters. They have to deal with a number of terrified pets who have escaped."

"Chester is microchipped. We had it done after a friend suggested it last year. Just in case. I couldn't bear to think of him out there running around, terrified and lost. I'm keeping all the doors shut. And my TV will be booming." Angela reattached the dog's lead. "So you're back from the big city. There were a few people who thought you'd stay there."

He heard the question in the statement and knew that whatever he said by way of an answer would spread through all the local villages by noon. "This is my home. There was never any chance that I'd stay there."

"Well, that's good to know." Her shoulders relaxed. "You wouldn't be the first to be tempted by the bright lights of Manhattan. We were laying bets at my knitting group that you wouldn't be coming back."

"Manhattan is always fun for a visit, but I wasn't tempted."

At least, not by the city.

An image of Fliss appeared in his head. She was laughing, the strap of her minuscule bikini sliding over her shoulder as she raced across the beach, her bare feet kicking up the sand.

He tapped a key on the computer and entered the details into the notes.

Nancy, the vet technician, handed over an information leaflet and showed Angela out.

She was back moments later.

"I overheard that last part of the conversation. Were you really not tempted to stay even for a moment? I have to admit if I had the choice between New York City and here, I'd take Manhattan." She struck a pose and broke into song, grabbing a syringe from the box to use as a microphone.

Seth rolled his eyes. "It's not enough that I have to

suffer the inquisition from the patients. Now I have to suffer it from the staff, too?"

Nancy stopped singing and put the syringe back. "It's just that when you leave, I leave, so I need some notice."

"I'm moving into my new house in the next week or so, and I don't plan on leaving it anytime soon." He closed the file. "Was Angela our last patient for the morning?"

"Smoke the kitten was back in, but you were tied up so Tanya dealt with him. She said to tell you to go to lunch. She has everything in hand."

Tanya, the other vet and his partner in the practice, was a wonder. "Good. I'll be on my cell if you need me."

"Hot date, Dr. Carlyle?"

"Not exactly."

But he was working on it.

CHAPTER SIX

"CAN YOU BELIEVE he actually showed up at the hospital?" Standing in the garden of her grandmother's cottage, Fliss updated her sister on the phone. "I mean, I came here to avoid him, and I'm seeing more of him than I did in Manhattan."

"I think it's adorable."

"It's not adorable! It added another layer to my totally craptastic day." Fliss rubbed her fingers across her forehead. "All right, maybe it was kind of him, but it was also inconvenient."

"Why?"

"I'd already told him I was you, and then there was Grams coming toward us in the wheelchair and—"

"No! You let Grams think you were me? Fliss, you *promised*!"

"And at the time I meant it! But then Seth showed up right at the wrong moment and I was trapped. *This* is what I mean. Not at all adorable." The phone crackled and Fliss paced to the top of a sand dune, trying to get a better signal. Her toes sank into the soft sand, and long grass tickled her ankles. She wondered what it was about this place that nudged her toward the impulsive.

"If you'd told him the truth when you bumped into him, you wouldn't have been trapped."

"I know. And I didn't intend to lie to him, but my

mouth took over and said I was you before I could stop it and now the whole thing is getting out of control. Are you mad at me?"

"No, but I'm not good with all this deception. I wish things weren't so complicated."

"Me, too."

"Are you sure Seth didn't recognize you?"

"Positive. He hasn't seen me in ten years. I guess that worked in my favor." And while part of her was relieved about that, another part was a little hurt, which made no sense at all. She'd known him without even turning her head to look at him. How could he not know her? "Having told him I was you, I didn't have any choice but to keep pretending I was you. It's just for a couple of weeks. What can possibly go wrong?"

"A million things! Fliss, if you keep pretending you're me, this thing is going to snowball."

"Are you kidding? It's sweltering here. No snowballs in sight." Her attempt at a joke fell flat. "Maybe you can come for a visit in a week or so and we can swap identities and Grams will never know."

"She's going to know. For a start we don't dress the same way."

"I'm dressing the way you'd dress if you were at the beach." She stared down at her flip-flops. "I'm wearing shorts and a tank top."

"I'm more likely to wear a sundress."

"I'm not wearing a dress. And I've seen you wear shorts."

"Are you keeping your shoes on?"

"Most of the time."

Harriet sighed. "Maybe you've fooled Seth, but do

you really think Grams can't tell the difference between us?"

"She was expecting you. People tend to see the person they expect to see."

"You have to tell her."

Fliss rolled her eyes to the sky. Yet another problem to solve. Usually life sent the boulders, but in her case she seemed to manage to throw them into her own path. "I will. Soon."

"How is she? I'm worried about her."

"Well, apart from the fact I almost died of shock when I saw her because 'a few bruises' turned out to be a massive bruise that covered pretty much the whole of her body, she seems remarkably like herself."

"And they're sure nothing was broken?"

"So they said. We're using ice on the bad parts."

"Which are the bad parts?"

"Actually, they're all bad. It's finding some body that isn't bruised that's the challenge. And talking of which, I should go and help her. We're doing it every few hours to reduce the bruising and swelling."

"You won't be coming home soon, then?"

"No." And now she was trapped here with Seth. The irony didn't escape her. "Poor Grams."

"Yes. Tell her the truth, Fliss. She'll understand that it feels awkward with Seth."

Would she? How could her grandmother understand something she didn't understand herself? It shouldn't be awkward, should it? Not after ten years.

Brooding on it, she ended the call and wandered back into the house. She removed ice packs from the freezer and then lifted a jug of iced tea from the fridge and took it to her grandmother, who was resting in the living room.

Sunlight spilled through the large windows, illuminating the soft, overstuffed sofas that faced each other across the room. The pale blue fabric was worn in places, but they were soft and comfortable—built for snuggling. Her grandmother had believed in the importance of reading time, and Fliss had spent many hours curled up with a book. She'd pretended she'd rather be outdoors on the beach, but secretly she'd enjoyed the quiet family time that was absent at home. Harriet had preferred Jane Austen or Georgette Heyer, but Fliss had veered toward adventure stories. *Moby Dick. The Last of the Mohicans.*

"Grams?" She paused in the doorway, and her grandmother turned her head, a smile on her face.

Fliss felt a stab of shock. "The bruising on your face is bad. Is it worse?"

"Just changing color." She held out her hand for the tea. "Don't fuss."

"I don't fuss." And then she remembered that if she was Harriet, she'd be fussing. "Poor you. Let me help you ice it."

She put a thin cloth between the ice pack and her grandmother's skin as the doctor had demonstrated. "I've never seen bruising like this."

"It will fade."

"Maybe you should stay out of the garden from now on."

"Nonsense. I was looking out of the window a moment ago, worrying about what's happening to my plants while I'm trapped here immobile."

"If you tell me which plants, I can do whatever needs to be done." Fliss poured tea into a glass.

"You're a good girl."

Fliss felt like a fraud. She wasn't a good girl. She was a liar and a fraud.

She had a sudden urge to blurt out everything to her grandmother, but she couldn't face seeing disappointment on her face. Or finding ways to dodge the inevitable questions about Seth.

"Anything you need," she murmured, and wandered back into the kitchen to throw together a salad for supper. As long as she didn't actually have to cook anything, she could keep this up for a while. Even she couldn't burn salad.

She was chopping tomatoes, focused on trying to make each piece as neat and uniform as Harriet would, when there was a knock on the door.

Her heart sank. She hadn't factored in visitors. This deception was spreading before her eyes, like a drop of ink spilled into water.

She tipped the tomatoes in with the lettuce and hoped whoever it was would go away.

"Harriet?" Her grandmother's voice came from the living room, and she bowed to the inevitable.

"I'll get it."

Hopefully it would be one of the neighbors with a casserole. At least then she'd only have to reheat. She was a champion reheater. And accepting a casserole could happen without worry about anyone suspecting her identity.

She opened the door, replacing her "why are you bothering me?" look with what she hoped was a reasonable imitation of Harriet's wide, welcoming smile.

The smile died on the spot.

It was Seth, standing shoulder to shoulder with another man she'd met only once before in her life. At her wedding.

Chase Adams.

Holy crap, she was totally and utterly screwed.

It didn't help that Seth leaned his arm against the doorjamb, all muscle and male hotness.

"Hi, Harriet, we just wanted to drop by and say that if you need any help, all you have to do is ask. You already know Chase, of course. He has a whole team of people who can fix anything that needs fixing in the house."

"We haven't met in person, but my wife, Matilda, talks about you a lot." Chase shook her hand. "It's good to finally meet you, Harriet. I'm sorry for your grandmother, but her misfortune is my fortune because it brought you here and I need a favor."

A favor?

Right now she wasn't in the mood for favors.

She just couldn't seem to catch a break.

"Good to meet you, too." More lies, all piling one on top of the other. She wondered how long it would take for the weight of them to topple the pile. With luck, they'd knock her unconscious when they fell. "How can I help you?"

"You know Matilda is due in four weeks, and you also know Hero is a bit of a handful. As you're going to be walking your grandmother's dog, I wondered if you'd mind walking Hero, too, while you're here. You can drop in and see Matilda at the same time. I know she'd be thrilled to see you. She hasn't had a chance to meet that many people here, so she'd be pleased to see a friend, and you already walk Hero back in Manhattan, so you know all his little quirks."

Fliss stared at him.

She didn't know any of that.

All she knew was that she was doomed.

"Sure," she croaked. "I can't think of anything I'd like more."

Except perhaps sticking her head in a bucket of freezing water and inhaling.

SETH STROLLED TO the car. "Thanks for your help."

"You're welcome." Chase paused by the car. "Matilda talks about Harriet all the time. The two of them have become friendly."

"And that's a problem because…?"

"It's not a problem. It's just that—" he turned to look at the house, a frown on his face "—Harriet didn't seem too enthusiastic at the idea of meeting up with Matilda."

Seth unlocked the car. "That's because that wasn't Harriet. That was Fliss."

"Excuse me?"

"You were talking to Fliss."

"So why did she say she was Harriet?"

"Because that's what she wants me to think."

"But—wait a minute. You're saying she's pretending to be her twin?" Chase stared at him, bemused. "Why? What possible reason could she have for doing that?"

"Me. I'm the reason. She's avoiding me."

"Avoiding—?" Chase shook his head. "But you're here anyway."

"Let me put this another way—she's avoiding having to have a conversation with me as herself."

"I've deciphered tax returns less complicated than

this. You were married! Why would she think she can fool you?"

"We haven't seen each other in ten years. She probably thought I wouldn't be able to tell the difference. That I wouldn't know."

But he knew. He knew *her*. Every detail.

"How long did it take you to work it out?"

"About ninety seconds. I mentioned cookies, and she panicked." It had been fleeting, but he'd seen it. It had been enough to convince him that he was looking at Fliss.

"She has a phobia about cookies?"

"No, but she is a terrible cook. They had to call the fire department after one of her attempts."

His friend grinned. "Does her grandmother realize?"

"I would imagine so. She's a pretty smart woman."

"So are you going to tell Fliss you know?"

"No. I'm going to let her carry on being 'Harriet' until she decides to tell me the truth."

"Why?"

Lulu rolled onto her back hopefully, and Seth crouched down to rub her belly. "First, because if we keep up the pretense then she has no reason to avoid me."

"None of this makes sense. If she was avoiding you, why would she be here in the first place?"

"She knew I was in Manhattan and didn't realize it was temporary. She came here to reduce the chances of running into me." And he wasn't sure how he felt about that. Was it a good thing or a bad thing? It was good that she was unsettled enough by his presence to go to those lengths. Not so good that she was so afraid of facing him she was prepared to conceal her identity.

Chase unlocked the car. "You have one hell of an effect on women, Carlyle. Next you'll be telling me she pushed Grandma down the stairs to give herself a reason to come here."

Seth laughed. "No, but I suspect she grabbed that excuse like a drowning man might grab a life preserver."

"So if Grandma is the life preserver, what does that make you? The big bad crocodile waiting in the water to eat her alive?" Chase paused by the car. "And tell me what the 'second' is."

"Second?"

"You said first you'd keep up the pretense so that she has no reason to avoid you. That means there's a 'second.'"

"Second is that while she is 'Harriet,' I hope to be able to tackle some issues she wouldn't discuss as Fliss."

"Are you going to kiss her?" Chase looked intrigued. "Maybe she'll be the first woman in history to break up with a guy because she's jealous of herself."

"I'm not going to kiss her. And we won't be breaking up because we're not dating."

"How long is this going to carry on?"

"Until she tells me who she is." Seth rose to his feet. "Do me a favor—play along, will you?"

"I'm no good at subterfuge. I almost wish you hadn't told me."

"You're going back to Manhattan. You won't see much of her anyway."

"What do I do about Matilda? Do I tell her the truth?"

"I think you should leave that up to Fliss."

"I don't want Matilda hurt." There was a steely edge to Chase's tone that only ever appeared when he thought someone was trying to take advantage of his wife.

"Fliss won't hurt her. I suspect right now she's on the phone to Harriet trying to work out a way to unravel this."

"I can't believe she came up with such a complicated plan."

"I don't think there was a plan. I don't think she came here intending to emulate Harriet. I think she came as herself, but then she met me on the roadside, panicked and said the first thing that came into her head."

"That doesn't seem strange to you?"

"No. It's classic Fliss. She puts the *imp* in *impulsive*."

Chase gave him a long look, the steel in his eyes giving way to amusement and sympathy. "I guess that keeps things interesting."

"It certainly does."

Chase slapped him on the shoulder and slid into the car. "You have one hell of a complicated love life, my friend."

Seth glanced toward the house. "Not yet, but I'm working on it."

CHAPTER SEVEN

"KILL ME. JUST kill me now." Fliss lay on the bed with her eyes closed. She felt as if she'd been tangled up in a coil of webbing and couldn't work her way free. "You need to come and swap places with me."

"So that I can sort out your mess? I don't think so."

"You're my sister."

"I'm doing this for your own good. You need to talk to him, Fliss." Harriet was firm. "This is the perfect time to do it."

It didn't feel perfect to her. "When Johnny Hill teased you about your stammer, did I make you punch him yourself?"

"That's different. I didn't want to punch him."

"I wanted to punch him enough for both of us."

"We have a different approach to problem solving."

Fliss sighed. "This is partly your fault. Since when have you been besties with Matilda Adams?"

"Since I started walking Hero. She's a writer, so she's often at home. Sometimes we have a coffee. I adore her."

"And you didn't think to mention it?"

"I'm sure I mentioned it."

"I don't think so. I would have remembered a business opportunity like that. Do you know how rich Chase is? I mean, the guy practically owns Manhattan."

"Yes, but they only have one dog, so I don't see the business opportunity."

"Neither do I yet, but there has to be one."

"Seth isn't exactly struggling."

"He's not a business opportunity. He's a bad decision from my past." One of the many. "Chase seemed pretty down-to-earth."

"So is Matilda. And they're so in love."

Fliss heard the note of envy in her sister's voice. That was the problem with never having been in love, she thought. It was all too easy to turn the idea into something wonderful, whereas the reality was more often than not painful. "I hope it lasts."

"Don't be a cynic. Are you sure Seth doesn't know who you really were?"

"He doesn't have a clue. What sort of things do you and Matilda talk about? Fill me in."

"You cannot pretend to be me when you're with Matilda. I really like her. This has to end right now, Fliss!" There was a sharp note in Harriet's voice that Fliss wasn't sure she'd heard before.

"If I tell her the truth she'll tell Chase, and he'll tell Seth."

"This is like a run in your panty hose. It starts small and then spreads."

"Which is why I never wear panty hose." Fliss rolled onto her stomach, and her hair slid over her shoulder. "What breed of dog is Hero?"

"A Doberman."

Fliss brightened. "That's one piece of good news."

"I will never understand you. Most people would be wary of that breed."

"They're misunderstood. I have sympathy for anyone who is misunderstood. And why are you worried? Is Hero likely to savage me?"

"No. I don't think anyone has told Hero he's a Doberman. He's having something of a breed identity crisis. He's more likely to lick you to death."

"Good."

Reminding herself it was business, and she was never going to say no to business, Fliss made sure her grandmother was comfortable and then decided she might as well make the acquaintance of Matilda and her hopefully not-so-scary dog.

The Adams residence was on a thirty-acre peninsula, with sweeping ocean views.

Fliss almost got lost driving there. Finding the turn-in was the easy part because there was no missing the wrought iron security gates. It was locating the house at the end of the wide gravel drive that proved challenging. She drove past hedged lawns and spied a tennis court on the edge of her vision.

"This drive is long enough to land a jumbo jet," she muttered, lifting her eyebrows as the house finally came into view. One glance and she decided that "beach mansion" would have been a better description than "beach house."

She parked her convertible, thinking that at least one thing about her looked at home in these surroundings. The fact that her car was rented was an irony that didn't escape her.

Knowing how wealthy Chase Adams was, she'd already formed an impression in her head of Matilda Adams. She'd be slim and elegant. Probably tall. Model-like in her proportions. One of those golden blondes who had hung around the beaches of the Hamptons when she was growing up. Girlie, with perfect hair and nails.

Having fixed that image in her head, it was a shock when Matilda opened the door.

She was tall, yes, but—

Fliss blinked. "Jeez. Is that—er—blood on your shirt? Did someone die? Disposing of a body isn't generally one of my services, but if the world is better off without whoever it was, I can make an exception."

"It's cranberry juice. Hero knocked into me and I spilled an entire glass over myself. You know what I'm like. Coordination isn't really my thing. Put me with an unruly dog, and together we have no chance. I was in the process of mopping up when you arrived." Matilda tugged at the damp fabric of her shirt. "Thank goodness it's you and not someone I'm trying to impress. It's so good to see you, Harriet! When Chase told me you were here, I couldn't believe it."

"You shouldn't believe it," Fliss said. "I'm not Harriet. I'm Fliss."

There. She'd said it. The first strand unraveled.

Matilda stared at her. "But Chase said—"

"Long story. Come to think of it, everything in my life is a long story. I don't seem to manage the short, simple version. Forget novellas, I'm *War and Peace* meets *Game of Thrones*, without the dragons and dead people."

Matilda brightened. "In that case come inside. I want to hear everything."

Fliss eyed the red stain on her shirt. "You're sure you don't want to kill me?"

"Definitely not." Matilda flung the door open a little too enthusiastically and almost smacked herself in the face. "I *love* stories. I make my living writing stories. You'll have to forgive my staring. You could totally be Harriet."

"Yeah, I get that a lot. Welcome to twindom." Fliss stepped into the spacious hallway and gazed around her in disbelief. "Wow. Sorry, is that crass of me? I probably should have pretended I see houses like this all the time. In fact I thought I had seen plenty of big houses. It's not as if there's a shortage around here. But this is—"

Matilda gave a slightly embarrassed smile. "It's a little overwhelming, isn't it?"

"A little? Make that a lot." She stared up at the domed ceiling. "The last time I saw a dome like that was in Florence, Italy."

"The first time Chase brought me here I actually got lost. I was looking for the bathroom and ended up in the guest residence. Don't even ask."

Fliss dragged her gaze from the dome. "You have a guest residence? Because you're in such cramped quarters."

Matilda grinned. "Three beds and three baths. Chase uses it to store his sailing gear. It's mostly full of wet suits and the odd sail in the middle of being repaired."

"What? No live-in staff?"

"We have a housekeeper who comes in from the village, but she doesn't live in. Chase likes his privacy."

"Yeah, must be hard having spontaneous sex if you have people lurking around every corner." She spoke without thinking and was about to apologize when there was a loud bark and a large black Doberman bounded out of the kitchen.

"And here's the other reason we don't have staff—

they can't handle my dog." Matilda braced herself and held up her hand. "Stay. *Stay!*"

The dog didn't stay. Instead he cannoned into her, tackling her around the knees, almost sending her flying.

"Whoa, that is one enthusiastic animal you've got there." Fliss grabbed Matilda's arm, steadying her. Then she grabbed the dog by the collar. "Well, hello. You must be my client. Hasn't anyone told you it isn't polite to tackle a pregnant woman?"

Hero wagged his tail so hard he almost removed her eye.

Matilda grabbed him and tried to persuade him to sit. "I apologize for his behavior. It's my fault. I don't like scolding him in case I crush his spirit."

"I think it would take a lot to crush his spirit." Like her sister, she knew animals. And she knew dogs. This one was bright-eyed, intelligent and mischievous. Her favorite type. "It's great to see a Doberman with a long tail."

"I found a breeder who didn't dock them at birth. I wanted him to have his tail. A tail is how a dog expresses himself and it's important to be able to express yourself, don't you think?"

"I do, and Hero is seriously cute."

She recognized a kindred spirit when she saw one. She knew all too well how it felt to have a continual urge to do the wrong thing. And she knew how it felt to have everyone think the worst of you.

"Chase wanted me to have security when he's working, but I couldn't think of anything worse than having a stranger in the house when I'm trying to work, so we compromised."

Fliss held out her hand to the dog and let him sniff her. "So you're a compromise, are you?" She smiled as he thrust his nose into her palm, and she slid her hand around to rub his neck. "Yeah, you like that, of course you do. You're a pushover, do you know that? A big, cuddly, oversized baby."

"Most people are terrified of him, but Chase thinks that if someone broke into the house he would lick them."

"Maybe, but the point about a dog like this is that he's a deterrent. The breed comes with a certain reputation. That reputation is often enough to make someone think twice." Fliss stroked her hand over the dog's head. "It's instinctive to him to protect those he loves. There's a reason they make great guard dogs and are often used in search and rescue."

"You know a lot about dogs."

"It's my job. Knowledge is power, and when I'm walking a strange dog I like to be the one with the power."

"He likes you. You have a way with him." Matilda seemed relieved. "Does that mean you'll be willing to walk him for me until I have the baby?"

"It will be my pleasure."

"I'd want it to be a business arrangement. I know how hard you're working to grow the business, and I wouldn't feel comfortable otherwise."

"I appreciate that. Does he have any bad habits I need to know about? Does he munch on small children? Growl at old ladies?"

"If anything he's too sociable. He greets everyone as if they're his long-lost best friend. It's the reason my cranberry juice is all over my shirt and not in my stomach."

Fliss petted the dog. "Enthusiasm is not a bad habit, although the way you're expressing it might need a little modifying. Dobermans are supersmart. They need consistent training and lots of exercise."

"I was taking him to classes in Manhattan before I got too big to comfortably move. Chase said you were also walking your grandmother's dog. Will you walk the two of them together?"

"Maybe. I'll see how they get on. Sometimes they benefit from a little company. Sometimes they're better on their own. Harriet and I personalize the service we offer and do whatever we think is best for the animal." She guessed that Hero might be the type who preferred to be the center of attention. "You have a nice dog there."

"Thank you." Matilda gently scratched his head. "Chase is worried I'm going to trip over him because I'm so clumsy. Which reminds me, I need to do something about this shirt. I look like a walking murder victim." She let go of Fliss's arm. "Let's go through to the kitchen. I have a mountain of cookies that need eating."

"Cookies? You love baking?" Fliss felt a rush of inadequacy. Was she the only person on the planet who didn't find baking soothing? "Harriet is the same. I'm beginning to see why the two of you get along so well."

Matilda laughed. "I'm nothing like Harriet and I *loathe* cooking. The sum total of my creative endeavor is writing. Whenever I cook I inevitably get distracted by the scene I'm working on and forget about whatever is in the oven. Which is probably why I burn everything. I've set off the smoke alarm twice this summer already. We're connected direct to the fire department, and Chase gives them a huge donation every year in order to smooth any frustrations they have for having me living on their turf."

"Really? So you had a team of hot firemen running through your house? If I knew that was a possibility I'd burn the toast every day. Wait. Come to think of it I do that anyway." She followed Matilda through the house, wondering if it would be rude to give in and let her jaw drop open. She thought about the guy standing next to Seth on her grandmother's doorstep. He'd been casually dressed. Relaxed. She never would have suspected he was a gazillionaire. "So if you don't bake, how did you end up with a mountain of cookies?"

"I mentioned to Chase that I had a craving for them, and ever since then he's been picking them up on his way home. He's so thoughtful, I don't have the heart to tell him I can't eat them all."

Fliss glanced at Matilda's bump. "You're sure that's a baby and not cookies?"

Matilda laughed and pushed open a door.

The kitchen was large and airy, positioned at the back of the house overlooking the garden and the beach.

Fliss thrust her hands into the pockets of her shorts and stared at the view. "This is incredible. How could anyone cook here and *not* burn everything?"

"It's even better from the second level. That's where most of the living space is. I'm always worried Hero is going to go leap off the balcony, so when I'm on my own we spend a lot of time down here. And we have quick access to the beach."

Private beach, Fliss noted. And Matilda Adams might not have much visible security in terms of beefy guys with dark glasses and discreet headsets, but she certainly had protection. The house was on its own spit of land, bordered by ocean.

And then there was the dog, of course.

Fliss was in no doubt at all that if his family were threatened, Hero would live up to his name.

"Does your beach connect with the main beach?"

"In one small area at low tide. Hero has been known to escape. Which isn't great, because as you know there are strict rules on the public beach. Up until ten in the morning they can be loose as long as they're under voice control. Hero struggles with that."

"We'll work on it."

"He's not great with authority."

"Don't worry. Neither am I." Fliss glanced around, noticing a laptop set up on a table by the window. Every available surface was covered in paper. "That's a lot of paper. Did your printer malfunction?"

"It's my next book. I printed it out to do a final read and then dropped it when Hero used me as target practice. I've been putting the pages back in order."

Fliss stooped and picked up a page that had fallen under one of the chairs. "Page two hundred and sixty-five."

"Brilliant! I was looking for that one." Matilda took it from her and added it to a pile on the countertop. "I should have printed it out a chapter at a time."

"So you make your living writing stories. What kind of stories? Anything I'm likely to have read?"

"I don't know. I write romance fiction, populated by strong, capable heroines who are nothing like me. Women who would *not* answer the door spattered in cranberry juice." She grabbed a cloth and mopped at her shirt.

"So are your heroes like Chase?"

Matilda blushed. "In a way. They're all versions of Chase, but don't tell him I said that. He's very private. He'd hate to think I'd put any part of him in a book. Tea or coffee?"

"Coffee, please. Black and strong." Trying not to think how it must feel to be that crazily in love with a man who loved you back, Fliss picked up another sheet of paper from the floor. "Page three hundred and thirty-four. Looks important. Sex scene. Wow. This is pretty hot. You wrote this?"

"Yes, and you shouldn't read it out of context!" Matilda tried to snatch it out of her hand, but Fliss held it out of reach as she read the first two paragraphs.

"Hey, you're good! So is this kind of thing embarrassing to write?"

"No." Matilda snatched it from her hand, tearing the paper in the process. "The type of sex I write about is always part of character development. It happens for a reason, and it always changes the relationship." She added the page to the others.

"And that reason can't just be because the character gets a little desperate?"

"It could be—" Matilda made coffee using a complicated-looking espresso machine "—but the reason they're desperate is probably to do with reasons a little deeper than that."

"I don't understand."

Matilda leaned against the counter, waiting while the machine did its thing. "So as a writer if I had a character who hadn't had sex in a while, I'd be asking myself why. There is always a reason."

"What sort of reason?" Fliss was fascinated.

"Maybe she was hurt in the past, in which case when she eventually has sex that's going to be a big deal and she's going to be dealing with those issues."

"What issues?"

"That's for me to figure out when I'm writing. I ask myself what's in the character's past. What do they want? Why do they want it?"

"I never realized it was so complicated. You think like this for all your characters?"

"Yes. That's what makes them real to me. I know how they'd act in any situation."

"Even I don't know how I'm going to act in any given situation, so you're one up on me. So what happens if the character doesn't know what they want?"

"Then they figure it out over the course of the book. And sometimes what they want changes, of course. That's the fun part of writing—working out what they'll do. Throwing in some surprises. And every book, every character, is different because no two people ever do the same thing even when faced by the same situation."

"You mean some people always do the right thing and some the wrong thing."

She knew all about that. She was the second sort.

"No, that's not what I mean." Matilda put the coffee mug in front of Fliss. "Who decides what is 'wrong'? Wrong by whose standards? What is wrong in our culture may be normal somewhere else. And people are never 'bad' or 'good.' They're just people. And 'good' people are capable of doing bad things and making bad choices. That's what makes people endlessly fascinating. For example, ask me if I'd steal and I'd tell you no, but if my baby was starving and stealing was the only way to keep it alive, would I steal then? Maybe. Who knows? None of us know how we'd act if circumstances pushed us to our limits. We don't always know what we're capable of doing, or becoming."

You're useless, worthless.

Fliss took a sip of coffee. "This is delicious, although that machine looks like you need two doctorates to operate it."

"That machine is a typical Chase gift." Matilda made herself tea. "We had a coffee in a coffee shop once and I enjoyed it, so he bought me the same machine. Had it shipped from Italy. All the instructions were in Italian, and I don't speak Italian. Adorable, but it took me three days, full time, to learn how to work it. And the irony is that since I got pregnant I can't bear the taste of coffee."

Fliss laughed, but she felt a little pang of envy. "You're lucky."

"Because of the quality of my coffee, or because I have a good man?"

"Both. So going back to the whole sex thing—" Fliss kept her voice casual "—what other reasons do you give characters for not having had sex in a while?"

"The simplest is that they just haven't met someone they like enough, but that doesn't make for interesting reading, so generally my characters have bigger issues. Maybe they have serious issues with intimacy. Maybe they're in love with someone from their past and no one else has matched up."

Fliss's heart beat faster. "But that would be crazy, right? I mean when something's over, it's over."

Matilda slid onto the nearest chair. "Are we still talking about my books, or is this about Seth?"

Instantly defensive, Fliss looked at her, fighting the impulse to leave the room. "You know about Seth?"

"I know the two of you were married. He and Chase have been friends a long time. Chase has helped remodel his house. But I guess you already know that."

Fliss shook her head. "No. I didn't know that." But it made sense. Chase was the one friend he'd brought to their wedding. The fact that there was so much of Seth's life that she knew nothing about felt odd. In some ways he was a stranger. A familiar stranger. And suddenly she had a fierce urge to know more. "So do you see him socially?" Really it was none of her business, and she had no idea why she was even asking that question. Seth Carlyle could have dinner with the whole of the Hamptons if he wanted to. Why should it bother her? Why should she even care?

"He's been here for dinner a few times. Once he brought Na—" Matilda stopped herself finishing the sentence, and Fliss gave a shrug, hoping the hideous lurch of her stomach hadn't been reflected in her expression.

"If 'Na' is a woman, you don't need to worry about me. Seth and I haven't seen each other in a decade. We're definitely history."

"Her name was Naomi, but they're not together anymore."

"Right." And that fact shouldn't interest her. It really shouldn't. It certainly shouldn't lift her spirits. It was inevitable that a man like Seth wasn't going to stay single for long. She suppressed the impulse to ask a thousand questions about Naomi.

"I was so relieved when they broke up."

"She was wrong for him?"

"Well, yes, there was that, and also the fact she made me feel totally crap about myself. You know there are some women who fall out of bed looking put together? Perfect hair. Perfect skin. Not an ounce of extra flesh anywhere. No accidents with champagne glasses or cartons of cranberry juice. Naomi was like that. She was really sweet, but I always felt she was privately amazed that someone like me hadn't been wiped out by evolution."

Fliss laughed. "So she broke it off?" Had she managed to make that question sound casual?

"No, Seth did." Matilda studied her carefully. "Seth always ends relationships."

Did he?

He hadn't ended theirs. She'd been the one to do that.

She felt a stab of guilt. Was she the reason he always ended relationships now? Had their short, painful marriage put him off commitment altogether?

Being afraid of commitment just didn't sound like him. But ten years was a long time, wasn't it? He'd probably changed.

She certainly had.

"So why was Naomi wrong for him?" Damn, why had she asked that? Now it was going to look as if she cared, and she didn't. She really didn't. It was of no interest to her who Seth dated.

"She was saccharine sweet. And a little manipulative, although it took a while for me to spot that. She got her own way through charm. She tried to manipulate Seth, but he wasn't having it. I felt a little sorry for her to be honest. I think she genuinely adored him, and it was a little uncomfortable to watch. The more she wrapped herself around him, the more he withdrew." Matilda sipped her tea. "Have we reached the part where you tell me why Chase thinks you're Harriet? You told him that?"

"Actually Seth did." Fliss stared into her coffee. "I got myself into a bit of a fix."

"Sounds like you could use a cookie." Matilda pushed the box toward her. "And a friend."

Fliss reached into the box and pulled out a cookie. She nibbled the corner absently and then frowned. "This is delicious."

"I know. If I could only ever eat one food again it would be this cookie. It's from Cookies and Cream."

Fliss chewed slowly, savoring the explosion of sugar and comfort. "No idea where that is, but I need a map right now."

"It's on Main Street, next to that boutique that sells all those gorgeous beach clothes, none of which I can squeeze into anymore."

"Harriet loves that place. And you're tiny apart from your bump."

"Are you kidding? I've been called many things in my life, but 'tiny' isn't on the list. The bump affects my balance. Most of the time I look like a cross between a drunken camel and a giraffe who swallowed a watermelon."

"You look nothing like either of those things." Deciding that willpower was overrated, Fliss took another cookie. "And in case you were wondering, this isn't emotional eating. It's 'these are too good to pass up' eating."

"I believe you. Now tell me why Seth thinks you're

Harriet." Matilda put her mug down. "You were married. He can't tell the difference?"

"Apparently not." And yes, that rankled. If real life was like a movie he would have looked into her eyes and known her instantly. "That's the downside of having a clone."

"But there must be a million upsides. I often thought about doing a twin story, but I assumed that in real life people would probably be able to tell twins apart." She studied Fliss. "But you two really are identical."

"Only on the outside."

"It's uncanny. But you're right, apart from looks, you don't seem to be much like each other."

"Even in looks, we have our differences. Harriet smiles. I scowl." Fliss reached across and closed the box of cookies. "You might want to move that to a locked cupboard. And don't let me see which one because I've been known to break into locked cupboards in my time."

"So do you do this a lot?"

"Eat cookies? It happens occasionally, especially when someone leaves an entire box out on the countertop." She took a bite. "Weird, when you think about it."

"I meant, do you pretend to be your sister?"

"Last time was when we were kids. Someone was bullying her." Remembering still had the power to make her angry. "They needed a little education on how to treat people."

Matilda's eyes gleamed. "And no doubt you educated them in style."

"I think my solution had certain elements of style." She waved the cookie, scattering crumbs. "Would have done it anyway, but I decided it would have more impact if they thought it was her."

"And she pretended to be you?"

"No. She wouldn't have allowed it. Harriet is straight and honest. I'm the manipulative one who thrives on deception."

Matilda raised her eyebrows. "What was the deception?"

"I arranged a diversion so she didn't know what I had planned. She didn't know until she found me trying to wash blood out of my hair in the girls' bathroom." Fliss put the cookie down and lifted her hair to reveal the evidence. "War wound."

Matilda reached for a piece of paper and scribbled some notes. "Sorry, but this has to go in a book. So if you haven't done it in a while, why now?"

She'd been asking herself the same question.

Impulse. Lack of judgment. None of the answers sounded impressive, even to her. "I came here to avoid Seth. And even saying that out loud makes me wince." She drained her coffee. "What sort of person is too much of a coward to say 'hi' to a man she hasn't seen in ten years?"

"One who still has complicated feelings. But I don't understand why coming here would help you avoid him. Seth lives here."

"That crucial piece of information happened to be missing when I made my decision. I saw him in Manhattan. He was working as a vet in the practice we use all the time. I assumed he'd moved there permanently."

"So you decided you'd get out of town," Matilda said slowly, "and then you bumped right into him."

"Within an hour of arriving here." She finished the cookie. "Which proves that karma is a bitch."

"Or that fate can be kind."

It was exactly the comment Harriet would have made.

"I can see why you and my sister are good friends. You're both romantics. And much as I hate to burst that little pink fluffy cloud you see the world through, I can tell you there was nothing romantic about our meeting. First, I thought I'd run over his dog—"

"Oh, that's Lulu. She likes to play dead."

"I know that *now*, but at the time I thought I'd killed her. Which almost killed me. There are plenty of humans I'd be happy to hit with my car, but I've never met a dog who deserved that fate. So there I was, shaking, when Seth steps out of the bushes. Instead of doing the adult thing and saying 'Hi, Seth, how are things with you?' I pretended to be Harriet."

Far from being shocked, Matilda looked delighted. "Oh, this would make the perfect meet-cute."

"Excuse me?"

"Don't you watch romantic comedies?"

"My favorite movie is *The Shining*, with *Psycho* a close second."

Matilda shuddered. "You're right. You really are different from Harriet. Anyway, if you thought you'd hit the dog, then you must have been feeling shaken and vulnerable."

"That's an explanation I can live with."

"Or maybe you just saw him and panicked because you weren't prepared."

"That, I find harder to live with."

"Why? If you haven't seen him in that long, it's an understandable reaction."

"Not for most people, but for me, yes. I have a long history of acting on impulse." If it hadn't been for that annoying tendency she might not have got up close and personal with Seth in the first place. "I'm working on it, but so far I'm a work in progress. And I'm not making much progress."

"You're too hard on yourself." Matilda shot her a look. "I based my last hero on Seth."

"You did?"

"Why not? He's handsome. And hot. And he's also a vet. That immediately elevates him to hero status for a lot of my readers."

Fliss stared at her. "That's all it takes? You can turn into a hero just by picking the right profession?"

"It's a caring profession. A hero who works in a caring profession starts off with plus points."

"Because you know he can de-worm your cat if the need arises?"

Matilda laughed. "You've changed the subject. I was saying that I totally understand why you would have pretended to be Harriet. We all do rash things when we're threatened."

"He didn't threaten me."

"No, but your emotions did."

Fliss decided Matilda saw a little too much for comfort. "Whatever the reason, I'm basically a coward who avoids potentially uncomfortable situations." She thought about Harriet, hiding under the table as a child. They'd each sought refuge in different ways.

"I don't think it's cowardice. It's because you still have feelings."

"I hate to disappoint you, Miss Romance Novelist, but until that encounter on the roadside, I hadn't seen Seth in a decade. Feelings are like plants. They need nurturing. And that's not me, by the way. I'm not a nurturer. I kill plants. Not intentionally, you understand.

It just happens. Things that live around me need to be able to care for themselves." She glanced at Hero. "Apart from dogs. Dogs, I can handle."

"And why is that?"

"Dogs only ever expect you to be who you are. They never want more from you. Unconditional love."

"But you felt something when you saw Seth."

"What makes you say that?"

"Because if you hadn't," Matilda said slowly, "you wouldn't have pretended to be your twin. I think the reason you ran is not because you didn't want to see him, but because you did."

CHAPTER EIGHT

SETH WALKED LULU on the beach, keeping her on the leash as they were past the time when dogs were allowed to run loose.

From the other direction, racing toward them was a Doberman.

Hero.

He glanced beyond him, expecting to see Matilda, but instead he saw Fliss.

Harriet, he reminded himself. Until she decided to end this charade, he had to remember to call her Harriet.

It rankled that she didn't trust him enough to reveal the truth, but that had always been the problem. Fliss kept her emotions behind barriers. He understood why, but that didn't make it any easier to handle.

In the meantime he was going to turn her subterfuge to his advantage.

Hero and Lulu greeted each other ecstatically, a whirl of fur, barks and wagging tails. Moments later Fliss arrived, breathless.

She was wearing running shorts, and her hair was caught in a sleek ponytail.

"Sorry." She looked annoyed that the dog had led her to him. "He slipped his leash. I called and he ignored me. I can see why Matilda struggles with him."

"No problem. These two know each other."

"Maybe, but a Doberman should be better trained than this one." She clipped the lead onto Hero, who looked at her reproachfully. "Yeah, that's right. This is not how I expected our first proper date to go. I'm the one in charge here, remember? I'm the boss."

Plenty of people would have been wary of a Doberman the size of Hero, but Fliss seemed completely at ease. It didn't surprise him.

He'd only ever seen Fliss scared of one thing, and that had been her father.

It had made him sick to the stomach to witness it.

He wondered whether she still saw him. Whether the man still had that much power over her.

"It's kind of you to walk him. I know Chase appreciates it."

"I can understand why he asked. This dog is too strong for Matilda. Sit." She spoke sternly, and Hero eyed her, weighing up his odds of getting away with ignoring her. Deciding they weren't good, he sat.

Fliss nodded. "That's better. I am going to teach you to listen because once that baby arrives, you're going to need to be more in control. It's a big responsibility being a family dog. Are you paying attention?"

Lulu, who was good at sensing atmospheres, whined and slunk behind Seth's legs.

Hero watched Fliss with big soulful eyes.

Seth watched her, too. He knew that at that moment she'd forgotten that she was pretending to be Harriet. In front of him was Fliss. The Fliss he'd known and remembered.

Their affair had been crazy, wild and hot. So hot that he'd often wondered if that had been part of the problem. If they'd spent less time having sex and more

time talking, would they have weathered those traumatic early months?

Probably not, because that would have required her
to open up. And she never opened up. She'd built defenses to keep her father out and in the process had kept
everyone else out, too.

He'd grown up in a loving family, with parents who
supported, encouraged but never interfered. They'd
raised him to understand the importance of hard work.
Of loyalty. Of love.

Everything he'd wanted had been at his fingertips.

And then he'd met Fliss.

"How's your grandmother?"

"Bruised. And a little frightened, I think. It's been
a blow to her independence, and I hate to see that. I'm
trying to rebuild her confidence." She lowered her hand
to the dog's head. "She's talking about making changes
around the house."

"What sort of changes?"

"Bed on the ground floor, that kind of thing. She's
wondering whether to have the apple tree taken down."
Her face was free of makeup, but the breeze and the sun
had whipped pink into her cheeks. She was subtly femi-
nine, with a narrowed tapered chin and defined cheek-
bones. He'd always loved the way she looked, but most
of all he loved that she was strong, intelligent and out-
spoken. Standing this close to her, there was no doubt
in his mind that this was Fliss. He'd long since given
up asking himself how he could feel sparks of chemistry with one twin but not the other.

"She tripped in the garden, so I guess it makes sense.
As for the house, if you need any remodeling, Chase
might be able to help with that."

"Yes, I heard he was building you a house." She shielded her eyes and glanced at the ocean.

Did she think that not looking at him would make it less likely that he'd recognize her?

"I used to come to this beach with Fliss." He saw her shoulders tense. "It was one of her favorite places."

Eventually she turned, but only to make a fuss of Hero. "There are some great beaches around here. So do you have an ocean view?"

"Yes. You should come and take a look sometime. We could share a beer and watch the sunset." They'd done that many times, the two of them, sitting on the sand, wrapped up in each other. She'd crept out of her grandmother's cottage and he'd been waiting for her the other side of the rusty gate.

Did she ever think about it?

Was she thinking of it now?

"Maybe I will." Her smile flashed, even as her eyes said *never*. "So you're not living in your parents' place?"

"For now, but it's temporary." And part of him wished he hadn't opted to stay there. The place seemed suffused with sadness. Maybe it was the silence, after years of large noisy family gatherings, but these days the house felt like an empty, echoing void. "Chase reckons I'll be able to move in next week. How long are you planning on staying?"

"I don't know. Until I'm no longer useful."

"Can Fliss manage without you?" He kept pushing, a little more each time, wanting her to trust him even though he knew she wouldn't. Protecting herself was second nature to Fliss, the instinct so deeply ingrained that she protected herself even when she didn't need to. She didn't know any other way.

He searched for some sign that she was uncomfortable with the lie, but her expression didn't change.

"Fliss will manage," she said. "She always manages."

How long did she intend to keep up the pretense?

He subdued that side of him that was tempted to confront her.

"I was going to grab a coffee and something to eat before going to the clinic. Will you join me?" He saw her hesitate as she searched for an excuse, and he wondered if her hesitation was because she didn't want to spend time with him, or because she was afraid of giving herself away. He felt a rush of frustration. Finally face-to-face with her, alone, and still he wasn't able to have the conversation that was so long overdue.

She looked away. "I have Hero—"

"It will be good for his training to sit patiently, and Lulu can teach him a few things."

"Like how to play dead and frighten the crap out of people?"

"That, too." He saw her fumble for an excuse, and give up.

"Sure, why not."

They walked along the beach, and he thought about the number of times they'd done exactly this, walked shoulder to shoulder, close. This time she was careful to keep a good distance between them. Before his relationship with Fliss, he'd thought, with the lack of depth that came with youth, that intimacy was a physical thing. It was naked bodies and carnal discovery. It was only with Fliss that he'd discovered that intimacy, real intimacy, was emotional. It was a sharing of thoughts, beliefs and secrets that deepened a relationship in a way that hot sex alone couldn't.

He'd thought he'd been on the way to having that with her, but there had always been a part of her he'd never been able to reach. Before he'd come close to doing that, everything had fractured. Like a vase dropped from a height onto concrete, it had seemed that there were too many pieces to put back together.

They found a table at the beach café, and the moment they sat down he realized his mistake. Here, in such a public place, there was no chance of privacy. Not that there was much chance of that anywhere in this community.

"Hi, Dr. Carlyle." Megan Whitlow was the first to approach him, smoothing her gray hair back from her temples. "Rufus seems a little better, but I'm wondering if I should have him checked again, just to be sure."

"Call Daisy," Seth said easily. "She'll make you an appointment."

Megan leaned forward, lowered her voice. "We're just all so happy you're back, Dr. Carlyle. You're an asset to this community."

"That's very kind of you, Megan." It was impossible for him to be anonymous here. Impossible for him to ask the questions he'd intended to ask. Patient, he listened as four different people approached and updated him on the status of their pets' health.

"You're popular. You don't even need to rent premises. You could run a clinic right here by the beach." Fliss picked up the menu, amused. "Still, I guess we should be relieved you're not a doctor. At least people aren't removing their clothes and updating you on their intimate problems."

"I should have picked somewhere else."

"No. I like it." Her admission surprised him.

"You do?"

"Yes." She glanced at the menu briefly and put it down again before sliding sunglasses onto her nose. "That's what being in this place means, isn't it? Community. It's the reason you chose to practice here and not somewhere like Manhattan. You used to talk about it. How ultimately this sort of practice was what you wanted."

"I don't remember ever discussing it with you."

There was a pause. "Fliss must have mentioned it." She'd made a swift rescue, and he decided not to press.

Not yet.

But soon. If she didn't tell him herself, he was going to have to make the first move.

"So you built a good business in Manhattan."

"It's growing fast." She talked about numbers, growth, strategy and plans for the future.

If she'd really been Harriet, she would have been telling him about the dogs, not their profit projections for the next quarter.

They ate a fragrant Thai salad, flavored with lemongrass and the tang of lime, and he watched as the sunlight played over her hair, picking out silver and gold.

They talked about neutral topics. Business—his and hers—life in Manhattan versus life in the Hamptons, dogs. Nothing personal.

"Dessert?"

She glanced at the menu and sighed. "Better not. I ate half a ton of cookies at Matilda's a few days ago, and I'm still feeling guilty." She put the menu down. "And you don't have a sweet tooth, so I guess it's just coffee."

Another slip.

He was working out how he could turn that to his

advantage when someone else approached the table. Only this time, he wasn't the target.

"Harriet?" The woman wrapped Fliss in a tight hug, and Seth saw her face freeze in horror.

It was obvious to him she had no idea who was hugging her.

He came to her rescue.

"Hi, Linda. How are preparations for the bake sale?"

"We're all set for Saturday. I hope you're going to stop by and spend a fortune. All in a good cause, the local animal shelter." She released Fliss. "I feel guilty asking for more support from you, Dr. Carlyle, given all that you already do."

Suddenly Seth had an idea.

Maybe it was a little unfair, but hey—if Fliss wasn't above a little subterfuge, then neither was he.

"Harriet makes the best chocolate chip cookies you've ever tasted. Isn't that right, Harriet?"

He smiled at Fliss and saw panic flash across her face.

Extract yourself from that, my beauty.

"Well, I wouldn't exactly say they were the *best*—"

"Because Harriet is too modest for her own good." He looked at Linda, whom he'd known for years. "You should talk her into making some for you."

"Now, that is a truly excellent idea." Linda whipped a little book out of her purse and scribbled a note to herself. "I remember the ones you made last summer. And your grandmother was boasting about what a talented cook you are. How could I have forgotten that?"

Fliss looked horrified. "Well, that's kind of you to say so, but I'm pretty busy right now what with taking care of my grandmother and walking Matilda's dog."

"How is Eugenia? I heard she had a fall. If she needs anything at all, I'm here for her."

"Well, that's very generous—"

"And I'm sure you'll be baking for her, seeing as she's ill and all, so I don't feel guilty asking you to make a few more for us to sell. Your chocolate chip cookies are famous around here. I don't know why I didn't think of it myself. Thank you, Seth!"

Fliss floundered and then bared her teeth in what was probably supposed to be a smile. "Sure. It will be my pleasure."

Seth smiled inwardly.

He was sure it was going to be anything but pleasure.

He wondered how she'd handle it.

Phone Harriet? Watch a video on YouTube?

Maybe he should call the fire department and warn them to get the hoses ready.

Their coffee arrived, and Linda left them in peace.

"It was good of you to offer."

"I didn't volunteer. You volunteered me." She poked at the foam on her cappuccino and sent him a furious look. "Why did you do that?"

He held her gaze. "I know how you love to cook and be part of the community, Harriet."

And because sooner or later she was going to have to admit who she really was.

He'd rather it was sooner.

Fliss slammed around the kitchen, sweating. The table and the floor were dusted with flour, and the first batch of cookies lay in a charred heap on a plate. The second batch was piled next to them. Not burned, but flat and greasy. She planned to bury the evidence later, after her next attempt. She should probably put the hospital on alert before anyone actually consumed one. By baking, she was risking mass casualties.

Damn Seth. Damn Seth and his community spirit.

It would serve him right if she fed the lot to him and let him deal with the consequences.

Next to her, Charlie whined.

"Are you kidding me?" She glanced down at the dog. "Trust me, you do *not* want to eat this. Take one bite and you'll end up at the vet clinic, and I won't be taking you, so I suggest you keep your jaws clamped shut."

Cross with herself, frustrated, she washed the bowl and started again.

Why had he volunteered her to do this?

Because he believed she was Harriet.

And whose fault was that?

Hers.

Never, under any circumstances, would she pretend to be Harriet ever again. She wasn't Harriet, and she never would be.

She checked the recipe again, trying to work out where she'd gone wrong the first time.

She could do this. She was smart. Capable. She should be able to make a batch of damn cookies without poisoning anyone or setting the house on fire.

"Do you need help?" Her grandmother spoke from the doorway, and Fliss gave a start of guilt. Given that there was no hiding the evidence of her incompetence, she had little choice but to brazen it out.

"You're supposed to be resting with your feet up." It was the reason she'd chosen this moment to bake. "What woke you?"

"I'm not sure. It could have been the clattering and muttering, or it could have been the smell of burning."

"Seth volunteered me to make cookies for the charity bake off." Fliss felt herself flush. Deceiving Seth was one thing, but deceiving her grandmother was something different entirely. "Sorry about the noise. And the mess. I'm not feeling myself today."

"You haven't been yourself since you arrived here," her grandmother said mildly. "You've been Harriet. Which, I understand, must be something of a challenge given that you're Fliss."

"You know?" Fliss stared at her, embarrassed. "How long have you known?"

"That you're Fliss? From the beginning, of course."

She felt a spasm of guilt. The spoon slipped from her fingers and clattered into the bowl. "How did you know? Because I can't cook?"

"I knew from the moment I saw you in the hospital parking lot."

"Was it the red car? I should have picked something more sensible."

"It wasn't the car." Her grandmother leaned down and brushed specks of flour from Charlie's fur. "You're my granddaughter. You think I don't know my own granddaughter?"

Fliss felt like a fool. "But if you knew, why didn't you say something?"

"I assumed you had a good reason for pretending to be your sister." She settled herself down in the chair. "And I'm assuming that good reason is tall, dark and too handsome for his own good."

Fliss retrieved the spoon. "I didn't intend to pretend

to be Harriet. That wasn't the plan. When you called that morning—that was me on the phone, not Harry."

"I know. What I don't know, is why you pretended to *me*. Why not just say who you were?"

"Because I needed to get away from Manhattan. Seth was working in the practice we use, practically around the corner from us. I didn't want to see him. When you called, it seemed like the excuse I'd been looking for."

"So why not tell me that when I called?"

"Because you didn't want me. You wanted Harriet."

Her grandmother studied her over the top of her glasses. "Is that really what you think?"

Fliss shrugged. "You called Harriet."

"I called her number first. I could just as easily have called yours."

"But you didn't. You wouldn't." Fliss pushed the bowl away from her. "And I don't blame you for that. Everyone wants Harriet. She's the kind, nurturing one. I'm the bad twin." She saw her grandmother's mouth tighten.

"That's your father talking. The first time I heard him call you that, I wanted to throw him out of my house and close the door behind him. I would have done it, except it would have been your mother who suffered."

Fliss froze. She wished she'd never made cookies. At least then, they could have kept up the pretense instead of having the last conversation on earth she wanted to have.

Her parents' relationship and their father's behavior were topics that'd always been ignored, swept aside like dust under a rug.

Fliss wanted to run for the door, but her feet wouldn't move. "He called me that because it was true."

"Do you really believe that?"

Fliss stared at the table, seeing the scars, remembering the scenes at the dinner table. She remembered her father shouting until his face took on a strange red tinge, somewhere between beetroot and tomato. There had been moments when she'd thought he might actually have a heart attack, and a few moments when she'd half hoped that would happen. And then it had, and it hadn't made any difference. In books something like that brought families back together. There were regrets and reconciliation. Real life hadn't happened that way. At least, not for her. "I should probably finish making these cookies. Or maybe I should just give up and buy a batch from Cookies and Cream. Or maybe I should confess to my sins."

"I never thought you were a quitter."

Fliss breathed and looked at her grandmother. "I'm not, but cooking and I don't mix. In fact it's the mix that's the problem."

"I don't think the cookies are the problem here at all. And anyway, they can wait."

"They can't. Thanks to my impulsive nature, I'm supposed to produce a batch for the sale this weekend. It's going to take me that long to figure it out." And suddenly baking cookies seemed appealing. Anything was more appealing than talking about her past.

"You're not the bad twin, Fliss."

She didn't want to talk about this. She absolutely didn't want to.

"Do you think I used too much flour? They're kind of sticky." She gave the mixture a desperate prod, but her grandmother wasn't about to be deflected.

"Maybe that's how it seemed to someone looking

on the surface. Someone who didn't know any better. But I saw how things were. It was hard for you all, and it was hard for me, too. She's my daughter. It didn't sit well with me knowing the love in that marriage was one-sided."

Jeez, this was too personal. It was as if her grandmother was poking around a locked door with a random key, hoping it would fit.

And Fliss had no intention of opening that door.

She made a desperate attempt to change the subject. "I don't pretend to be an expert on love. I'm good with numbers and difficult dogs. Emotions—they're not really my thing." But she should make more of an effort, shouldn't she? Particularly as her grandmother was clearly determined to have the conversation. She was about to scoot away from it again but then decided that, as her grandmother had apparently forgiven her for the deception, the least she could do was offer her something back. "You're right. My dad didn't love her enough. Or if he did, he had a weird way of showing it." And it must have been hard for her mother, too. Fliss could all too easily imagine how hard. She thought about Seth and immediately pushed the thought away.

She didn't want to think about Seth. And she certainly didn't want to dwell on his feelings for her.

She wasn't going there.

Her grandmother removed her glasses slowly. Her hair was snowy white, emphasizing the livid bruises on her skin. "That's how you saw it?"

"How else?" Of course her mother had loved her father. Otherwise why would she have tried so hard to please him? "She was always trying to keep him happy. She had this voice that she only ever used around him, like a cross between melted honey and sugar syrup. And it annoyed him. He used to say 'stop trying to placate me,' and she'd say, 'I just want you to be happy, Robert.' But he was never happy. Didn't matter what she did, he was never happy." And she'd often wondered whether he'd always been like that. Had he been an angry child? Difficult? His parents had died when he was in his teens, so she'd never had anyone she could ask. "You spent time with them. You must have seen that, too."

Her grandmother picked up her glasses. "Yes. I saw that."

Then why was her grandmother giving her that strange look?

Fliss had the distinct feeling she was missing something.

"I know they got married quickly because Mom was pregnant with Daniel." Was that what her grandmother was hinting at? Her mother had always been quite open about it. "I know it was a whole whirlwind thing. Romantic and a little crazy."

Her grandmother gave her a long look and then gave her a smile that was more than a little strained. "Yes, it was all very quick."

"Maybe my dad thought she trapped him or something. Maybe that was why he was always so angry with us. Me in particular. I always assumed he didn't want kids."

"That wasn't the case at all."

Fliss shrugged. "That was how he acted."

"Fliss—"

"It doesn't matter anymore. We're not even in touch. He made it clear he didn't want to see me anymore."

What she didn't tell her grandmother was how he'd

made it clear. She'd never told anyone about that time, after his first heart attack a few years ago, that she'd visited him in the hospital.

She'd gone on her own, lied to everyone, even her twin. Taken a train and a bus and arrived at the hospital soaked through because it had been raining so hard. It was as if the weather had been mirroring her mood.

She'd pushed open the door of her father's room, seen beeping machines and her father, frail and vulnerable in the bed. Her coat had clung to her, the rain dripping onto the floor like tears.

He'd turned his head and for a moment they'd just stared at each other. And then he'd said four words. Not, "I love you, Fliss," or "Good to see you," but *"What do you want?"*

That had been it.

What do you want?

And she hadn't been able to tell him what she wanted because she hadn't known. She hadn't understood why she'd come in the first place, to visit a man who had always seemed to find her existence close to intolerable. And she hadn't understood how his indifference could still crush her after all this time.

What *had* she wanted?

Had she honestly thought he'd open his arms and embrace her? When had he ever done that?

She'd retreated from the room without saying anything at all and returned home quietly, relieved she hadn't told anyone where she was going. Because of her secrecy, she'd been spared uncomfortable questions. Like the ones her grandmother was asking now.

"I really need to make these cookies. And I don't know how I'm going to do it."

Her grandmother rose to her feet, her hands closing over the edge of the table as she steadied herself. "I always find a problem is halved when it's shared."

Was her grandmother making a point? If so, Fliss chose to ignore it.

"Depends on who you're sharing it with and what the problem is. If you tried to share a cooking problem with me, it would be doubled, not halved."

"In this case you're the one sharing the cooking problem with me. We'll do it together."

"You're supposed to be resting."

"You think a few bruises are going to stop me from baking?"

"If I thought that, I would have bashed myself on the skull a few hundred times with a wooden spoon."

Her grandmother laughed. "You're not getting away with it that easily. Move over. You can follow instructions, can't you?"

"I suppose so. Unfortunately this cookie dough didn't. I said to it *turn into a cookie*, and look what happened." Fliss stared doubtfully at the mixture. "You think we can make this work?"

Her grandmother took the bowl. "No. I don't think we can make this work. It's a mess. But when you've made a mess you put it aside and start again."

Another metaphor, Fliss thought. The day seemed to be full of them.

She looked at her grandmother, knowing her help was more than she deserved. "I didn't mean to switch identities. I was going to tell you right away, but then Seth showed up at the hospital—"

"And you didn't want to face him as yourself."

"Because I'm a coward."

"You're many things, but I don't think a coward is one of them. I'm sure you have your reasons. If you'd like to share them, then I think you'll find I'm a good listener. If you'd rather bake, let's bake."

Fliss had a sudden urge to tell her grandmother how she was feeling, and the urge surprised her. She was so used to keeping everything inside. And that was the way she preferred it.

She felt a rush of guilt. "I'm sorry I lied to you."

"I understand. You got yourself in a state over Seth and you decided it was easier to run from your problems than face them. I don't suppose there are many people who haven't done that at some point in their lives." Her grandmother picked up the bowl again. "On second thought, I think we might be able to rescue this. Your dough is too soft, that's all. Did you weigh the flour?"

"Vaguely. Some of it went on the floor. A lot more went on the dog."

"Fetch me the flour."

"If Harriet was here, she wouldn't need help. She's a better cook. No, scratch that. She's better at everything. Cooking, caring for other people, caring for herself if it comes to that—" Fliss stared miserably into the bowl. "In fact the only thing I'm better at is math and messing up."

"They do classes in messing up? Education has changed since my day."

Fliss managed a smile. "I never needed classes. I was always a natural. If there was a bad decision to be made, I made it."

Her grandmother measured the flour and added it to the bowl. "You think Seth was a bad decision?"

Fliss felt her eyes sting. Damn. What was happening

to her? And it wasn't as if they were chopping onions or anything. There was nothing she could blame. "Of course it was a bad decision."

"Why? You didn't love him?"

Double damn. How did she answer that? She decided her grandmother deserved a little honesty from her after so many lies. "I loved him."

"So why was it a bad decision?"

"Because I ruined his life." And she'd lied to him, too.

"So if you ruined his life, why is he hanging around?"

"He isn't hanging around. He lives here. He can't exactly avoid me. And anyway, he thinks I'm Harriet. Come to think of it, he'd be better off with Harriet. She's a better person than I am."

Her grandmother shot out her hand and gripped Fliss's arm. "Oh no, honey, you've got it all wrong. She's not better. She's just different, that's all."

"Different in a better way."

"It's your father who made you think that. He played the two of you off each other. Messed with your heads. You're a smart girl. I could never understand how you couldn't see that. Now move over. We have a ton of cookies to make, and they're not going to make themselves."

CHAPTER NINE

"So if I were a character in your book, how would you fix me?" Fliss lay on the sand next to Matilda, who kept shifting positions on the blanket.

"Do you need fixing?"

"There are days when I wish I was more like Harriet."

"I think it's wonderful that you're different. I envy you having a twin. I would have done anything for a sibling. That was part of the reason I wrote stories. For company. You were born with company."

"Yeah, that part is pretty cool." Fliss stared out across the ocean and then realized Matilda was still wriggling next to her. "What's wrong? Do you need to pee or something?"

"I always need to pee, but no, it's not that. I've had this backache for a few days and I can't get rid of it." Her phone rang, and she rummaged in her purse. "Do you mind if I take this? That will be Chase telling me what time he'll be home." She answered the call, and Fliss watched as her friend's expression changed from delight to disappointment. It was like watching a light go out. "*Of course* I don't mind. Don't be silly! I'm totally fine here… It's not even due for another month, and that's if it arrives on time—and everyone says first babies are always late. Don't worry about a thing. I'll have a lovely indulgent evening watching Netflix. Are you having dinner with your father? Don't let him upset you. I'll see you tomorrow and we can talk about everything then. Love you, too."

Fliss felt a stab of envy and dismissed it.

Talking about everything sounded like her idea of an evening of horror.

She waited for Matilda to end the call. "Chase not coming home?"

"Buried under work and he has an early meeting scheduled tomorrow. It would be crazy for him to come home. He'll grab a quick dinner with his father while he's there. That's more duty than pleasure."

"They don't have a great relationship?"

"It's complicated."

Fliss knew all about complicated. "You shouldn't be on your own."

"I'll be fine." Matilda shifted again. "I'll take a bath."

"Should you see a doctor or something? I can drive you to the hospital."

"I'm pregnant, not sick."

"Then I can drive you to the maternity center."

"I'm fine, honestly." Matilda shifted again. "Just another of those Braxton Hicks contractions. I've been told all about them. They can feel real but they're not."

"I don't want to leave my grandmother alone for the night, or I'd offer to stay." Fliss pondered. "You could come and stay with us."

"That's kind, but nothing is going to happen." Matilda shifted again, and Fliss stood up.

"We should go back to the house. Whatever is going on, sitting on the beach is hardly comfortable for you."

"I like the ocean air, and Hero likes playing with

Charlie. And being with you takes my mind off the fact that I feel like a whale. Tell me more about being a twin."

"What do you want to know?"

"Did people treat you as individuals? Did you wear the same clothes?"

"Not unless it was a school uniform. And I cut three inches off the hem of mine, so even then we didn't look the same."

Melissa laughed. "Keep talking. You're giving me the most wonderful idea for a book."

Fliss recoiled. "I don't want to be in a book."

"You won't be. I use the elements that suit me and make up the rest. Real life is never as interesting as my stories."

"Unless it's my life. And we've definitely talked enough about me."

"You don't like talking about yourself, do you?"

"Not much. And it's your turn. How did you meet Chase?"

"At a very glamorous event on a rooftop in Manhattan."

"Wow." Fliss stooped to pick up a shell. "You hang out with some seriously cool people."

"Not true. I was a waitress. I had no idea who he was. In fact I didn't even see him at the party. I spilled a bottle of very expensive champagne, and I was fired on the spot. I was leaving the building when this superhot guy stepped into the elevator with me."

"And you introduced yourself?"

"Not exactly. At that moment I was a bit disillusioned with being me, so I pretended to be someone else."

Fliss was intrigued. "Who?"

"The heroine I was writing in my book. I'd given her all the qualities I would have liked to have myself. She was confident and never clumsy…" Matilda's voice trailed off and she stared at the water for a moment. "Anyway, we had this amazing night. And then real life intruded. He found out who I was. I found out who he was."

"Wait a minute," Fliss said slowly. "So you're telling me you pretended to be someone else? I thought it was just me who did that."

"At least you pretended to be a real person. Mine was fictional. That was worse. Before I met Chase, all I knew about him was that he was a collector of rare books and that he had a library in one of his houses. A library! My idea of book storage was to push them under my bed."

Fliss thought about Matilda's beach house. The space and luxury. And her interest was the library. "So you were after him for his books?"

"Not exactly. His brother owned a publishing company, and I was desperate to send him the manuscript I'd been working on. I had a cunning plan, but like most of my cunning plans it didn't quite work out the way it was supposed to."

Fliss looked at the diamond sparkling on her friend's finger. "Seems to me that it worked out perfectly. Fairytale ending."

"It was. And the weird thing is, it was more romantic than anything I've ever written." She took a sip from her water bottle. "I should probably be getting back. I have to finish my proofs before this baby comes."

Fliss ignored the tug of envy and walked with her back to the house. "Call if you need me."

"I won't need you. Hero has had two walks today. We'll both be fine."

"I hope you're right because delivering babies isn't one of my skills."

SETH STROLLED AROUND the empty master suite of his new house. Without furniture to absorb the sound, his footsteps echoed on the oak floorboards.

The room was light, with high ceilings and glass doors opening onto a balcony, and he already knew where he was going to put his bed. Against the wall, facing the view. He was on the edge of the ocean, close to the nature preserve. When he opened the windows, all he could hear were the birds and the soft lap of the water on the sand.

The house might be empty, but already it felt like a home.

Chase had done well.

And there was something to be said for living somewhere new, with no history or memories clinging to the walls.

He'd had his furniture shipped from his house in California and it had been sitting in his parents' home for six months.

It was time he had it moved.

His phone rang, and he smiled as the caller ID flashed up.

"Chase? This is a coincidence. I'm admiring your handiwork. The house is looking great. I'm moving in on the weekend."

"Sounds good."

"I need to think about furniture." He'd walked through every room and decided that many of the things he'd brought with him from his place in California weren't going to look right here. "I need to think how to fill the space."

"Fill it with people. It's a family house. Maybe it's time you thought about a family."

"Have you been talking to my sister?"

"No. I just believe in marriage."

"This from a guy who was determinedly single until last year."

"I was single for a reason. I hadn't met the right person. Once I did, everything seemed different. I'm a convert."

Seth strolled to the window. The setting sun sent shafts of light over the ocean. "Want to come over and share a beer?"

"That's why I'm calling. I'm in Manhattan and I'm worried about Matilda." Something in his tone made Seth pause.

"Is there a reason to worry?"

"I'm not sure. She's not answering her phone. She's probably left it somewhere, or dropped it in the bath, but I can't stop worrying. I was meant to be home tonight. I don't like leaving her alone this far into her pregnancy."

"Do you want me to go check on her?"

"Would you? Thanks." Chase sounded relieved. "I owe you."

"You don't owe me anything. I'll call as soon as I get there." He scooped up his keys, checked that the doors to the balcony were secure and whistled to Lulu.

FLISS SAT ON the beach, watching as the setting sun spilled golden light across the sand.

She'd left her grandmother engrossed in a TV show

while she'd taken Charlie to the beach for his final walk of the day.

On impulse, she called Harriet. "Grams knows I'm me and not you."

"Good. So it's all fine? I knew it would be."

Her sister was always so calm. Nothing seemed to ruffle her. She said it was working with animals that soothed her, but Fliss knew it was her nature to be calm. It was as if after living with their father, nothing could ever stress her again. Nothing could ever be that bad.

"I'm sorry I did that."

"Don't apologize."

"Don't be so understanding."

"All right, I won't." Harriet was laughing, but Fliss felt a twinge. She thought about what Matilda had said about being an only child.

Harriet was her best friend.

How would she have gotten through life without her sister?

"I still have to unravel the whole Seth thing. Haven't worked out how to do that yet, but I need to do it before I get roped into more cookie making for the sake of everyone's digestive systems."

Harriet was still laughing. "I'm glad Grams helped you with that."

"Yeah, it was pretty cool. She's a good cook." Fliss rubbed her toes in the sand. "She's been teaching me a few things."

"And you hate every minute?"

"That's the weird thing. No."

"It's not weird. I used to love cooking with her because she always listened to me. Didn't matter how long it took me to get the words out, she was never impatient. After living with Dad it was heaven. Did you talk to her about Seth? Did you tell her how you feel?"

She didn't know how she felt about Seth. And she certainly didn't intend to talk about it. "No need. I'm fine."

"You should talk to her. She's very wise."

"Did she ever talk about Mom with you?" Fliss frowned. "She said something."

"What?"

"It was weird." Fliss watched as Charlie chased across the sand in front of her. At this time of day he was allowed off the leash, and he weaved in great loops, as if he was tracking something. "She said it was hard seeing your daughter in love with the wrong man."

"What's weird about that? Dad *was* the wrong man for Mom. She was too gentle for him. Too compliant. She spent her whole life twisting herself into pretzel-like shapes trying to please him. And I empathize. He had the same effect on me. Every time he yelled, I couldn't force a word out. Do you remember?"

"Trying not to." She remembered her sister crouched under the table with her eyes squeezed shut and her hands over her ears. She remembered her father growing more and more angry when Harriet couldn't speak smoothly. *Vicious circle*, she thought, with the emphasis on *vicious*.

And she remembered Daniel intervening. Standing firm between his father and his sisters, as he always had, and incurring his father's wrath because of it. And when he'd left home to go to college, she'd taken on that role.

Would they be as close as siblings if it hadn't been for their childhood?

If they'd grown up in a happy family, would they have flown the nest and spread out? Or would they still be living close to one another, looking out for each other?

"Well, Mom was no different. We all tried to keep a low profile. Apart from you, of course. You goaded him."

Fliss lay back on the sand, watching as the sky darkened. "I still think there was something else. Grams looked at me in a funny way. Like I was missing something."

"You're imagining it."

"I don't think so. I'm not the one who digs around for emotional stuff. That's you. I try to pretend it isn't happening."

"It's unusual to hear you admit that."

"Yeah, well, nothing that's happening around here is usual. And Grams was definitely hiding something. And now, of course, I need to know what it is. Because that's human nature. Did Mom ever talk to you about her and Dad?"

"Not really. Only that she got married quickly."

"Because she was pregnant with Daniel. But we already knew that. Mom told me about it once when she was lecturing me on contraception. She told me that you never want to get married unless both of you feel the same way."

And she'd ignored that advice, of course. The way she ignored all advice.

As a teenager she'd done the opposite of everything anyone had suggested.

"Poor Mom. Still, she's happy now. Did you see the photos she posted of Antarctica?"

"Yes." Fliss brushed the sand from her legs. Maybe Harriet was right. Maybe she was imagining things. And if there was something in her mother's past, that was her business.

People had a right to secrets. They had a right to keep their thoughts and feelings inside if that was what they wanted.

It was exactly what she did.

"So when are you going to tell Seth the truth about who you are?"

"I don't know. Maybe I won't need to. You had lunch with him, by the way, at the beach café."

"I like that place. What did I eat?"

"You had the Thai salad."

"Did I enjoy it?"

Fliss grinned. "It wasn't bad. A lot of people came up to me and said how pleased they were to see you. You're loved, dear sister."

"I hope you didn't do anything to ruin my reputation. What were you wearing?"

"Nothing. I dined naked."

"I'm hoping you're joking."

"I thought your reputation needed spicing up a little. I did wear sunscreen."

"So you're telling me I had lunch in the beach café, and all I wore was factor twenty?"

"And a smile. A big smile."

"Fliss!"

Fliss grinned. "Calm down. I wore a sundress. It was almost decent."

Harriet choked on laughter. "Well, that's punishment enough for teasing me. I can't remember when I last saw you wear a dress."

"Yeah, it felt weird."

"And what are you wearing now?"

"Well, since Grams knows who I am, and I'm not likely to bump into anyone else tonight, I'm wearing my ancient cutoffs with a crop top. My abs are on display."

"Disgraceful, Felicity."

Fliss was about to respond when she noticed another dog speeding along the beach.

It looked like—

No, it couldn't be. Not out here on the beach on his own.

But—

"Crap." She sprang to her feet, the phone still in her hand. She could hear Harriet's voice asking her what was wrong. "I need to go. Hero seems to have escaped. Matilda must have forgotten to close the kitchen door. Talk to you later." She slid the phone into her pocket, put her fingers in her mouth and whistled loudly.

Hero skidded to a halt, sand flying, and turned his head in her direction.

She cupped her hands to her mouth and shouted his name, relieved when he changed direction and sped toward her.

"Whoa. What are you doing out here all on your own? And what's the hurry?" She made a fuss over him. "Does Matilda know you've escaped? You're supposed to be babysitting her tonight."

Hero turned away, but she grabbed his collar.

"Oh no, you're not running off again." She was almost pulled off balance as the dog strained and tugged. "You run away and suddenly you want to go home?" She adjusted her hold and braced her legs.

Hero whined and nudged her thigh.

"I have no idea what you want me to do, but you need to calm down. All this energy, and you've already had two long walks today. You're the reason I can wear a top that shows my abs. I'll call Matilda to let her know I've found you. She'll be worrying." Keeping one hand on Hero's collar, she called Matilda's number.

The phone went to voice mail.

"That's weird." She frowned, and then remembered that this was Matilda. She'd probably lost the phone. Dropped it in the bath? Maybe she was taking a bath. Did she even realize she'd left the doors to the house open? "I'm beginning to see why Chase wanted her to have security. I guess I'm going to have to take you home myself."

She whistled to Charlie and walked briskly until she reached the part of the beach that was private. Because the tide was low, she was able to walk straight onto the stretch of sand that fronted the Adams property.

As she'd suspected, the glass doors that led to the kitchen were open. She stepped through them and saw the cup on the tiled floor, lying in pieces in the middle of a pool of liquid. Next to it was Matilda's phone. Also in pieces.

Fliss paused. Why had she dropped everything?

And then she heard a sound upstairs, a dull thud, and the hair rose on the back of her neck.

Intruders?

Her mouth tight, Fliss grabbed a heavy iron skillet from the stove and nudged Hero away from the broken mug with her toe.

"Find Matilda. Go! Fetch. Seize. Whatever."

The dog shot off without any more encouragement

and Fliss followed, the skillet in one hand, her phone in the other.

She was about to dial 911 when Hero barked and she heard Matilda give a howl of pain.

She took the stairs two at a time, followed the noise and found Matilda on her hands and knees in the bedroom. "Did they hurt you? Where are they? Are they still in the house?"

Matilda looked at her, her eyes glazed with pain, unable to speak.

Fliss dropped to her knees in front of her. "What happened? Oh God, what did they do? Say something."

Matilda shook her head, but no words emerged.

They must have attacked her. Winded her. "Did they push you? The doors were open downstairs. I saw the broken cup. And your phone. Are the intruders still in the house?" Fliss brandished the skillet like a weapon. "Because I'll tear them limb from limb. They will be so damn sorry they—"

Matilda grabbed her wrist and gasped out one word. "Baby."

"I know you're worried about the baby, but I'm sure she's going to be fine. We're going to—" She yelped as Matilda gripped her arm more tightly.

"Now!"

Now?

Fliss froze, every muscle in her body paralyzed. Her arms and legs wouldn't move. Neither would her mouth. With immense difficulty she forced the words past stiff lips. "You mean the baby is the reason you're on the floor in agony? But it's not due yet. It can't come now."

Matilda gave another moan of pain and Fliss moved,

her need not to be left to deal with this galvanizing her into action. She put the skillet down.

"Who do I call? The hospital? Chase?" Someone. Anyone. The phone almost slipped from her shaky, sweaty hands, and she gave a hysterical laugh. At this rate the floor was going to be littered with broken phones.

Matilda tried to speak. "No time."

No time? Fliss felt hot and then cold. "That can't be right. Even if it is coming now, babies take ages to arrive."

Please let it take ages to arrive.

She couldn't do this.

She really couldn't do this.

She was the wrong person in every single way.

If this baby really was coming, then Matilda needed someone skilled and responsible with her. Someone who would do all the right things.

Fliss knew she wasn't that someone.

She did all the wrong things.

She felt a shocking pain in her arm and realized it was Matilda's nails.

Holy crap.

She'd never doubted that childbirth was a painful experience, but she hadn't realized the pain extended to bystanders.

"That's right." She gritted her teeth. "Hold on. Hit me. Anything. Whatever helps." With her free arm she reached out, grabbed her phone and dialed 911. Maybe having a baby wasn't an emergency, but it seemed like one to her. And no doubt they'd call whoever they needed to call. The best she could hope for was that reinforcements would arrive before the baby.

"They'll be here in under ten minutes." Relief flowed through her. Ten minutes was no time at all. She wasn't going to have to do this by herself. All she had to do was hold the fort and keep Matilda calm until help arrived.

That was easier said than done. Whatever was happening to her was clearly overwhelming. Matilda was hit by wave after wave of pain, with no room to breathe. Tentatively Fliss placed her palm on her friend's rounded abdomen. It was like touching a rock.

She grabbed her phone again and typed *having a baby* into the search engine.

A stream of websites sprang onto her phone, offering baby classes, pregnancy advice.

Fliss stared at the screen in frustration.

Muttering under her breath, she added the words *right now* to her search request and saw something about breathing pop up.

She thought back to a TV series Harriet had watched based on a maternity unit. They'd gone on and on about breathing.

Feeling pitifully inadequate, she rubbed Matilda's shoulder. "Remember your breathing." That was what they said, wasn't it? "In through your nose and out through your mouth. Everything is going to be fine. You can hold on ten minutes, right?" *Please say yes.*

Matilda said nothing. She couldn't catch her breath to speak.

Instead Fliss saw her hold her breath and push. "Are you pushing?" Panic ripped through her. "Don't push. Whatever you do, don't push."

"Have to." Matilda panted out the words, and Fliss looked at her in horror.

This couldn't be happening. Not like this. Not now. She needed only ten minutes! How hard was that?

"Hold your breath. Think about other things."

"Can't." Matilda gasped out the word, her fingernails almost digging holes in Fliss's arm. It was so painful she almost joined her friend and yelled.

Fliss felt sweat cool her skin. *Ten minutes.* That was all the time she needed to delay this thing from happening. "Don't push, don't push. Do I at least have time to do an internet search on 'what to do if a baby comes too fast'?"

Matilda's gaze met hers, and Fliss saw the panic in her friend's eyes.

Her own panic evaporated in an instant.

She put her arm around Matilda's shoulders and gave her a hug. "It doesn't matter. We don't need the internet. Women have been doing this for centuries without the help of Google. It's natural. Babies are born every minute, right? No worries."

She hoped she sounded more convincing than she felt.

It was dawning on her that she was going to have to deliver a baby.

Why her? Why did she have to be the one in this position?

And then she realized it was Matilda who was in this position, not her, and she felt a stab of shame. She might be bad at some things, but never would she abandon a friend in a crisis.

"It's okay, really it is." She hoped Matilda couldn't see that her hands were shaking. "It's all going to be fine. Wait there a second—I'm not leaving you, but if it's really coming now then we have to get ready for it."

She pulled her arm away from Matilda's grip, sprinted to the bed and grabbed pillows, cushions and the comforter. She flung them on the floor next to her friend.

What else?

She didn't have a clue.

Matilda grabbed her, gasping, and Fliss tried to think straight. Logic. She was good at logic. "Get closer to the floor. Here, lie on these cushions. It will be more comfortable." And that way if the baby popped out fast it wasn't going to start life bashing its head on reclaimed oak.

Her mind was racing ahead. Was she supposed to cut the cord? No. She wasn't going to touch the cord. But what if the baby wasn't breathing?

She should probably wash her hands, in case she had to handle it.

She shot into the bathroom and scrubbed her hands as best she could, and took clean towels from the neat pile. She barely had time to register that Matilda's bathroom looked like something from an upscale spa, before she heard her friend groan in agony.

She shot back into the room.

Hero was next to her, looking worried.

Fliss empathized.

"Move away, Hero. I'm no expert but I don't think dogs are allowed in the delivery room."

Matilda sent her a panicked glance. "I can feel the head."

And suddenly Fliss realized that whoever was coming, they weren't going to get here in time. She was all Matilda had.

She felt a wash of calm.

"Well, that's exciting."

"I'm scared."

"Don't be. Everything is fine." She gave Matilda's shoulder a squeeze and then knelt down and saw that there was indeed a head. Was she supposed to check whether the cord was around the neck or anything? She didn't want to risk touching anything she shouldn't touch. Before she could decide, Matilda gave another groan and the baby slid out into Fliss's hands.

She was so shocked she almost dropped it. She held the baby's slippery body, and emotion choked her. She'd never allowed herself to think about this part. How this must feel, holding new life in your hands. Beginnings.

She'd never been so grateful for her ability to lock her emotions away, but even she struggled to conceal her feelings this time.

Somehow she managed it, and she put the baby carefully in Matilda's arms and wrapped a towel around them both.

Then she propped cushions around Matilda to support her.

"She's not crying—" Matilda gasped out the words, and Fliss felt another flash of anxiety.

Did babies always cry? Weren't any of them born happy?

She rubbed the baby with the towel, and the newborn started to howl at the same time she heard footsteps on the stairs.

She turned, expecting to see an EMT or someone from the hospital, but instead it was Seth.

He was the last person she'd expected, and she gave a weak smile, ridiculously relieved to see him. Anyone.

"Typical. You arrive when it's all over. Your timing is terrible."

CHAPTER TEN

SETH TOOK IN the situation with one glance.

Matilda, the baby and Fliss. He wasn't sure which of them looked the most traumatized.

Matilda looked exhausted, but Fliss looked worse, her cheeks unnaturally pale.

The fact that she looked relieved to see him told him just how stressed she was.

Deciding to deal with Matilda first, he dropped to his haunches. "Well, this isn't quite what I expected to find when Chase asked me to check on you. I gather this baby was in a hurry. How are you doing, honey?"

"Okay, I think." Finally Matilda was able to catch her breath and speak. "He asked you to check on me?"

"You didn't answer your phone. Chase was worried, so he called me and I said I'd come over."

Matilda's gaze softened. "He's overprotective."

"I don't think so. Looks like he made a good call." He noticed the skillet and frowned. "What's that doing there?"

"I don't know." Matilda looked at Fliss, who was staring into the middle distance, lost in thought.

"What? Sorry? Oh—" She stared at the skillet as if she'd forgotten its presence. "I brought it up from the kitchen."

Seth wished he could read her thoughts. "What were

you planning to do? Fry her breakfast while she was in labor?"

"I didn't know she was in labor," she snapped. "I thought there was an intruder, and that was the only weapon at hand. I was getting ready to knock someone unconscious."

Matilda gave a choked laugh. "I wish you'd done it to me. I could have done with the pain relief. And you still haven't told me how you came to be here."

"Hero found me on the beach." She glanced at the dog, who thumped his tail, soaking up the approval with style. "I brought him home and found the door wide open and a mug and your phone shattered into pieces on the kitchen floor. I assumed you'd left the door open and someone had taken advantage. Then I heard you scream, so I grabbed the skillet."

Despite her exhausted state, Matilda shot her a look of admiration. "I would have hidden in the closet and called 911."

"So would most people." Seth didn't want to think about what might have happened had it really been intruders and Fliss had faced them armed only with a skillet. He made a mental note to talk to Chase about increasing security.

"I heard you moan and I thought they were hurting you."

Matilda's eyes filled. "You were willing to risk your life for me?"

"Hey, don't get mushy." Fliss looked alarmed. "I like a good fight, that's all."

Seth wondered whether this was a good moment to point out that Harriet wouldn't hit someone with a skillet even if her life were threatened. She would have thought it through and measured the risks. Then she would have called 911 right away before even thinking of another plan.

Fliss rushed into action and then thought things through.

It had been one of the things he'd loved most about her. And the reason everything between them had unraveled.

She was glaring at him, apparently forgetting to maintain her sister's identity. "What was I supposed to do? I heard a thump from upstairs, and then she screamed. I thought she'd been attacked, and when I got upstairs she wasn't saying anything to me—"

"I couldn't. I couldn't breathe through the pain. It was agonizing. And intense. I wasn't anticipating anything like that."

Seth propped another pillow behind her, wondering if Matilda knew that her rescuer was Fliss, not Harriet. "Precipitate labor. You had no warning?"

"I've been having pains for days, but I thought they were normal pains. Then I was in the kitchen and suddenly the pain was overwhelming. I dropped my cup and my phone. Fortunately the pain eased long enough for me to get upstairs. I was going to call Chase from the bedroom, but then I was hit by another pain, and this one didn't go away. Will the baby be all right? Has it hurt her being born so quickly?" Matilda looked anxiously at the baby and Seth took a look at her.

"She looks happy and content to me."

"I was all set to go to the medical center. My bag is packed and everything."

Seth heard the sound of wheels on the gravel.

"Sounds like the cavalry is here, so you'll be making that trip anyway."

"It hardly seems worth going to the hospital now."

"It's worth it. I'll call Chase and he can meet you there." Seth stood up. "Does your daughter have a name?"

Matilda held the baby closer, the vision of a contented new mother. "Rose. Rose Felicity Adams." She smiled. "Felicity, because if it hadn't been for Fliss, I wouldn't have got through it."

There was a tense silence.

He met Fliss's gaze, and she looked away quickly, as if she knew it was all over.

"Thank you," she said. "I'm touched."

Matilda smiled, oblivious to the bomb she'd dropped. "I've never seen you this emotional. Now you're the one having trouble speaking." She reached out and took Fliss's hand. "Thank you. Will you take care of Hero for me until Chase gets here?"

"Of course. He can come home with me. He earned his name today. If it hadn't been for him, I wouldn't have come looking for you."

There wasn't time for any more conversation because at that moment the medical team arrived and Matilda and the baby were bundled into the ambulance.

Seth waited until they were out of sight and then went in search of Fliss.

He found her upstairs in the bedroom cleaning up. She was hauling sheets and towels into a pile, even though half of them hadn't been anywhere near the baby.

She must have heard his footsteps, but she didn't pause to look at him. "I'm going to drop this lot in the laundry room. I'll deal with it tomorrow. I need to get back to Grams. If I take Hero, will you secure this place?"

That was all she was going to say?

He thought he saw something glisten on her cheeks. Was she crying?

He reached out to grab her, but she dodged him. It was possible she hadn't seen his hand, but more probable that she'd chosen not to take it.

He watched as she walked quickly out of the bedroom, Hero at her heels.

He ached for her. He wanted to drag her into his arms and force her to tell him how she felt, but he knew he had to take this at her pace, so instead of grabbing her again he thrust his hands in his pockets and forced himself to take it slowly.

This was Fliss he was dealing with. Fliss, who hid every feeling. Who never talked about things. Who fought battles on her own, her own way.

Mouth tight, he followed her downstairs and found her in the laundry room.

"Fliss—"

"I'm tired, Seth. It's been a pretty busy evening." She kept her back to him. "I'll lock up here and take Hero to my grandmother's, so you can take off if you like."

And he was willing to bet that was exactly what she was hoping he'd do.

The fact that she still wasn't looking at him told him a lot about how bad she felt. That and the raw emotion shimmering in her voice.

"Talk to me." He tried gentle, the same approach he would take with an injured animal. No sudden moves.

"Nothing to talk about. The baby is fine. Matilda is fine. What is there to talk about?"

"We could start with the fact that you're shaking." He could make out the delicate lines of her profile. He saw that she was on edge, and he understood the reason. "We could talk about the fact that if I wasn't here, you'd be crying."

"Never been much of a crier." She stuffed the laundry into the machine. "But if I did shed a little tear of emotion, that would be understandable, wouldn't it? It's not every day a baby is born in front of you in less time than it usually takes me to swallow a hamburger."

He studied her expression, trying to work out how best to tackle this. Direct? No. She'd definitely run. Oblique, then. Carefully. "Can't have been easy."

"It wasn't, but she handled it like a trouper."

"I was talking about you."

"I was just the spectator."

"Didn't look that way to me. And she did name her daughter after you, so she obviously felt you played an important role."

"She named her after Fliss. I'm Harriet."

He didn't know whether to feel sympathy or pity. "Are we seriously going to do this?"

Her shoulders slumped. "All right, you win. I'm Fliss. Are you happy now?"

"Do I look happy?"

"You're mad that I pretended to be Harriet. You feel deceived."

"I wasn't deceived. I've known almost from the first moment that you weren't Harriet."

"You did?" Finally she looked at him. "As a matter of interest, what gave me away?"

"The fact that I wanted to take you to the beach, strip you naked and have sex with you. I've never felt that way about your sister."

Her mouth fell open with shock. "Seth—"

"There's a chemistry between us I can't explain, and it doesn't matter how many dresses you wear, or perfect cookies you manage to produce, I'd still know which twin I was talking to."

"If you knew, why didn't you say something?"

"Because I assumed you had your reasons for hiding from me. I have a pretty good idea what those reasons were, but maybe it's time you shared them. I told you the truth. Now it would be good if you did me the same favor and told me the truth."

He saw her hesitate and thought, for a fleeting moment, that for once she might be about to open up and let him inside her head.

And then she gave a brief shake of her head. "Nothing to share. It just seemed simpler to pretend to be Harriet. You should be grateful. I was sparing us both an awkward moment."

"Why would it have been awkward? Because we haven't spoken in ten years? Because the last time we were together, you were walking away from me? Because you walked away without talking to me about how you were feeling? I'm used to that, Fliss. It's your survival instinct kicking in. It's the way you operate. The only way to stop you running away when the going gets tough is to block the exit. It's the reason I'm standing in this doorway."

"If you know that, then you'll kindly step out of my way." She shoved his chest, and he stepped to one side.

Not because he was willing to end the conversation, but because he was worried about her.

He'd seen Fliss stressed before, but never quite like this.

"Fliss—"

"You were great back there. I'm glad you arrived when you did. Now go open champagne. Beer. Something." She turned to walk away, and this time he closed his hand over her shoulder.

"You're upset."

"And this is how I handle being upset."

"I know how you handle being upset. I know better than anyone how you push people away. Talk to me."

"You really pick your moments." There was a flash of anger in her eyes. Anger and something else. Panic? "Jeez, Seth, like I don't have enough trouble coping with the present, and you choose this moment to bring up the past?"

"When your past is head-butting your present, I can't think of a better time to talk about it."

"Well, I can." She stalked past him and he watched for a moment, trying to imagine Harriet wearing denim cutoffs and a tummy-revealing tank.

"Did you really think I wouldn't know you?" His words acted like a brake.

She stopped walking and there was a sudden stillness in the air.

For a moment he thought she was going to turn and face him, but she didn't.

"You never really knew me, Seth."

What the hell was that supposed to mean?

He'd known her better than anyone.

He opened his mouth to demand an explanation, but

she was already walking out of the house, Hero and Charlie at her heels.

He watched her go, feeling useless.

DAMMIT, WHAT WAS happening to her?

Her heart was racing, her mind was racing and her thoughts and emotions were a tangled web. There was Matilda, and the baby, and Seth. Always Seth.

It had been over for ten years, but he was still in her head. She'd never gotten him out of her head.

And now he knew who she really was, so there was no more pretending.

She'd have to face him soon, but it didn't have to be now when she was at her lowest. If they were going to have the conversation he seemed to want, then she needed to be strong, and right now she didn't feel strong.

She felt weak and vulnerable and she hated it.

Although part of her had been relieved to see him, another part of her wished he hadn't shown up.

Why now? Why tonight? She could have handled things one at a time, but not altogether.

Her stomach churned. She felt physically sick.

She should have gone home, but she knew her grandmother would take one look at her and start asking questions, so instead she headed straight for the beach, Hero and Charlie at her heels.

Seth was right that she always ran from her emotions. Unfortunately right now it wasn't working. Whether she walked or ran, moved left or right, her emotions came right along with her.

There was a hot ball of fire lodged in her throat, and she realized with a lurch of horror that she was going to cry.

She couldn't remember the last time she'd cried.

She never cried.

She had no experience in holding back tears because she'd never had to hold back tears.

She was afraid if she let them out, they'd choke her, but she couldn't keep them in. She was going to drown, right here on the beach, not from being out of her depth in seawater but from being out of her depth in misery.

She brushed at her eyes, furious, telling herself it was sand that was making her eyes water. Sand.

She couldn't go back to the cottage like this.

She needed to pull herself together.

But how?

She hadn't expected to feel this way.

What was *wrong* with her?

If she'd been Harriet she would have been cooing over the baby, admiring tiny fingers and the unexpected shock of dark hair. But she wasn't Harriet, and she couldn't handle it. She couldn't handle all the feelings that holding Matilda's baby had unleashed. She'd looked down at that tiny bow mouth and those long lashes, at that shock of hair, and she'd felt as if someone had ripped her heart out.

She heard a strange sound and then realized it had come from her throat.

The sobs came without her permission, and she sank down on the sand, sheltered by the dunes, and cried so hard it felt as if her chest might split in two.

She sobbed for everything that might have been and hadn't been, for the future she'd wanted so badly and lost.

Drowning in her own misery, she didn't feel Hero nudging her, worried. But she did feel strong hands lifting her.

Seth.

He'd followed her. Well, of course, he'd followed her. He had never known when to stay away.

He lifted her as if she weighed nothing and pulled her onto his lap.

She heard the crash of the ocean and the deep, soothing murmur of his voice as he stroked her hair gently and let her cry.

She wanted to crawl away and hide, but his arms were tight bands of security. And they felt good. He felt warm and strong and comforting, so she stayed there until she'd cried herself out, her hand locked into a fist in the front of his shirt.

There was a dull ache in her head and her eyes felt swollen. She was relieved it was almost dark. "I'm sorry."

He stirred, but he didn't release her. "What are you sorry for?"

"For howling on you."

"Don't be."

"I never cry. I don't know what the hell is wrong with me."

"Yes you do." When she said nothing, he smoothed her hair back from her face. "I know you hide your feelings from the world, but do you hide them from yourself, too?"

"It was just the stress of it all. Matilda's baby."

There was a long pause, and then she felt his arms tighten around her.

"We both know this wasn't about Matilda's baby." His voice was soft in the darkness. "It was about ours. Our baby."

CHAPTER ELEVEN

SHE LEAPED TO her feet as if she'd been scalded.

This time he didn't try to stop her, even though he could happily have gotten used to the feel of her on his lap. For a moment, as he'd felt her relax into him, he'd had a tantalizing glimpse of the possible, but now the barriers were up again. She put a firewall between herself and the world.

"I can't believe you're bringing that up now. I don't want to talk about it."

"I know. You never do, but this time you're going to." He stood, too, determined that this time she wasn't going to walk away. "You owe me that. You owe me a conversation." He closed his hands over her shoulders and she tried to shrug him off.

"We've been divorced ten years. I don't owe you anything. Dammit, Seth, this is my problem. I handle it the way I choose to handle it."

He wondered if she even realized that she didn't really handle difficult things. She buried them.

"Do you know what the real problem is? The fact that you think it's *your* problem. It was my baby, too. The fact that you had a miscarriage was *our* problem, Fliss. Ours. But you refused to share it. You shut me out."

She pressed her fingers to her temple. "Well, whoever's problem it was, it's in the past so there's no point in talking about it now. I can't do this. Don't push me on it."

He knew that this was exactly the right time to push her. If he waited for her to pull herself together again, to regain her strength, she'd do what she always did. Retreat, leaving him on the outside. It was a cold, lonely place, and he was damned if he was going to find himself exiled there again.

"If it's in the past, why were you crying yourself dry?"

"Because I'm tired."

"That's only the second time in my life I've seen you cry." He wondered if she'd remember the first time and saw from the quick look she sent him that she had.

"I have a lot on my mind right now. I need to think. It would help if you didn't stand so close."

"My standing this close is bothering you?"

"Yes, it's bothering me!"

"I'll take that as a good sign."

"How can it be a good sign?" She shook her head. "Leave me alone."

"I did that once before. It was a mistake. Everyone makes them, but I generally try to avoid making the same mistake twice." And with her he'd made big ones. Huge. He'd thought he was so mature. So experienced. But he hadn't had the experience or maturity to handle a woman as complex as her.

Now he did.

She dug her hands into the pockets of her cutoffs. "It wasn't a mistake. You did the right thing." She'd kicked off her shoes and was barefoot, but that didn't surprise him.

She'd spent half her summers barefoot, her toes dusted with sand.

It had taken him a while to figure out that when she came to the Hamptons she wasn't just throwing off her shoes, she was throwing off her life.

"No, I didn't. I did what you wanted me to. Not the same thing. And by the time I realized my mistake I couldn't get near you. Between your sister and your Rottweiler brother—" He saw alarm flash in her eyes.

"He doesn't know about the baby. I never told him."

"I figured that out a long time ago. What I had a harder time understanding was why you didn't tell him."

"Because he was already mad at you. If he'd known I was pregnant—"

"I would have handled it. I would have handled him."

She shook her head. "Daniel has always been protective, but back then—"

"I understand. He's your big brother. It was his job to stop you being hurt, but once we got involved it was my job, too. I would have protected you."

"I didn't want that. I ruined your life, Seth. You should hate me."

He couldn't have been more shocked.

"This is the reason you've been avoiding me? Because you think you ruined my life?"

"Partly."

"Do I look ruined to you?"

Her gaze met his. "No."

"Because I'm not. I'm older and wiser, I hope. But not ruined." He could hear the rapid snatch of her breath above the rolling crash of the waves.

"Do you ever wish—" She stopped, that tantalizing

half sentence hovering in the air between them, leaving him wondering what the other half would have been.

Over the past ten years he'd wished a thousand things. He'd wished their relationship hadn't been so intense, that they'd met later when they were both ready for it, that he'd thought less about his own pain and more about hers. Most of all he'd wished he hadn't let her walk out of his life.

Regret was a solid ache behind his ribs.

"Do I ever wish—?"

"Nothing. Forget it. I have to go. Grams will be wondering where I am."

He could see the faint trace of tears on her cheeks and the outline of her mouth.

He knew how that mouth would feel under his. How it would taste.

But he wasn't going there.

Not yet.

Last time they'd done everything the wrong way. Passion had overwhelmed everything. Next time he was determined it was going to be different.

And there was going to be a next time.

"Does your grandmother know you're Fliss?"

"Are you kidding? Who do you think made the cookies?"

He was relieved to see her sense of humor flicker back to life, and he smiled in the darkness. "I'll take you home."

"I have a Doberman. I don't need an escort."

He ignored that. "I'm taking you home, and I won't follow you in on one condition—"

"What?"

"You have dinner with me tomorrow and we talk properly then."

"Last time I shared a meal with you I ended up baking cookies."

"I'm not talking about dinner in a restaurant. I'm talking about christening my new kitchen."

"You're moving in?"

They'd arrived back at his car, and she slid into the passenger seat.

"I'm sleeping there tonight. On the floor."

"If my memory serves me rightly, you have about ten bedrooms at your parents' house. You don't need to sleep on the floor."

He almost told her then. Told her how it felt being in the house knowing his father was never going to walk through the door again.

Instead he focused on driving, negotiating the darkened lanes that led to her grandmother's house.

He pulled up outside. Lights were burning in the downstairs windows, and he thought about the times he'd lurked by the gate at the back of the house, waiting for Fliss. It seemed like a lifetime ago.

"Does seven thirty work for you?"

"I'm not cooking for you, Carlyle. And if you value your health, you won't push it."

"I'll do the cooking."

"I have to babysit Grams." There was a desperate note to her voice, as if she knew she was running out of excuses.

"That's why I suggested seven thirty. Gives you time to settle her down."

"She might need me."

"You'll be on the end of a phone."

She unfastened her seat belt. "You don't give up, do you?"

Once, but not anymore.

This time he wasn't giving up until he got what he wanted.

And now, after months, maybe even years, of wondering, he knew what that was.

"Seven thirty. I'll cook."

THE PHONE WOKE her and she fumbled for it, knocking a book onto the floor.

There was a whimper from the bed, and Charlie scrabbled to his feet and licked her face.

He'd followed her up to the bedroom when she'd arrived home, and hovered there, as if he sensed something different about her and was afraid of leaving her alone.

And she'd discovered she didn't want to be on her own. So she'd pulled Charlie onto the bed and slept with her arms wrapped around his solid body, comforted by his warmth and his presence. Only with animals had she ever felt able to truly relax her guard. Hero had slept across the door, apparently determined to live up to his name.

She stroked Charlie's silky fur with one hand and checked the caller ID with the other.

Harriet.

"What time do you call this?"

"Six in the morning. Did I wake you? You're usually up by now."

"Is everything all right?" Fliss rubbed her eyes, suddenly worried about her sister. "Is there a problem?" Her head throbbed from crying.

"Not with me. I heard the news! Matilda called me. You're a heroine."

"She called you?" Fliss groped on the nightstand for painkillers. If this was how a heroine felt, she didn't want to repeat the experience in a hurry. "How is she?"

"Doing well, thanks to you."

"I didn't do a thing."

"That wasn't how she tells it."

"I was just in the right place at the right time." Or the wrong place at the wrong time, depending how you looked at it. She swallowed the pills along with a glass of water.

"She said Seth was there, too. And that she blew your identity. She's feeling guilty and worried about you."

"No need." She put the empty glass down. "Turns out Seth knew who I was all along."

"Really? So why didn't he say anything?"

"He was waiting for me to tell him."

"Did you talk?"

No, I sobbed myself dry on his shoulder. "We exchanged a few words."

"That's it?"

Fliss sighed and forced herself out of bed. Still holding the phone, she padded into the bathroom and stared at herself in the mirror.

"Jeez. I can't believe I look this bad when I didn't even have a drink. There is no justice." She still had streaks of mascara under her eyes, and her hair looked as if she'd dived headfirst into a bush. "I'm all dressed for Halloween, and it isn't even July."

"Are you avoiding my question?"

Fliss scrubbed at the smears of black under her eyes.

"I don't even remember your question. That's how bad I feel."

"I want to know about Seth. And I want to know how you are. It must have been difficult for you."

"No." She might have stood more chance of convincing her sister if Charlie hadn't picked that moment to bark.

"Who is that?"

"It's Charlie. Who else would it be?"

"What's he doing in the bedroom? You barely tolerate Charlie."

Fliss thought back to the night before, remembering how she'd lifted the dog onto the bed and held him on her lap until he'd settled down. "He was hard to shake off, and I was too tired to fight it."

"That doesn't sound like you. Are you upset?"

"As long as he doesn't howl, I'm fine."

"I'm not talking about Charlie, I'm talking about the baby. That must have been tough. Are you doing okay? Talk to me."

"Nothing to talk about. The baby is fine, I'm fine, Seth's fine. Everyone is fine." Fliss stared into the mirror, relieved her sister couldn't see her. Her face still looked a little puffy.

This, she thought, *is what a liar looks like.*

"You know I'm here if you need to talk to someone."

"Thanks, but there's nothing I need to talk about." The last thing she wanted was for Harriet to worry about her. Fortunately hiding her feelings was easy, or it had been until last night.

She felt a prickle of annoyance.

Why had Seth come looking for her? Why hadn't he just left her alone? If he'd guessed how upset she was, and clearly he had, then why couldn't he have left her to deal with her emotions her own way?

Given a little more time, she would have pulled herself together and no one would have been any the wiser.

"I'll be two minutes," she told Charlie, and stepped into the shower. Two minutes of needle-sharp hot water helped a little. Not a lot, but enough to help her face the day.

She took Charlie and Hero out for a quick walk, and when she returned her grandmother was already seated at the table, sipping her coffee.

"You're up early, Grams." Fliss fed the two dogs.

"So are you. Especially given how late you were last night."

"You're waiting up for me? I'm a little too old for that, don't you think?"

"You're never too old to enjoy the fact that someone cares about you."

"Good point." Sunlight poured through the windows, and Fliss could hear the faint crash of surf through the open windows. The fresh air did more for her aching head than all the Tylenol on the planet. "I walked the dogs. Came across Hero on the beach so I went to investigate." She put a slice of toast in the toaster and wandered to the fridge. "Turned out Matilda had her baby."

"I heard. I thought it wasn't due for another few weeks?"

"It wasn't, but nature thought differently." She pulled out butter and a jar of her grandmother's homemade plum jam.

For as long as she could remember, there had always been a jar of her grandmother's plum jam in the cupboard.

"Toast is burning," her grandmother said casually, and Fliss sprinted across the kitchen, cursing.

"It's toast! How can I burn toast?"

"Because you were thinking about other things."

Fliss wasn't about to argue with that. She'd been thinking about Seth. The baby. Matilda. The baby. Seth. The baby. Seth.

Seth, Seth, Seth.

"Damn." She retrieved the charred toast. "Looks like something spewed from the center of a volcano."

"Turn the temperature dial down. Start again. Cooking requires you to stay in the moment. That's why it's relaxing. So you drove her to the clinic?"

"No time." Instead of throwing out the toast, she scraped away the top layer and spread the surface with butter and plum jam. "She was having the baby right there. This jam is good. You could sell it and make a fortune." She chewed, savoring the sweetness and the flavor. The taste took her straight back to those long summers where she and Harriet had filled baskets to the brim with plums and apples. Fliss had eaten them, right there and then, with the sun beating down and the juice running down her chin.

Harriet had preferred to save hers to cook with their grandmother.

They'd spend hours preparing the fruit, stirring, testing and tasting until finally pouring the jam into jars that Harriet had labeled in her neat, careful writing.

It was typical of Harriet to want to lap up every morsel of family time and store it, like a squirrel, for the winter when they were back in New York.

Fliss had preferred to spend her time outdoors. For her, the beach had felt like freedom.

But by doing that, she'd missed out on spending time with her grandmother.

She studied her, noticing how blue her eyes were and how her hair, now white, fell in pretty waves around her face.

She'd seen enough photos of her grandmother as a young girl to know she'd been a knockout.

"Is it my imagination or is the bruising a little better?"

"It's better." Her grandmother finished her coffee. "If you like the jam you can take a couple of jars back to the city with you when you go. And you can take one over to Matilda. Tell me more about what happened."

Fliss swallowed the last of her toast and gave her grandmother a vastly edited version of the previous night's events. Which meant she included most of the facts, and left out all the emotions.

"You delivered the baby?"

"No. It delivered itself, and I caught it." And she could still feel it in her hands. *Warm flesh, vulnerability. So tiny.* She pushed away the memory and shrugged. "Finally putting all that softball I played in college to good use."

"And Chase wasn't there?"

"No. Missed the whole thing. Isn't that exactly like a man?"

"So did the midwife come to her?"

"Midwife and an ambulance, but Seth arrived first." She said it casually, as if it was no big deal, and her grandmother looked at her keenly.

"Seth? But Seth still thinks you're Harriet?"

"Not anymore. Matilda named the baby Rose Felicity." She slid another slice of bread into the toaster and turned the dial down a notch. "Even I found it hard to talk my way out of that one. And it turns out he knew all along." She hovered by the toaster, watching it. What sort of a person couldn't cook toast? "Probably shouldn't have rented a car in a shade of fierce red. Harriet would have gone for soft blue."

"So what happens now?"

Fliss chose to deliberately misunderstand the question. "I need to make a trip to the store to buy a baby gift for Matilda. Which means I could do with some help, because buying baby gifts isn't on my list of skills." Sadly her attempt to take evasive action didn't work with her grandmother.

"I meant, what happens with Seth?"

It was a question that had been playing on her mind since she woke up.

She'd come here to escape emotion and encountered more than she would in Manhattan.

Fliss ejected the toast. "I expect he'll buy her a gift, too." She caught her grandmother's eye and sighed. "What do you want me to say? Nothing happens with Seth. It's all in the past. Over. Done. History."

"Honey, if it was all in the past you wouldn't have run here from Manhattan and you wouldn't have pretended to be your sister. Maybe you should stop running and talk to him."

"Now you're starting to sound like him." Fliss poked the spoon into the jam. "He wanted me to go over to his place tonight for dinner."

"And you're going."

"I haven't decided."

"Why wouldn't you go?"

"Because I'm here to look after you."

"I promise not to dance around the garden naked or get into trouble in any way. Don't use me as an excuse."

Fliss paused, the toast halfway to her mouth. "You danced naked in the garden? That actually happened?"

Her grandmother's eyes twinkled. "Maybe. Maybe you're not the only one who had a liking for skinny-dipping."

Fliss took a bite of toast. "You're a surprise. Tell me more."

"Not unless you tell me about Seth. Trust is a two-way street. I'll show you my secrets if you show me yours."

Fliss sighed. "What do you want to know? Seth was a mistake. We all make them. I was young. Now tell me about skinny-dipping. Did Gramps dare you?"

"No. I dared him." Her grandmother's voice was brisk. "He didn't know whether to be scandalized or impressed."

"You and Gramps obviously had an interesting marriage."

"Oh, we weren't married. Not at that point. Before that night, he'd never seen me naked."

Fliss choked with laughter. "You're *bad*. How did I never know this about you?"

"You're not the only one capable of breaking a few rules, Felicity. And anyway, rules seemed pointless back then. There was a war on. People were dying. It seemed as if the world had gone mad. None of us knew what was going to happen in the future. It seemed right to grab happiness wherever we could find it. Nowadays people are so busy working toward the future and thinking about tomorrow, they forget how precious the present is."

"Wow, Grams, that's profound for seven in the morning." Fliss poured herself another cup of coffee, readjusting her image of her grandmother.

"All I'm saying is that you should grab the opportunity to spend time with Seth."

Living in the present and thinking only of the moment was the reason she'd wound up pregnant at eighteen. But her grandmother knew nothing about that.

"It's complicated—"

"Love always is. Doesn't mean you should give up on it."

"Who said anything about love?"

"Sex, then."

Fliss choked on her toast. "Excuse me?"

"Don't look so shocked. How do you think your mother arrived on this earth?"

Fliss tried to delete the image from her brain. It was bad enough thinking about one's parents having sex, without thinking about grandparents. "Um—okay, but I don't intend to have sex with Seth either. That's not going to happen."

Her grandmother removed her glasses. "I'm going to ask you a question. Being you, you'll probably dodge it, but I'm going to ask it anyway."

Fliss squirmed, her heart sinking. "What?"

"Have you ever met a man that made you feel the way Seth did?"

It took her a moment to answer because the word seemed to be stuck in her throat. "No."

"And that doesn't tell you something?"

"Yes, it tells me I was a teenager with my head in the clouds, seeing things the way I wanted to see them. Artistic interpretation."

"Maybe, or maybe it's telling you something else."

Fliss thought about the way it had felt when Seth had her and dismissed it.

She wasn't going there again. Not even with an unreasonably large helping of sexual chemistry thrown into the mix.

"It tells me I'm practical about relationships. Realistic. I'm not like Harriet."

"You think it's unrealistic to expect to find someone who loves you and who you love back?"

"I think it's hard to find that. Relationships are often one-sided, as you said the other day. One partner invariably feels more than the other. Mom did, and look where it got her."

Her grandmother was silent for a long moment. Then she drew breath, as if she was about to say something.

But she didn't.

Instead, she stood up.

Fliss realized how tired she looked and felt a pang. "Why are you up this early? You should have slept in. What can I do for you? Once I've walked Charlie and Hero, I thought I'd make a start on the garden. I'm going to call a tree surgeon to deal with the apple tree."

"That would be helpful."

"And I'll change the sheets on your bed."

"Thank you."

Fliss bit her lip. "Is there anything else I can do for you?"

Her grandmother paused by the doorway. "You can go and have dinner with Seth. Hear what he has to say."

"Why? What's the point of going over old ground? There's nothing there, Grams. It's history."

"Maybe, but if you don't go, you won't know. Go to

dinner. Clear the air. Have that talk you've been avoiding. Tell him how you feel."

There was no way she was going to tell him how she
felt. Not after last night.

He'd already caught her at a vulnerable moment.
She wasn't going to put herself in that position again.

But if she didn't let him have the conversation he
wanted he was never going to leave her alone.

This way she could keep both her grandmother and
Seth happy.

And all she had to do was listen.

She'd let him say whatever it was he wanted to say,
and then she'd leave.

"All right. I'll go to dinner."

Dinner. Not sex. Not a relationship. Two people
clearing the air. Putting the past behind them.

That was all it was.

CHAPTER TWELVE

FLISS WASN'T THE only one who had a sleepless night.

Seth did, too.

He'd been called in to operate in the early hours of the morning. A dog had been hit by a car. Summer people, driving too fast on unfamiliar roads, buoyed by good spirits, both the sort that came from spending summer at the beach and the sort that was served at the beach bar. That side of it wasn't his business.

His responsibility was the dog and the owner, because when an animal was involved there were always two patients.

It was a reminder of the grim side of his job, but also the good parts.

He thought the animal stood a good chance.

By the time he was satisfied he'd done what he could, the sun was rising and it hardly seemed worth going home, so he sat in his office with strong coffee and tried not to think about Fliss. Instead he tackled a mountain of paperwork, reasoning that doing it now would give him the time he needed to devote his weekend to his new home.

Home.

It didn't feel that way yet, but hopefully in time it would.

He stared at the lab report, but instead of numbers

he saw Fliss's face, streaked with tears, and felt her fingers clutching the front of his shirt. Even then she'd tried to hide her emotions, but he'd felt them, and he'd shared them.

The door opened and Nancy, one of the vet techs, stood there. "You had a busy night."

"I did." He stood up and stretched. "What time is it?"

"Ten minutes until clinic, and it's going to be a busy one."

"Thanks. All I needed was strong coffee and a little good news."

"Hey, you're in demand. That's good news. And I can manage coffee if it would help."

"Thanks, but I can make it myself." He'd always done everything himself, a legacy from a time when people's first response to him was to assume he was wealthy and entitled.

The wealth was a privilege, he knew that. It had also been a lens, a filter, through which people viewed him.

It was one of the reasons he'd chosen to study veterinary medicine. Here he was mostly judged on his ability to deal with animals. When a couple brought in their family pet, bleeding and broken, they didn't give a damn who his father had been.

And, as a vet, he'd learned that what enriched a life was the many small everyday things that so many took for granted. He'd seen a child's face crumple with emotion when given a first pet. He'd seen a millionaire broken over the loss of a dog.

For a while he'd worked with large animals, then very sick animals, and he'd ended up here, running a small animal practice. Part of the community.

It felt right.

"Rufus is looking good, Mrs. Terry." He checked the wound he'd sutured a week earlier. "It's clean and healing well. Can't have been easy keeping him out of mischief this week. You've done a good job."

"I'm so relieved. We've had him since he was weeks old. Billy found him abandoned on the side of the road. The kids have grown up with him. I don't know what we'd do without him."

"Fortunately I don't think you're going to need to worry about that today." Seth handed the dog back to his owner.

Losing a pet was hard. He understood that. He found it hard, too. It was the part of the job he hated.

He worked his way through a busy clinic and then stopped at the store on the way home. Crusty bread, heirloom tomatoes, mushrooms—he almost cleared the shelves of produce, adding in a couple of steaks at the last minute.

The steaks earned him a curious look as Della, the store owner, bagged his items. "Either you and Lulu are eating well, or you have company tonight."

"We always eat well, Della." He handed her his card, hoping that would be the end of it. He didn't mind being the subject of discussion, but he wasn't sure Fliss would feel the same way.

"You're a good cook, Dr. Carlyle, just like your mama. She used to come in here and pick out everything individually. She had an eye for the best. We miss seeing her around. You send her my love when you talk to her next and tell her we're all thinking of her." She returned his card and Seth picked up the bags.

"I'll do that."

She winked at him. "Whoever you're feeding tonight is in for a treat."

He kept his smile polite, and left the store and Della with all her questions behind him.

Preparing and sharing meals had been an important part of his upbringing. Everyone was expected to participate, and the big family kitchen in Ocean View had been the heart of their home. Food had been fresh, healthy and colorful. Bell peppers, their skins charred from the grill, piled in colorful heaps, glistening with olive oil. Fat olives, which always reminded him of the one vacation they'd taken to Italy, exploring the family roots. Every meal was a work of art, his mother's skills as an interior designer showing even when plating food.

The easy conversation over good food was the thing he missed most since his father had passed. Now each gathering was suffused with sadness and the undeniable fact that something was missing.

His mother had kept going, trying to fill a gap that couldn't be filled with other things. Nothing had fitted. Seth knew that gap was always going to be there. The best they could hope for was that they would eventually adjust to it. The family was a different shape now. They had to get used to that.

He unpacked the food in his new kitchen, filling the shelves of the empty fridge. He didn't know if Fliss was going to join him, but if she did he didn't want to be forced to go out. He wasn't going to run the risk of someone derailing their conversation. He knew she'd snatch whatever excuse she could not to talk, and he was determined not to hand one to her.

With the last of the food safely stowed, he grabbed a beer from the fridge.

The place was finally starting to feel lived in. It didn't feel like home, but hopefully it would feel that way in time.

He took his beer out onto the deck, Lulu by his side.

This was privilege. Owning your own place, close to the water, with nature as your closest neighbor.

Even this close to the ocean it was still stifling, the air refusing to release any of the warmth that had built up during the day.

The deck wrapped itself around the back of the house. Light danced across the wooden boards, creating shadow and shade, and he leaned on the railing, staring out across the dunes to the ocean. The only sounds were the plaintive call of a gull, the whisper of the wind and the faint rush of the waves on sand. From here he could appreciate the beauty of the sunset over the Peconic Bay, his only companions the swans and osprey.

And Lulu.

Her ecstatic barking announced Fliss's arrival even before he heard the wheels of her car crunch on gravel, followed by the slam of a car door.

Moments later she appeared around the side of the house, Lulu running circles around her feet.

She stooped to make a fuss of the dog, teasing her, murmuring words Seth couldn't quite hear but which sent Lulu into tail-wagging ecstasy.

With a last tickle of her fingers, Fliss straightened and looked at him.

All sounds faded. It was as if the world had shrunk to just the two of them.

He wanted to reach out and haul her close, but he forced himself to keep his free hand on the railing.

He'd thought it was a good idea to ask her to his home, but now he wondered if a restaurant full of people might have been easier. Or maybe nothing about this meeting was ever going to be easy.

He watched as she took the steps up to the deck where he was waiting.

His heart pounded, but seeing her in shorts always did that for him. These skimmed her thighs and showed off the long, tanned length of her legs.

He lowered the bottle he was holding, even though his mouth felt as dry as dust. "You found the place with no problem?"

"One wrong turn. Almost landed the car in a ditch. You're hidden away down here. You managed to find the one patch of land that isn't crowded with summer people."

"That was the idea. The land borders the nature preserve. This cottage used to be owned by an artist. He converted the top floor into an incredible studio. North light." He watched the way the sunlight danced over her hair. She'd always had the most beautiful hair. Silver in some lights. Pale gold in others. If the artist who had owned the cottage were still living here, he would have whipped out a canvas and a brush. "I wasn't sure you'd come."

"Why wouldn't I?"

"You've been going to considerable lengths to avoid me."

She gave a casual shrug. "It's not the first time I've pretended to be my sister."

"I know you turn hide-and-seek into an art form, but surely even you can't expect me to believe all that had nothing to do with avoiding me."

"I really don't—"

"I saw you, Fliss. That day outside the clinic when you were hovering, making up your mind whether to come in or not. I was on my way outside to talk to you when you dropped to the ground. I was about to dial 911, and then I realized you'd done it to avoid me."

"I lost my balance."

If he hadn't been so exasperated he might have laughed.

Instead he pressed his fingers to the bridge of his nose and forced himself to breathe slowly. "Fliss—"

"*Okay*! I wasn't totally excited about seeing you. And yes, I snatched the opportunity to get away from Manhattan so that I didn't bump into you, and then I bumped into you anyway, which just proves that karma is an insensitive bitch."

He let his hand drop. "Why was it such a big deal? You couldn't just have said, 'Hi, Seth, how are things?'"

"If I could turn the clock back that's probably the approach I'd take, but at the time I thought I'd killed your dog and then I heard your voice and you sounded—" she snatched in a breath "—and I saw you and you looked— It flustered me."

Flustered was good. He could live with flustered.

Her gaze slid to his, and he saw the flicker of something there before she looked away again.

"So you decided to pretend to be Harriet."

"If I'm honest, there wasn't a whole lot of planning behind that strategy. It was more of an impulse. A conditioned response."

"The conditioned response being to avoid me?" He waited, refusing to allow her to dodge it and finally she scowled.

"So I wasn't comfortable seeing you. Turns out I'm clueless when it comes to ex etiquette."

"That exists?"

"I don't know! But I didn't know how to handle it."

"So you pretended to be Harriet, which made it a different conversation."

"That was the idea. A different conversation was exactly what I wanted. Goal achieved."

"But you're here now. As yourself. And this time we're having the conversation *I* want."

"Yes. So let's get it over with." The expression on her face suggested she was about to be dragged off to a torture chamber. "If there are things you need to say, although I can't imagine why there would be after all this time, then you need to say them. Go right ahead."

You need to say them.

What he really wanted was for *her* to talk to *him*, but he knew that wasn't going to happen in an instant. You couldn't change the habits of a lifetime overnight, and Fliss had been keeping things to herself for her entire life. He needed to be patient. And persistent. Last time he'd given up and walked away. This time he wasn't doing that. Not until he'd explored what might have been. If losing his father had taught him one thing it was that life was too precious to waste a single moment doing things that didn't matter with people who didn't matter.

Fliss mattered to him. She always had.

He knew that now. What he didn't know was why it had taken him so long to follow up on it. There had been plenty of reasons why walking away from it had seemed like the right thing. They'd been too young, it had all happened too fast—the list was long, and topped off by the fact that she'd never returned his calls. Nothing on that list had explained why he hadn't been able to leave her behind.

She hovered, wary, her weight on her toes. She reminded him of a deer, alert for danger, ready to run at a moment's notice.

And he wasn't going to give her a reason to run.

"Do you want a tour?"

"A tour? Of your house?" She relaxed slightly, as if she'd been given a reprieve. "Sounds good. Great idea."

"You're my first visitor, apart from Chase, and he doesn't count given that he's had eyes on the place every week since the project started."

"Have you spoken with him?"

"Yes. He flew back last night the moment I called him."

"The advantage of helicopter travel."

"He's with Matilda in the hospital, but I think she'll be coming home today."

"I wondered. I would have texted her, but of course she dropped her phone. And I didn't want to get in the way by showing up at the hospital."

He wondered if that was all it was. The image of her face when he'd walked into the room and seen her with Matilda's baby was welded into his brain.

"I doubt they would have minded." He picked up the empty beer bottle and strolled through to the kitchen. "He'll be calling you. To say he's grateful would be an understatement."

"Why would he be grateful? I didn't do anything."

"You did plenty. If it weren't for you, Matilda would have been on her own."

"Hero takes the credit for that. He came to find me on the beach. That dog is supersmart."

"You stayed with Matilda through the whole thing."

"Believe me, if there had been anyone else within shrieking distance I would have been out of there." She made it sound like a joke, but he knew she wasn't laughing.

"But you stayed. And it must have been hard for you." He was probably the only one who had any idea how hard. He could imagine how it must have ripped open wounds she'd carefully sealed and exposed feelings she'd kept hidden.

"Not hard at all."

He thought back to the way she'd sobbed on him the night before and felt a rush of frustration. "Fliss—"

"Obviously I don't know anything about delivering babies, but Matilda seemed to manage that part just fine by herself. I was little more than a cheerleader. All I had to do was say, 'Yay! Go you! Wow, a baby!' That kind of thing."

It was like trying to crack his way through a reinforced steel wall. She had defenses that would have been the envy of any security force in the world.

The fact that he understood her reasons didn't make it easier to handle.

"So last night on the beach when you were drenching my shirt, sobbing as if your heart was going to crack— which part of cheerleading was that?"

"Witnessing the beginning of a new life is an emotional thing."

Last night he'd caught a glimpse of the feelings she was keeping locked inside, and it hadn't been pretty.

He wanted to ask if she'd slept, if she'd shed more

tears, but the answer to that was visible in the bruised shadows under her eyes, and he knew that the emotional events of the night before had stolen her sleep in the same way they had his.

She paced around the kitchen, admiring, touching, and gave a low murmur of approval. "Nice." She ran her hand over the countertop and glanced at him. "Chase did this?"

She looked exhausted,.but he decided there was no point in asking more questions she would evade.

"Not personally. He has a good team." He opened the fridge, forcing himself to be patient. Haste had destroyed the fragile roots of their relationship last time. He wasn't going to let that happen again. "Drink?"

"Please. Something cold. Nonalcoholic, as I'm driving. I need to keep my eye out for dogs who lie down in the middle of the road." She gave Lulu a pointed look. "How do you train a dog to play dead? Maybe that's a way we could expand. Dog training."

"You're looking to expand?"

"Yes. We practically own dog walking on the east side of Manhattan. I've decided we need something else. I was thinking maybe dog grooming, or even boarding."

"Do you have premises?"

"No. That's the downside." She shrugged. "But also the upside because I'm tired of falling over paperwork in our apartment."

"You share with Harriet?"

"Yes, of course. We live in Manhattan. An apartment to yourself is the stuff of dreams. And we're in tight quarters. Harriet hates paperwork or anything to do with accounts, so she pushes it into a corner and pretends it isn't there. Before I can process it, first I have to find it."

"You can't run the business online?"

"A lot of it is online, but there's still paper."

"Do you have to expand? Why not just keep the business small?"

"Now you're starting to sound like Harriet. She's happy the way things are. I handle the accounts and the clients, she handles the animals and the dog walkers. So maybe dog training might be the way forward. Heaven knows, we'd have enough clients who would benefit."

"Do you ever refuse to walk a dog?"

"In theory, but in practice I've never met a dog Harriet couldn't handle. She's a wizard when it comes to animals. That's probably another reason why we should expand our offerings to include training."

"But Harriet couldn't train every dog."

"Are you trying to burst my bubble?"

"No. I'm presenting a strong counterargument. If you can't challenge me, maybe it's not a sound business proposition."

"The weakness is in needing new premises. That increases our fixed costs and our risk."

"You've never been afraid of risk."

"No, but this business means a lot to me, and it's not just mine. It's Harriet's, too. I know how much this job means to her." She glanced at him. "She started off studying veterinary medicine just like you."

"I didn't know that."

"I think you inspired her. But she hated the way some owners behaved toward their pets. After this one guy told her there was no way he was going to throw away good money having his dog put down when he could die for free if left alone, she lost her temper."

"Harriet?"

"You don't believe me?" Fliss's eyes gleamed. "You want to see my twin's steely side? Mess with an animal."

He took a can of soda from the fridge. "What happened?"

"She gave up. Probably the best thing that could have happened, although she didn't see it at the time. I'd just finished business school, so I decided we should do something together. I did all the things she hated—paperwork, phone calls, face-to-face with strangers, that kind of thing. She did all the things she was great at—dealing with difficult animals, recruiting dog walkers, convincing clients that no one cared about their pets more than we did. And it was true. We were doing pretty well, getting by, and then about a year ago Daniel heard about this start-up. Urban Genie. Three women offering concierge services. Turns out there's a lot of demand for dog walking. He recommended us. We've had almost more business than we can handle ever since."

She'd set up the business as a way of protecting her sister.

"And now you want to be even more busy."

"What can I say? Making money, growing, being a success—it gives me a thrill. Winning new business is my adrenaline rush." She paused by the island, looking at the neat heaps of chopped vegetables. "When you said you'd take care of dinner, I wasn't expecting this. What would you have done if I hadn't showed up?"

"Eaten alone. Put some in the fridge for tomorrow. Maybe invited the neighbors." Dealt with his disappointment and frustration. "I'm a Carlyle. We like entertaining." He handed her the Coke. "Do you want a glass?"

"No, this is good. Thanks." She snapped open the can and drank. "You have neighbors? I didn't see any. The nearest house is back up the lane."

"The Collins family. He runs a boat business, she's a teacher. Two children, Susan and Marcus. And they keep two ponies."

"Wow. You're a real pillar of the community, Dr. Carlyle."

"That's the point of living somewhere like this. It doesn't have to be anonymous."

"I like being anonymous."

"Why?"

She took a slug of her drink and watched while he cooked. "It's easier when people don't know your business. I walk into a store in Manhattan and no one knows who I am. I like that. Maybe it's just me. I prefer to keep my life private from strangers."

She preferred to keep her life private from everyone. Including him.

"Sometimes it's good to have connections. And everyone who isn't family is a stranger until you let them in." He cooked without consulting a recipe, confident enough in the kitchen to be able to keep the focus on her.

"As we both know, I'm not great at letting people in. Dogs, no problem. Humans—that gives me more of a problem." It was the first time he'd heard her admit it.

"Not everyone is out to get you."

"Maybe not." She scanned the food. "So all this food

is just for us? Because it looks as if you've invited the whole of the Hamptons."

"I may have overcatered. It's a family trait."

A smile flashed across her face. "I remember being in your kitchen with about eighteen other people. Your mom didn't even flinch. Your house was always full of people, and the food kept coming."

"Blame the Italian blood. Food has always been central to family life in my house."

She eyed the food on the countertop. "And you're continuing that tradition. I didn't know you liked to cook."

There were a lot of things she didn't know about him and plenty he didn't know about her, but this time he was determined things were going to be different. Last time they'd rushed their way through most of those small, subtle things that fed a relationship and made it grow and deepen. They'd bypassed some aspects altogether in their race to satisfy raw sexual attraction.

It was like having arrived at a destination without having taken the time to enjoy the journey. Only now was he realizing how much he'd missed.

If he'd understood her better, would they still be together?

"My mother always insisted that we sat down at the table at least once a day. Breakfast could be taken on the run, but dinner never was. It didn't matter what we were doing, we were all expected to be there. Eating those meals, talking over food, was something that glued us together as a family. If it hadn't been for that we might not have spent time together." And he instantly felt a flash of guilt because the one thing he did know about her was that mealtimes in her house had been an incendiary affair. "I guess that happens a lot in a family with divergent interests. Given the choice, Bryony would have spent her whole time at the stables with the horses and Vanessa would have been with her friends."

"How are your sisters?"

"Bryony is teaching first grade and loving it, and Vanessa is married and determined to see everyone else in the same blissful state."

She smiled. "You two used to fight all the time."

"Still do." He decided not to elaborate on what the biggest cause of their discord was. "We're not as close as you, Dan and Harriet."

"And your mom?" Her gaze skated to his. "Losing your dad must be hard on her."

"It is. They were together for more than forty years. She's lost her soul mate. But she's doing better than she was. Having grandchildren helps." He saw the question in her eyes and realized how much of each other's lives they'd missed. "Vanessa has two children. A girl and a boy, age six and eight. Vanessa works part-time as an accountant and Mom takes care of the kids when they're not at school. I reckon it helps her as much as it helps my sister."

"So you're Uncle Seth. And I bet you're good at it." She leaned against the counter. "Beach games, hide-and-seek, you're a hands-on type of uncle. Six and eight. I'm guessing lots of sport. Taken them surfing yet?"

"As it happens, yes."

"I bet they loved it."

"Tansy loves it. She's the eight-year-old. It's hard to get her out of the water. Cole would rather dig in the sand for dinosaurs."

"Which you've conveniently buried?"

"Sounds about right. How about your family? How's Harriet?" He forced himself to ask the question. Not that he didn't care about Harriet, but he cared more about finding out as much as he could about Fliss. "Does she know you've been impersonating her?"

"Yes." She paced the kitchen, on edge, and then spun to face him. "Okay, I thought I wanted to avoid this but it turns out I can't, so can we just get it over with?"

"Which part? The part where we update each other on the parts of our lives we've missed, or the part where we enjoy dinner?"

"The part where you say whatever it is you feel you need to say. Just do it. Give it to me straight. I hate suspense and tension. At least, I love it in movies and books, but I hate it in real life so let's just get this done. You're mad at me. Ten years is a long time to store up anger, so just let it out and then we can move on."

"Fliss—"

"Don't feel awkward about it. You think I don't know? I messed up, Seth. I messed up in a giant, huge way. *Mega* mess-up. And you suffered for it. I wrecked your life, and I'm sorry." She pressed her fingers to her forehead and muttered something under her breath. "That didn't sound sorry, did it? But I am. Jeez, I am so bad at this. Are you going to speak?"

"You said the same thing the other night." And he'd thought of very little else since. He couldn't make sense of it. "Why would you think that? Why would I be mad at you?"

"You want a list?"

She had a list?

"Yes. Let's hear it." He wanted access to everything

going on in her head. Even more so now he'd been given a glimpse.

"It was all my fault."

"The fact that you got pregnant? I was there, too." And he remembered every detail. Small things. The softness of her skin. The crash of the waves. Touch and sound. The way she'd felt and tasted. Nothing in his life had ever felt so right. "How could it have been your fault?"

"We wouldn't have had sex at all if it hadn't been for me."

Did she really believe that?

"Fliss—"

"Can we stop pretending and remember how the whole thing went down? You tried to stop me ripping your clothes off. I have a distinct memory of hearing you tell me it wasn't a good idea and that we shouldn't do it."

"Because I was worried about you. Not me. You were upset that night. You didn't talk about it, but I knew you were upset. Your father had arrived unexpectedly. He'd said something—you wouldn't tell me what. Whatever it was made you cry."

"He didn't make me cry." Her tone was fierce. "He never made me cry."

"You mean you never let him see you cry. But I saw it, Fliss. I saw what he did to you. How his words made you feel." And he'd wanted to step through her front door and confront her father. He would have done it if he hadn't been sure she would have been the one to bear the consequences.

There was a long silence, and then she lifted her chin

and looked at him. "I have a confession. Something I probably should have told you a long time ago."

He could hear the crash of the waves through the open doors.

"I'm listening."

"I told you I was protected. Taking the pill." She looked away and stared at the food instead. "It was a lie. I wasn't. I said it because I—I was afraid you might stop. And I really, *really* didn't want you to stop."

He waited. "That's your big confession?"

"I lied to you, Seth."

"I know. I always knew."

Shock flashed across her face. "How?"

"You were pregnant. It was pretty easy to figure out. And if there was blame, I share it, too. I should have used a condom."

"You didn't think you needed to."

"I should have used one anyway. The reason I didn't is the same reason you lied about taking the pill. Neither of us was thinking much about that side of things. Our relationship was always a bit like that, wasn't it? It was like trying to hold back a storm." And he knew instinctively that part hadn't changed, that if he touched her they'd reach flash point as fast as they had the first time.

"I trapped you."

"That's not how it felt."

"Oh, come on." She paced to the doors, and for a moment he thought she was going to walk out. Then she paused. "One crazy summer, that's what it was. Sex. Hormones. A teenage rebellion moment."

"Seriously? You're pretending it was teenage rebellion?" He saw her cheeks darken with color.

"It was never supposed to end up the way it did. We never should have gotten married."

"It was the right thing to do."

"Mr. Good Guy."

He gave a harsh laugh. "I don't think so. I got you pregnant."

"That wasn't your fault."

"Why are you always so determined to take the blame for everything?"

"Because it was my fault! I hurt you. Vanessa said—" She broke off, and he stilled.

"Vanessa? My sister spoke to you about it?" Why had that possibility not occurred to him? What had happened to his thinking?

Her gaze slid from his. "Forget it."

"Tell me."

"Why? It's all history now. It's not going to help."

"I want to know what she said." He stood firm, in this instance every bit as stubborn and immovable as she was.

"Nothing I didn't already know. That I wasn't the right person for you. And a few other things."

Knowing Vanessa, he could imagine what those other things might have been, and he tucked the anger away and made a mental note that next time he spoke to his sister he was going to leave subtle at the door.

"My relationships are not my sister's business."

"She had your best interests at heart."

"Maybe, but that still doesn't make it her business."

"She cares about you and didn't want to see you hurt. And I hurt you."

"You were hurt, too."

"I was fine."

Something inside him snapped. "Were you fine? Because I wasn't. I wasn't fine, Fliss! And I'm willing to bet you weren't fine either."

"Seth—"

"I understand why you hide your feelings. You don't want to make yourself vulnerable. You're afraid of being hurt. I know how much your father hurt you. He virtually trained you to keep every damn feeling inside. I get that. What I don't get is why you would hide your feelings with me. Why you wouldn't talk to me. And why you won't talk to me now."

The color drained from her face. "I am talking. What else do you want me to say?"

"I want us to talk about what happened. Really talk. Not gloss over the emotion. Last night you came close to falling apart and you won't even admit it."

And he wanted her to be honest. He wanted her to peel back those layers of protection that kept him from understanding her.

"I've told you it was a long day, and I'm not a midwife and—"

"Dammit, Fliss—" He crossed the kitchen in two strides. When she tried to sidestep he planted an arm on either side of her to block her escape. "Do *not* run."

"I don't know what you want from me."

"The truth. Let's start there, and I'll go first. Losing our baby hurt. It hurt more than I could ever have imagined possible. People talk about a miscarriage as if it's nothing, as if a baby is replaceable. But it didn't feel like nothing. Not to me, and I'm guessing not to you either. We hadn't told anyone you were pregnant, so there was no one I could talk to and share my feelings with, except you. And you were determined not to talk. I couldn't get near you. I don't even know what happened that day you lost the baby. I went to sleep and you were in my bed and I woke up and you were gone. Then I got that call from Harriet saying you were in the hospital."

She stared at him for a long moment and then lowered her eyes so that she was staring at his chest. "I woke early and went for a walk on the beach. I had this horrible pain and I knew I was bleeding. I panicked and called Harriet."

"Why didn't you call me?"

"She's my sister."

"This was *our* baby, Fliss. We were married! You should have called me right away."

"I was hoping I wouldn't have to."

"What does that mean?"

"I was hoping they could do something." Her voice cracked. "I hoped they might perform a miracle. Something, anything, that would make our baby stick. That's what they said to me when they tried to make me feel okay about it. They said some babies just don't stick and there isn't always a reason they can find. Maybe that's true, but to me it felt like karma. I'd got you into this situation and now I was being punished. I felt as if I deserved it for ruining your life."

"Seriously? That's what you believed?"

"Yes."

"And you didn't think to ask me what I felt about it all?"

"I didn't need to. I knew that without the baby, there was nothing left."

He was so shocked it took him a moment to process what she'd just told him. "So you thought the baby was central to our relationship? That by losing it, we'd lost whatever we'd had?"

"Yes." She lifted her gaze to his. "You want honesty, Seth, so let's be honest. If it hadn't been for the baby, we wouldn't have got married."

"Maybe not then, but—"

"We wouldn't have got married." Her tone was firm. "What we shared would have ended up being a steamy summer affair. I would have returned to Manhattan. You would have gone back to college. That would have been it. And maybe one summer in the future we would have met up on the beach and had another fling for old time's sake, I don't know, but I do know it wouldn't have had a happy-ever-after."

Outside, beyond the glass, the sun was setting, sending golden light flowing across the kitchen. For once, Seth didn't care about the sunset.

"I had no idea you felt that way. Our marriage was real, Fliss."

She gave a choked laugh. "We got married in Vegas."

"It was real."

"Seth—"

"Were you happy that day?"

She looked startled by the question. "I—this isn't—"

"Were you?"

"Yeah." Her voice was a croak. "I was happy. It was fun. There was that crazy dress we rented and that crowd of tourists taking photos. Harriet was terrified our dad would guess what we were doing and show up. Most of the photos we took have her looking over her shoulder into the crowd."

He didn't tell her that he'd had the same thought. He

didn't tell her about the security firm he'd employed to keep a discreet presence in the background.

"I was happy, too. And I was afraid that if we waited and asked permission, your father would find a way to stop it. I was worried he'd guess you were pregnant."

And make her suffer.

"You married me to protect me. Vanessa kept telling me you were a knight in shining armor. A gentleman."

If his sister had been given access to his thoughts at that moment she would have been forced to rethink that belief.

"She wouldn't have thought that if she'd seen me ripping your clothes off behind the sand dunes." He thought about the night they'd had sex on the beach and knew she was thinking of it, too.

"I unleashed your bad side. I trapped you."

She really thought that? It explained so much. "I never once thought you'd trapped me."

"We got married because I was pregnant. That's the truth. And I'm still shocked you took me to Vegas. I always saw you as more of a Plaza-in-June kind of guy."

"Ouch." He took her face in his hands. "Do you really know so little about me?"

"Are you trying to convince me you've always dreamed of marrying in Vegas?"

"Guys don't tend to dream of weddings. I was more interested in the woman than the setting."

And he was still interested in the woman. More than interested.

"Not all girls dream of weddings either. After watching my parents in action, it wasn't something I was in a hurry to emulate. But I bet you thought you'd do it some day. Pretty girl. White dress. Big family wedding. I deprived you of that."

"The wedding was for us, not my family. We were the only two people who mattered. In fact I'd even say you *spared* me a big family wedding. For that, I've been forever grateful. Vanessa's wedding almost gave my mother a nervous breakdown. I had no idea choosing a dress and a few flowers could be so stressful. I always thought a wedding was supposed to be a happy occasion." He hesitated. "Ours was. Whatever came after, that day was happy."

"Yes. And then we told people and suddenly it didn't seem quite so shiny." She looked tired and defeated. "Your mom was devastated when we told her what we'd done, although she hid it well. She was always very kind to me."

"She likes you a lot." He paused, wondering, asking himself questions he never had before. "Would you have wanted that? The Plaza in June?"

"No." She shook her head. "That stuff doesn't matter to me."

"I remember Harriet trying desperately to add some romantic touches to our wedding. She was the one who found the flowers—"

"She did that to satisfy her own image of what a wedding should look like."

"Why didn't you turn to me?" His emotions were too raw to be contained. "When you lost the baby, why didn't you tell me how you felt?"

She was silent for a long time.

"I couldn't. I felt so raw and exposed. As if my insides had been ripped out. It was the most terrifying thing that had ever happened to me. For the first time in my life I didn't know how to handle my feelings, and that made me feel vulnerable. Talking to you would have made me more vulnerable."

He knew she believed it. And knew that was the root of their problem. "I'm glad at least you were able to talk to Harriet. At least you weren't alone."

There was a long pause. "I didn't talk to Harriet either. Not about that."

It was the last thing he'd expected to hear, and in that one sentence she revealed more than she'd ever revealed before and it made him realize that even he had underestimated the degree to which she protected herself.

"But she picked you up from the hospital—"

"She knew what had happened, but not the details. She tried to get me to talk, but I couldn't. I just couldn't."

"I assumed—" He broke off, processing it. "I thought you told each other everything."

"If I'd let her see how bad I was feeling, she would have felt bad, too. I didn't want her to feel a fraction of what I was feeling."

"That's a twin thing?"

She gave a faint smile. "No. I'm not talking about some weird, spooky thing where we feel each other's pain secondhand. I'm talking about how it feels to see someone you love in agony."

"Losing a baby is an emotional experience."

"It wasn't just the baby. I knew, even as it happened, I'd lost you, too."

And she'd talked to no one. Harriet hadn't got any closer than he had. He didn't know if that made him feel worse or better.

"So you've never talked about it? Not with anyone?"

"No. I dealt with it my own way."

He suspected she hadn't dealt with it at all.

Her gaze shifted to the door, and he decided that if he pushed her any more she'd be gone.

"Let's eat." He stepped away and picked up a couple of serving platters.

She eyed him. "That's it? We're done talking? Is it over?" The anxiety in her voice made his heart ache.

"You make it sound like dental work."

Most women he knew loved talking. Vanessa did. Naomi had loved it.

Fliss made it sound as appealing as a visit to a tax attorney.

"We're done." *For now.* There was plenty more he wanted to say, needed to say, but it could wait.

"I'm not that hungry."

"You will be when you've tasted what I'm cooking. It's an Italian recipe handed down from my great-grandmother. A Sicilian caponata."

"I have no idea what that is, but I'm sure it's delicious." On the outside she looked fragile. Her face was slim, her features fine and delicate. The outside bore no clues that she was as tough as Kevlar.

He threw steaks on the grill while she carried the rest of the food to the table on the deck. He'd positioned it to make the most of the sunset and planned to spend every free evening out here until the temperature dropped too low to allow it. He told her about the construction. The thought and work that had gone into transforming the house.

"The view is incredible."

"I love it. Are you missing Manhattan?"

"Strangely enough no. It's a pleasant change to wake

to the sound of sea and surf rather than blaring horns and dump trucks."

"You always did love the sea. I wasn't sure how much of that was because it was time away from your father."

She didn't flinch. "That was an element, but it was more than that. I loved the feeling of being right on the edge of the land." She took a mouthful of food and gave a moan of pleasure. "This is delicious. Do you remember that time we played beach volleyball? There was a crowd of us and we all tumbled into your house and your mom produced all this food. It was one of the things I envied most about your family."

"The food?"

"Not the food exactly. More what the food represented. Family mealtimes. It was a time to spend quality time together. All those people. Laughing. All helping. *Hand me the salt. Pass the sugar. Bryony, can you fetch the ham from the fridge?* It was like choreographed happy families. I used to think about it when I was back in New York." She spooned more food onto her plate.

"That's what you thought? That we were the perfect happy family? I seem to remember Bryony and Vanessa fighting at the table over something most days, and my mother getting more and more exasperated with them."

"I remember that, too, and it was one of the things that seemed so enviably normal to me. We never argued with each other at the table," she said. "We never used to talk at all."

It was the first time he could remember her ever offering a glimpse into her family life.

"Talking was considered rude?"

"No." She paused, her fork in her hand. "Talking was considered a risk. Whatever you said, there was a chance it would set my dad off. None of us wanted to do that, so we sat in silence. Apart from my mom. She kept up a stream of false happy chatter that drove Dad insane. I mean I could literally see him boiling. His face would go from pale to puce in less time than it took her to serve a slice of pie. I wanted to tell her to stop talking, to leave him to simmer in his bad mood, but I was almost always in the firing line so there was no way I was putting myself there on purpose. But I could never work out why she tried so hard. I mean, why didn't she just stay silent like the rest of us?"

"Maybe she wanted to keep trying."

"That's the conclusion I reached. She loved him. And no matter how much he made it clear he didn't feel the same way about her, she just wasn't willing to give up on that. No matter what he did, she stuck with him. Soothed. Placated. I guess some people would think that was good. Not me. Watching it drove me insane. I couldn't work out where her pride was. He clearly didn't love her, so why didn't she just accept that instead of working so hard to please him?"

It was more than she'd ever told him before, and he wondered if it was because she was talking about her mother's feelings rather than her own. Her mother's marriage, rather than their short-lived car crash of a relationship.

"She never thought of leaving him?"

"In fact she did." She hesitated, as if making up her mind whether to elaborate or not. "Daniel told me Dad threatened to take us. Which surprised me, frankly, because the way he acted made it pretty clear he didn't want us around.

"Our mealtimes were so tense it was easier to cut

the atmosphere than the food." She finished her drink. "We weren't allowed to leave the table until everyone had finished eating. The three of us ate so fast we used to give ourselves indigestion. Didn't make a difference, because if my father hadn't finished none of us moved. Mom was so nervous she invariably dropped something. That would set him off. There—" She sent him a look. "You say I never talk about things, and now I bet you're wishing you hadn't said that."

That wasn't what he was wishing.

"You never talked about this before."

"I didn't want people to know. I hated the thought of people talking about us, especially here, where we created our own little world every summer."

"Would it have mattered?"

"Once people know where your weakness is, they can hurt you, so yes, it mattered."

He wanted to tell her that not everyone was like her father. That there were still plenty of people out there who would have sympathized and supported. Maybe even restored a little of her faith in human nature.

She leaned back. "You're a good cook. Your mom would be proud."

"Your mom must be, too. How is she doing? They're not still together?"

"No. They got divorced the year Harriet and I left home. Daniel helped her. She moved back here for a while to live with Grams. For a while I was worried about her. She seemed listless. I guess she'd been with my dad for so long it was hard for her to contemplate a life without him. But then suddenly she seemed to blossom. It was like watching a completely different person. She was full of the things she was going to do and the places she was going to see. She volunteered in Africa for a while. Earlier in the year she went to South America with friends she met at a support group she attended. Now she's in Antarctica. It's as if she's trying to make up for lost time. How about your mom?"

"She's doing a little better, considering, but she's lost a lot of weight—" he paused "—and most of all she has lost her smile. She used to smile a lot, and now you can tell she only does it to make an effort, to stop us worrying. It's a huge adjustment. And it was a shock. Unexpected. It's going to take a while for her to be comfortable in a life that doesn't have my dad in it. It's hard on her."

"And hard on you, too." She reached across and took his hand. The gesture was spontaneous, and he knew that if she'd thought it through she probably wouldn't have done it because it revealed quite clearly that she still felt something for him. The warmth in her eyes thawed the places inside him that had felt frozen for months.

"It's been very hard."

"You're the man of the house."

"In a way." He curled his fingers over hers, not wanting to lose the contact. "And talking of the house, we're selling it."

"Oh." Her eyes darkened with sympathy. "That's tough. I know how you love that place."

"Yes. But it's what my mother wants. There are too many memories there."

"And you find those comforting, while she finds them distressing?"

He wondered how she could see that so clearly when

people who were closer to him, his sister, for example, failed to understand.

"She's trying to start creating a few positive memories that don't have him in it. That's the only way not to constantly view the world as if something is missing. It's the reason the family aren't joining me here this summer. They've rented cabins by a lake in Vermont."

"Something different." She nodded. "Have you spoken to a Realtor about selling the house?"

"Not yet. I was going to do that this week, but Chase thinks he may know a private buyer who is interested. Cash."

Her eyebrows lifted. "Only Chase would have a friendship circle that includes someone who could buy that house for cash."

"I get the sense he's a business associate rather than a friend."

She was silent for a moment. "I'm sorry, Seth. And I'm sorry I didn't get in touch when it happened. If I'd known—"

"What? You would have pretended to be Harriet and called me?"

"Maybe I would have. I don't know. I don't know what I would have done, and whatever it was I probably would have messed that up, too. But for what it's worth, I really am sorry. Your dad was a good man." She pulled her hand away from his, and he resisted the temptation to snatch it back.

"And I'm lucky to have had him. Given what you've been through with yours, I shouldn't be complaining."

"Of course you should. You've lost something irreplaceable. Something truly special and valuable."

"Are you in touch with your father?"

She dropped her gaze, her expression unreadable. "No."

"Then you've lost something, too."

"You can't lose something you never had." She stood up quickly. "I'll clean up, and then I should go."

"Wait—" He reached out and caught her wrist before she could pick up a plate. "Leave that. It's a beautiful evening. Let's walk."

"Now? It's dark."

"That never used to stop you. In fact it used to be our preferred time for going to the beach."

The look she gave him was loaded with memories. "That was then. This is now. We're both a little old to be creeping around in the dark, climbing out of windows and meeting up in the sand dunes."

"I had in mind walking out of the door and heading for the beach. There's a full moon and we can take a flashlight. And since when has the dark ever bothered you?"

She laughed. "It doesn't."

"So if it's not the dark that bothers you, then what does?"

"You. You bother me, Seth."

"I'd rather you were bothered than indifferent. It means you still feel something."

"Maybe it means you're annoying. Were you always this stubborn?"

"Always. I used to hide it better." He held out his hand. "So that you don't trip in the dark."

"I'm not Matilda." She hesitated and took it.

They strolled on the sand, the dog at their heels.

At the edge of the dunes she bent to slip off her shoes. It was something about her that hadn't changed at all. She did it without thinking, but this time he stopped her.

"Don't. There might be glass or rubbish on the sand."

"Older and wiser." But for once she left her shoes on and carried on walking. She stopped at the water's edge and tipped her head back. "I'd forgotten how much I love the place at night. Look at the stars."

He looked at the twinkle of lights against velvet black. And then he looked at her.

He was tempted to throw control into the ocean and kiss her, but that was what he'd done last time, and unraveling the consequences hadn't been easy.

This time he was determined to take a different path to the same destination.

This time they were taking it slowly.

"I'm going to ask you a question. And you're going to answer me."

"Am I? What if I don't like the question?"

"You're going to answer anyway."

She made a murmur of irritation. "You come across as all calm and civilized, Carlyle, but it's all a ploy. Stealth interrogation."

"Some call it conversation."

"When you prefix it with a warning, it becomes interrogation. I thought we were done. I thought the hard bit was over." She sighed. "Go on then, ask."

"What do you think would have happened if we hadn't lost that baby?"

She stood there, strands of her hair blowing in the wind. "I don't know."

"I do. We'd still be together."

She stilled. "You don't know that."

"I do. Because I wouldn't have given up on us."

"So why did you?" She anchored the strands of hair

with her fingers. "If you really cared that much, why didn't you come after me?"

"I called your number. Left about a thousand messages. You chose not to return a single one of them." And that, for him, had been almost the worst part. Not just that she wouldn't talk to him, but that she hadn't thought, or cared, that he was hurting, too.

"That's not true." She shook her head, puzzled. "I didn't get any calls."

"Well, I know for sure I didn't dial a wrong number."

She was silent for a moment, thinking. "For the first few weeks after I left the hospital, I wasn't very well."

That thought hadn't occurred to him. "Physically? There were complications?"

"Yes. I had an infection. My temperature was sky-high. I was out of it for a while."

"You had to tell your family you'd lost the baby?"

"I didn't tell them. The doctor who treated me kept it confidential. But it was the lowest point of my life. I'd lost you. The baby. And on top of that Dad used the fact that we'd broken up to remind me that I was useless and no sane person would want me. He said you'd obviously finally come to your senses."

Seth felt the anger rip through him. "But when you recovered, didn't you check your phone?"

"Yes, but there were no messages."

Seth cursed under his breath. "He must have deleted them." Why hadn't that possibility occurred to him? The answer, quite simply, was that his own experience was so different he'd always been one step behind.

"He never told me you called, and I took the fact that you didn't as confirmation of everything I already believed. That the marriage was a mistake."

And behind the scenes she'd had her father endorsing that. There was a horrible logic to it all.

"And I was hurt that you wouldn't turn to me. That you were keeping me at a distance. Trust, closeness—those things are fundamental in a marriage. The fact that you didn't turn to me told me you didn't trust me. That you didn't feel close enough to be able to share your low moments with me." And he'd let his own stubborn pride and grief stop him thinking clearly. He'd allowed people to persuade him that the best thing was to move on. He'd allowed other people to influence his decisions.

"Even if we had talked, the truth is I didn't know how to open up. Even if I'd known, I probably wouldn't have dared do it."

"If you didn't trust me, then that was on me."

"No, it was on me." She sounded tired. "I don't know how to have the sort of relationship you just described. I don't recognize it. You learned about trust and love by watching your parents. Want to know what I learned from watching mine? How to protect yourself. How to make sure I was never exposed. I learned that if I kept my feelings to myself, no one could use them against me. I learned that emotions make you vulnerable, and that expressing them makes you even more so. I didn't learn how not to be hurt, but I learned how to hide the fact that I was hurt." She paused. "You were right about that night at the beach, when we had sex. I was upset."

"Because your father had shown up unexpectedly."

"He said some pretty awful things, and I ran out of the house."

"You're implying I was a bandage? That we never would have had sex if you hadn't been upset?"

"No, but you're an honorable man, Seth. You always were. And then when I told you about the baby and you told me that getting married was the only solution, I took advantage of the fact that you were honorable. I should have said no."

"You assume I was being honorable. Maybe I was being selfish. Maybe," he said slowly, "I didn't want to let you go and the baby provided a convenient excuse."

She stared at him for a long moment, as if that possibility hadn't occurred to her. "Whatever it was, it's all history now."

Not to him. "Did you miss me? This last ten years, did you think about me?" He'd put her on the spot. Cornered her, and he saw the brief flash of panic in her eyes and heard the uneven snatch of her breath.

"Ten years is a long time. I barely thought about you."

"You think you're an expert at hiding your feelings, but you're not as good as you think, Felicity Knight." Or maybe he knew her better than either of them thought. He had a feeling she might find that knowledge scarier than his question.

"I don't see the point on dwelling on the past."

"Agreed. Which is why we're going to focus on the present."

She relaxed a little. "Good plan."

Deciding he'd spent too much of his life giving her space, he pulled her against him and took her face in his hands so that he could look into her eyes.

Her eyes, he'd discovered, were the only way he stood a chance of understanding what she was thinking, and right now they were wide and shocked.

"What are you doing?"

"I'm focusing on the present." Step by step, he told

himself. Slow and easy. "Come sailing with me tomorrow, Fliss. Just the two of us. The way we used to."

"I can't."

"Why not?"

"Because—" she gave a helpless shrug "—first you say you want to focus on the present, and now you want to wind back the clock?"

"No. I don't want to re-create what we had back then. I want to discover what we have now." He saw the anxiety in her eyes turn to panic.

"We don't have anything now. Whatever we had is in the past!"

"Is it? Have you been serious about anyone since me?"

"What?" Her lips parted. "Well, I—I don't—"

"I haven't either. There's been no one."

"Are you telling me you haven't dated for ten years? Because I'm not going to believe you."

"I've dated."

"Me, too. I've been on plenty of dates since you and I broke up. I live in Manhattan! Part of the most exciting city in the world. New York has more hot guys than you can throw a stick at." The sass was back, and he held back the smile.

Because it was getting harder and harder not to kiss her, he let his hands drop. He lowered them to her shoulders, but that didn't help ease the ache, so he released her.

"I think you might be getting the guys mixed up with the dogs. Are you telling me you've dated every man in New York?"

"Not *every* guy. There might be a couple of guys in Brooklyn who haven't had that good fortune."

"And yet here you are—single."

She scowled at him. "What are you suggesting? You think the fact I'm single has anything to do with you?"

"Does it?" He had the satisfaction of seeing her flustered.

Her mouth—that mouth that he couldn't stop thinking about—opened and closed. "Definitely not. Marriage just isn't on my bucket list, and you're letting the whole 'I'm a veterinarian' thing go to your head."

"Who said anything about marriage? I'm single, too."

"Are you blaming me for that? Are you saying I damaged you for life?"

"Not damaged, no. But when you've had something really good, it can be hard to settle for less."

The sound of her breathing mingled with the soft sound of the ocean.

"What we had was pain."

"What we had was good. And we let circumstances, and other people, damage what we had. You talk about blame, but I blame myself for that."

"You're starting to freak me out. Stop looking at me like that." She stepped back, hands raised. "I'm bad news, Seth." With that, she turned and strode back along the beach toward the house.

I'm bad news.

He wondered who had told her that. Her father or his sister? Had Vanessa in her tactless, interfering way somehow scraped against feelings that were already raw?

He caught up with her by the car.

"If you're bad news, then you're my type of bad news." He braced his arm against the door so that she couldn't escape until he moved. "I have the afternoon off tomorrow. I'll pick you up. We'll take a picnic."

"That's ridiculous. I—"

"Does two o'clock work for you? I should be done by then. The wind and tide will be perfect."

"It doesn't matter! I'm not going to—"

"Dress casual. You know the score."

"Dammit, Seth! We can't just—this is ridiculous—" Her voice came to a stuttering halt. "Grams is having friends over for lunch."

"So she doesn't need you there."

"I promised to walk Charlie."

"I have a clinic in the morning, so you'll have time to do that before I arrive." He held out his hand. "Give me your phone—"

She sighed and then handed it over.

He entered his details into her contacts. "Text when you've finished doing whatever you need to do for your grandmother. I'll work on the house until I hear from you."

"If I did come, and I probably won't because I'm going to be busy, where would we go?"

"Sailing in Gardiner's Bay, the way we always used to."

And she would come, he was sure of it. Fliss loved the water too much to say no. The first time he'd taken her and her sister out on a boat was the only time he'd seen Fliss speechless.

She'd stood in the bow, her hair streaming out like a pennant, legs braced against the roll of the boat.

A repeat of that, he hoped, would be enough to tempt her.

Without giving her more time to conjure up more excuses, he whistled for Lulu and strolled back toward the house.

Generally he wasn't given to keeping score, but if he did he definitely would have won that round.

CHAPTER THIRTEEN

ROSE FELICITY ADAMS lay asleep in Matilda's arms. Hero lay across the doorway, his head resting on his paws.

"He won't let us out of his sight," Matilda said. "Chase is worried I'm going to trip over him."

Fliss hovered at the edge of the room watching her friend. She'd never seen anyone so content. It was hard to believe the drama of a few nights before had ever happened. True, she looked tired, but there was a light in her eyes, and a smile of pure happiness hovered around her mouth. Fliss wished she could feel half as relaxed. Instead she felt restless and unsettled.

And it wasn't seeing the baby. For some reason she didn't entirely understand, the raw feelings of loss and grief that had poured out of her that night of the birth hadn't returned. Somehow they'd diminished, the sharp edges worn away by the tide of her emotion. Emotional erosion.

No, it wasn't baby Rose who was the cause of her current feelings.

It was Seth.

I want to discover what we have now.

What did he mean by that? They didn't have anything now. Except confusion and a whole lot of new stress. She'd thought a conversation would be the end of something. Instead it seemed that it was the beginning. But the beginning of what?

Life would have been simpler if she'd stayed in Manhattan. Or if he'd stayed in Manhattan. Or if he'd been born less attractive. The moment she thought it, she dismissed it. It wasn't about the way he looked but the way he *was*. Persistent and damn stubborn. *Decent and caring.*

And stubborn.

Other people mostly respected her boundaries. Seth seemed determined to invade them. Was that a legacy from his childhood? His family had always been open and communicative. Even when they'd been involved in a shouting match, they'd been communicating. It wasn't just food they'd shared in the Carlyle household, it had been feelings. Feelings had been right there at the table along with glistening tomatoes and ripe goats' cheese. To her, it had felt alien and unfamiliar. When they'd tried to include her, she'd answered as briefly as possible, her smile stretched and stiff. She hadn't been able to switch off that side of her that constantly asked *why do they want to know this and how are they going to use it against me?*

She wanted desperately to be part of their group, to fit in, but nothing in her past had trained her for this. Her childhood had taught her not to engage. How to deflect any possible intrusion into her feelings. But Seth hadn't been put off by those barriers. And it seemed nothing had changed.

The fact that he wanted to see her again made her nervous. Uneasy. Exposed. It was like setting the alarm on your house, knowing that the person watching from outside had both the key and the code and could walk in at anytime.

She shouldn't have gone to his place for dinner. That had been a bad move. If she'd just had the conversation on the side of the road that day, instead of pretending to be Harriet, she wouldn't be in this mess now. There was nothing remotely disturbing about a conversation conducted in blazing heat with traffic pounding past, kicking up dust. They would have sweated it out and gone their separate ways. Awkward moment done.

Instead, there had been the intimacy of his house. Just the two of them and a thousand heated memories she definitely hadn't needed in the room with her. And as if that wasn't torture enough, it had been followed by that walk on the beach, something they'd done so many times before.

Moonlight over the ocean.

Why had she agreed to *that*?

He hadn't touched her, and yet she'd wanted him to. Yet another thing that made no sense. The feelings should have faded by now, but instead they continued to throb, unrelenting and raw.

Frustrated by all the things she couldn't control and didn't understand, she glared out the window and jumped as Matilda cleared her throat.

"Is everything okay?"

"Of course. Everything is perfect." If you ignored the fact that she hadn't slept well since Seth arrived back in her life. The stress was starting to age her.

"You seem tense."

"It shows? Am I going gray?" She grabbed a handful of hair and examined it. "I'm going to be old and haggard before my time."

"You're a long way from old and haggard. Is it Seth?" Matilda looked worried. "Is it my fault for inadvertently revealing you're not Harriet? I feel terrible about that."

"Don't. I was planning to confess anyway." Maybe. Or maybe she would have legged it back to Manhattan. Would he have followed her if she'd done that? And would she have wanted him to? Her thoughts spun randomly, like leaves caught in a gust of wind. She never knew quite where they were going to fall. "And it's pretty cool having a baby named after me."

"I blew your cover. And now Seth knows."

Another person would have told her that Seth already knew. They would probably have laughed about it, the laughter tinged with embarrassment. But Fliss wasn't that person. "I should have done it a long time ago, but I was so tangled up in my own lies I didn't know how to get out of it."

"Was it very awkward? I want details."

She didn't do details. "We talked."

And while he was talking she'd been preoccupied by the shape of his mouth and the thickness of his eyelashes.

How was it right that one man could be so attractive? There was no justice in the world. If there was then she should have been able to spend an evening with Seth without feeling as if her emotions had been dumped in a cocktail shaker and treated with a total lack of mercy.

She didn't know whether it was his eyes or his smile, but something about him turned her inside out.

Or maybe it was that confidence. She'd always envied that confidence. The fact that he was so *sure*. She assumed it came from having parents who encouraged and believed in him. Parents who were proud.

She, on the other hand, was a seething mass of uncertainty. And she hated feeling that way. Surely she should have shaken it off by now.

What did it matter that no one in her family had ever been proud of her? She had a business and an apartment, albeit small and shared with her sister. And she'd paid for all of it herself. Her father had never given her a single cent. *She* was proud of herself. That was all that should count.

"I need you to translate something for me." The words blurted out of her mouth, surprising her.

"I've never been good at languages." The breeze floated through the open window, taking the edge off the heat.

"I'm talking about men. You understand men."

Matilda burst out laughing. "Fictional men. I understand my characters, but that's because I'm the one who made them up. And I hope I understand Chase, at least most of the time."

Chase had been the one who had led Fliss into the house, and he'd hovered close to Matilda and the baby until she'd gently shoed him off to do some work. The look he and Matilda had shared had made it clear to Fliss that they'd forgotten she was even in the room.

Once again she'd found herself envying their close connection. "Do you tell Chase everything?"

"Yes. It's what makes it so good. I don't have to hide who I am from him, he knows and loves me anyway." Matilda settled the baby more comfortably. "So what is it you need me to translate? Body language or a situation?"

"You told me the other day that you think through the reasons people act the way they do. So that's what I want to know. The reason." She'd been thinking about it all night. Her brain had gone around and around until she'd felt dizzy with thinking. And still she couldn't make sense of it. She'd spent a decade thinking things were a certain way, and now that they were different she didn't recognize what she was looking at. "I need to understand why Seth is behaving the way he is."

"I'm going to need a little more information."

"It's the first time I've seen him in ten years—"

"As yourself."

"Excuse me?"

"You've seen him as Harriet."

Fliss sent her a look. "Are you going to keep interrupting?"

"Sorry."

"He invited me to dinner. Why do that? Why go to the trouble of dinner for what might have been the most awkward encounter of the decade?"

"*That's* why you're so distracted." Matilda nodded, as if Fliss had just shared something momentous. "I'm guessing it was because he didn't want to rush it. Dinner ensures that you have time to say what needs to be said. He took you to a restaurant? What type of restaurant? Romantic, or neutral territory?"

"It wasn't a restaurant. He invited me to his home. He cooked."

"I love a man who can cook." Matilda tucked the blanket around the baby. "And cooking for you at home is more personal than a restaurant. Intimate."

"That makes no sense. Why would he want it to be personal and intimate?"

"Perhaps he thought it was better for your relationship to spend time together without anyone else around."

"What relationship? *This* is why I'm confused. Our relationship was over ten years ago, and even when it was running hot we didn't do dinners." But they'd done romantic moonlight walks on the beach. And they'd done other things, too. Things she couldn't stop thinking about.

"So what did you do first time around? How did you spend your time?"

Fliss looked at the baby. "She's too young to hear it."

"Right." Matilda laughed. "I get the picture. It was more hormones than head or heart."

There had been heart, Fliss thought. On her side, at least. There had been so much heart she'd found it difficult to pick herself up afterward. But that wasn't something she shared.

"Last night he cooked, then we had a walk on the beach and talked."

"Seems straightforward. So which part of that needs deciphering?"

"The things he said weren't the things I expected him to say."

Matilda looked at her. "If you're expecting some input from me, you're going to have to give me more."

"I assumed he was mad at me. I mean, he should have been mad at me."

"Why? What did you do?"

Fliss stared out the window, letting her mind slide back to the past. "It doesn't matter. All you need to know is that he wasn't mad. And—he surprised me, that's all." And she'd surprised herself with what she'd revealed. "I thought he'd say his piece and then I'd leave. I thought that would be the end of it. And every time I saw him after that I'd wave and say, 'Hi, Seth.'"

"But—?"

"He wants to see me again." Fliss let out a breath. "I didn't see that coming. He should be staying away from me."

"It doesn't look to me as if that's what he wants."

"But what does it *mean*? He said he wanted to spend time with me. So is that time as a friend, or time as more than a friend?"

"Do you always think this much about relationships?"

"Yes, but that isn't the point. The point is that I don't have a relationship with Seth."

"But clearly he wants one."

"*Why?* Where is this all going?"

"I don't know. Maybe all he wants is friendship. Or maybe he doesn't know either. Maybe he just wants to spend time with you and see how it turns out."

And how *would* it turn out?

"I thought the whole point of having the conversation we had last night was to get it out of the way so that we could move forward. And now he wants to rewind the clock. It's confusing, and I don't like feeling confused. It's stressful."

Melissa smiled. "Do you always overthink everything?"

"Sometimes." When it was something that could hurt her? Always.

The baby looked so peaceful, her eyes closed.

Fliss envied the simplicity of her life. At that moment she would have swapped places.

Matilda stirred. "Could you hold her for a moment while I run to the bathroom?"

Fliss thought about the way the baby had felt in her arms. "You don't want to put her in her crib? She's asleep. Seems a shame to wake her."

"Exactly. The moment I put her in the crib she wakes up, and I don't want her to wake up. And anyway, it's an excuse for you to have a cuddle with your namesake."

Fliss had been searching for excuses *not* to have a cuddle, but admitting that would have required explanations she didn't want to give, so she took the baby carefully, hoping that her bruised heart proved more robust than the last time she'd handled little Rose. "I hope I don't wake her up. I haven't had that much to do with babies."

There was an ache inside her. Regret? Longing?

If you hadn't lost the baby we'd still be together.

Was that true?

The thought made her feel sick. It brought back all the "if onlys" she tried never to allow into her head.

"You'll be fine." Matilda vanished from the room, stepping carefully over Hero, who didn't shift his gaze from Fliss and the baby. He'd obviously decided that Rose was now his priority.

"You think this is easy?" Fliss stood without moving, desperate not to wake the baby. "Try putting your paw on a thorn and then pressing down hard. That's how it feels."

Hero yawned.

"I would have expected a little more sympathy, given all the outstanding walks you've had from me. You owe me."

Still watching her, Hero settled his nose on his paws, a benign bodyguard.

Matilda reappeared and took the baby from her. "So where's he taking you?"

"Sailing."

"Oh, lucky you." She slotted Rose onto her shoulder as naturally as if she'd been doing it forever. "Chase loves sailing with Seth."

She'd loved it, too.

"It's crazy, isn't it?"

"No. He's a skilled sailor. He and Chase got into difficulties once out in the bay, and it was Seth who got them out of it."

"I wasn't talking about the sailing. I mean, it's crazy to do something a second time when it went badly wrong the first time."

"Are you worried about him, or yourself?"

"Both of us."

Even in the last twenty-four hours, things had changed.

The discovery that he'd tried to contact her and that no one had told her was another piece of the jigsaw that explained some of the events back then.

"Maybe I should have invited him to join me for lunch with Grams and her friends. That would have scared him off."

Matilda transferred the baby to her other shoulder. "Seth doesn't strike me as a man who scares easily. You, on the other hand—"

"What? What about me?"

Matilda hesitated. "You don't sound as if you're planning a date, that's all. You sound as if you're preparing to defend yourself from attack. You're not exploring the possibilities of a relationship, you're formulating a battle plan."

A battle plan?

Fliss thought about it while she walked Hero on the beach in front of Matilda's house, and was still thinking about it when she returned to her grandmother's house.

Her grandmother was in the kitchen with four women Fliss knew vaguely from the summers she'd spent here as a child.

"Sorry to disturb you. I came to walk Charlie. Everything okay, Grams?"

"Everything is good, thank you. You remember Martha? She owns the bakery on Main Street, although her daughter is mostly running it now. And Dora, who you'll remember from the doctor's office, and Jane and Rita, who used to live down the road but moved to East Hampton. You all know my granddaughter." She eyed Fliss, taking her cue from her, and Fliss gave a faint smile.

She'd given up on subterfuge.

"I'm Fliss," she said. "Hello, ladies." She murmured a generic greeting, hoping that Dora had forgotten the time she'd visited the clinic with poison oak, having brushed against the leaves on her way to meet Seth. "You seem to be having fun. Cookies from Cookies and Cream?"

"Of course. They're the best. Apart from the ones your sister makes, of course. And we only do this twice a month, so we're allowed a treat."

"Twice a month? So this is a regular thing?"

"We meet once to play poker, and once for our book group. We prefer to meet at lunchtime because we all go to bed early."

Fliss stared at the cards on the table. "Poker?"

"We are the Poker Princesses, didn't you know?"

Fliss hoped her mouth wasn't open. "No," she said. "I didn't know."

"Why so surprised?" Her grandmother studied her over the rim of her glasses. "You think poker is something played by men throbbing with testosterone in a smoke-filled room, is that it?"

"I wouldn't say no," Jane murmured and Fliss grinned.

"It's true you don't exactly fit the vision in my head."

"It keeps our brains sharp and it's fun, even though Rita usually wins."

Dora tutted. "Because none of us can ever read her expression."

"That's the Botox," Rita said cheerfully. "And I like the sound of men throbbing with testosterone. Could we invite a few for our next session?"

Fliss laughed. "Are you playing for cookies?"

"Goodness no. Money." There was a gleam in her grandmother's eye. "What's the point otherwise?"

Fliss decided there was plenty she still had to learn about her grandmother.

"I'll take Charlie and leave you all to your gambling habit."

"Thanks, honey." Her grandmother put her cards down on the table. "She's been walking Hero for Matilda and Charlie for me twice a day. He's looking better for it. Lost a bit of weight and he's calmer. Better behaved. She takes him to the beach and lets him run."

Dora glanced up. "I thought it was Harriet who was going to come and stay with you until you're back on your feet."

"Turned out it was Fliss." Her grandmother's voice was calm. "Which was lucky for me. She's sorted out all my paperwork and my finances, which were in a horrible mess. And she's great with Charlie."

Rita looked confused. "I thought Harriet was the one who has the gift with animals."

"Fliss has a gift, too. And she's not as soft as Harriet. They know they can't mess with her, which is a good thing. And she has a savvy business brain, does my Fliss. She's built a thriving business from nothing, and in New York City, where thousands of businesses go under daily."

Fliss felt a rush of gratitude. She wasn't used to people defending her. She was usually the one doing the defending.

"If we're moving on to that subject, I need more tea." Jane helped herself. "When your grandmother starts, there's no stopping her. If we let her, she'd spend our entire poker session boasting about you."

Fliss smiled. "I think you mean Harriet."

"No, dear, I mean you." Jane stirred her tea. "She talks about you all the time. So much so that sometimes we have to give her a warning. We all boast about our grandchildren, but she does it longer and louder."

Fliss felt a rush of confusion. "She talks about me?"

"Of course. She's very proud of you."

"You never met a stronger, braver, more determined woman than my Felicity." Rita and Dora chorused the words together and then burst into laughter.

Her grandmother sent them a cool look. "Is there a reason I shouldn't boast about my granddaughter?"

Her grandmother talked about her with her friends? Boasted about her? *She was proud?* To her horror, Fliss felt her throat thicken. "I'd better take Charlie. He's waiting by the door."

Dora took a sip of tea. "You're lucky, Eugenia. I wish there was someone who could help walk my Darcy. I've kept his walks very short since my arthritis started playing up. He does miss the beach so much."

Fliss was relieved at the change of subject. The lump in her throat dissolved without causing further problems. "I could walk him for you."

Dora lowered the cup. "Would you?"

"Why not? I'm here, I have time on my hands, and I'm already walking Hero and Charlie."

"If she does, then you'll pay her," her grandmother said. "And you'll pay her a fair rate."

"I'm starting to understand why you've never sold this place to all the people who come knocking," Rita said. "You drive a hard bargain."

"My house has never been for sale. Nor has my friendship. And you can laugh all you like, but my granddaughter is not running a charity. She runs her own business, you know, in Manhattan."

"*The Bark Rangers*," all four women chorused, and this time Fliss smiled.

"You know about us?"

"Every detail. We have celebrated every new milestone right along with you," Dora said. "And I'm happy to pay. I'd expect nothing less. Would you do it for me, honey? Darcy is very social and he's not getting out enough."

Fliss took Charlie's lead from the cupboard by the door. "Of course. What breed of dog is he?"

"He's a Labrador. A great big softie. Twice a day would be good, if you think you can fit it in. And he's a very indiscriminate eater, so you have to watch that. Your grandmother is right. You're a good girl."

No, Fliss thought. She wasn't a good girl. But she was happy to walk dogs. "Not a problem. I'll give you the questionnaire we use, then meet Darcy and work out a plan. I can start tomorrow if you like."

"Thank you. I guess all that walking is why you have such a great figure."

Feeling more comfortable among them, Fliss leaned forward and stole a cookie from the plate on the table. "Which book are you reading for your book group?"

"Matilda's latest."

Remembering the pages she'd read, Fliss lifted her eyebrows. "They're pretty racy."

"That's why we read them. There was a time when we used to find our excitement between the sheets, but now it's between the pages. And talking of excitement—" her grandmother studied her over the top of her glasses "—I didn't hear you come home last night. How was your date?"

"She had a date?"

Five pairs of eyes were suddenly fixed on her with interest, and Fliss paused with the cookie halfway to her mouth, wishing she'd left when she had the chance.

"It wasn't a date."

"He invited her over and cooked her dinner." Her grandmother glanced at her friends. "In my day we called that a date."

"Grams—"

"It must have been a date," Dora said, "because she doesn't want to talk about it. When you don't want to talk about a man, it's a sign that you're interested."

"Who was the man?" The question came from Rita, and Fliss started backing toward the door, panic rising along with the color in her cheeks.

"It was no one—"

"Seth Carlyle." Her grandmother picked up her cards and studied them. "Our sexy vet."

"The most eligible man in the Hamptons," Dora said. "It's time someone snapped him up."

"She already snapped him up once before," Jane muttered. "Your memory is failing you, Dora."

Fliss squirmed. "I'm not snapping him up, Rita. I'm not doing anything at all with him."

"Shame. So you're not seeing him again?"

She'd thought about it all day and decided it was stupid to see him again. There was a difference between a casual encounter and going sailing. She'd been planning on texting him. "It was casual, that's all." She tried to forget the way Seth had looked at her when they'd stood side by side on the beach.

Jane looked interested. "So you saw his new place?"

Fliss opened her mouth, but her grandmother spoke first.

"I'm glad he has his own place. Ocean View is beautiful, but it can't be easy rattling around in that big old house without his father."

"I agree." Dora nodded. "The boy needs to sell it."

But he didn't want to, Fliss thought. Selling it was going to break his heart. He felt as if he was giving away all those memories.

"Boy?" Martha raised an eyebrow. "Maybe my vision is better than yours because I don't see a boy. Our vet is all man. Those shoulders!"

"And his arms."

"For me it's those dark eyelashes and the stubble," Rita murmured. "The man has more sex appeal than I'd know what to do with."

Fliss opened her mouth and closed it again. She'd known exactly what to do with it.

She still did, which was another reason to keep her distance.

"It's the Italian blood. *Mama mia.* He's a strong man, but so gentle with the animals. Sometimes if I use my binoculars and stand on a chair I can see him running on the beach," Jane confessed and Dora smirked.

"I see him regularly since Darcy's arthritis got worse."

Rita gave a little cough. "I overheard Mrs. Ewell in the library the other day confessing that half the women in this area take their pets when they're not really sick, just so that they can talk to Seth. He has such a calming way about him. In a crisis that man is rock solid."

Fliss gaped at them. "You're saying people take their animals when they're not really sick?"

The women exchanged glances. "It's been known," Jane said, polishing her glasses.

"Well, I envy the woman he ends up with."

"Me, too." Jane slid her glasses back onto her nose and glanced at Fliss. "Does he kiss well, honey?"

"Jane Richards!" Her grandmother intervened. "She hasn't kissed him since she was eighteen. She's not going to remember how he kissed."

She remembered. She remembered the feel of his hands and his mouth. The rip of sensation. The liquid heat that had pooled in her belly.

"I don't remember." Her voice sounded strangled. "No recollection."

"Oh." Jane looked crestfallen. "When he kisses you again, we want to hear all about it. And don't look at me like that. There's nothing wrong with enjoying a bit of sex talk. Especially when talking is all I get these days. Books, movies, conversation. That's it."

"True." Dora nodded. "But we're embarrassing Fliss, so I think it's time we minded our own business."

"When have you ever minded your own business, Dora Sanders?"

"Maybe I haven't, but I'm afraid that if I upset Fliss, she won't walk Darcy."

"I can't wait to walk Darcy." She couldn't wait to

get out of here. Fliss grabbed Charlie by the collar and made for the door. "Nice to meet you all."

"When you've walked Charlie, you should join us. When we finish our game we're ordering Chinese from the Jade Garden and watching *Sex in the City*."

"You can give us the young person's view."

Fliss blinked. "That's kind, but actually I'm busy this afternoon."

Five pairs of eyes fixed on her face.

"You're seeing Seth?"

"In fact I am. We're going sailing." What harm would it do? It was a perfect afternoon for sailing, and if the alternative was hanging around for poker and sex talk, she was definitely out of here.

Seth, she thought, was the lesser of two evils.

There was a low murmur of approval from the women at the table.

"Not so casual, then," Jane murmured.

"Don't rush home," her grandmother said. "When we're finished here I'll be having an early night so I won't be good company."

Were they suggesting that she stay the night with Seth? "I won't be—"

"Live while you're young," Dora urged and Jane nodded.

"Before your hips creak."

"Go get him, honey," Rita said, punching the air with her fist.

Fliss fled.

DORA WAITED UNTIL the door slammed. "Success."

"Do you think so?" Martha looked doubtful. "Far be it from me to tell you how to handle your own grand-daughter, Eugenia, but I think you almost overplayed your hand there. Especially the part where you tried to get her to stay the night with him."

Jane nodded. "Doesn't do to interfere. That never turns out well."

Eugenia slapped her cards on the table. "With my own daughter, I didn't interfere enough and I should have done. If I have one regret in life, it's that."

Dora put her cards down, too. "You're too hard on yourself. What could you have done?"

"I don't know, but I should have done *something*. That's what. I knew that marriage wouldn't work out, and I stood by and let it happen."

"That's not how I remember it. She made her own decisions, Eugenia. She did what she thought was right for her. And since when did children ever listen to their parents? Even grown children. She probably wouldn't have listened to you anyway."

"Maybe not, but I wish I'd tried." Eugenia looked at the door, where Fliss had recently disappeared. "When a marriage goes wrong, it doesn't just affect one person. It reverberates. It's like an earthquake. It destroys some structures and weakens others."

"Fliss doesn't seem weakened. She's a strong girl. If nothing else, her childhood taught her how to protect herself."

"That's what worries me." Eugenia removed her glasses and rubbed her eyes. Since her fall she felt tired. More tired than she had in a long time. It had shaken her feeling of security, made her fear a time she might need to depend on people for help. "She protects herself a little too well. No one can get close to her. She holds everything she feels inside because that bastard my daughter married made her feel worthless."

Jane gasped. "Eugenia! Sex talk and poker isn't enough for you? You have to use that language, too?"

"If I could think of another word that fitted, I would have used it."

"You did what you could. You threw him out of your house."

"But she went back to him. She always went back to him."

"Love is a complicated thing."

"Particularly when it's one-sided." Eugenia rubbed her fingers over her forehead. "I should have sold this place and given her the money for a divorce."

"You offered. She didn't want that."

"If I'd sold it without telling her, she wouldn't have had a choice."

"And she would have lost the place that was her sanctuary. And a sanctuary for the kids. Every summer she brought them here."

"And at the end of every summer they left again. Back to hell."

"He abandoned his family a decade ago, Eugenia. Why are you talking about this now?"

"Because his legacy lives on. I see it in the way Fliss lives her life."

"Maybe our sexy vet will change that."

"Maybe." Eugenia made a decision. It seemed so clear, so obvious, she wondered why she hadn't done it before. She sat up a little straighter. "And maybe he needs a little help. And I'm going to give him that help, even if it means releasing a few skeletons from the closet."

"A few? How many skeletons do you have in there?" Jane frowned. "If you're saying what I think you're saying, then those are your daughter's secrets, Eugenia.

Not yours. If there are things she chose not to tell Fliss, then it's not your job to do it. It's not your business."

"That's where we disagree. When her secrets affect her daughter, my granddaughter, it becomes my business. There are things Fliss believes that are just all wrong. And in my opinion my daughter should have set her straight a long time ago. There were things she should have said that she never did. It's not good for a child to grow up believing something to be the truth when it isn't."

"She must have had her reasons for keeping it quiet."

"She did. Just as I have my reasons for coming out in the open." She picked up her cards. "Now let's play. I want to win big tonight."

"Poker days are always so exciting," Martha said. "Even though we don't often finish the game."

Jane glanced up. "Are we really going to watch *Sex in the City*?"

"Of course not."

"Then why did you tell her we were?"

"It was the only thing I could think of that would make leaving the house more appealing than staying."

"Did you see her face? Why is it young people think sex is something just for them? How do they think they got here in the first place?"

"I think we should watch it." Jane was hopeful. "Just in case she comes home early and finds we were fibbing."

CHAPTER FOURTEEN

"POKER AND SEX TALK? They actually called it that?" Seth drove down the narrow roads that led to the water.

He'd been surprised when she'd texted him, asking him if they could meet earlier.

She'd sprang into his car and muttered "*Drive*" without offering any explanation until now.

He'd been mildly amused by the irony. For years she'd been avoiding him, and now she was treating him like a getaway vehicle.

"Yes. I heard the words clearly before I went into shock. I mean, their combined age must be close to four hundred."

"So they have a lot of experience between them."

"I know. And I'm not sure how deeply I want to think about that." She glanced back over her shoulder. "They probably have their noses pressed to the window right now watching us through binoculars."

"Would it bother you?" He didn't mind if the locals were interested in his life, as long as they didn't try to influence it the way Vanessa had.

He'd spoken to her the night before, immediately after Fliss had left. It had been the harshest conversation he'd ever had with his sister. With hindsight he probably should have waited until his temper had reduced from a boil to a simmer, but the thought that Vanessa might have in any way contributed to tearing apart his relationship with Fliss had driven aside restraint.

Remembering the conversation, he tightened his hands on the wheel.

Fliss glanced at him. "Is something wrong? You look angry."

"Not angry." He forced himself to relax.

"Good. For a moment there I wondered if you'd overheard their conversation. They talked about you in lurid detail. Doesn't that terrify you?"

"You're forgetting I've lived here for a while. I'm used to them. And then there's the fact that I don't scare easily."

"Then you're made of tougher stuff than I am. They scared the hell out of me. I'm not used to talking about personal stuff, particularly not with five women all of whom were over the age of eighty." She slid her sunglasses onto her nose. "You still sail a lot?"

"Whenever we get the chance." He glanced in his mirror and saw Lulu looking back at him, loyal and devoted. He was hoping she played her role well and helped Fliss to unwind.

Fortunately she seemed relaxed enough at the moment.

"Matilda said you and Chase sail together."

"Sometimes. And sometimes I sail with his brother Brett. Sometimes I just take Lulu." He parked at the pretty waterfront and heard Fliss sigh.

"I love this place. They have the most spectacular Fourth of July fireworks display. Grams used to bring us."

"I saw you a few times." And he'd watched her, seen her face glow as she'd watched the night sky light up with a glittering explosion of stars. "We used to come here, too. My dad was a member of the yacht club."

She turned to look at him. "You must miss sailing with your father. I know you loved that. I used to sit on the beach and watch the two of you."

The pain was sudden and acute, like a kick in the gut. "Yes. It was the time we both used to unwind. He was the one who taught me. Took me out on the water before I could walk. He had so much knowledge about the waters around Gardiner's Bay and Shelter Island."

"And he passed that on to you."

"Sometimes he took Vanessa, and I used to hate that because it was something I did with him. It was ours. I didn't want to share it with my sister. I was fiercely jealous." He glanced at her. "I bet you can't understand that. You shared everything with your sister."

"And nothing with my father. I guess every family is different."

"I guess it is." He parked and sat for a minute fighting off the memories that swooped and swirled around him. "Once a year we used to compete in the yacht race. My father was so competitive." It made him smile to remember it. "Sometimes we just used to go out on the water and spend the weekend harbor hopping."

"Is it worse sailing without him or does it help?"

"It helps. It definitely helps."

"Then let's sail. Let's do this." She gave his hand a squeeze and opened the car door.

Lulu sprang out, tail wagging approval, game for anything.

And so was Fliss. It was one of the things he'd always loved about her, the fact that whatever anyone suggested her answer was always yes.

He watched her tease and play with Lulu, talking to her, telling her she was a beautiful girl and clever.

Grateful for those few extra moments, he shook off the dark cloud, climbed out of the car and removed the cooler and a large bag from the trunk.

"I hope you're hungry."

"As it happens I am, which is just as well because overcatering seems to be a habit of yours. You inherited your mother's hospitality gene." She straightened. "I didn't know you kept your boat at the yacht club. What about your private dock?"

"I might move it there eventually, but right now it's convenient for me to keep it here."

Lulu was running in circles, tail wagging.

"Someone is excited." Fliss stooped to fuss over her again. "How long have you had her?"

"The boat or the dog?"

She laughed. "Lulu."

"Six years." Seth slammed the car door and carried the gear to the boat. "She was the star of a long-running TV series. She was injured filming a stunt, and they brought her to my clinic."

"This is when you were working in California?"

"Yes. We got talking about how she'd have to be retired and how hard it would be to find a home for her. She gave me a look. Big eyes. Sorrowful. I was completely taken in. It was only later I learned that 'sorrowful' on demand was one of her party tricks."

"So you kept her. Lucky dog."

Seth glanced at Lulu, who could brighten his day with each friendly wag of her tail. "I was the lucky one. She's a real character. And because she did so many things when she was working in movies, she's game for anything. She's so brave." Another thing she had in common with Fliss.

"She's not purebred Labrador?"

"Part Labrador, part retriever."

Lulu sprang onto the boat with a single joyful bound.

Fliss stayed on the dock, studying the boat from bow to stern. "This isn't the boat you used to sail."

"I've had this about six years."

"You had a little sloop. A classic wooden sailboat that your dad spent every weekend restoring. He was always trying to track down certain types of wood or canvas. I was always surprised that a lawyer would know so much about boatbuilding."

"It was a hobby. And he was an incredible craftsman. The boat was his relaxation. His way of leaving the city and the job behind."

"What happened to the sloop?"

"He sold it. Life got busier and we didn't have the time to keep maintaining it." And he missed those days. Those easy, lazy weekends where the only sounds had been the clink of masts and the soft slap of water against the hull of the boat. "This boat is easier to sail. And she's fast."

"How fast?" Fliss's eyes gleamed. "Are we going to get a speeding ticket?"

"You'd like that."

"It would be an adventure. It's been a long time since I was on a boat. Does that matter? Am I going to need to help?"

"I can sail her singlehanded if I need to. She has a self-tacking jib and auto-whisker pole."

"No idea what that is, which proves that whatever you taught me, I've forgotten."

"You don't have to know anything. I'll tell you what to do. You just have to follow orders." He stepped onto the boat and stowed the cooler. "Think you can do that?"

"If the alternative is taking an unscheduled dip in the ocean, then yes. You know how to motivate a girl." She paused and glanced at him, and there was a wistful look in her eyes. The look she gave him made him pause.

"What? Now you're scared that you'll drown? Don't be. I'm a good sailor and you can wear a life jacket."

"It's not that."

"Then what?"

She shrugged. "This feels—this was one of my favorite things." It was as close as she'd come to talking about their relationship, and he stopped what he was doing and listened.

The wind and the tides could wait. If Fliss was talking, he was going to let her talk.

"The sailing?"

"The few times you took us all out with you on the boat. I loved it. I used to wish it was just the two of us." She shook her head. "So is this a date, or am I sharing a sport you love?"

"Call it what you like. Whatever makes you get your butt onto this boat, that's what it is." He lightened the mood and saw her grin. He loved her smile, the way her mouth tilted and her eyes sparkled with anticipation. "I'm hoping you'll get on this boat before the sun sets. Of course, if you'd rather not, there's always sex and poker back at your grandmother's house. Your choice."

"The choice is meant to be between the devil and the deep blue sea. The two aren't meant to be one and the same."

"Am I the devil in this scenario? I'm making you nervous?" He sensed it was him and not the sailing.

"Only because I don't know the rules. I don't know what this is. I don't even know what I'm doing here. Oh, what the hell—" She puffed a strand of hair out of her eyes and sprang onto the boat, lithe as a cat. "I choose the devil and the deep blue sea."

"I'm not the devil, and presumably you're here because you want to be." He put his hand on her shoulder and saw her smile falter. "We're doing some of the things we never did before, that's all. And there are no rules."

Her gaze met his, and the smile returned. "Am I going to get seasick?"

"I seriously hope not because I have food in the cooler." He let his hand drop, and she swept her hair back from her face and settled her sunglasses on her nose.

"Of course you do. Your name is Carlyle. So this is just two people enjoying a pretty afternoon on the water. Sounds good. Certainly sounds more appealing than poker night with reruns of *Sex in the City*."

He guided the boat out of the marina and into the bay. To the west were the twin forks of Long Island, to the right the open wafer, the shape of Gardiner's Island in the distance.

Fliss stood next to him, feet planted apart, steadying herself against the gentle rise and fall of the boat. "I used to dream about that first time you took me out on the water. You have no idea how much I envied you. I envied your tight loving family, too, of course, but I also envied you the boat. Being out on the ocean felt like freedom to me. You could have just carried on sailing and never come back."

It was a thought that would never have occurred to him, but clearly it had occurred to her.

For him the summer had been an escape from life in the city. For her it had been an escape from life with her father.

"I saw you watching me. You always sat in the same place. On the sand, tucked between the dunes."

She turned. "You saw me?"

"We all saw you." He judged the wind and made an adjustment to the sails. "Although I admit I probably paid more attention than most."

"You did?"

"Sure. You had great legs. I'm shallow like that."

"That was it?"

"Your butt was cute."

She punched him on the arm. "How do you know you weren't looking at Harriet? From that distance, you wouldn't have been able to tell."

"I could tell. You never wore shoes. Everywhere you went, your feet were bare."

"I liked it. Still do. It gives me a feeling of freedom. Makes me think of the beach. I do it at home, too. It drives Harriet insane because she's always falling over my shoes." She paused. "I didn't know you noticed me. I thought I was one of the crowd. Daniel's sister. You were always surrounded by girls. Older than me. They had confidence, flippy hair and not a single bruise on their personality."

"I knew you existed." He kept his eyes on the horizon, hoping that if he kept it low-key she'd keep talking.

"You really thought the first time I noticed you was the night of your eighteenth birthday?"

"Until that night we were always in a group."

"Sometimes in a group there's one person who stands out. You were that person for me."

"Because of my legs and my butt?"

"No. Not because of that."

She was silent and suddenly he wished he hadn't chosen to take her sailing. Sailing demanded concentration, and what he wanted to do was concentrate on her. He didn't want his hands on the boat. He wanted his hands on the woman.

But that would be the wrong thing to do. Too fast, too intense, and they risked blowing what they had all over again.

"I didn't know."

"Your brother knew. He warned me away from you. Told me you'd been hurt enough."

"He talked about our home life? Daniel?" She sounded astonished, as if the possibility hadn't occurred to her.

"A couple of times. He'd had a beer or two and there had been some incident at home. From what Daniel told me, your father preferred ripping into you than eating his dinner." And he'd listened, feeling his friend's frustration, his hands balled into fists as he'd wondered what type of guy would find tormenting his daughter to be a sport.

"Daniel tried to get me to keep quiet, but I couldn't. If I'd stayed silent, it probably would have ended sooner, but I couldn't keep my mouth shut. Harriet hid under the table with her hands over her ears. I argued with him. The more I argued, the madder he got. My dad always had to win every fight. He had to have the last word. He wanted to see me cry, and I refused to ever cry." She gave a soft laugh. "Some days I thought I was going to burst holding it all inside, but I would rather have burst than let him see he'd upset me. I'm stubborn like that."

"I knew things were difficult for you, but I didn't know the details." And he hated hearing it, but he hated not hearing it even more. He wanted to know. In some ways dealing with Fliss was like dealing with a sick animal. They didn't tell you what was wrong. You had to search for clues. It was a jigsaw puzzle, and up until today he'd had nothing but missing pieces.

"It's the way it was. I just felt so bad for my mom. She loved him *so* much. She worked so damn hard to please him, and he didn't even give her a morsel of affection in return. That was the worst part for me. Made me realize that loving someone isn't enough. They have to love you back, and you can't make that happen. Wanting it isn't enough. I didn't realize Daniel had told you."

"Why wouldn't he? We were good friends."

"Before I came along and ruined it."

"He was protective of you. I don't blame him for that. And he was worried I'd hurt you."

And he *had* hurt her.

It had been unintentional, but he'd hurt her nonetheless.

The wind blew them along, and he kept his gaze fixed on the horizon. Other sailboats dotted the horizon, two or three abreast as they bounced over the waves. Sleek yachts, the thoroughbreds of sailing, that wouldn't be seen once the summer season ended. As the weather cooled and the wind whipped at the water, those boats would be replaced by fishing vessels loaded with nets and ice chests.

Fliss made a sound of annoyance. "I didn't need him to police my relationships. But I did feel bad that I ruined your friendship."

"I was responsible for that." They slid through the waves with barely a whisper, the boat accelerating under his touch. "And so was he, by not listening when I tried to talk to him. But when it came to you he had a protective streak as wide as the Atlantic Ocean."

"I know. He still does. Did you know that he's getting married? They haven't fixed a date yet, but it's serious."

"A woman called Molly? I met her when they brought her Dalmatian to the vet."

"That's right. She's been good for Daniel. I've never seen him like that before. She brings out the best in him."

"I guess that's how it's supposed to be." He sailed the boat across to the island, turned the boat head to wind and dropped the anchor. "Grab the cooler. I raided the deli on my way home from the clinic. There's cold chicken, fresh salad and a sourdough loaf."

"Are we going ashore?"

"No. We'll eat on the boat."

"How about swimming?" Her eyes gleamed. "Are we doing that?"

"Did you bring a bikini?"

"As it happens I'm wearing one under my clothes. I promised Harriet no skinny-dipping."

"Damn." He handed her a plate. "If I'd known that, I would have invited a different woman. You're no fun."

"That's me. Staid and sensible." She peered into the cooler. "This looks delicious."

"What's your grandmother eating tonight?"

"Nothing I made, so you can relax. Her friends brought her dinner. Dora made a casserole that would feed the whole of the Hamptons. I've decided I want that when I'm ninety." She sat down and stretched out her legs, tilting her face to the sun. "A bunch of great friends who will talk about everything, including sex, and feed me. I used to wonder why Grams didn't move from here, but I'm starting to understand why she'd stay."

"Dora?" He divided the food onto two plates. "Owns a chocolate Lab called Darcy?"

"You know her?" She took a bite of chicken and purred like a contented cat. "This is delicious."

"I'm the vet. I know everyone. Darcy is my patient. Nice temperament."

"That's good to know because starting tomorrow, I'm walking Darcy."

"You are? So that's three dogs now. Maybe you should extend your business to cover the Hamptons."

Fliss swallowed and stared at him. "There are already plenty of dog-walking businesses here already."

"Upscale ones that will give your pooch a spa day or fly it in a helicopter to Manhattan. I'm willing to bet there are plenty of people who'd use a quality, trustworthy outfit like the Bark Rangers. And for those people who shuttle between here and Manhattan, you offer continuity."

She helped herself to more chicken. "That's an interesting idea. It hadn't occurred to me to formalize it. I mean they're paying me, of course, but I hadn't thought of it as a permanent arrangement." She licked her fingers, frowning slightly. "It can't be. I don't know how long I'll be staying, but no more than a few weeks."

"In Manhattan you don't do all the walking yourself, do you? You could recruit people."

"Yes, and that part is hard work because we need reliable dog walkers. Do you know anyone who might be interested?"

"I'm pretty sure my vet tech might be interested. She loves dogs and she could probably use the money. And she has a couple of friends who work part-time. I could ask around if you like."

"Thanks. I've thought about extending the business, but this option hadn't occurred to me." She finished the chicken and tore off a chunk of bread. "You think I could recruit enough dog walkers to enable me to run it from Manhattan?"

"Why not? You don't do it all yourself in Manhattan, do you?"

"No. But it's taken us a long time to build up a reliable team."

"So start small. Build it up slowly. See how it goes. If it doesn't work out, it doesn't work out."

They talked it through while they finished the picnic.

"I need to crunch some numbers." She wiped her fingers, then pulled her phone out of her purse and made some notes for herself. "I need to work out how many dog owners there are, and how many are likely to use the services of a reliable dog walker."

"There are plenty of dogs. If you drop by the office tomorrow I can give you a number. We're not the only vet clinic, of course, but it would give you an idea."

"Could I put an advertisement on your bulletin board?"

"Sure."

"I might be able to expand the business simply by walking the dogs of my grandmother's friends."

"If you're walking Darcy, you'll probably need to check him for listening devices."

She grinned. "You think she'll bug the dog in order to eavesdrop on my love life? That's an interesting idea."

"Never underestimate how far the locals will go to find out what they want to know. Are you saying Dora didn't grill you?"

"Until I was charred. Cooked right through. They wanted to know everything about you."

Knowing her as he did, he doubted they'd extracted much information from her. "So what did you tell them?"

"I told them there's nothing happening between us. Because there isn't." Her gaze flickered to his and then away again. "They think you're hot, by the way."

Seth almost fell over the side of the boat. "Excuse me?"

"According to them you're the most eligible man in the Hamptons, and that's saying something." She eyed him. "Martha thinks you have great shoulders. Dora likes your arms. For Rita it's your eyelashes."

"My eyelashes?"

"Don't look to me for an explanation. I don't get what they see in you. Personally, I don't find you attractive at all." She secured a strand of hair behind her ear. "Never did."

He loved her sense of humor. The fact that it was reemerging now told him she was relaxing with him. "Right. So all that sex we had—"

"I don't remember ever having sex with you. You must be thinking of someone else."

"Maybe. She was a cute blonde who used to climb out of the kitchen window because the back door creaked."

"Yeah? She sounds like trouble. You should have stayed away from her."

"We weren't good at staying away from each other." And then later, when it had all gone wrong, he'd stayed away when he should have gotten closer.

They'd done it all wrong, he realized.

He stood up, cleared up the remains of the picnic and she helped.

"I blame hormones."

"Hormones?" He stowed the rest of the food in the cooler. "You're telling me you would have done those things with anybody?"

"Yeah, pretty much. We bad girls don't much mind who we're bad with."

"So I was just in the right place at the right time."

"That and teenage experimentation. I was a bad influence on you."

He decided this wasn't the time to dispute that. Instead he stooped and moved the rope before she could trip over it. "We should make a move before it gets late."

"If I go home now they'll still be there and I'll have to face the inquisition. I'm not sure I have the strength for it."

He raised the anchor. "After what you told me, I'm not sure I'm ever going to be able to look them in the eye again either."

"They won't notice. They're not looking at your eyes. Apart from Rita, who is obsessed with your eyelashes."

"Stop. You're starting to make me nervous." He tried to focus on sailing the boat back to the marina.

"Now you know how I felt." She pushed her hat down onto her head. "And they're reading one of Matilda's books for their book group."

"That's nice. Supportive."

"Have you read Matilda's books?"

"I can't say I have." He headed back across the bay, the waves slapping gently at the sides of the boat. It was a perfect evening, and there were plenty of other boats on the water. "I go more for thriller and crime than romance."

"They're pretty hot."

"Seems like you learned something new about your grandmother today."

"I learned a couple of things, and one of them was that I don't know my grandmother as well as I thought I did."

"Which surprised you the most? The fact that they read Matilda's books or the fact that they play poker for money?"

She was silent for a moment. "The biggest surprise was that she's proud of me." She leaned on the rail of the boat and stared across the water. "Never knew that before."

He glanced at her, but all he could see was her profile. "You didn't know your grandmother was proud of you?"

"No. It never occurred to me for a moment that she was proud of me. Why would it?"

It seemed a strange question to him. "She's your grandmother. It goes with the territory." And then he saw her expression and was reminded that her territory had looked nothing like his. And that had been part of the problem. Handling Fliss had been like landing in a different country without a map or a phrase book. "I'm sorry. Give me a minute while I pull my foot out of my mouth."

"Don't. Don't ever tiptoe around me. I don't want that. The truth is I didn't give her a reason to be proud."

Her comment made his heart tighten in his chest.

Did she really believe that? "I'm sure you gave her plenty of reasons."

"No. I was always the one causing trouble."

He wondered how much to say. How far to push it. "And you did that to take the attention from your sister."

She turned her head and met his gaze. "Excuse me?"

"You kept your father's attention on you so that he didn't start on Harriet."

"Daniel told you that?"

"He might have mentioned it, but it wasn't hard to work it out. You always stepped in front of Harriet. Physically, when necessary, but I guess with your father you had a different tactic in mind. You were the equivalent of a flare, tempting the heat-seeking missile off course." He waited for her to deny it. To shut him down and close him out as she always did.

Instead she gave a soft laugh. "You're right. That's what I did. And it worked."

"Now we've finally got that straight, could we also reach the point where you stop calling yourself the bad twin? I hate it. It isn't who you are. And it certainly isn't the way I see you."

"Those were his words, not mine."

Seth kept his hands tight on the wheel and his eyes

fixed on the horizon. "He didn't know what he was talking about."

"He knew. He knew how to wound. And once he'd wounded he knew how to make that wound hurt like the devil. I grew up accepting that I couldn't please him, and somewhere along the way I stopped trying. As long as he left Harriet alone, that was fine by me."

"And you wonder why your grandmother is proud of you? What exactly did she say? She told you straight out?"

"No. It was her friends, really. They started to tease her. They repeated her words. Chorused it. As if they'd heard her say the same thing time and time again. I thought they meant Harriet. Whenever there was praise floating around, it was usually for Harriet. And that didn't bother me," she added quickly, "because she deserved it."

"So did you, for a million reasons and certainly for stepping in front of her all the time."

"I didn't do that for praise. I did it because I loved my sister and hated to see her suffer. She had a terrible stammer as a child. The more he yelled, the worse her stammer, and the more she stammered, the more her confidence dropped. It was a vicious cycle." It was obvious that thinking back to that time distressed her.

"And now?"

"She hasn't stammered for a couple of years." There was warmth in her voice. "We have a great circle of friends, a cool apartment even though it's on the small side, and she loves her work."

"And she has that work because of you." And the apartment, he suspected. "You're the driving force."

"We make a good team. And Harriet is tougher than

she looks. And maybe she wouldn't have set it up if she'd been on her own, but she's as essential to the business as I am. She's so happy working with the animals. The clients, both human and canine, all love her."

He wondered if she even realized the extent to which she put her sister first. At the first sign of threat or danger, she stepped in front of her. It seemed to him that it was something she did instinctively, without thinking or maybe even noticing.

"Do you ever wonder what your relationship with your father might have been like if you hadn't always protected Harriet?"

"It would have been exactly the same." She paused. "I came to the conclusion that it wasn't us, it was him. Something in him made him angry. I didn't expect him to be proud of me. I've never expected that from anyone, so tonight when Grams said that—I felt as if someone had stuffed a tennis ball in my throat. Couldn't breathe. Couldn't swallow." She frowned. "Since I've been here I'm starting to realize there's so much about my grandmother that I don't know. There are things I'd love to ask her."

He leaned against the rail of the boat, watching the dying rays of the sun flicker across her hair and face. "Like what?"

"I'd like to ask her about my mother. I want to try to understand why she tried so hard at a marriage that wasn't working. I want to understand why my father, who didn't love her at all, wouldn't let her go. He used us to blackmail her into staying, but why did he even want that? Why not just cut loose so they could both rebuild their lives? He could have met someone else. So could she."

"You never talked to your mother about it?"

"Harriet tried a couple of times. She wouldn't talk about it. She said she wanted to think about the future, not the past. And she's probably right. It's best to focus on the present." She threw him a smile. "And talking of the present, how do I handle the inquisition when I get home?"

"Maybe they won't be too interested in the details."

"Are you kidding? They wanted to know how you kissed."

He didn't know whether to be amused or appalled. "What did you tell them?"

"I told them I couldn't remember."

He reached out and yanked her toward him, catching her off balance. She landed against his chest with a thud and a gasp, and for a moment he could smell the fragrance of her hair and skin. His last coherent thought was that if his plan had been to keep his distance, this was the stupidest move of his life. Then he was kissing her, or maybe she was kissing him. It was a blur of hands, lips and need, hers and his, equally matched as it always had been. Everything about it was urgent. A rush of hunger, a burn of desire, and through it all there was the delicious thrill of kissing her again. Only with her had he ever felt this. Everything was exaggerated and more intense. He felt the light curve of her breast and the pounding of her heart beneath his hand. It wasn't enough. He wanted more, and he tugged at her shirt and felt her hands tugging at his. She was all sleek lines and smooth curves, her skin smooth and warm. He tasted sweetness and desperation on her lips, and felt desire rip through him like flames through a dry forest until all he wanted to do was strip her naked and take her right here and damn the consequences.

But they'd damned the consequences the last time, and he'd spent a decade regretting it. If he carried on, they'd be back where they started, doing what they'd done before. And what they'd had before wasn't enough for him. This time, he cared about the consequences.

Seth dragged his mouth from hers, yanked her top back down and thrust her away from him, turning his attention back to the boat.

It took him a moment to find his balance. To remember how the hell to sail a boat.

She was obviously the same because she caught the wheel to steady herself and then looked at him, her eyes dazed, strands of hair over her eyes. "What are you doing? Why the hell did you just do that?"

It was a good question.

It took all his effort to produce an answer that wasn't going to scare her senseless. "I thought I'd remind you how I kiss so that next time they ask you, you'll be able to answer."

Yeah, right.

"I didn't need you to do that! It wasn't fair of you to do that." She touched her fingers to her mouth, as if she could still feel his kiss.

He could feel it, too. He felt it on his lips, in his bones and in his heart.

"Maybe I don't always play fair." He held her gaze for a moment and then turned his attention back to the harbor in the distance. "Maybe I'm not the good boy you always thought I was."

"What are you saying? That you want to have another wild affair? Another hot, sizzling summer in the Hamptons, is that it? Live in the present."

He adjusted the heading of the boat. "No. That's not what I want." This time he wanted more than the present. He wanted a future. "Sex changes everything. It's what we did last time. I don't want this to be like last time."

"This? There isn't a 'this,' Seth. There is no '*this*.'"

"No?" Keeping one hand on the wheel, he used the other to tug her close. He held her there for a moment, eye to eye, mouth to mouth. "Let's be clear about one thing. I didn't stop because I was afraid of being hurt again. I stopped because this time around I don't want sex to be the focus." He released her quickly and turned his attention back to the boat, careful to stay within the deep-water channel passing west of Cedar Point.

Sag Harbor was crowded, and he needed all his concentration to navigate back to the yacht club.

He wished he hadn't started a conversation he couldn't finish.

His timing, as always, was less than perfect.

Or maybe with Fliss there was never going to be a perfect time. And maybe if he waited for that moment, he might miss it altogether and lose.

He'd lost her once. He had no intention of losing her again.

Mindful of wind and tide, he sailed into the yacht club, rigged the lines and fenders for docking and backed into a slip.

Fliss still hadn't spoken a word.

Lulu, tail wagging, sprang onto the pontoon and waited expectantly.

Still Fliss didn't move.

"What did you mean—" her voice sounded croaky, as if she was recovering from the flu "—you don't want sex to be the focus?"

"I still have feelings for you, Fliss. I want to find out what those feelings are." He hadn't intended to say it. The yacht club was busy, and not only were they in public but it was too soon, much too soon, to say what he wanted to say. But now the words were out and there was no taking them back.

She opened her mouth and closed it again, so he figured he might as well keep talking.

"The sex was always the good part, but it clouded everything else. It stopped us being close."

"We were—"

"I don't mean close in that way. I mean close in other ways. The ways that glue a couple together and hold them there when something tries to pull them apart. An important part of that is talking. Confiding. You never did much of that. On a good day you gave me access to maybe ten percent of what was going on in your head. This time around I'd like the ninety, and you can hang on to the ten."

He saw her throat move as she swallowed.

"This is crazy. Us getting involved again after everything that happened? Crazy."

And not being involved was driving him crazy.

"Why is it crazy?"

"Because—" She shook her head. "It's too late, Seth."

"Too late for what we had then, but I don't want what we had then."

There was a flare of panic in her eyes. "What *do* you want?"

More. Everything. *All of it.* "I want to spend time with you, and this time we're keeping our clothes on."

"I'm not the person I was ten years ago."

"Neither am I. I'm older and wiser, for a start."

She ran her tongue over her lips. "You don't know me, Seth."

"I've learned more about you in the past week than I found out during all those long hot summers."

"Half the time I was with you I was pretending to be Harriet."

"And that told me something. It told me you still hide when you're scared." He paused. "And it told me I'm not the only one who still has feelings. You have them, too."

"Of course I have feelings! I'm annoyed, confused—"

"For me. You have feelings for me." That silenced her. "If you didn't you wouldn't have gone to such lengths to hide."

"I felt guilty. I wasn't even sure you'd want to see me. In a way I was protecting you."

"And you were also protecting yourself."

She snatched in a breath. "And why wouldn't I? We *hurt* each other, Seth. And maybe some of that was misunderstanding, bad timing—I don't know—but it was bad."

In that single moment he caught a glimpse of just how bad.

"So we know not to do that again next time."

"There is no next time. No present and no future. Only the past." She snatched up her things, almost tripping over her feet in her haste to get off the boat.

"Fliss—"

"I'm not doing this again. I can't."

She all but fled, her sneakers pounding the wooden boards.

Look back, he thought as he watched her run. *Look back*.

But she didn't. She kept running, knocking into people in her haste to get away from him.

Lulu looked at him and barked.

"I know. She's gone, which means I don't get to ask my next question, which involved sharing a bottle of champagne on the beach and watching the sun go down. The whole thing didn't go quite as I planned it."

He hadn't meant to kiss her, at least not then.

She'd probably go back to hiding behind corners when she saw him coming. Maybe she'd even go back to Manhattan.

With a sigh, he sprang off the boat.

Lulu licked his hand. Sympathetic.

He glanced up one more time and saw Fliss pause at the entrance of the harbor. And then she looked back, a single glance over her shoulder.

His gaze met hers and held.

She stood for a moment, and then turned again with a flip of her gold hair and vanished.

"Or maybe I didn't mess it up," Seth murmured.

Maybe this was just the first, necessary step.

CHAPTER FIFTEEN

HE'D KISSED HER. Why had he kissed her?

The anger burned through her in a scorching, sizzling, furious heat. She was so mad at him. And under the anger was confusion and a lurch of fear.

He expected to get involved again? After last time? Did he have no idea what it had done to her? Did he really think she'd ever put herself through that again?

Worthless, stupid—she'd be both those things if she stepped back into the path of a train that had already flattened her once.

She scowled, her feet pounding the path as she ran.

She could have called a cab, but she was too angry.

A relationship? He wanted a relationship? He wanted to start again? As if all they'd done ten years ago was wave goodbye in a friendly way and agreed to a sabbatical. As if her heart hadn't ached every second, of every minute, of every day for years after.

The thought of putting herself through that again—

Right now she didn't want a relationship.

Right now she wanted to push him in the water and drown him.

Had he done it on purpose? Yes, it had to be on purpose. He knew that every time he kissed her it muddled her brain. It was like a hit-and-run. He'd kissed her and then left her to stew in the heat of her own raging hormones.

It was a low trick.

Muttering, furious, she pushed open the door to her grandmother's house.

Had the rest of the Poker Princesses gone? She hoped so because she wasn't in the mood to give them a report of her date with Seth.

And she wasn't sure she didn't have *he kissed me* written all over her face.

Hearing sounds from the kitchen but no conversation, she walked through to find her grandmother with her head in her hands.

"Grams?" Forgetting her own problems, she dropped her bag and ran toward her. "What happened? Where is everyone?"

Her grandmother lifted her head. "They left a while ago. We had so much fun, but I didn't quite have the energy to get myself to the living room. Don't worry about me."

"I *am* worried about you."

"They said it was normal to feel tired after a head injury."

"They also said you should rest. Shall I help you up to bed?"

"I do not need to go to bed. I'm not an invalid."

"Then I'll make up the sofa for you. You can look at the water for a while, or we could talk." She was surprised by how appealing the thought of that was. "You could show me photos of Mom when she was little." Fliss eased her out of the chair and they walked together to the living room. "Put your feet up. I'll clear the kitchen and bring you some tea. Can I fix you something to eat?"

"No, honey. I ate enough of Dora's delicious casserole to fill me up for days."

"All right, then. I'll be back when I've cleaned up."

"You don't have to clean up my mess."

"I'm great at cleaning up other people's messes. It's my own I struggle with." She left her grandmother with the remote control for the TV and went back to the kitchen.

Cleaning up worked off the rest of her anger and confusion.

She clattered pans, loaded the dishwasher, emptied the trash, all the while thinking about Seth.

She polished the stove until it shone and then took iced tea to her grandmother.

"I cleaned your kitchen."

"I'm grateful for that clarification because for a moment there I was worried you were demolishing it." Her grandmother took the glass from her. "You leave the house to go on a date with Seth, smiling, and then you return and start breaking things. Is that something you'd like to talk about?"

"Nothing is broken." But her heart would be if she listened to him, if she let herself fall the way she'd fallen the first time. "And there's nothing to tell."

She sat down opposite her grandmother, but her emotions were too all over the place for her to stay sitting, so she sprang up again and started tidying magazines. Her grandmother subscribed to two crafting magazines and a gardening magazine, so there was plenty to keep her occupied.

"Something he did, or said, flustered you and made

you angry." Her grandmother took a sip of tea. "And then there's the fact that Seth picked you up but didn't drop you home after your day together. He's too much of a gentleman to make you find your own way, so you must have chosen to come by yourself."

"He isn't that much of a gentleman."

"I may be old, but you'll find that age often comes with wisdom, and that can be an advantage. There's also the added bonus that you don't have to protect me and you can certainly trust me. I hope you know that."

Fliss discovered she did know that. "He wants us to see each other again. But if it didn't work out the first time, why would it work out this time?"

Her grandmother put her cup down slowly. "So it's not that you're not interested, it's that you're scared."

"Is that so surprising?"

"No. Love can be scary. We put our heart in the hands of another. That requires trust. But the alternative is that we go through life without love, and that's not a great option either."

"I know. I saw Mom live through that. I saw what it was like to love a man who didn't love her back. Dad was the only man for her. I guess that's why she never gave up trying." Something in the way her grandmother was looking at her made her feel uncomfortable. "What have I said? She found herself in the same situation as me. She was in love with Dad, got pregnant—" The words fell out before she could stop them, and she stared at her grandmother, mortified, wondering if she could snatch the words back. "I mean, that part wasn't the same, obviously—"

"You think I didn't already know you were pregnant?" Her grandmother studied her over the rim of her cup. "I never believed that whirlwind romance story. Not for a moment."

Fliss stared at her, paralyzed by shock.

She'd held the secret close to her for so long. At the time she'd been worried some people might have guessed, or at least wondered, but then she'd lost the baby so it hadn't seemed to matter anymore.

The fact that her grandmother knew made her feel panicky. Exposed.

"I—"

"You don't have to sit there working out what to say to me. You don't owe me, or anyone else, an explanation. You were pregnant, but you were also in love. Why not get married?"

Her grandmother made it sound so simple. So logical.

The feelings of panic receded.

"I had feelings, it's true." The depth of those feelings was something she kept to herself. "And Seth Carlyle is a good, decent guy."

"You think that's why he married you? Because he's decent?"

"It was hardly something he would have done otherwise."

"You sound very sure about that." Her grandmother took another sip of her tea. "It didn't occur to you that he might have married you for another reason?"

"There was no other reason. It was exactly like Mom's situation." And because of that she'd never been given the opportunity to find out if Seth might have fallen in love with her given time.

Her grandmother handed over her empty cup. "Take that to the kitchen for me, honey. Then go to my bedroom. Under the bed you'll find a box. Bring it to me."

"What's in the box?"

"You'll find out."

"You should be resting."

"I am resting. Go. There's something in that box I want to show you."

Fliss was intrigued enough not to ask any more questions, and pleased to have an excuse to leave the room. She couldn't believe she'd told her grandmother about the pregnancy. The only two people who knew about it were Seth and Harriet.

She found the box under the bed, along with a family of dust bunnies. It made her smile. Her grandmother had always prioritized living her life over cleaning. She'd swum in the ocean every day until she was seventy. And some of those swims had been naked. Who would have thought it?

Brushing off the box, she took it downstairs. "It was wrapped in a ton of cobwebs. I ruined dinner plans for at least five spiders. How long has this been here?"

"A long time." Eugenia took the box and set it down in front of her. "Your mother said she never wanted to see it again. It made her think of things she didn't want to think about."

Fliss went from mildly intrigued to downright curious. What had her mother not wanted to think about? It must have been important for her to keep the memories in a box as a memento. "But you kept it?"

"I understood why she wanted me to dispose of it. She was afraid your father might find it, but some things are too important to be discarded. Fortunately even your father wouldn't have had the gall to come into my bedroom on the rare occasions he showed up here. It's been there for more than three decades. I've never opened it, but I assume the contents are intact."

"Does Mom know you kept it?"

"I told her after she finally left your father. She didn't want it. As far as she was concerned, the past was the past. She was only interested in building a future."

Fliss wasn't sure she wanted to see something her mother hadn't wanted her to see, but her grandmother was already opening the box, revealing a stack of letters and photos. "What are those?" She reached across and took the letter from the top of the pile.

"They're letters to your mother, from the man she was in love with."

Fliss studied the beautiful loopy script. "I never would have guessed my dad was the letter-writing type."

"The letters aren't from your father."

"Who are they from?" Confused, Fliss reached for one of the photos and stared at it, uncomprehending.

It was a little faded, and a little crinkled at the corners, but the image was still perfectly clear.

In her hand was a photo of her mother, laughing up at a man. It was obvious from the way they were looking at each other that they were in love. Nothing wrong with that, Fliss thought numbly. The only thing wrong with that photo was that the man her mother was smiling at wasn't her father.

SETH WAS SEEING his last patient of the morning when Nancy, the vet tech, walked into the room.

"There's someone to see you."

"I'm nearly done here." He turned his attention back to his patient, a French bulldog with breathing problems. "The shape of his head and the flat face—the technical term is brachycephaly—isn't natural. It's a look that has been developed by selective breeding, and it often causes health problems for the dogs."

"I didn't know that." Mary Danton looked upset. "They're such fashionable dogs and I thought Maximus was adorable. So that's why his breathing is so noisy and why he gets so tired on walks?"

"Yes. He has an elongated soft palate and smaller openings in his nose. He's finding it hard to breathe."

"I thought the noises he makes are normal for the breed."

"Plenty of owners think that. And some vets," he added, thinking of a colleague he'd clashed with back in California.

"Is there anything at all you can do for him?"

"I can remove some of the tissue obstructing his airways and widen his nostrils." Seth reached for paper and a pen and drew a rough sketch, showing Mary what he meant.

She studied the drawing. "You mean surgery? Would that help?"

It took another ten minutes to talk through the options, then he walked Mary and Maximus to the reception area to make an appointment.

Fliss was waiting there with Hero.

He'd been hoping she'd come to him. He'd made himself wait, but one more day and he would have gone to her.

He turned back to Mary. "Bring him in tomorrow. We'll do it right away." Then he dropped to his haunches to make a fuss of the dog. "There, buddy." He stroked the animal's head, feeling the floppy folds of skin around his face. "We're going to make this better for you, I promise."

Leaving Mary and Maximus in the capable hands of their receptionist, he gestured to Fliss. "Come in."

She followed him into the room. "Maximus is a cutie. And he loves you."

"He's a great dog. I hate to see him struggling."

"Breathing issues?" She paused in front of a poster urging people to get their pets vaccinated. "We see that a lot among our clients with brachycephalic dogs. We have to plan walks accordingly because the dogs are so tired breathing they can't walk far. So you'll operate?"

He talked it through with her, surprised at how knowledgeable she was. Even more surprised that he was able to concentrate enough to string words together.

She was wearing those cutoff jeans again, the ones that made her legs seem endless. Her arms were bare.

"You're busy. I came at a bad time."

He wouldn't have cared what time it was, as long as she was here. "Not a bad time. I've finished for the morning."

"And judging from your face it's been a busy one."

"Started the day by pulling three feet of string from a cat's intestine, and it was all downhill from there." He was more interested in finding out about her. He sensed something was wrong. "So what can I do for you? I presume you don't need the services of a vet." He dropped to his haunches and made a fuss of Hero.

"I've been thinking about what you said, that's all."

He straightened slowly. "You have?"

"Yes. I'm going to explore the possibility of extending our business to cover the Hamptons."

The business?

He wondered if she'd thought about the other things he'd said. "I thought you said your stay here was temporary."

"I was thinking I could stay on a little longer. See if it's viable. And that way I can keep an eye on Grams for a while."

"You're staying on so you can keep an eye on your grandmother?"

She turned her attention back to the poster. "It's the right thing to do. Not that she really needs me. The house is full of people most of the time."

"Your grandmother has a lot of friends. So you're not staying for any other reason?"

"What other reason would there be?" Her tone was casual, but then she glanced over her shoulder and gave him a wicked smile. "You might have something to do with it. But only a small, tiny part of the reason, so don't get any ideas."

He already had plenty of ideas.

"Just for the record, what changed your mind? My cooking, my boat, my shoulders or my eyelashes?"

Her smile widened. "All of those, but mostly your dog. I'm crazy about Lulu."

"Harriet doesn't need you back in Manhattan?"

"It's quiet right now. A lot of people have left the city to escape the heat and the tourists. And I can manage all the paperwork, invoicing and business side of things from here. I've set up in our old bedroom. I need to advertise my services. You said I could put a card up on your board in the waiting room?"

"Of course. Do you want a pen and paper?"

"No need. I've already had some printed." She whipped some cards out of her bag and offered him one.

He glanced down at the card in his hand. Slick. Professional.

The Bark Rangers. Professional dog walking, bespoke caring service.

"You had these printed since we went sailing. It's only been a few days."

"I already had the artwork. I just needed to tweak it. I used the printer on Ocean Road. He was good. And he fed me cookies while I waited, so it was a good deal."

"Where else are you planning to put them?"

"I've put one in Country Stores, and I'm planning on dropping a few more off once I've taken Hero back to Matilda."

He watched as she prowled to the other side of the clinic, full of nervous energy.

Something was wrong.

"You can leave a couple of extras with me. I'll take them with me on my calls."

"Do you have time for lunch? I was thinking we could pick something up and eat it on the beach. Lulu could join us. We could talk."

She wanted to talk?

"About anything in particular?"

"Not really." Her gaze slid from his. "I'm practicing saying what's on my mind a bit more, that's all."

"What's on your mind?"

"Nothing specific."

He didn't believe her for a moment. "I'm not too busy. And eating it on the beach sounds good." He picked up his keys before she could change her mind, exchanged a few words with the receptionist and headed for his car. "Have you seen Matilda?"

She slid into the car next to him. "Yes. She seems to have taken to motherhood pretty easily."

He glanced at her face, wondering if that was the problem. "Does it hurt, honey? Seeing the baby?"

"No. It really doesn't. I think I cried the last emotion out of myself that night at the beach. I love little Rose. She's adorable."

"Then what's wrong? And don't tell me nothing, because I know it's something."

"It's nothing important. Everything is great."

If he had a dollar for every time Fliss had told him she was "fine" or "great" he could have bought every mansion in the Hamptons.

He started the engine. "You're right, you need more practice. Generally when people talk about problems, they actually describe what they are. That's the first step."

She rubbed her hands over her legs. "My grandmother said some things, that's all. Not that important."

Important enough to bring her to his clinic in the middle of a working day.

"Is everything all right with her?"

"Yes. She saw the doctor yesterday, and he's happy with the way she is healing. The bruising is fading. She gets pretty tired, but they say that's normal. And she seems to have some of her confidence back. We've been doing a lot of baking."

"We?" He found a space on Main Street, between a carload of summer people and a beat-up pickup loaded with fishing gear. "You cooked?"

"You'll be pleased to hear my skills are improving."

"Wait there. I'll be back in a minute with food. We can eat it on the beach." He headed for the weathered shingled building that housed the Ocean Deli and was back in under five minutes. One advantage to being the local vet was that you were shunted to the front of the line.

Fliss was sitting exactly where he'd left her, staring straight ahead.

Whatever it was her grandmother had said to her, it had certainly had an impact.

"Fliss?"

"What? Oh—" She blinked and took the bag of food from him, stowing it on her lap. "Sorry. I was miles away."

He drove back to the house, parked, and then they walked with the picnic down to the beach beyond his house.

They sat on the steps that led down to the beach, and he handed her a sandwich. "Turkey, lettuce, tomato and bacon. Now tell me."

She paused. "Maybe I should—"

"Tell me or I will strip you naked and drop you in the water. It's freezing, by the way." He took a bite of his sandwich. "Whatever is on your mind, just say it, Fliss. Maybe it won't be as hard as you think."

"My grandmother told me some things, that's all."

"Things?"

"About my mother. Things I didn't know. I always assumed—"

He waited, forcing himself to be patient, reminding himself that to some people talking was like ice-skating. It was something that had to be learned, and you were bound to take a few falls along the way. "What did you assume?"

"She was pregnant when she got married. I always

knew that. I assumed she married him because she was in love with him and that she hoped that it would be enough. Hoped that one day he'd love her back. Pretty straightforward." She still hadn't touched her sandwich. "Turns out that wasn't what happened."

"She wasn't pregnant when she got married?"

"Yes, she was pregnant. But it wasn't that my father didn't love her. The problem was that she didn't love him." She stared at the water, her sandwich still untouched. "My mother was never in love with my father."

"Are you sure?"

"Yes. When my father first met my mother she was in love with someone else. And they couldn't be together. Wife and family," she added, in response to his unspoken question. "Grams told me she was a mess after he went away. And then she met my father."

"At a time when she was vulnerable."

"Yes. And my dad was crazy about her. *He* was the one in love. I never suspected it. Not for a moment. How could I have got it so wrong?"

"Not that I spent much time with them, but your father didn't behave like a man in love." He thought about his parents' relationship. The shared smiles, the laughter, even the fights had been infused with love and respect. From what he'd gleaned from Daniel, neither quality had been evident in the Knight household.

"When I first arrived here, Grams made a comment—she told me it was hard watching your daughter love the wrong man. I thought she was talking about my father, but she wasn't. I probably shouldn't be telling you this. I'm not even supposed to *know*."

"Why aren't you supposed to know?"

"Because it's my mother's secret."

"She never discussed it with you?"

"No. And I wish she had. It might have helped me understand a few things. Grams says when she was eighteen, she fell in love."

The same age she'd been when their relationship had become serious. "Did she tell you about him?"

"He was an artist. He moved here for six months to paint. He was married, although Mom didn't know that at first. He used to eat all his meals at the café where my mother worked. She loved painting, so he helped her. Gave her advice. Even bought one of her paintings."

"I didn't know your mother painted."

"I knew, but I didn't realize she was so serious about it. Anyway, he stayed until January, and then he confessed that his wife and family were back in Connecticut. They were in the middle of a trial separation, but it was obvious they were still very much together. Grams said she thought my mother was going to break. He was her first love. In her heart, she'd painted a picture of their future together."

Seth said nothing.

He knew all about painting pictures of the future.

He leaned forward and removed the sandwich from her fingers before she dropped it. "So he moved away, and what then?"

"My mother was devastated. She stopped painting. Grams was worried sick about her. And then one day my father walked into the café, and that was it. He'd come to the Hamptons with some friends for the weekend. Saw my mother and pursued her ferociously. She turned him down. She hadn't recovered from her last relationship. She was vulnerable. My father was successful, charismatic and persistent. Older than her. He refused to give up. That was one of his traits. Never giving up." She rubbed her palms down her calves, an anxious gesture. "I remember mealtimes at the brownstone in Manhattan. He used to lay into me in a verbal attack and he didn't stop until the meal ended. We fought so badly there were times I wanted to hide under the table with Harriet."

"But you didn't." He knew she would have forced herself to sit still and take whatever was thrown at her, to deflect his attention from her more vulnerable sister. "So your dad persuaded your mom to date him?"

"He wined her, dined her, and in a weak moment she slept with him. And got pregnant. My father was thrilled. Not because he wanted children, but because he loved her so much he was willing to do just about anything to keep her with him." She sounded sad. "I always knew her life had been hard, but I misunderstood so much of the details."

"Did your grandmother try to intervene?"

"Yes. She tried to talk her out of it. Told her my father could still be part of the child's life without marriage, but Mom didn't want that. She felt she owed it to the baby—Daniel—to give it a proper family. Grams asked her if she loved my dad, and all she would say was that he was a good man." Fliss frowned. "And that seemed weird to me. I wanted to know what he was like back then. Was he as impatient? As angry? Grams says there were signs things weren't right. The way he pursued her. He wasn't thinking about what was right for her, just what was right for him. Grams thinks he really believed she'd fall in love with him over time."

"But that didn't happen."

"No. And he grew more frustrated. Bitter."

"Why didn't they divorce sooner? Did she talk about that?"

"He refused. He knew she'd married him because of Daniel, and then Harriet and I came along, and he used the three of us as a weapon. He told her that if she divorced him, she wouldn't be taking us. I already knew that part, but I see now that it was another way of keeping her. He couldn't get her to love him, so he was willing to use any other means at his disposal. Daniel always said it was because she couldn't afford a lawyer, but Grams told me if it had been a matter of money she would have sold the cottage in a heartbeat. In the end she waited until we'd left for college."

"And Daniel helped her find a lawyer."

"Later. Much later." She stared at the ocean. "Maybe that's why he was so angry all the time. He knew my mother didn't love him. Not that I'm excusing him, because there are no excuses, but it helps to understand a little. I can't believe I'm saying this, but I almost feel sorry for him. And up until now I think I only thought about my parents in relation to me. I saw them as my parents, not as individuals with their own hopes and dreams."

"I would think that's pretty common. And parents often hide things from their kids anyway."

"And sometimes they hide the wrong things. I wish she'd told me."

"Why do you think your grandmother told you this now?"

"Because I was comparing what happened with us to what happened with my mother. I thought she got pregnant and married a man who didn't love her."

It took a moment for her words to sink in, and when they did he felt a lurch in the pit of his stomach.

"You think I didn't love you?"

She shot to her feet. "I shouldn't have said that. I don't know why I did. Forget it." She sped down the steps to the beach and was halfway to the water by the time he caught up with her.

"Wait!" He grabbed her shoulder. "It seems to me that you didn't only misunderstand your parents' relationship, you misunderstood ours."

"Seth—"

"It's my turn to speak. And if you run off now I'm going to be following you, so don't waste your energy. I didn't marry you because you were pregnant. The only thing that the fact you were pregnant influenced was the time and the place."

"But—"

"The truth is I never got over you. I tried. Believe me, I tried. Over the years there have been women, I'm not denying that, but none of them has gone anywhere, and do you know why? Because none of them were you. I didn't marry you because you were pregnant, Fliss. I married you because I loved you." He tightened his hands on her shoulders, forcing her to look at him. "I loved you."

CHAPTER SIXTEEN

FLISS STARED AT HIM, mute. He'd *loved* her?

No, that wasn't possible.

She remembered something he'd said that night she'd gone to his house for the first time.

Maybe I didn't want to let you go and the baby provided a convenient excuse.

"That's not true. It can't be true."

"I told you. I said those words to you." There was a note of frustration in his voice. "You know I did."

"You said them when you knew I was pregnant. Not before."

He cursed under his breath. "Then that was bad timing on my part, but it didn't make the words any less than the truth."

"But can you understand how it might have seemed to me? I tell you I'm pregnant, and you tell me you love me and that we should get married?"

He was silent. "Yeah," he said finally. "I can see that."

"I thought you were saying it to make me feel better about the fact I'd trapped you."

His mouth tightened. "I don't think communication was the best feature of our relationship, but we're going to change that."

She felt her throat thicken and her eyes sting.

He'd loved her? He'd truly meant those words?

Oh God, if that was true then she'd thrown that away. She'd held the very thing she wanted in her hand, and she'd crushed it without ever knowing it could have been hers.

She sniffed and gave him a little push. "Your timing sucked, Dr. Carlyle."

"It did. It definitely did. But my timing has improved with maturity."

"It's too late. Whatever the truth was back then, it's history. I'm not good at relationships, Seth. All that opening up and trusting—that's not me. I want to, but I can't."

"You can. All you have to do is trust me. And this time I'm going to prove to you that you can. I'm going to prove I'm not your father. I didn't spend enough time dealing with those issues. I didn't understand how deeply everything he said had affected you. I judged your actions based on my own experiences of family, not on yours."

She felt the warmth of his hand stroke her back. "You make it sound so easy, but it isn't." Her voice was muffled by his shirt. "I'm not good at laying feelings out there."

"Because you're afraid someone is going to tread all over them in heavy boots." He smoothed her hair. "I get that. And we'll work with it."

"How?"

He eased her away from him. "Same way you get better at anything. Practice."

"You want me to practice telling you things about myself? I'm five-four, have a black belt in karate and bench-press one-twenty."

"Those are facts. I want feelings. Tell me how you're feeling right now."

"A little bit sick? A whole lot terrified?"

"Because you're afraid you're going to end up hurting the way you did last time, but that's not going to happen."

"You don't know that."

"I've told you how I felt about you back then. Maybe it's time you told me how you felt."

Until recently, she'd never revealed the extent of her feelings for him to anyone.

Her grandmother probably suspected. But that didn't mean she was ready to share how she'd felt with anyone else. Especially not Seth.

He eased her closer. "All right, let's try this a different way. In the ten years since we broke up, have you been serious about anyone else?"

"Why does that matter? There's nothing there, Seth. Whatever we had was gone." The flutter of her heart and the ache behind her ribs told her she was lying, but she wasn't ready to tell him that. And maybe she never would be.

There was sharing, and then there was exposing. There was a difference.

To admit to him that she still had feelings, strong feelings, would be exposing. And her instinct to protect herself was more powerful than her desire to share.

"You've already told me more than you ever have before. For example I didn't know your mom was pregnant when she got married. That explains a few things about the way you acted back then. Why you jumped to the conclusions you did. It shows me how much I didn't understand. That's going to be different this time."

This time?

She pulled back reluctantly. "Why would you want to put yourself through this again? I'm trouble, Seth."

"I know." He gave a soft laugh. "It's one of the things I like most about you."

"My father would—"

"No." He covered her lips with his fingers, his eyes darkening. "What your father thinks about anything has no relevance to us. Not ever."

"It's not just my father. Your sister warned you about me."

"Then it's a good thing I never listen to my sister." He took her face in his hands, forcing her to look at him. "The only two people who matter are the two people in this relationship. That's us. I can be patient. I can wait while you learn to trust that I'll be careful with your feelings, but don't ever let anyone else influence how you feel about us. There's no one else."

No one else.

He meant it. He really meant it.

And she was tempted. So very tempted.

How many times had she lain in bed under the protective curtain of darkness, wondering what would have happened if she hadn't got pregnant that night? How many times had she wished for a chance to find out?

He was giving her that chance.

She thought about how hurt she'd been last time. If it all went wrong, could she survive it again?

"I HAVE SOMETHING to tell you." Fliss lay on her bed in the attic, listening to the sound of the ocean through the open window as she talked to Harriet on the phone.

"Now I'm nervous. I've barely heard from you in the last couple of weeks, and whenever I don't hear from you I get a bad feeling. It usually means you're hiding something from me. Is Grams okay?"

"She's good. Her friends are around here the whole time. It's busier than Times Square in July."

"She said you'd been busy, too."

"Walking dogs." *Seeing Seth.*

Yesterday they'd gone surfing on the beach. The day before that they'd spent the evening at the Beach Hut, eating lobster dripping with butter.

Just the two of them. Alone. She ricocheted between terror and delicious excitement.

"So what did you want to tell me?"

"You know how I mentioned expanding the business? What do you think about branching out to the Hamptons? Half our clients escape here in the summer months."

"But they already have dog-walking services there that they use."

"Not all of them. I remember Claudia Richards saying that she wished there was a company like ours based here."

"That's one person."

"I'm already walking five dogs."

"One of those is Charlie. Don't tell me you're charging Grams to walk her dog."

"She insisted on paying."

"Fliss! You can't take money from our grandmother."

"Try telling her that. She's more stubborn than I am. Once she makes up her mind about something, she doesn't budge." She couldn't believe how close she'd become to her grandmother over the past few weeks. "She says that I'm losing work because I'm here with her, and so she's going to at least pay me for the dog walking. And her friends are paying me, too. At this rate I'm going to be walking half the dogs on the South Fork."

"I can't imagine you with pampered pooches. Are you charging double?"

It was a relief to hear her sister laugh. "No. And I'm not walking any pampered pooches. These are all real, down-to-earth dogs."

"And you're thinking of making this permanent?"

"Why not? I've run the numbers and I think we have a scalable business. If you agree, then we can make it official."

"But how would this even work?" Harriet sounded anxious. "You're going to be coming home soon. How would you manage it then?"

Fliss paused. She'd spent hours thinking about the best way to say this. "I was thinking I might stay on a little longer."

"You said Grams was okay."

"She is."

"So why stay? If you stay, you'll keep bumping into Seth."

Fliss stared at the wall. "I've been bumping into him quite a bit in fact."

"Oh. That must be awkward for you."

"Not that awkward. In fact, mostly on purpose."

There was silence on the end of the phone. "You mean you've been seeing him?"

"Well, I wouldn't exactly—" Fliss transferred her phone to the other hand. "Yes, I've been seeing him."

"How much of him?"

"So far he's been clothed the whole time, so not much."

"I meant, how *often*?"

"Which proves that although we look identical on the outside, our minds are entirely different. I thought you were asking me how much of him I'd seen in the flesh." And the answer was not enough. Apart from that brief moment on the boat, he hadn't even kissed her, and it was starting to drive her crazy. "I've seen him every day. Twice on some days." There was another long silence, and Fliss frowned and glanced at her phone to check they were still connected. "Are you still there?"

"I'm here." Her sister's voice sounded strange. "Why didn't you tell me?"

"Nothing to tell. I went to his house for dinner the night after Matilda's baby was born. He said he wanted to clear the air. Then he took me sailing. We talked." She'd thought about telling her sister what her grandmother had told her about their mother, but decided it was best to wait until they were together in person. "I've seen him a few times since then. Lunch. Dinner. We went kayaking once. That was fun."

"You're *dating* him? Is this serious?"

Serious? Fliss felt a flicker of alarm. "No! We're just friends. Hanging out."

"Friends with benefits."

"No benefits. At least, not the ones you're talking about. Seth had this idea that we should focus on other things for a while." And she'd started to wonder how long "a while" was.

"Are you sure this is a good idea? I'm worried."

"Don't be."

"He *hurt* you. I don't want to see that happen again."

"You've got that the wrong way around. Look, it's been ten years. It's all behind us."

"If it's behind you, why did you pretend to be me and escape from Manhattan?"

"I'm a drama queen."

"Have you talked about it with him? No, of course you haven't. You never open up, not even with me."

Fliss frowned. If Harriet had a clue just how much emotion she'd protected her from, she'd be relieved. "I have told him a little. The downside of keeping everything to yourself is that misunderstandings so easily occur."

If she hadn't kept everything to herself, she might have believed he loved her.

If her mother hadn't kept everything to herself, they might have understood more about why the marriage was so difficult.

Had their mother lied to protect them, or herself? It was something she'd thought about a lot.

"So you've talked to him?" There was an edge to Harriet's voice that Fliss couldn't ever remember hearing before.

"A bit. I'm a work in progress."

"That's great." Her tone suggested otherwise, and Fliss wondered if Harriet was worried about her revealing too much to Seth.

She was a little uneasy about it, too. Talking freely was a whole new thing to her. Part of her wanted to confide in Harriet, but she didn't want to worry her more than she already had.

"Tell me what's been happening with you."

"First, tell me more about Seth."

"Nothing to tell," Fliss said, and felt the lie stick in her throat.

HE MADE A point of spending as much time as possible with her. Even on the days when he'd had a long day in the clinic, he saw her, if only for a few hours. He'd thought about it and decided that trust came with familiarity, and familiarity came with contact. Lots of contact. That worked just fine for him. He'd even dropped in to see her in her grandmother's house, and found them working side by side in a kitchen that smelled like heaven.

He'd accepted the offer of coffee and sat at the table watching while Fliss had rubbed butter and flour together, the look of concentration on her face absolute.

When she'd pulled a batch of finished cookies out of the oven, concentration had given way to pride.

Her grandmother had broken one in half to check the texture, and declared them perfect.

Seth had eaten four. It didn't bother him a bit whether she could cook or not, but he liked the fact that she was growing closer to her grandmother. The way he saw it, opening up took practice, and as long as she practiced on people she could trust, that could only be a good thing.

"Saw you and Fliss together on the beach again." Jed Black lifted his daughter's kitten out of the crate and put him on the examination table. "She's a fine-looking girl."

"She is."

If seeing Fliss meant he took some teasing from the

locals, well, he was willing to live with that. In fact he would have said it was part of living in a community, and he enjoyed being part of a community. He liked seeing the same families, caring for the same animals throughout their lives. He enjoyed his work with the local animal shelter and appreciated how willing the locals were to take on abandoned pets.

"Those big blue eyes and those long legs are enough to threaten a man's concentration."

"Nothing wrong with my concentration, Jed. What's the problem with the kitten? Looks healthy enough." He stroked the animal, feeling the kitten quiver under his fingers. If Fliss knew how interested the community was in their blossoming relationship, would she take off back to Manhattan?

He hoped not.

He focused his attention on the Black family's kitten and gradually worked his way through the animals in his waiting room. He had several cats, a dog with a limp and a rabbit with dental issues.

His last patient of the day was another cat, this one hissing and spitting as the owner tried to put him on the examination table.

Nancy came to help him, using a towel to stop the cat from hurting himself.

"I got him from the animal shelter," Betsy Miller said. "They told me no one ever gives him a second look because he's ugly and bad-tempered."

"You were looking for those traits?" Seth examined the cat's throat, his ears and abdomen while the animal twisted and smacked him with his paws. "I know, buddy. You don't like being here. I get it, I really do. Some days I feel the same way."

"I was looking for an animal who needed me. Seemed to me this fellow needed me badly. Needed someone who would look past his behavior and see what was behind it."

"If only everyone was as astute as you, the world would be a better place." Seth took the cat's pulse. "It's pounding. Not much surprise there." For some reason the animal made him think of Fliss. Scratching when something scared her. Hissing to keep people at a distance.

Gradually the cat relaxed, finally compliant as he finished his examination.

"He likes you," Betsy said, and Nancy nodded.

"Animals always like him. He's patient, that's why. And he moves slowly. No sudden movements. That's a good thing."

Not always.

With Fliss, he'd moved too slowly. Waited too long. But he was about to fix that.

CHAPTER SEVENTEEN

"ONE THING," SETH SAID, as they lay on their backs on the sand. This time they'd dropped anchor near the island and swum to the beach, Fliss gasping at the chill of the water.

She rolled onto her stomach and smiled.

One thing.

It was a game they'd started playing, where they each told each other one thing the other didn't already know.

Thanks to that game, she'd discovered that Seth had moved to California to try to distance himself from everything but had stayed only two years. She found out that he still didn't want to sell Ocean View, and that his relationship with his father had been closer than even she'd thought.

Her heart ached for him.

"When I was eight, I wanted to know what kissing felt like so I trapped Ricky Carter behind the bike sheds."

"Doesn't count. Not personal enough."

"You didn't see the kiss."

He grabbed her and rolled her on her back on the sand. "Who is this Ricky Carter? I want his address and phone number."

"Last heard of somewhere in Florida."

"Good thing. Now tell me something personal. And make it count."

"When you kiss me, it's nothing like kissing Ricky Carter."

"When I kiss you like this, you mean?" He lowered his head to hers, and she felt her stomach jump and her heart flutter. He kissed her often, and each time was more exciting than the last. It was as if he was slowly building the tension, racking it up inch by inch until she was wound so tight she was afraid she might explode.

She'd stopped thinking she should fight her feelings, stopped listing all the reasons why this was probably a mistake.

Slowly, he lifted his head. "Ricky had better not have kissed you like that or he's a wanted man." His voice was low and lazy, the look in his eyes making her squirm with anticipation.

She knew he was holding back, and she couldn't help wondering how long that was going to last. Sex clouds things, was what he'd said, but she couldn't help thinking that not having sex clouded things, too. It stopped her being able to think straight. Cut through all the strings that held together her defenses.

"It was how I imagine it would feel to drown. I needed a life jacket."

He grinned. "Sounds like I have serious competition."

He'd never had any competition. That was the problem.

She moaned as she felt his mouth on her neck and the light scrape of stubble against her skin.

"Now you."

He lifted his head just enough to speak. "I hate mushrooms on pizza."

"That doesn't count."

"If I'm the one eating the pizza, it counts. I can eat mushrooms in any other dish, but they shouldn't be anywhere near a pizza."

"I get the message." She could feel the press of his body against hers. "Pizza, no mushrooms. Now tell me something personal."

He lowered his head and continued his exploration as far as her collarbone. "I'm determined." His mouth lingered there. "When there's something I want, I don't give up until I get it."

Was he talking about their relationship? Or something else? The things he was doing with his mouth made it hard to focus.

"You wanted to be a vet, and now you are."

He paused and lifted his head, looking at her from beneath those long lashes that had made him the talk of the town. "That's one example. There are others."

She wanted to know all about them. She wanted to know everything.

In the past few weeks she'd learned so much about him, like the fact he had the respect of the whole community. Everywhere she went it was "Dr. Carlyle this" and "Dr. Carlyle that." And among some quarters, respect came closer to adoration. Whatever details she didn't hear while shopping in Country Stores were filled in by her grandmother's friends.

It was through them that she'd learned he ran an outreach program helping the local animal shelter and that he actively encouraged the locals to adopt rescued pets rather than going to breeders.

Through them she'd learned that he'd risked his life to lead four horses out of a burning barn and that he'd once done two house calls to check up on a teenage girl whose cat had died.

Seth himself hadn't told her any of those things, not even in their "one thing" conversations, but that didn't surprise her. He was a man who did what needed to be done because he believed in it, not because he was trying to impress.

He loved animals, and if there was anything he could do to make their lives better, he was going to do it.

"How old were you when you decided you wanted to be a vet?"

"Eight. I was hiking with my dad and we found this dog tied to a stake in a yard. The owners had moved and not taken him with them. He was skin and bone. Showed no interest in being rescued, but my father rescued him anyway and took him to the animal shelter. I went every day to visit and care for him. I saw what a great job they did. How they coaxed this terrified animal into trusting them. It seemed like magic to me. And I wanted to learn how to do it." He stroked her hair back from her face. "I never forgot that dog because he taught me something important."

"Which was?"

"That it's important to look beyond the superficial. That most behavior comes with a reason."

This time she knew he wasn't talking only about the dog.

Her heart beat a little faster. "What was his reason?"

"That dog was fierce and angry, but once he realized no one was trying to hurt him, he stopped being angry and he was the most docile, loving dog you ever met."

"Did he eventually go to a good home?"

"Yeah, I like to think so." He lay back on the sand and shielded his eyes against the sun with his arm. "He lived with us for fourteen years. Best damn dog we ever had. I still miss him."

She lay watching him, thinking that no other man had ever affected her the way Seth did. He slammed through her willpower with his handsome face and his sexy smile, and he sneaked under her defenses with his patient kindness.

Strength, for Seth, wasn't who could shout loudest or act meanest. It wasn't fists or fight, although she had no doubt he could defend himself if the need arose.

No, strength was doing the right thing no matter what the cost.

She sometimes wondered if part of his appeal, at least at the beginning, was that he represented the complete opposite of her father.

He kept up a steady flow of conversation, telling her stories about his mother, about Vanessa, about the time Bryony had fallen off her horse and broken her arm. She told him more about her time in college, about all the adventures her mother was having now, and about Daniel's relationship with Molly. She almost told him about the visit she'd made to her father, that night in the rain, but she wasn't ready to share that story with anyone yet, not even with a good listener like Seth.

And he was a good listener. He paid attention, not just to what she said but what she didn't say, and beneath the apparently easy conversation was the ever-present awareness, an intense chemistry and sexual tension that shimmered between them.

It felt easier talking to him than it had the first time, and she didn't know why that was.

Aware that it was getting late, she sat up and dusted the sand from her arms. "One thing. Last time. You go first."

"Hey, I just told you fifty things. It's your turn."

"Definitely yours. You're confused."

"That might be that top you're wearing. The sight of semibare breasts has a strange effect on my brain." He leaned toward her, and she gave him a push.

"One thing. Your turn."

He paused and his gaze dropped to her mouth. "I'm glad you decided to hide from me in the Hamptons."

"I didn't do a great job of hiding."

"I'm glad about that, too."

Discovering she felt the same way made her heart miss a beat.

She had no idea where this was leading. No idea what she was going to do when she got there.

But for the time being, she was enjoying the ride.

SETH SPENT THE following day in surgery and then drove back to the house to shower and change before fulfilling an obligation he'd been dreading. He'd almost hoped for an emergency to give him an excuse not to show up.

He'd put it out of his mind while he was operating, but now that was over he discovered he didn't have the self-discipline to hold back the thoughts. He knew all about the stages of grief, and he'd experienced each one. Shock, denial, anger—he'd gone through the roller coaster of all the emotions after his father had died.

And now he had to sell Ocean View, which felt like the last connection with his father.

Pulling up outside his house, he was surprised to see Fliss's car.

His mood lifted, and then he realized with a pang that whatever she'd planned wasn't going to work for him.

He planned to do what needed to be done and then sit out on the deck and share his low mood with the sunset. Maybe a beer.

He stepped out of the car, wishing he could just drag her up to the bedroom and not leave for at least a week. But he wouldn't ever treat her as a distraction. Or a cure.

"I wasn't expecting you."

"*One thing—*" She raised one finger, playing the game that had become routine. "I love doing the unexpected. I thought I'd surprise you. Your turn. And make it a good one. Something really dark and dirty." She leaned against her car, eyes gleaming with humor and invitation until she saw something in his face. Humor quickly melted into concern. "What's wrong? Did you lose a patient? I heard the Jenkinses' dog was hit by a car."

"The dog is going to be fine, although he spent two hours in surgery." And he'd spent almost as much time reassuring and soothing Lily and Doug Jenkins, who had been distraught at the prospect of losing a much-loved pet.

Maybe it was the pressure that had given him a thumping headache, and not the prospect of selling memories of his father to the highest bidder.

"You're a bit of a hero, Dr. Carlyle. You should be celebrating."

He'd never felt less like celebrating. "Not tonight.

There's somewhere I need to be." And she didn't need to be part of that.

She eased away from the car and walked across to him. "I'm new to this game, but I'm pretty sure this is the part where you tell me what's bothering you."

"I'm meeting Chase at my parents' house. That friend I told you about who may be interested in buying it? He wants to take a look around."

"Oh, Seth." She put her arms around him and hugged him. "I didn't know you'd made the decision. And I had no idea it would happen this fast."

Breathing in the scent of her hair and feeling the lean lines of her body pressed against him made him wish he could just take her inside, switch off his phone and block out the world.

"It's fine."

She gave a short laugh and eased away so that she could look at him. "I'm the one who is supposed to hide feelings, not you."

"True. In that case, yes, I admit this sucks."

"Why not wait a while? What's the hurry?"

"It's what my mother wants. I talked to her last night. Seems like I'm the only one who isn't in a hurry to let it go." He sighed. "My father loved the place. I know it sounds crazy, but it feels like I'm losing part of him all over again."

He'd told her about that night his father had died, right through from his mother's frantic 2 a.m. call to the mad dash to the hospital. And he'd told her about his feelings when he realized he was too late and wasn't even going to get to say goodbye. Regret chasing regret. Things he wished he'd said, and hadn't. Time he wished he'd spent, and hadn't. The realization that control is an illusion. That tragedy picks its victims randomly and without mercy. That a perfect life could change in an instant and that time, once gone, was gone forever.

All useless, wasted, pain-inflicting thoughts.

"Couldn't you delay things until you've had time to get used to the idea?"

"If we're going to do it, then it's better to do it sooner rather than later. We need to sell it before it starts to need a ton of upkeep, and if Chase has a potential buyer then I can't afford to ignore that."

"In that case I'll come with you."

"I don't want you to do that. It's not going to be fun."

"We're friends. Friends are there for the tough bits as well as the easy bits." She locked her car and shoved the keys in her pocket. "Let's go."

He found that he didn't want to argue. "With luck, I'm going to have the easiest sale in the history of real estate. Mom won't have to worry about money again."

"But you don't care about the money," she murmured. "You never did. With you it's never about the money."

"I was lucky enough not to have to think about it."

"Plenty of people don't have to think about it, but still think about it all the time. It dominates everything, influences all their decisions. Are they doing the right thing? Behaving the right way? Wearing the right clothes? Being seen in the right places, mixing with the right people? You never cared about any of that. And you won't care that the market is good, or whether Chase has got you a great deal. You do care that you're selling your family home, somewhere you spent summers and Thanksgiving for more years than you can remember."

He remembered them. He remembered all of them.

"The place is full of memories. For Mom, that's hard. But for me—" He hesitated and she nodded.

"I understand. It's somewhere you still feel close to him. Selling it feels like handing those memories on to someone else."

"It's about what's right for Mom, not me. I'm not the one who matters here."

"You matter to me." She slid her hand into his, and he stroked the backs of his fingers over her cheek.

The sun had dusted her nose with freckles and lightened her hair, making her eyes seem bluer than ever.

He wondered how she could possibly think she was the "bad" twin.

She was one of the most fiercely loyal people he'd ever met and straight as an arrow. For some reason he found himself thinking of Naomi, and her complicated manipulation.

Fliss was straightforward. She didn't play games.

If Chase Adams was surprised to see Fliss, he kept his feelings to himself. Instead he gave her a hug, thanked her again for what she'd done for Matilda, assured her he was deeply in her debt and then turned to introduce his friend.

Todd Wheeler was an investment banker who worked on Wall Street. His phone rang constantly. It would have driven Seth insane, but Todd seemed to regard it as a normal part of his day.

"Wheeler." He answered the phone in blunt, crisp tones. "No… That's right… That stock is going through the roof—"

Seth didn't care what happened with the stock as

long as Todd had the money to buy his house, but the man didn't seem interested.

Was a guy really going to part with a substantial portion of his capital for a place he'd barely glanced at?

Todd ended the call and Seth managed a polite smile. "Busy day?"

"Normal day." Todd glanced at his watch. "Let's do this."

Seth refrained from asking if he was sure he had the time. Instead he walked through the rooms, the emptiness of the house enveloping him.

He probably should have been giving an effusive sales pitch, filling the echoing silence with patter about why this house was perfect, but he couldn't summon the energy.

In the library Todd took three more phone calls in rapid succession and Fliss glanced at Seth and rolled her eyes.

The face she pulled made him feel better.

Later, he decided, they'd go back to his place and walk on the beach.

When Todd finally dropped the phone back into his pocket for the fifth time, Seth showed him the rest of the downstairs. He lingered in the formal dining area, where his mother had hosted more noisy dinner parties than he could remember, then walked through to the large kitchen that had been the heart of the home and had sweeping ocean views.

When Todd took another phone call, Seth started to wish he'd let Chase show the house without him. He could feel his father in every room.

He remembered the last Thanksgiving they'd spent together here as a family. Naomi had joined them, and from the moment she arrived it had been obvious to him he'd made a mistake inviting her. She'd read too much into the gesture and he'd heard her giggling with Vanessa. It was obvious they'd been plotting together, and that he was the subject of the plot.

She'd been waiting for him to propose.

When he hadn't, she started dropping hints. When he hadn't taken those hints, she'd grown more and more exasperated. And then moody.

Seth had left her with Vanessa and gone sailing with his father. This late in the year the waters around Gardiner's Bay had been choppy, and they'd needed all their skill and experience to keep the boat on course. It had been both terrifying and exhilarating, and they'd had one of the best days sailing Seth could ever remember.

And he remembered another thing, too. He remembered his father saying that choosing a partner was one of the most important decisions a man ever made. That you should choose someone who wanted to run with you, not hold you back.

Seth knew his father didn't think Naomi was right for him, and he'd agreed.

It was one of the last serious conversations he'd had with his father, and it had been the beginning of the end of his relationship with Naomi. It was the day he'd stopped looking for someone who made him feel the way Fliss did and resolved instead to find Fliss.

His father's death shortly after had reminded him that life was too short to spend it with the wrong person.

They moved upstairs to the bedroom suites, and he heard Todd asking Chase a question about rental yield.

Rental yield?

For Seth, owning property wasn't about financial return, but emotional return. He didn't measure real estate in terms of square footage but in terms of lifestyle.

It was the reason he'd chosen his place on the edge of the nature preserve.

He'd seen the potential. Not for a financial killing but for a future that was good. Somewhere he could plant roots. Somewhere to make memories. And yes, somewhere to have a family one day. He still wanted that. Maybe, on one level, he'd always wanted that.

Todd was on the phone again, so Seth opened the French doors and walked onto the balcony. The house faced over dunes that sloped down to a wide sandy beach. He'd played there with his sisters, acted as referee as they'd quarreled and argued about things so small and insignificant he couldn't even remember them.

All he heard now was the gentle hiss of the waves as they hit the sand.

He heard footsteps behind him and felt Fliss's hand on his arm.

"That man is driving me insane. Is he really your only buyer? Because if it's okay with you I'd like to kill him. I promise to keep the blood to a minimum. I thought I might push him off the balcony or drown him in the pool, along with that damn phone of his."

He hadn't thought he was capable of smiling today, but he found he was smiling. "I guess he has a job to do."

"His job right now is to look at this house."

"He's not going to buy the house, Fliss." And it was only now, when it was obvious it wasn't going to happen, that he realized how badly he'd wanted this part to be over. If Todd walked away, he'd be faced with end-less months of dealing with a Realtor.

Strangers would tramp through the house, leaving footprints on his memories.

Fliss tapped her foot on the floor. "If he put the phone down for five minutes he might be able to focus long enough to fall in love and decide to buy it."

"Guys like Todd Wheeler don't fall in love with houses. He thinks only in terms of return on invest-ment. He's not seeing a potential home, he's seeing eight thousand square feet of oceanfront property with easy access to a heliport."

Fliss narrowed her eyes. "Hmm. We'll see about that." She stalked back into the house, leaving him with no choice but to follow.

Not that he was afraid she actually would drown Todd Wheeler in the pool, but he wouldn't put it past her to do some damage.

She marched through two of the upstairs bedrooms before she finally tracked down Todd and Chase in a guest room overlooking the gardens.

"Excuse me." She planted herself in front of Todd and offered up a friendly smile. "Could I talk to you for a moment?"

Seth paused just outside the doorway and saw Todd frown.

"Sure." Then his phone rang and he glanced down at it. "I need to answer this, so if you'll excuse me—"

"No, in fact I won't." Her smile fixed, Fliss removed the phone from his hand. "My advice is to make them wait. They'll be more interested."

Guessing that it wouldn't do much to ingratiate himself with his buyer if he laughed, Seth moved out of sight.

He couldn't be bothered to call Todd out, but it seemed that Fliss intended to.

"You should focus all your attention on the task at hand," she said, "which is deciding whether or not you're interested in this house. Because once you walk out of that door, it will all be over and let me tell you, if you lose this place you will kick yourself. And if I were your wife, and frankly I'm glad I'm not because I would never want to be in a threesome with a cell phone, I might be tempted to kick you, too. You will never again have the opportunity to own a property with as much potential as this one."

"I'll need to talk to an architect before I can assess that."

"I'm not talking about its potential as a building project. I'm talking about its potential to add quality to your family life. I'm helping you to see something you don't seem capable of seeing by yourself."

"Look, the property is great, but it's not the only property on the market. There are several larger beach properties I have to see."

Seth felt a thud of disappointment. It was as he'd suspected.

"Larger?" Fliss obviously wasn't ready to give up. "How many children do you have, Todd? Ten? Eleven?"

"Two."

"And are you planning to live with extended family? Your mother-in-law, perhaps? A whole stream of cousins?"

"Just the four of us." His tone was cautious. "I don't see what that—"

"I'm trying to work out what you would do with more space than this. With four of you, you could move in here and not sleep in the same bedroom for a week. You can entertain lavishly—there's even a guest cottage. When your kids hit their teenage years there is enough space to give them a wing each if they turn moody. Sure, you could buy something with more room, but why?"

"It's called investment."

"So you're not looking for a home, you're looking for profit."

"That's a factor." He studied her for a moment. "I understood from Chase it isn't even on the market yet."

"A house this special doesn't need to go on the open market. The appeal that dragged you down here in the middle of your very busy working week is the same appeal that has had other buyers knocking at the door. Seth only agreed to let you see it first because you're Chase's friend. So I guess it boils down to one basic question. Are you in love with the house?"

"In *love*?" He shot her a bemused glance. "Real estate is a financial decision, not an emotional one."

"This isn't a piece of real estate, Todd, it's a *home*. As a matter of interest, how do you propose to present this to your wife? 'Hi, honey, I bought us a house but don't bother unpacking or getting too comfortable because if the value increases enough I'll sell it right out from under you.' Is that what you're planning? Because if so, I feel sorry for her. And your kids. What are their names? How old are they?"

"Grant is six and Katy is eight."

"A boy and a girl. And you're buying this because you want to be able to spend summers at the Hamptons. I bet they're going to just love the beach." Her tone warmed. "They'll spend time playing hide-and-seek in those dunes just beyond the house. Sandy feet, sun on their faces, happy children. *Lucky* children."

Seth frowned.

She'd painted a picture so clear he could taste the salt air and hear his sisters' laughter. Hear his mother warning them to wipe their feet so that they didn't trail sand into the house.

Todd said nothing.

"Maybe you'll take Grant sailing, like Seth's father did." Fliss's tone was desperate, and Seth wondered why she didn't just give up. Did she really think she could convert Todd Wheeler from hard-nosed businessman to family guy in one conversation?

"Fliss—"

"Has he told you they used to spend every spare hour here doing up their boat? Not down at a boat-yard, but at the dock right there in front of the house. Or maybe it will be Katy who loves being on the water. And when you're spending time messing around with boats, whether it's on dry land or the water, it's not about the boat, Todd. It's about the time you're spending to-gether, the conversations you have while you're varnish-ing planks or sailing a boat into the wind. Whatever you do, however you spend your time in this beautiful home, those are the things your kids will always value about your relationship. They're the moments Grant and Katy will remember, not how much money their dad made on a property when he sold it. This house isn't just bricks and wood, it has a heart and a soul."

Her words were met with silence.

This time, it seemed, Todd had nothing to say.

Neither did Seth.

He realized she wasn't trying to convert Todd, or reform him in any way. She was selling his house, and she'd done it with as much passion and conviction as if she'd been selling her own.

She'd painted a picture like an artist, skillfully weaving visions of an idyllic lifestyle until Seth would have bought the house himself had he not already owned it.

Todd frowned. "I don't think—"

"Think of it like this." She didn't give him time to speak. "When you invest money, you expect a return. But who says that return always has to be financial? This house is an investment in quality family time. Happy moments become happy memories, and they last forever. Nothing can ever take that away, not even a crash in the market. Take your son sailing, teach your daughter to surf, and they're going to be remembering those things into adulthood. And when they leave, they'll take all those memories with them. If that's not an investment, I don't know what is."

They'll take all those memories with them.

Seth felt a pressure in his chest.

He'd thought the memories belonged to the house, but Fliss was right. They belonged to him. They were inside him and they would always be inside him, no matter where he went or what he did. Selling a house wasn't going to change that.

Swallowing down the emotion, he walked into the room and Chase reappeared at the same moment, full of apologies.

"Sorry, that was Matilda. She wanted me to pick up a few things on my way home. Have you finished? Is there anything else you need to see, Todd?"

"No. I need to get back to the office." He gave Fliss and Seth a brief nod. "Thanks."

Seth said nothing. He couldn't stop thinking about what Fliss had said.

"I'm driving Todd back to the airport." Chase slapped Seth on the shoulder. "I know you said you were working over the holiday, but are you free in the evening? Matilda and I are having a few people over. We're keeping it low-key as Rose is so little and Matilda is tired. My brother, Brett, will join us if he can, and a couple of other friends."

Seth forced himself to concentrate. "I'm on call during the day. Tanya is covering the evening."

Todd raised his eyebrows. "Are people really going to need a vet on the Fourth of July?"

"It's always a busy few days for us. First there's the heat—people leave pets in cars and forget about them while they're barbecuing on the beach. They feed them table scraps, they have people around who leave doors and gates open so pets escape. And don't even start me on fireworks. And it doesn't end there. The day after when the yard is full of debris, the dogs eat it."

Chase looked surprised. "I had no idea."

"Neither does half the population, which is why I'm always busy."

"You can bring your phone to our place. Fliss?"

"Grams and I are cooking lunch for her friends. I'll be clear by five o'clock easily, and Grams goes to bed early."

"Great. Then the two of you should come over."

The two of you.

Seth noticed that Chase had bracketed them together, as if they were an item. It was typical Chase. Another friend might have been delivering a caution. Reminding him this hadn't worked out the first time and that he was risking heartache for a second time.

Chase understood that some things were so important they were worth every risk.

He smiled at his friend. "Are you cooking?"

Chase looked offended. "Hey, I can grill. But as it happens, no. I've hired a chef. Do you know Eva?"

Fliss nodded. "She's part of Urban Genie, the concierge business in New York that is responsible for the stratospheric growth of our business. Is she cooking? Because if the answer is yes, then I'll be here."

A few minutes later, the car pulled away and Seth watched as they disappeared from view.

Everything felt different. Everything had changed. The sky looked bluer, the air felt fresher and his head, which had been enveloped in a cloud since the death of his father, felt clear for the first time in months.

When he glanced around the kitchen, the dark fog of memories had lifted.

And he knew who was responsible.

He turned to Fliss. "You sold my house."

She stepped closer and put her hand on his arm. "Are you upset? You weren't even sure you wanted to sell it."

"Neither was I, but I am now. All those things you said to Todd made sense to me. I thought the memories were part of the house, and listening to you made me realize they're part of me. And although I've lost him, I haven't lost the memories or the legacy. I'll always have that. Thank you for making me see it." He felt her wrap her arms around him.

He wondered why other people didn't immediately see her warmth and generosity.

He'd seen those eyes blaze with fierce determination when she'd stepped in front of her sister to defend her. He'd seen her step in front of her brother, too, no matter how big her opponent. But until today she'd never stepped in front of him.

"You were amazing. Bold, fearless, honest and right." He turned to her, wondering how much to say. Was it too soon? "Do you know the best part about this?"

"That despite extreme provocation, I'm not up on a murder charge?"

He smiled. "The best part is that you did it for me."

"You said you wanted to sell it. You *need* to sell it. I understand that, so I was trying to do everything I could to make it happen."

"You defended me. Fought for me. You stepped in front." He stroked his fingers across the line of her jaw. "You do that with people you care about. I've seen you do it with Daniel and with Harriet."

There was a long silence, disturbed only by the call of a seagull and the rush of the ocean.

"I care about you." She spoke softly. "I've always cared about you."

There was so much he wanted to say, but he knew he had to take it slowly. "I always cared about you, too. Right from that first day when I saw you watching over Harriet on the beach. There was a girl teasing her about her stammer."

"That happened a lot. And the teasing made poor Harriet worse. I don't have much patience with bullies."

"Or men who are addicted to their mobile phones, it seems."

"Todd was a dumbass. I wanted to take his damn phone and shove it up his—"

"I think I can imagine where you wanted to shove it."
He tugged her against him. "Let's go back to my place.
I can pay your commission with dinner."

"What if Todd doesn't buy it?"

"Then you owe me. And I'll be calling in the debt."

She peeped at him from under her lashes. "I can
think of a different way for you to pay me."

"Felicity Knight, are you making an indecent suggestion?"

"Maybe. I'm trouble, didn't you know?"

"I might have heard that about you. Why do you
think I'm here?" He slid his hand behind her neck and
lowered his head.

Their mouths collided, and he groaned and sank his
fingers into her hair. It spilled over his hands, and he
stroked his thumbs over the smooth lines of her jaw. He
wanted to explore every delicate inch of her. He wanted
to unpeel her shorts and that provocative tank top and
discover all the things that had changed since the last
time he'd touched her.

He felt her hands on his shirt, tugging, and then felt
her palms slide up his spine.

Heat shot through him. He tasted the excitement on
her lips and felt her press against him.

Another minute of this and they'd both be naked.

He eased away, wondering if he was crazy.

She was obviously wondering the same thing because she steadied herself and looked at him dizzily.
"You're stopping?"

"That's right."

"Why?" She slowly withdrew her hands, tugging his
shirt down and taking a step back. "You're still worried
that my brain will stop working once we're naked?"

"It's a factor." Although it was his brain he was worried about.

"You have too much willpower, Seth Carlyle. How did I ever manage to corrupt you the first time?"

"I wasn't doing much thinking back then." But he was doing plenty of thinking now.

He wanted her, right there and then, in this house that held a lifetime of memories, but he knew that was only the start of what he wanted. And he realized that what Vanessa didn't understand was that he couldn't fall in love with Fliss again, because he'd never fallen out of love.

He'd given her his heart at the age of twenty-two and he'd never taken it back.

CHAPTER EIGHTEEN

SHE WAS SILENT on the drive back to his house. Silent and desperately conscious of every movement he made. His hands on the wheel, the muscular length of his thigh close to hers. He was big and handsome, and keeping her hands to herself was proving as difficult as it had when she was a teenager.

She was starting to wish she hadn't agreed to dinner. She certainly wasn't going to be able to eat anything. The tension had created a tight knot in her stomach.

She felt like a teenager, her heart all fluttery and her palms damp.

How crazy was that?

She tried to keep her gaze fixed straight ahead, but somehow she found herself turning her head to look at him. His shirt was open at the neck, allowing her a tantalizing glimpse of his tanned throat.

"You're quiet."

"I'm okay."

"Fliss—"

"All right, I'm not okay. I don't know if sexual frustration counts as a medical condition, but if it does I have an advanced case of it. You don't want us to focus on the sex, and that's just fine in theory, I get it, I really do, the principle I mean, not the sex, obviously I'm not getting the sex—"

"I think—"

"*Let me finish!* I'm struggling to get my words out here. All I'm saying is that I've reached the stage where the sex is getting in the way because it's all I can think about. And it's making me crazy." She closed her eyes. "Forget dinner. I think you'd better take me home. I'll take a cold shower. Watch a nature program on TV."

"You want to watch a nature program?"

"No, but I don't think I'm going to be safe around you. I feel a 'bad Fliss' moment coming on. You don't want to be near me when that happens."

"Or maybe I do."

He swerved into his drive, sending loose stones flying. Seconds after he turned off the ignition, he grabbed her and yanked her up against him.

The look in his eyes made her heart pound.

"I thought you didn't want this."

"I want this. I was showing restraint."

"Restraint is overrated." Her hands tore at his shirt, clumsy in her haste. "Seth, I really want—"

"Me, too, so quit talking and let's get inside. Whatever other sins we committed in the past, or may commit in the future, I don't want one of them to be having sex on the front porch in front of all my neighbors."

They stumbled out of the car, and somehow he opened the front door of his house. They all but fell through it and then he was kissing her, opening her mouth with his. She felt the erotic slide of his tongue against hers, and it felt so sinfully good she wondered how she could have survived so long without this.

Why had it never been like this with anyone else?

Why had no other man ever made her feel this way?

Still kissing her, he pushed her back against the wall

and kicked the door shut. He pinned her there, trapping her legs between his and caging her with his arms, and she gave a shiver of excitement because whatever she'd started it was clear he intended to finish it.

She wrapped her arms around his neck and he dropped his hands to her waist and then her thighs, his body still pinning hers against the wall. She felt hard muscle and strength and whispered his name, urging him on as she trailed her mouth from his lips to the roughness of his jaw. Her breathing was as unsteady as his and her heart pounded with almost brutal force as his hands slid beneath her panties. Sensation shot through her, turning her limbs heavy and weak. She wanted him so badly it was indecent, and she moaned as she felt the slow, skilled invasion of his fingers. His mouth silenced her, his kiss deep and deliberate. She wanted to speak, to tell him how good it felt, how much she'd missed him, but her thoughts were tumbled and confused and she couldn't form the words. She'd never felt like this before. Nothing had ever felt like this. She wanted him so badly that when he withdrew his hand she almost sobbed, but then she realized he was simply removing clothing that was getting in the way.

Her panties hit the floor. Her bra followed.

She fumbled with the buttons of his shirt and opened it.

She'd seen him on the beach, in board shorts and in even less, but she couldn't get enough of looking at him.

Her body remembered his, remembered the feel and the taste. She knew every inch of him, but recognized the changes. His shoulders were broader, his muscles more clearly defined. He was strong, steady and sure of himself.

Years of separation fueled their desperation. They ripped off the rest of each other's clothes, although Seth paused long enough to grab something from the pocket of his jeans. Haste made them clumsy and Fliss murmured a protest, and then he was lifting her, his hands hard on her thighs as he pressed her back. Desire was so intense it was almost suffocating. She wrapped her legs around him and cried out as he drove into her, the sound a mix of shock and pleasure as she felt her body yield to the thickness of him. She was engulfed in a storm of sensation, each upward thrust sending her senses spinning. She felt crazily out of control, dizzy with it, and gripped the muscles of his arms, trying to hold on to something as her body yielded to his demands. But whatever he took, he gave back a thousandfold until she was shivery and helpless.

She'd never known excitement like it, and she wondered if there would ever be a time when the chemistry between them calmed to something more serene and gentle. Right now the excitement was savage and urgent, a cascade of erotic sensations that built and built until she felt herself tip over the edge. Her body shuddered against his, and he captured her cry of pleasure with his mouth as he hit the same peak.

It was a long time before either of them moved. She stayed where she was, her forehead resting on his shoulder.

Finally he lowered her to the floor. Still holding her with one hand, he slid the fingers of his other hand under her chin and lifted her face to his. She gazed up at him, dazed, wondering how a look could feel more intimate than what they'd already shared.

His hand slid behind her neck, cradling her head

while his thumb gently stroked her cheek. "Are you all right?" His voice was soft, his gaze intensely personal.

"I'm not sure. Best not to let go of me for a minute."

"I was holding back."

"Really? I didn't notice." She was glad she was trapped between him and the wall because she wasn't sure her legs would have held her without help.

"I meant, I was trying to postpone this happening."

"I know. And this might be a good time to tell you I question your reasoning."

"I had a master plan. First we were going to date. I was going to get you talking to me. Persuade you to share."

"We dated. We talked. I've shared." More than she ever had with anyone else. Thinking about it was more than a little terrifying. "Then what?"

"I was going to take it to the next stage. And before you ask me, I hadn't exactly figured that out, but it was going to be romantic. It wasn't going to be sex against the wall before you'd barely made it through the door."

"It worked for me." She could have stared at him all night and all day. The Poker Princesses were right. He had incredible eyelashes. "Tell me more about your plans for romantic."

"I hadn't got as far as making firm plans, but they definitely involved a comfortable bed."

"The wall seemed to work perfectly well." Although she was only now realizing that parts of her ached. "Maybe we could go for a more comfortable option next time."

He smoothed her hair back from her face. "Did I hurt you? Because I swear I heard something crunch when we hit the wall."

"That was my willpower." She lifted her head, viewing him from between the tangled strands of her hair. "Now maybe I can stop thinking about sex and focus on all the other stuff you want us to focus on."

"You think that's going to work?"

"Sure. In time. Once all the hot stuff has cooled. Of course, that might take a while." She tested her legs, surprised to discover that they seemed able to hold her. "You used a condom. It seems at least one of us has learned our lesson from last time. Do you always carry that with you?" She asked the question casually, and he tugged her back to look at him.

"You think I'm prepared to have sex with every woman I meet?"

"I don't know. It seems as if every woman you meet thinks you're cute, so I guess it's good to be prepared." After what had happened between them she couldn't blame him, and she hated herself for asking the question as much as for the insecurity behind it. "I'm sorry, it's none of my business."

"It's definitely your business." His eyes darkened. "And the answer is I'm prepared, and careful, but only since you moved here. Before that I generally managed to get through my working day without jumping on women."

His words left her with a warm glow. "You're saying it's just me that has this effect on you?"

"Seems that way."

She stroked her hand over his shoulders, feeling taut muscle under her fingers. "We could try this again. Your way."

He glanced sideways. "Lulu is wearing your bra."

"Do you think we shocked her?"

"Nothing shocks Lulu." He turned his attention back to Fliss, kissed her slowly and thoroughly and then eased away. "Let's go upstairs."

"I think I might have dropped my tank top on your doorstep."

"It will be a deterrent for visitors." He scooped her up, and she gasped.

"What are you doing?"

"I don't want to have sex on the stairs, and that's what will happen if you walk up the stairs in front of me."

They made it upstairs, stumbling and laughing, and fell onto his bed, their bodies lit by moonlight.

He touched her with skilled, practiced hands, every move slow and drawn out, designed to pull maximum pleasure from the moment. It was agonizingly intimate and totally different from anything they'd shared before.

The darkness was filled with soft sounds and low murmurs. He wanted and demanded everything, and she gave him all that and more, and when she finally reached the peak she was afraid she might shatter.

Afterward they lay there, close, eyes locked, her legs trapped by his.

He ran the pad of his thumb over her forehead. "I'd forgotten your scar. You never did tell me how you got it."

She shrugged. "Fell into a tree."

"Yeah? Because you seem pretty competent walking around whenever I watch you. And lately I watch you a lot."

"I was fighting."

"Why were you fighting?"

"It felt like more fun than doing a boring English

assignment." She saw the look in his eyes and sighed. It was typical of him to know there would have been a reason. He looked for good in people. It was part of the man he was. "Someone was mean to Harriet."

"So you leaped in and defended your sister."

"His name was Johnny Hill. He was captain of the football team and a real bully. He made her cry. No one makes my sister cry."

"So you were stepping in front of her, the way you did with me this evening."

It was true, and it made her realize that she was in deep. It made her stomach lurch to contemplate how deep. If there had been a life preserver handy she would have grabbed it. "So what if I did?"

He slid his hand behind her neck and took her mouth. "You care."

"Maybe I do." Admitting it felt scary. Admitting it meant stripping away armor and making yourself vulnerable.

"And you care about your sister. You care enough to protect her." His fingertips gently traced her scar. "I think that makes you Good Girl Fliss."

"The school didn't think so. I was suspended for a while, which meant I couldn't watch out for Harriet. I was more careful after that." She changed the subject, preferring not to dwell on what was happening with her feelings.

"No more fights?"

"I kept them off the school premises." She turned on her side, her hand on his chest. "Now it's your turn. Show me your scars, Carlyle."

"I don't have scars. At least, not on the outside."

"And on the inside?" She felt his hand stroke her hair.

"I never stopped thinking about you, Fliss. You've always kept a piece of my heart."

His words stole her breath and sliced through her. It made her think about all the time they'd lost and what might have been. "I'm sorry I hurt you."

"I hurt you, too. We both made mistakes. I think it's called being human."

"I should have said more. Opened up more."

"When a person has spent their whole life putting up barriers, it's difficult to trust people enough to lower them."

And suddenly it seemed important to make him understand.

She eased out of his arms and sat up. "My dad knew exactly how to control people. He understood their weaknesses and he used them. He wanted to hurt. Pretty early on I realized that, and I was determined never to let him see that he'd hurt me. The more indifferent I was, the worse he became." She shook her head. "Maybe I should have crumpled at the first insult, but there was no way I was doing that. He preyed on weakness. On vulnerability. The only way to survive him was to never let myself be vulnerable. So I hid. Not like Harriet, who hid under the table or in her bedroom, I hid inside myself. I built these walls. I even used to imagine I was in a castle and the enemy was coming. I'd pull up the drawbridge and they'd be trapped outside. That's how I used to picture my dad."

He sat up, too, pulling the covers around them. "As the enemy?"

"There were days when it felt that way. He taunted me that I was no good, useless, so I spent my whole adult life proving him wrong. How crazy is that? In a way I let him control me. I wanted to show him I could be financially independent and successful. And I worked so hard at hiding my feelings, and got pretty good at it. I think I was afraid that if I lowered that drawbridge to let you in, my defenses would be down. I couldn't let that happen. I needed to protect myself. I saw my mom vulnerable. And Harriet. I didn't want to be vulnerable, too."

"And now? You've started opening up. You've lowered that drawbridge and let me in. Told me things you've never told me before. And have those castle walls come crashing down?"

She gave a half smile. "Still standing."

He nodded, his gaze thoughtful. "You know, someone who crosses that drawbridge isn't always the enemy. You were afraid to let down that drawbridge because you thought the person on the other side would attack you, but I'm not attacking you, honey. I'm on your side. Think of me as reinforcements."

"My father used to tell me I'd never do anything with my life." She breathed. "I've never told anyone that before. I was always afraid that if I said it aloud, someone might agree."

"Fliss—"

"I worked hard because I wanted the freedom and independence that came with owning and running a successful business, and I wanted Harriet to have that, too. And I worked hard because deep down I wanted him to be proud. I really wanted him to tell me he was proud, and that he'd been wrong about me. He never did. Never has."

"You don't need him to tell you that." He pulled her into the circle on his arms. "You know he was wrong."

"I wanted to hear him say it. I went to see him in the hospital, hoping for some dramatic reconciliation. It always happens in the movies." Her voice was muffled against his chest, and she felt his hand smooth her hair gently.

"I'm guessing in this case life wasn't like the movies."

"Some people might have used that experience to reconnect with people. Not my father." She paused. "It didn't soften him or make him repent in any way. I showed up at the hospital and he asked me what I wanted. It was a good question, and I realized right then that all I really wanted was his approval, and I was never going to get it. To him I was always useless, hopeless, a disaster." She felt Seth's arms tighten around her. "He pushed me away, and it hurt more than anything that had gone before. I've never told anyone that before. No one else knew I went to see him, not even Harriet."

"If he pushed you away, that was his loss."

"It was mine, too, but it's a loss I have to learn to live with." She lifted her head. "I'm glad I told you."

"So am I."

"Talking. Opening up. It feels good. Better than I thought it would. I think I could get to like it."

"Good. Because I'm definitely liking it." He pressed his mouth to her neck. "And I'm liking other things, too."

So was she. And as he pulled her down again she realized that during all those years she'd spent trying to find someone else, she'd been wasting her time. She didn't want someone else. She'd never wanted anyone else. All she'd ever wanted was this. Him.

Seth.

CHAPTER NINETEEN

TIME PASSED IN A BLUR.

Fliss found more clients, walked more dogs, built up the business. In this case the community grapevine worked to her advantage. Word-of-mouth meant she was as busy as she wanted to be, but she still found time to be with Seth.

They drove to Montauk and watched the surfers at Ditch Plains, and she found it hard to remember that she was only a few hours from the city. At least part of every day she went without shoes, felt the sand between her toes and breathed in the smell of the ocean.

They ate at the marina restaurant, where daily seafood specials were the order of the day, and sometimes they frequented the airy waterfront bar that served cocktails.

They took the ferry to Shelter Island and explored tidal creeks, woodlands and marshes. They rented kayaks and saw diamondback terrapins and fiddler crabs, blue herons and egrets. Later, with muscles aching, they found a beach restaurant and ate clam chowder and blackened fish tacos while they watched the sunset. Here, far away from the celebrity magnet of South Fork, there was an unmanicured wildness that she loved.

But her favorite times were the hours they spent sitting on the deck of Seth's house, watching the sun dip down over the water.

By the Fourth of July she had completely adjusted to the pace of life.

The day dawned sunny, and Fliss pulled on shorts and a T-shirt and found her grandmother in the kitchen measuring pecans into a bowl. The smell of baking came from the oven and a mound of apples sat in the middle of the table waiting to be peeled.

"The bruising is fading." Fliss kissed her grandmother on the cheek. "How are you feeling?"

"Less stiff. I might live to annoy you for a few more years."

"I'm counting on it. And so are your friends. You still have several seasons of *Sex in the City* to get through. Wouldn't want to miss that." She poured herself coffee and suppressed a yawn.

Her grandmother glanced at her. "Someone is in a good mood. Do you want to tell me about it?"

Fliss curved her hands around the mug. "Definitely not. Your heart couldn't take it."

"My heart's as strong as yours." Her grandmother measured flour into a large bowl. "It's good to see you smile."

"Why wouldn't I smile? The sun is shining, I have eight clients in the Hamptons and two more calls to deal with. I like spending time with you, and it turns out I'm not such a bad cook. Life is good."

"So you're not planning on going back to Manhattan anytime soon?" Her grandmother made a well in the center of the flour. "I expected you to stay a week."

"Well, it hasn't been that long." Fliss made a calculation in her head and felt a stab of shock as she realized just how long. How had that happened? One sunny day had flowed into another until the whole summer seemed a blur of sunrises and sunsets. "I enjoy living with you. You're good company."

Her grandmother studied her over the rim of her glasses. "Are you trying to convince me you're here because of me? Because entertaining though the Poker Princesses are, I have a feeling the reason for your continued presence might be a certain young sexy male who is good with animals."

Not just animals. "He's part of the reason. And you were the one who pushed me toward him, so you can't judge."

"Do I look as if I'm judging? I'm pleased for you. Now stop talking and get peeling. There's a knife on the table. Peel the apples, then slice them. And I want them thin. No shortcuts."

"What time are the Poker Princesses arriving?" Fliss stole a pecan from the bowl on the counter. "I need to prepare myself for the inquisition."

"They'll be here at midday. And if you stop picking at the food there might be something left for them to eat."

"You're a hard taskmaster. I like cooking with you." And no one was more surprised about that than she was. It wasn't so much the cooking, she thought, as the shared activity. "Harriet's going to be surprised when I make her pancakes. At home, she's the one who does the cooking. Daniel and I do the eating."

"She's a real homemaker, your sister. Now that Daniel is with Molly, there's only Harriet left alone. I'd like to see her with someone special. Is she dating?"

"Wait a minute. What do you mean, the only one left alone? What about me?"

"We both know it's only ever been Seth for you." Her

grandmother picked up the recipe to check something, and Fliss stared at her, heart pounding.

"Do we? I never said that. We haven't talked about a future or anything. We're seeing each other, spending time together, that's all."

Her grandmother put the spoon down. "Does he know that?"

"I don't know. It feels scary," she confessed. "He was hurt because of me. And I hurt, too. I'm terrified we'll end up hurting each other again. I couldn't put him through that. And I couldn't put myself through that. It feels like a huge risk."

"Wonderful things almost always require that you take a risk. And love is a wonderful thing. It's what adds richness to our lives. Not everyone is lucky enough to find it, or sometimes they find it but they can't do anything about it. I'd say if it comes your way then you should grab it with both hands. I suspect Harriet would do pretty much anything to have what you have."

A serious case of the jitters? Sick tension?

She'd never thought love was as simple as Harriet seemed to think it was. Harriet thought all you needed were the feelings and the rest was easy. To Fliss, all of it was hard. The feelings, and what those feelings meant.

But even she had to admit that what she had with Seth was special.

"I'm thinking of persuading her to try online dating. Harriet, I mean. She's not keen."

Her grandmother winced. "I don't blame her. I can't imagine going on a date with someone I'd never met face-to-face."

"It's the way things are done now. It's not ideal, but it's hard meeting someone when everyone is busy."

"She doesn't still stammer with strangers?"

"Not for years. She's more confident. In her comfort zone."

Her grandmother put the sugar and flour back in the cupboard. "And what happens when she isn't? How does she cope?"

Fliss frowned. "That doesn't happen. I do the accounts and all the new business contacts, anything she finds stressful. She handles the animals and all the dog walkers. We each do the things we're good at."

"If you only ever do the parts you're good at, how will you ever grow and improve? Take your cooking skills as an example. Your pancakes are perfect," her grandmother said, "which proves that with patience and practice we can become good at things."

"You're suggesting I tell Harriet to do the accounts and call a hundred strangers? She'd freak."

"I'm suggesting we are always capable of more than we think."

Fliss had a feeling her grandmother wasn't talking only about Harriet.

"That may be true. I haven't burned anything in a week, have you noticed?"

"I've noticed a lot of things. Like the fact you've never stopped protecting your sister." Her grandmother moved the bowl out of reach before Fliss could help herself to more. "Also that you're busy and your paperwork is all over my kitchen table. You might like to move it before we cover it in apple peelings."

Fliss tidied the papers and moved them from the table to the countertop. "Of course I protect her. I'm her sister."

Her grandmother said nothing. Instead she peered

at her recipe. "I need six eggs. Could you break them into a bowl for me?"

"Sure." Fliss found the eggs while her grandmother dropped a stick of butter into the bowl. "That's what sisters are supposed to do, isn't it?"

"You're saying she protects you, too?"

"No. I'm the oldest." Fliss broke eggs into a bowl and studied the result with satisfaction. "See? A month ago I would have spent hours picking out shell. Now, no shell. Are you proud of me?"

"You know I'm proud of you. Always have been."

"I didn't know that until you said it the other day."

"I should have told you sooner. I remember sitting here biting my tongue while your father said you were useless, and that you'd never amount to anything."

Fliss disposed of the eggshells. "I remember that, too. I remember Mom saying he should be proud of me, and him saying that if I gave him something to be proud of then he'd be proud."

"And you've been trying to make him proud ever since. Setting up the business. Growing it. Some of that was for yourself, and some for your sister, but I'm sure a large part of the motivation came from a drive to prove your father wrong."

She thought about her visit to the hospital. "He doesn't even know. Certainly doesn't care."

"I'm not talking about proving it to your father. I'm talking about proving it to yourself. You drop enough acid into the pool, eventually you're going to poison the water."

Fliss stared at her, the blood thrumming in her ears. "What do you mean?"

"Those things your father used to say to you—

some of them stayed, didn't they? Like an infection that wouldn't heal. Those words sank in, and you've been trying to prove him wrong ever since. You might want to think about that. And you might want to stop listening to that voice in your head that tells you you're not good enough, that Seth deserves better because he couldn't get better than you, that's a fact. Start looking at the person you are, not the person your father made you think you might be."

Fliss swallowed.

Was her grandmother right? Was that how she looked at herself?

For years she'd told herself that every choice she made, every decision and path she followed, had been driven by a desire to convince her father he was wrong about her.

The truth was, she'd been trying to convince herself.

SETH HAD A quieter day than he'd expected. He could have stayed at home and answered calls from there, but he opted to catch up with paperwork in the clinic. He had one urgent call to deal with a cat who had been hit by the wheel of a bicycle, and another to deal with a dog who had swallowed a child's button. Other than that, it was remarkably calm.

Tanya, his partner, arrived early. "You're spending too long in this place."

"You're here, too."

"That's different. My kids are grown." She removed the stethoscope from his neck. "Go, Dr. Carlyle. Party, party, party."

"If you need me—"

"I'll call. Relax, Dr. Carlyle. Have fun."

Seth drove home, showered and changed, and then picked Fliss up from her grandmother's house.

She slid into the passenger seat, and her short skirt slid up her thighs, revealing long legs brushed gold by long summer days. She was a thousand times more relaxed than the person he'd met on the road that first day.

They drove to Chase and Matilda's and walked together across the grass toward the back of the house that overlooked the dunes.

Seth caught a glimpse of the ocean, an empty stretch of golden sand, heard the crash of the waves and the sound of laughter and decided he was lucky.

A job he loved, good friends and a life by the water. What more could a man want?

Fliss, he thought. That was what he wanted.

Chase, for all his wealth and success, was the same. It was one of the reasons they'd been friends for so long.

He strolled across the grass watching as Fliss took baby Rose from a tired-looking Matilda.

"There was a time when disturbed nights used to mean something more exciting." Chase handed him a beer. "My mother tells me we should leave her to cry, but I've never been good at hearing a woman cry. A few more broken nights and I'll be the one crying."

Seth grinned. "A couple of weeks old and she's already wrapped you around her little finger."

"Sounds about right." Chase gestured. "I assumed you'd prefer the beer over the frozen margarita."

"You presumed correctly."

"Chase!" Matilda called to him across the gardens, and Chase removed Seth's empty beer bottle from his hand.

"I'm needed. Eva is doing all the salads and desserts, but I'm in charge of the grill." He strode across to Matilda, and Seth noticed Fliss standing on the deck, a glass in her hand. She was laughing at something Matilda had said. Looking at her, it was hard to believe she was a city person. She certainly didn't seem to miss it.

Over the past few weeks the one thing they hadn't talked about were her plans for returning to Manhattan.

He hoped that her love of the ocean would persuade her to stay. Even better, her love for him.

He was surprised to see that she was still wearing her shoes, although they weren't shoes exactly. Jeweled flip-flops that showed off her lightly tanned skin and polished nails. He was willing to bet money that as soon as the guests relaxed a little more those flip-flops would be lying abandoned and she'd be standing in bare feet.

"Seth!" She waved and beckoned him over. "Have you met Eva? She runs Urban Genie, a concierge company in Manhattan with Paige and Frankie. They're over there, by the gazebo. Half our clients have been referred by them."

Seth exchanged words with Eva, while thinking only of Fliss.

He wanted to ask what her plans were. Whether she'd thought about going back.

Later, when they'd all gorged on grilled shrimp, steaks and corn dripping with melted butter, Matilda disappeared to try to get Rose to sleep.

The sun was already dipping down behind the horizon, fiery red, and the evening had a mellow vibe.

Seth helped Chase clean up and then snagged two bottles of beer and went to find Fliss.

There was no sign of her, but he saw her flip-flops

abandoned by the edge of the dunes and followed the footprints to the beach. Small footprints. Delicate. His own footprint would have covered it twice.

Small, yes. And delicate. But also fierce. And he was glad about that. It was hard to handle what life threw without at least a touch of fierce in the armory.

He saw her sitting on the sand, just far enough away from the ocean to keep those pretty toes dry.

Fireworks exploded in the distance, lighting up the night sky.

He sat down next to her, looped his arm around her shoulders and they watched them together.

As the last shower of stars cascaded down to the water, he pulled her in and took her mouth.

"What was that?" She sounded breathless.

"It's Fourth of July. I'm allowed to kiss you on Fourth of July."

"Trying to create a different type of fireworks?"

"Maybe."

"Did you call your family?"

"Yes. I spoke to my mother. They seem to be enjoying Vermont."

"It's a pity you were working and couldn't join them. Bad luck that you had to work."

He sat for a moment, watching as the last of the fireworks died, leaving a velvet-black sky studded with stars. "It wasn't bad luck. I didn't have to work, I asked to."

She turned her head. "You didn't want to have a family gathering?"

"I've promised myself I will spend Thanksgiving with them, but right now—no, I didn't want to have a gathering on Fourth of July without my father there.

And I didn't want to hurt their feelings by telling them that, so I arranged to work. That probably makes me selfish."

"I think it makes you human." She leaned her head on his shoulder. "And both your sisters are there, so it's not as if your mom is alone. You don't have to feel guilty for thinking about your own needs, or coping with it the way that feels right to you."

She never judged. He'd never felt he had to live up to some perfect, unreal image she had of him.

"The next job is to clear the house of Dad's personal items. The furniture can stay until it's sold but all the other things—books, papers, sailing things—sorting through those won't be fun."

"We'll do it together."

Together.

He wanted to ask how long she was planning to stay. Whether they had a future.

He waited, silent, hoping, but she said nothing. Just stared ahead, deep in thought.

"I love it here."

"Me, too."

What exactly did she love? Was it the beach? Or him? Him and the beach?

"Could you live here?"

She stilled. "Maybe."

If he told her how he felt would she run or would she tell him she felt the same way?

He wasn't willing to take the chance that it might be the former.

He'd waited so long to hear her say the words he wanted her to say, he decided he could wait a little longer.

CHAPTER TWENTY

Fliss worked her way through the Carlyle mansion, room by room, packing personal items carefully into boxes. Occasionally she broke off from what she was doing to check on Seth, who was clearing a different room.

She knew how hard this was for him and she wanted him to know that she understood.

She'd felt the shift in their relationship. Sharing thoughts and feelings had created an intimacy that hadn't been there the first time. Everything was deeper and more intense.

"Do you want this?" She held up a vase that she privately thought was ugly and was relieved when Seth shook his head.

"It's hideous. Put it in the Goodwill box." He peered at it more closely. "On second thought, I think it might be something Bryony made at school. Put it in the box for my mother to check in case she wants to keep it."

She thought again about how difficult this must be for him, clearing through his family history, deciding what to keep and what to give away.

But love wasn't an object. Love was a feeling, and these days she knew all about feelings.

She picked up another book, and a photo slipped out of the pages and fell to the floor.

Bending to retrieve it, she saw that it was a photo of her and Seth on their wedding day.

Her hand shook as she held it. She remembered the baking sun and the sheer craziness of it all. Her smile was so big it was a wonder it even fit in the frame, and Seth was laughing and so damn handsome she remembered people nearby turning to stare at him.

She remembered feeling as if she was walking on air, the reality of their circumstances cushioned by an almost unbearable excitement for the future.

Most of all she remembered feeling hope, and when she'd lost the baby she'd also lost that hope.

She'd never thought she'd get a second chance.

Or maybe the truth was that she hadn't thought she deserved one.

She stared at the photo and saw the love she'd felt clearly visible in her expression.

She'd loved Seth then and she loved him now. Maybe she'd never stopped loving him. She didn't know, and it no longer seemed to matter.

Emotion rippled through her. She didn't entirely recognize it. Excitement? Terror?

"Fliss?"

She hadn't even realized he was standing in the doorway. "Seth—"

"Are you all right?" He glanced at the photo in her hand and smiled. "Where did you find that?"

"Inside one of your father's books." She wasn't ready to talk to him yet. She hadn't got used to the way she was feeling.

"That explains why I couldn't find it all those years ago when I was looking. Don't lose that. I love that photo."

"I love it, too." Her mouth was so dry she could hardly speak. She would have liked a bit more time to work out the best way to say what she needed to say, but maybe it was best like this. "Seth, there's something I need to—" She broke off as Seth's phone rang. She wasn't sure whether she felt frustration or relief. "You should get that."

He answered it, and she saw his expression change as he listened. "I'll be there right away." He ended the call. "The Christies' dog was kicked by a deer."

Fliss winced. "Deer hooves are sharp. Go."

He reached for his keys. "What was it you wanted to say?"

"It can wait." And waiting would mean she had more time to think it through. "I hope the Christies' dog is all right. I'll be here when you're done."

It gave her time to plan. To make it romantic.

She didn't want to blurt out those words while surrounded by dusty books and reminders of his father.

She'd tell him that later when it was just the two of them. She'd buy a bottle of champagne and put it in the fridge.

They could take it down to the beach.

As the door closed behind him, she turned her attention back to the books, stacking them carefully in boxes and labeling them.

Her heart felt lighter than it had in a while.

She was in love. And this time she wasn't afraid to tell him.

In fact she couldn't wait to tell him.

She straightened, rubbed her aching back and walked down to the kitchen for a glass of water.

She drank a glass straight down without pausing and still had the empty glass in her hand when the phone rang.

It was the landline.

She frowned. Should she answer it?

Yes. It might be important. It might be someone trying to get hold of Seth.

She picked it up and heard a woman say, "Hello?"

She recognized the voice instantly, and part of her was tempted to hang up. Another part of her knew this was an encounter she had to handle at some point.

"Hi, Vanessa," she croaked. "It's Fliss."

There was a pause. "Fliss. It's been a while."

"I'm helping Seth pack up some of the things in the house. He's not here. He's performing surgery on a dog that was kicked by a deer."

"Oh—well, I've been wanting to talk to you for a while."

Fliss sat down hard on the nearest kitchen chair. "You have?"

This was going to be bad.

Really bad.

"I owe you an apology."

"Excuse me?" Fliss assumed she'd misheard. "I didn't catch that."

"Apology. Last time—that phone call I made. All of it." Vanessa's voice sounded strange, slightly thickened. "I wasn't—friendly."

That, Fliss thought, was an understatement. "You didn't like me."

"That's not true. Seth is my brother. It's true that sometimes we fight and annoy the hell out of each other, but I care about him. I love him. And after you walked away from him last time—"

Fliss's mouth was so dry she could hardly form the word. "What?"

"I was worried about him, that's all. It took him a long time to get over you, Fliss. He was not in a good way. You *hurt* him."

Fliss felt an ache behind her ribs. "I didn't mean to."

"I believe you, but he was hurt. I think the fact that he couldn't talk it through with you drove him crazy. He didn't know how to handle it, so he threw himself into work. You're probably the reason he graduated top of his class. It was two years before he even went on another date."

Fliss felt a stab of shock. "Two years?"

"Yes. And then he moved to California. As far away from everything and everyone he knew. He said it was a fresh start, but I think he just couldn't bear to spend time in the places you'd been together."

Fliss stared ahead of her.

He hadn't dated anyone for two *years*?

He'd moved to California because of her?

She'd had no idea she was the reason. He hadn't told her that.

He'd told her that he was hurt, too, but he hadn't mentioned the extent of it and she hadn't ever given much thought to the detail. Because she'd been so sure he was marrying her only because of the baby, she'd assumed that it wouldn't take him long to get over her.

"Are you sure?" Her voice sounded croaky. "He didn't date for two years?"

"It might have even been longer. Bryony and I wheeled every single female we knew past his nose, but he wasn't interested. To begin with I think he simply didn't notice them because his head was still full of you, and then I think he was wary of getting involved again."

Fliss felt as if she'd been plunged into ice water.

He'd stopped going out. He'd moved to the other side of the country because of her.

She'd broken his heart.

"But then he met Naomi. So he was fine in the end."

"Not really. They got along just fine and she was crazy about him. I assumed he was still wary about handing over his heart after what happened with you. It did seem as if it might happen. I thought they might have a chance, but then Dad died and everything fell apart."

"He and Seth were close."

"I know, and it was after that Seth changed. He broke it off with Naomi and moved back east. He took that temporary post in Manhattan so that he could see you."

"Not *just* for that reason."

"Yes, for that reason. Think about it, Fliss. Seth is not a city person. He did it so he could see you again, and he wanted to see you because he has never stopped thinking about you. I think, after my father died, he needed to reach out and find out if there was anything between you still. The fact that you're in the house now tells me there is. And that scares the hell out of me. *Not* because I don't like you. Honestly? I admire you a lot and I'm sure that in different circumstances we'd be friends, but I'm *worried*." She paused. "I know you grew up with trouble at home."

Fliss tensed. "Vanessa—"

"No, please let me finish. I can't find an easy way to say this, so I'm just going to say it and hope you'll forgive me for being direct. I know you don't talk to people easily. I understand that, I really do. But Seth is the type of person who *needs* that. He is the most straightforward guy I know. He doesn't play games. Last time he had no idea how you were feeling, and it drove him insane. He was so hurt that you wouldn't talk to him. And I'm worried that it might be all great now, but that if there's a problem in the future and you walk away, I don't know how he would get through that a second time. I don't want to watch him go through that again."

Fliss swallowed.

Seth was putting all his faith in her, and she wasn't good at this, was she?

They'd messed up before. What was to stop them messing up again?

What if she couldn't be what he wanted her to be?

What if, when things got tough, she couldn't open up enough for him?

What if she *hurt* him?

Doubt eroded the certainty that had been there only moments before.

"Fliss? Are you still there?"

"I'm here."

Ninety/ten. Fliss stared straight ahead. She'd been doing okay, hadn't she?

But she hadn't really thought about the stakes. About what would happen if this went wrong.

"You're probably wondering why this is any of my business, but he's my brother. I've seen you defend Harriet, so I think, hope, that maybe you understand why I would do the same for Seth."

"I do understand."

If anyone hurt Harriet the way it seemed she'd hurt Seth, she'd break them in half.

"Are you angry with me?"

Fliss stirred and stood up. "No. You love him. You're protecting him. And you're right, I'd do the same in your position."

"All I ever wanted was to see him happy. Seth is like my dad. He wants a home and family. He wants to settle down with someone he loves. For him, that's you. If you don't feel the same way, if you can't give him what he needs, then you need to tell him. And you need to tell him soon."

Fliss hung up the phone and wandered like a sleepwalker back to the library. The thought that she'd hurt him so badly once before left her feeling as if she'd been flayed raw.

The happiness she'd felt had gone. All that was left was a kind of sick panic. Doubt slid into every corner of her mind. That inner voice that she'd worked so hard to silence was suddenly shouting so loudly she could hear nothing else.

What if she couldn't be what he needed her to be?

She sank to the floor among the jumble of boxes that were part of Seth's past. He was clearing it out, getting ready to step into the future.

He wanted her to be part of that future.

SETH WALKED BACK into the house and dropped his car keys on the counter.

"Fliss?"

There was no answer. Had she left? After ten back-breaking hours of clearing out and hauling boxes, he wouldn't have blamed her.

Hearing a noise from the library, he followed the sound,

and saw Fliss stacking books. Something about the stiff set of her shoulders didn't seem quite right to him.

"Fliss?"

She paused for a moment and then turned. There was a smudge on her cheek and she looked exhausted.

"Hi. How was the surgery? Is the dog okay?"

"The dog is fine. You, on the other hand, don't look fine. You need to stop now. You're tired." But something told him the look on her face had little to do with packing boxes.

She closed the box she was filling and wiped her palms on her shorts. "You're right. I should probably go. I need a shower."

"While you're doing that, I'll make you dinner."

"Not tonight. I was thinking of going back to my grandmother's."

She'd been fine when he'd left. Smiling, laughing, distracting him as she'd dived elbow deep into boxes of books.

Was this because she was tired, or had something happened?

He picked up the boxes she'd packed and piled them in the hallway.

"What's wrong?" He stacked one box on top of another in the hallway, sifting through the possibilities in his mind. It couldn't possibly be anything to do with him. "Is Harriet okay?"

"She's fine." She hauled another box out of the library, not looking at him.

"Fliss—"

"Actually she's not okay." She straightened and turned to face him. "She needs me. I'm going back to Manhattan tomorrow."

"What's wrong with her?"

"She isn't coping. It was unfair of me to think she'd be able to manage the business without me there."

It took a moment for his brain to compute what she was saying. "Wait. You're talking about going back permanently?"

"That's right."

He was stunned. Whatever he'd expected, it hadn't been that. "But yesterday you were saying how much you loved it. How you could live here."

"Blame it on sun and sangria."

"We weren't drinking sangria."

"It was a figure of speech." She pushed her hair away from her face, leaving another dusty streak on her skin. "I hadn't thought it through."

She was leaving?

He was still trying to work out what she wasn't telling him when she brushed past him, her keys in her hand.

"Wait." He followed her and put his palm against the door to stop her leaving. "What aren't you telling me? What's wrong?"

"I'm fine."

"You're doing it again. Shutting me out. You're imagining yourself as the castle and you're pulling up the drawbridge, but you don't have to do that with me. You *never* have to do that with me. I'm not a threat to you." Unless… And suddenly he knew what was going on and he wondered how it had taken him so long to see it when he knew her so well. "You're afraid."

"Why would I be afraid? There's nothing to be afraid of."

"Isn't there?" He stepped closer. "How about the fact

that you love me? That's a pretty scary reason right there."

Her eyes flew wide. "I never said—"

"No, you never said." And he'd waited, and waited, to hear those words. Waited for her to open up and share her feelings with him, and tried not to mind when she hadn't. "The fact that you haven't found the courage to say the words doesn't mean you're not feeling them. You love me. At some point over the past few weeks you've realized that, and now you're afraid and looking for a way of protecting yourself. That's why you're rushing back to Manhattan."

"That's not true."

"Isn't it?" It seemed pretty clear to him. "I've been waiting to hear you tell me how you feel about me, but you haven't. And if you'd talked about that, told me how scared you were, we could have dealt with it. But you're not sharing anything with me. I love you. I really love you, but if you won't share your feelings, if you constantly throw a smoke screen over what's going on inside, like you are now, we're not going to make it. We're never going to make it, Fliss."

He waited for her to say something, to tell him how she felt, but she said nothing and in the end her silence was more painful than words would have been.

He thought about the last few weeks, the summer they'd spent. She'd started talking. Opening up. He knew he was in love with her and he'd been sure she was in love with him. But now, when her back was literally against the wall, she'd reverted to her default setting of keeping everything to herself.

So sure, he tried one more time to reach her. "I know you're scared—"

"I'm not scared."

Exasperation gave way to bone weariness. What more did he have to do to prove to her she could trust him? What else was there for him to do? Nothing. The rest had to be up to her. And she couldn't do it. It seemed he'd been wrong about that. "So that's it, then."

There was an agonizing pause. "I guess so."

He wanted to argue. He wanted to hold her there until she told him the truth, but he knew in his heart, his aching, fractured heart, that if she wouldn't trust him with her feelings, her fears and her heart, then they had nothing.

"Be careful driving. The roads are busy."

"I will." There was another painful pause. "We had a fun summer."

A fun summer?

He hadn't intended to say anything else, but he couldn't help it. "We both know it was more than a fun summer, but you'll pretend it didn't mean anything, because that's the way you choose to handle difficult things." Frustration pricked holes in his patience. "You won't share the fact that you're hurting deep inside, and I know you are hurting. This relationship isn't over because I don't love you, or because you don't love me. It's over because you won't share your fears with me. You won't let yourself be vulnerable. And no matter how much we love each other, if you won't talk to me then this is not going to work. And I can't put myself through this again. I won't." He moved his hand from the door and opened it for her, the ache in his chest almost too much to bear. "Goodbye, Fliss."

CHAPTER TWENTY-ONE

FEELING LIKE ROADKILL, Fliss let herself into the house. She'd checked her mirror and knew she looked like hell on the outside. The inside felt even worse. She felt as if she was torn and bleeding, her heart and her hopes ripped into shreds. Given that she seemed to have lost the ability to hide her feelings, she was hoping her grandmother might be having a nap. Or maybe even have ventured into town with one of her friends.

That hope was dashed when the kitchen door opened.

Fliss braced herself, but to her surprise it wasn't her grandmother who stood there. It was her sister.

"Harriet?" *No!* She couldn't do this. Not right now. Could today get any worse? She forced herself to smile, trying to remember everything she'd once known about hiding. "I wasn't expecting you."

"Spontaneous visit." Her sister scanned her face. "What's wrong?"

"Nothing is wrong. I'm fine. Now tell me why you're here."

"I was worried about you."

"Me? I've never been better. Why didn't you just text me or call? I could have saved you a journey." And maybe spared herself the exhaustion of putting on an act. She couldn't do this now. She had no reserves left.

"Chase gave me a ride in the helicopter."

"So you've joined the jet set." Fliss dropped her purse, conscious of her filthy appearance. She'd been hoping to lock herself in the bathroom and let tears flow in the shower, but it seemed that indulgence would need to be postponed until later. "Where's Grams?"

Maybe her grandmother could occupy Harriet while she vanished to the bathroom and pulled herself together.

All she needed was a few minutes. A few minutes to remind herself how to pull up that drawbridge.

"She's upstairs. What have you been doing? You're covered in dust."

"I've been helping Seth clear out his parents' house." She walked into the kitchen and made herself a coffee, hoping the caffeine would restore her energy levels. "Now tell me why you're really here. I know you. You don't fly from Manhattan without good reason. Love the shirt by the way. You look great in green."

"I'm worried." Harriet looked at her steadily. "You're seeing Seth again."

Fliss sat down. "We're friends, that's all." And probably not even that. It felt as if she'd been kicked in the chest.

"But Grams said—"

"You know Grams. She's a romantic. She wants a happy ending."

Harriet stared at her. "What aren't you telling me?"

"Nothing. I'm telling you everything. Ninety/ten, that's me."

"Excuse me?"

"Nothing." Fliss stood up, almost knocking over the chair. "I ought to go and shower."

"Fliss—" Harriet reached out a hand, and Fliss

brushed her away. She was so close to the edge that she knew that if her sister as much as touched her, she'd fall.

"I'm filthy. Need to wash off this dust."

"You're upset—"

"Truly I'm not." And then she noticed the box, open on the counter. "I see Grams told you about Mom. A bit of a shock to the system. I always thought she was the one who loved Dad. Not the other way around. Poor Mom." And poor her. What was she supposed to do with all these feelings? Put them in a box and shove them under the bed as her mother had done? If only it were that easy. "I'm surprised she kept a secret that big."

Harriet held her gaze. "Why would you be surprised? Keeping secrets is a family trait."

"What do you mean by that?"

"You keep things from me."

"That's not true." Her heart was pounding. She rarely fought with her sister. Even as a child, they'd fought only when no one else was attacking.

"You're hiding things from me now. I came here because I was really worried about you getting involved with Seth again. I thought you might need someone to talk to."

"Nothing to talk about." There it was. The ability to hide it. She was starting to remember how it was done. Deny. Conceal. Smile. Rinse and repeat. She could do this.

Harriet leaned forward. "Something has happened! Why won't you *talk* to me? Why won't you tell me?"

Because not in a million years did she want Harriet to know how bad she was feeling.

"Nothing happened."

"Right." Harriet thumped her mug down on the table

and stood up. "Go take that shower. I'm going for a walk."

"What? Why? No!" Fliss stood up, too. What the hell had just happened? "Don't walk out. What is wrong? You're not behaving like yourself."

Harriet fumbled with the back door. "And you are behaving *exactly* like yourself."

"Excuse me?"

Her sister turned, her eyes brimming with hurt. "Do you know why I came here? I came because I was worried. Ten years ago you were so badly hurt I was actually scared. Yes, that's right. I was *scared*, Fliss." Her voice shook. "I thought you were going to snap. Break."

"I was—"

"Do *not* tell me you were fine, because we both know that's not true. You were hurt, but you didn't talk to me and I accepted that because I know that's the way you prefer to deal with things—" She drew in a shaky breath. "But then a few months ago when Daniel told us Seth was back in Manhattan, I know what that did to you. You didn't sleep. You didn't eat properly. You pretended you didn't care, because that's what you do, but you cared. Knowing that you might bump into him at any moment pushed you right to the edge again. And the worst part of all that? Knowing that you still don't turn to me. Even now, when something has obviously happened, you won't turn to me. Once, just once in your life, why can't you admit how you're feeling?"

She'd been doing that. And where had it got her? "You don't need to worry about me, Harry."

"But I do." Harriet's voice cracked. "Do you think I don't know when you hurt? Just because you don't trust me enough to talk about it doesn't mean I don't know."

"I trust you." Her mouth felt dry. Her hands were shaky. "There's no one I trust more in the world."

"Then why don't you share what's going on inside you?"

"Because I don't need to."

"Oh, for—" Harriet bit her lip, turned on her heel and left the room, leaving Fliss staring after her.

"Wait! What the— I try and protect you—" But she was talking to herself.

"Maybe she doesn't always want to be protected," her grandmother said from the doorway. "Maybe, sometimes, she'd like to be the one doing the protecting. That's what sisters do, isn't it? That's what you told me."

Fliss felt her throat thicken. "I don't want her to worry. I don't want her to be hurt. Is that so wrong?"

"A person can't get through life without being hurt. Hurting is part of being human. Feeling pain is part of being human. We learn to cope with it, just as Seth is doing. What makes it bearable is having people around us who care. Who love."

"I care about Harriet. I love her!"

"And she cares about you and loves you. But do you ever let her do that?"

Fliss swallowed. "I try to be strong."

"Maybe, instead of being strong, she wants you to let her in."

You hide ninety percent and show ten.

It wasn't the same thing, she thought. With Seth it had been all about protecting herself. With Harriet, it was all about protecting her sister.

Everyone, it seemed, wanted her to spill her feelings. Her grandmother poured coffee into a mug and handed it to her. "Take a shower. Wash your face. You look terrible."

"I feel terrible. I've messed everything up. I've upset Harriet and I've lost Seth." The words tumbled out, and the next thing she knew she was being hugged by her grandmother. "I was hoping to talk to you about it, but I walked through the door and Harriet was here. And I tried to pretend everything was fine—"

"You can talk to me," her grandmother soothed, "but I think it would be even better if you talked to your sister."

"She doesn't want to talk to me." But Fliss knew she had to try.

Her head throbbed, but she took the shower her grandmother had suggested, changed into clean shorts and walked down to the beach.

Harriet was sitting on the dunes, Charlie next to her.

For the first time ever Fliss felt nervous around her sister.

"Harry?"

Harriet turned her head, and Fliss saw that her eyes were red from crying.

"I'm sorry." Harriet pulled Charlie closer. "I didn't mean to walk out, but you make me crazy sometimes. You think I'm so weak and pathetic I'll break at the slightest pressure."

"That's not what I think!" Fliss sank down onto the sand next to her, the long grass tickling her calves. "I love you and don't want you to be hurt. I can't bear it when you're hurt. I want to protect you from that."

"And how do you think that makes me feel? Let me tell you it's bad seeing your twin, your sister, the person you are closest to in the world, suffer. But what's worse is knowing that you won't share it with me."

Fliss's eyes filled. "I didn't want you to feel bad."

"So instead I was left to imagine how you must be feeling, which is worse. I'm not fragile, Fliss. I lived through the same childhood you did. And I know you protected me, so did Daniel, and I'm grateful for that, but the one thing I don't need protecting from is your emotions. That's totally different. And I know you're also protecting yourself, but it doesn't feel great to know you don't trust me to be careful with your feelings. I'm hurt, Fliss, because even though we're sisters, twins, you still don't trust me enough to let me see you at your most vulnerable."

Fliss saw the tears in her sister's eyes and felt her own throat close. It was bad enough that she'd screwed up her relationship with Seth, but now she'd upset Harriet. She'd made her sister cry. Her sister, whom she'd always tried to protect from hurt.

It was the final straw.

"I'm sorry. I never thought I was hurting you by not telling you how I felt. I thought I was doing the right thing. And I trust you. I do trust you, but—" She choked on the words. "I hurt. I hurt so badly, Harry." She felt her sister's arms come around her and then she hugged her tightly, holding her while she sobbed and gave Harriet a hiccuping account of everything that had happened. She let it all spill out, telling her things she'd never told her. About Seth. About the baby.

Finally she sniffed and eased away. "I bet you're wishing you'd never asked me to tell you what was wrong." She wiped her cheeks with the back of her hand.

"I don't wish that. Do I hate seeing you in pain? Yes.

But I don't want you to be in pain on your own. You're my sister. You've always looked out for me."

Fliss sniffed. "I'm older than you."

"By three minutes."

"Those three minutes came with responsibility. I feel like I'm never going to be able to smile again. These last few weeks—" She leaned her head on her sister's shoulder. "It was magical. Magical. And I messed everything up. I love him so much and it terrifies me."

They sat shoulder to shoulder, looking out across the ocean.

"Vanessa shouldn't have called you."

"I would have done the same. Everything she said was true." Fliss scrubbed her cheek with her hand. "She loves her brother. I respect that."

"Does he know you love him?"

"I never actually told him, but he knows. He said that if I was going to shut down when things got tough then it would never work, no matter how much we love each other."

"And he's probably right about that," Harriet said.

Fliss winced. "You're the romantic one. You're supposed to tell me that it's all going to be fine and that we're going to live happily ever after. You're supposed to believe that."

"I do believe that, but I think you have to want it to happen. And make it happen. I never said it was easy."

Fliss sniffed. "Isn't he supposed to ride up here on his charger and sweep me into the sunset?"

"You'd get sand in your eyes. And you'd probably argue about who was going to sit in front, and the horse would get bored and stomp on you."

"So what are you saying? I should ride over to him on my charger?"

"I think what I'm saying is that it's time to make a decision. How much is love worth to you? What price are you prepared to pay?" Harriet stretched out her legs. "Plenty of people go through life and never find what you have. Mom. Me. You *have* found it."

"And I've ruined it."

"No." Harriet scrambled to her feet. "You need to stop feeling sorry for yourself and get over there and tell him how you feel. You've never actually said those words to him. Say them! You need to find out if this can work."

"He already told me it wasn't going to work."

"Because he was hurting. He saw you scurrying back into your fortress. I know it's scary, but you're brave, Fliss. I've seen you stand up to people twice the size of you. Look at how you were with Dad! You're brave when it comes to defending other people, so for once in your life go and be brave for yourself."

"Whatever happened to sympathy?"

"That comes later, when you've tried and failed. But first you need to try. What you have is too rare and special to let it go without a fight."

"You're right, I'm afraid." Fliss sucked in a breath. "I'm afraid to tell him how I really feel. I'm finding it hard to change the habit of a lifetime. I don't think I'm very brave at all."

"You're the bravest person I know." Harriet reached down and pulled her to her feet. "And it's natural to want to protect yourself. You probably always will. But don't do it from me. And don't do it from Seth. Go and talk to him."

"It feels like walking a high wire with no safety net."

"I'm your safety net," Harriet said, wrapping her in her arms. "I'll catch you if you fall."

SETH WAS SANDING paint in one of the bedrooms when he heard someone at the door. Even vigorous activity hadn't improved his mood.

He dropped everything and pulled open the door.

She stood there, looking more demure than usual in a flowered sundress.

"Fliss—"

"No. I'm Harriet, so don't kiss me or do anything that is going to embarrass both of us." She stepped inside without waiting for an invitation, which made him wonder if it really was Harriet or if this was Fliss playing another game.

Harriet wouldn't just march into his house uninvited, would she? And then he took a closer look at her face and realized it really was Harriet.

"What's happened? Is Fliss all right?"

"Well, it's hard to know, isn't it? This is Fliss we're talking about. She doesn't exactly wear her feelings emblazoned on a T-shirt. I'm sure it would help us both if she did. I'm here because I assume you still care about her."

"What's that supposed to mean? Of course I care."

"If you care, why did you push her away?"

"Because she keeps her feelings in solitary confinement, under lock and key, and even I don't have access."

"So she got scared," Harriet said slowly, "but before that phone call she opened up to you, didn't she? She opened up in a way she never has in her life before with anyone. And that includes me. Do you have any idea how hard that was for her? Do you *know* how long I've been trying to persuade her to talk to me? It feels like most of my life. And finally, *finally*, she does it and it ends like this."

He felt as if he'd been doused in ice water. "What phone call? I don't know anything about a phone call."

Harriet stared at him. "Never mind. It doesn't matter now. What matters is that this summer you persuaded her to drop her guard. And then when she had a little wobble, and was feeling at her most vulnerable, instead of being patient and encouraging her, you hurt her."

He frowned. "I didn't—"

"I haven't finished." Harriet stepped forward, eyes sparking, and he wondered how he ever could have thought she was even-tempered and mild.

He might have been looking at Fliss.

"It's uncanny—"

"What is?"

"Never mind. You were in the middle of explaining to me all the ways in which I've messed up."

"That's right. She opened up, and the result was that she got hurt. And instead of understanding that, instead of seeing that she'd fallen and needed time to pick herself up, you pushed her down again. You showed her that you couldn't be trusted to be there for her, which is going to teach her never to open up again. And I am scared, really scared, of what that means for her future. If you can't reach her, no one ever will."

"Tell me who made the phone call."

"Vanessa. But before you get all flinty-eyed, it was a good phone call."

Harriet planted herself in front of him and Seth realized how much she'd changed.

They'd all changed, him included.

"I should have known something had happened. And you're right, I shouldn't have pushed her away. I was wrong, but then it seems I was wrong about a lot of things, including you. I didn't know you had a steely side."

"Well, now you know, and given neither of us knows how deep it runs or just how far I'd be prepared to go to defend my sister, you'd better not hurt her."

He gave a faint smile. "From now on I'll be sleeping with the doors locked."

"Hurt my sister, and that's probably a good idea."

IT HAD TAKEN her two hours of walking on the beach to pluck up the courage she needed to drive to Seth's. Two hours of going over it in her mind and in her heart and measuring risk.

And it was a risk.

When she finally arrived back at the beach house, Harriet was in the kitchen cooking with their grandmother.

Both of them glanced up.

Fliss looked at her sister. "Are you all right? You're flushed. As if you've been rushing around."

"The heat of the oven." Harriet brushed flour from her fingers. "How was your walk?"

"Good. It helped me think. I—" She wrapped her arms around herself, trying to pull together the last strands of her courage. "I need to go out for a while."

"No problem." Calm, Harriet carefully arranged sliced apple in a dish and added cinnamon and brown sugar. It was only once she heard the front door close that she sank onto the nearest chair and looked at her grandmother. "What if I made a mistake?"

"You did the right thing, honey. And it was brave. I can't believe you drove over there and confronted him."

"I can't believe it either. I shook the whole time."

"No stammer?"

"No stammer. And it felt good. Protecting her for once felt good. Now we just have to see if she can stop protecting herself long enough to tell him how she feels."

It took Fliss ten minutes to drive to Seth's house, and all the way she had to stop herself turning around.

What if he didn't answer the door? Or, worse, what if he answered the door but didn't want to talk to her? He'd told her it was over and they had no future.

What if he'd meant it?

She hammered on the door before she could change her mind, hoping he hadn't gone for a walk because she wasn't sure she could put herself through this a second time.

He opened the door and the sight of him, so damn handsome in dark jeans and an open-necked shirt, glued the words to her mouth. They were in there somewhere, but she just couldn't get them out.

Dammit, why couldn't he have had paint in his hair or dust on his jeans? But she knew it wouldn't have made a difference because it wasn't the outside of the man she loved, it was the inside.

"I came to say some things."

He opened the door wider. "Good, because there are some things I'd like to say, too."

"I need to go first." She paced into his kitchen and turned, keeping the island between them. "When I first heard you were in Manhattan, I was terrified. I dreaded bumping into you. I thought, I really believed, that I ruined your life. No—" she saw him open his mouth and lifted her hand "—let me finish. Let me speak. If I don't do it now, I might not be able to do it. I'm telling you how it was, that's all. I felt guilty, and I carried that around with me, and I carried around the thoughts about what might have happened if we hadn't lost our baby. Back then, I couldn't tell you how I felt. I felt so bad, there was no way I was sharing that with anyone. And I was still living at home, under my father's scrutiny, and that wasn't a good place to be. I had no idea how to open up to anyone. Not even you, or maybe I should say especially you because I knew that you could hurt me more than anyone. I didn't see you, or hear from you, in ten years and then suddenly there you were."

"Slow down. You're talking too fast."

"This is the only way I know to get it out there. I had no idea how to handle the fact you were in Manhattan, so I did the cowardly thing, took the easy way out, and came here. And then you were here, too. It threw me." She stooped and petted Lulu, needing the comfort. "And what threw me even more was how persistent you were, and then hearing how you'd really felt all those years ago. And I realized how much I'd lost by not talking to you. By not being honest."

Seth stirred. "I made mistakes, too. I should have thought about how you might be feeling, what you might be thinking, but even though I knew a little about your father, I used my own upbringing, and family, as a measure. In our family we talked and shared, even when it was loud and noisy. No one ever needed to hide. And I knew you found it hard to say how you were feeling, but I didn't know how hard. And I had no idea what was going on in your head. If I'd known—"

"Let's not do *if*s. Let's admit we made mistakes. And the important thing, and the reason I'm here—" she swallowed "—is that I don't want to make that mistake again. This time I want to spell it out, so we both know. So there is no mistake. You want the ninety percent— I'm giving you a hundred. I'm telling you exactly how I'm feeling so that there is no misunderstanding."

He paused. "So tell me."

"I feel like crap, Seth. We've spent an amazing summer, we've laughed and yes, you made me fall in love with you, dammit, or maybe I never fell out of love, I don't know—" She felt Lulu pull away from her and slink across the kitchen. She didn't blame the dog for wanting to get away from all the emotion. She did, too. She was confused, mixed up and dizzy with love, but her overriding emotion was terror. "I thought it was all going great, I exposed my heart to you—"

"You didn't. You didn't expose your heart. You protected it."

"I exposed my heart. Maybe I didn't say the words, but I showed you. You knew. You *saw*. And then when I was about to tell you, you were called out. And that was all fine. But then Vanessa called, and she told me how badly I'd hurt you—"

"She shouldn't—"

"No—" She raised her hand. "She was right to call me. She was protecting you, and I understand why she would do that. But up until that moment I hadn't really thought about how what happened affected you. I thought you married me because of the baby, so it didn't occur to me that you might be going through the same agony I was going through. And when Vanessa told me how it was, I felt terrible. So guilty. Just horrid that *I'd* done that to you. I had a little emotional crisis." She paced toward Lulu, who backed under the kitchen table, knowing danger when she saw it. "I knew I never, ever wanted to hurt you again, and right then I lost all confidence in my ability to be the person you need me to be."

"Fliss—"

"It wasn't opening up and telling you things that made me vulnerable, it was opening up and loving you. That was the part that scared me. I was a crab without a shell, an armadillo without the armor. And it scared me so much that for a while there I wasn't sure I could handle it. And I knew that if I couldn't handle it, then you were gong to get hurt. And I thought maybe you'd be better off with someone like Vanessa's friend Naomi."

There was a pause. A silence and then he breathed.

"Can I talk now?"

Part of her wanted to just leave, but she remembered what Harriet had said about hearing him out. About knowing. So she'd listen. And then she'd know. Then she'd walk away. Then she'd fall apart.

She could get through another half hour, if that's what it took, although she might have holes in her palms from the way she was digging her nails into her own flesh.

"First, I'm not interested in Naomi. It's true that over the years she spent a lot of time at our house, she's Vanessa's closest friend, and yes, she and I were together for a while. She's a good person. Not hard to like."

Fliss shot to her feet. "You see? She's perfect for you."

"Sit *down*."

"She sounds like a sweet woman."

"And when have you ever seen me eat dessert?"

She thought about it. "I guess she might drive you a little insane after a while. She probably wouldn't fight with you. And fighting keeps you young."

The corners of his mouth flickered. "When I lost my father, I realized I didn't want any more relationships where I didn't feel enough. Relationships that felt like a compromise. Settling." His gaze held hers. "The moment I worked that out, I ended it with Naomi. I was honest. I knew what I wanted. Who I wanted." His gaze locked on hers, and Fliss felt her knees turn liquid.

"Dammit. Keep going and you'll have me feeling sorry for her." She stooped and hugged Lulu again, holding her close, taking comfort from her warm body. "Vanessa said you were looking for the same relationship your parents had. That you'd never find it."

"I'd already found it." His voice was soft. "I found it years ago, but I was stupid enough to let it go. There's never been anyone but you, Fliss, and when my father died I knew, *I knew*, that I had to find you, and find out whether there was anything there. Life is too short and precious to fill a single moment of it with 'what if?' So I took the job in Manhattan."

"Why didn't you just bang on my door?"

"Because I knew that wouldn't work. I've had ten years to think about what happened. Ten years to focus on all the ways I screwed up."

"I was the one who—"

"We both screwed up. But we're not doing that again. So here's my hundred percent. I love you. You have to believe that I love you. You have to trust me on that one."

Her heart was so full she could hardly speak. "I do

believe you. I do trust you. I love you. One hundred percent, I love you. And I'm far more scared of losing you than I am of telling you that."

For the first time since she'd walked into his house, he smiled. "Then how about letting go of my dog and showing me?"

Fliss kept her arms round Lulu. "I love your dog."

"I love her, too. She will always be part of our family, but right now I'd rather she took a backseat. This isn't her moment."

"Our family?"

"Yes. That's what we are. It's what we're going to be."

Her head spinning, she gave Lulu a final kiss and stood up.

The next moment she was in his arms and Seth was kissing her.

"I've always loved you."

"It was sex—"

"And then it was love. So much love I didn't pause long enough to think about whether I was moving too quickly. Whether what we had was strong enough to stick. When I lost you, I didn't know how to live with the pain. You say you felt guilty, I felt even more guilty. I got you pregnant, we lost the baby. I was hurting. I knew you were hurting, too, but I didn't know how to reach you."

"If I'd been braver and shared more, maybe we wouldn't have broken up. But I really felt that without the baby there was nothing to hold us together."

"A baby isn't glue, Fliss. Plenty of couples have a baby thinking that will fix a rocky marriage, and then wonder why it never does. Invariably it makes things worse. Love is the glue. Love is what holds a relationship together through good times and bad."

"I've spent my whole life protecting myself, and I never thought about the other side of that. That by not letting people in I blocked love as well as hate." She eased away from him. "I had a fight with Harriet earlier. The first fight I can remember us having since we were kids. Actually it was less of a fight than her yelling at me. She gave me the full hundred percent. Told me how hurt she was that I wouldn't confide in her, that I protected her. I hardly recognized her, but she got me thinking and I realized she was right."

"Did she tell you she came here?"

"Harriet? *What?* No. When?"

"Earlier. She threatened me, and I can tell you your sister is scary when she's angry."

"Angry? You must have that wrong. Apart from the one fight we had earlier, Harriet is the kindest, gentlest person on the planet."

"That's what I thought and I'm sure that's true, except in certain circumstances."

"What circumstances?"

"When she thinks her sister is in trouble." He tightened his arms around her. "She stepped in front of you. She stepped, and she wasn't moving until she'd made me promise I wasn't going to make you cry. In the interest of full disclosure and the one hundred percent, I thought I should mention it. She probably doesn't want you to know she came, so don't tell her."

"And Vanessa probably doesn't want you to know she called, so don't bring that up either." She leaned her head against his chest. "I want to know what you're thinking. I want to know what's in your head. All of it."

"I love you. That's what's in my head. And in my heart." He stroked his fingers over her chin, and her eyes filled.

"I love you, too." Tears spilled onto her cheeks, and he brushed them away with his thumb.

"Don't cry. For pity's sake, don't cry. Harriet will kill me."

"These are happy tears."

"I don't want tears at all. I never want to see you cry, and I definitely don't want to make you cry."

"Not even when it's in a good way?"

"Never. I just want to see you happy. I'll move back to Manhattan if that's what you want."

"You'd do that for me? Even though you love it here?"

"I want to be with you. I'll do whatever works for you."

"What if it worked for me to stay here? To build up a business here. It's not as if it's far from Manhattan. I can hitch a ride on Chase's helicopter whenever I need to get back."

"Or Todd's."

She gasped. "He's buying the house?"

"Seems likely. He called earlier. He's bringing his family to see it this weekend. Wants us to join him for dinner."

"Well, look at us, mingling with the wealthy. I might have to change out of my shorts." She grinned up at him. "I could get used to living here, in your house by the water, with Lulu."

"Are you sure? But if you're going to stay here, what about Harriet?"

"She doesn't want me to protect her." Fliss let out a

breath. "I think that's going to be hard. Maybe it will be easier if I'm not breathing down her neck all the time."

"It wouldn't drive you crazy living here? The Poker Princesses will want to know every detail."

"I was thinking I could distribute a monthly newsletter, to save them the trouble of asking or listening to rumors. You could pin it to the bulletin board in your clinic. We could call it *Straight from the Horse's Mouth.*"

He laughed. "If you're going to be living here, you'll need to bake cookies."

"I'm an expert, although I'm not telling anyone how many batches were abandoned before I reached that lofty status."

He lowered his forehead to hers. "You'd be prepared to stay here? Live here? With me?"

"Always."

He lifted his head and glanced around him, a smile on his face.

"Before today it was a house, and now it feels like home."

"Because you've sold Ocean View. Because you've finally moved in properly."

"No." He shook his head. "Because you're here. You make it feel like home. I love you."

"I love you, too. I thought I was the wrong woman for you, but that's because for a very long time I saw the woman my father saw. Deep down I believed all the things he said about me. It was like looking into one of those mirrors that distorts everything. And that was partly the reason we never would have made it the first time around. Because I really did believe I wasn't good enough, that I was Bad Fliss, that I'd ruined your life."

"And now? Do you believe that now?"

She shook her head. "No. I spent most of my life proving to him that I wasn't that person, and somewhere along the way I proved it to myself, too. I just didn't realize it until recently."

"I want to marry you. Again. As soon as possible." The look he gave her did strange things to her insides.

She felt excitement and a sharp twist of desire, but most of all she felt love. "I want that, too."

"This time it's not going to be Vegas."

"I don't care where it is, as long as you're there." She kissed him, happiness overflowing in generous waves. "But please don't tell me you're thinking of the Plaza in June. Because I might have to hurt you."

"I was thinking beach wedding. Lobster bake. Dancing in the moonlight. Matilda will probably spill champagne, and you probably won't wear shoes. How does that sound?"

She wrapped her arms around his neck. "I think that sounds perfect."

* * * * *

THANK YOU

MY BIGGEST THANKS go to Flo Nicoll, my editor, for enduring my endless questions on life as a twin on a short flight to Berlin. She's probably thankful we weren't flying to Australia.

I'm grateful to my publishing teams in both the UK and the US who do so much to put my books into the hands of readers and to my agent, Susan Ginsburg at Writers House for the wise advice.

I'm grateful to all my wonderful readers, particularly those on Facebook who are always so willing to help with details like dog names. If not for them, all the dogs in my books would be called Rover.

Last but definitely not least, my family for enduring life with a writer with patience and humour.

*If you loved this book,
you won't want to miss the next!
Turn the page for a sneak peek of
MOONLIGHT OVER MANHATTAN,
the next magical book in Sarah Morgan's enchanting
FROM MANHATTAN WITH LOVE series!*

CHAPTER ONE

THIS WASN'T HOW a date was supposed to end.

If she'd known she was going to have to climb out of the window of the ladies' room, she wouldn't have chosen tonight to wear insanely high heels. Why hadn't she spent more time learning to balance before leaving her apartment?

She'd never been a high heel sort of person, which was *exactly* why she was now wearing a pair of skyscraper stilettos. Another thing ticked off the list she'd made of Things Harriet Knight Wouldn't Normally Do.

It was an embarrassingly long list, compiled one lonely October night when she'd realized that the reason she was sitting in the apartment on her own, talking to the animals she fostered, was because she lived her life safely cocooned inside her comfort zone. At this rate she was going to die alone, surrounded by a hundred dogs and cats.

Here lies Harriet, who knew a lot about hairballs, but not a whole lot about the other kind.

A life of sin would have been more exciting, but she'd picked up the wrong rule book when she was born. As a child she'd learned how to hide. How to make herself small, if not exactly invisible. Ever since then she'd trodden the safest path, and she'd done it while wearing sensible shoes. Plenty of people, including her twin sister and her brother, would say she had good reason for that. Whatever reasons lay in her past, she lived a small life and she was uncomfortably aware that she kept it that way through choice.

The *F* word loomed big in her world.

Not the curse. She wasn't the sort of person who cursed. For her, the *F* word was *Fear*.

Fear of humiliation, fear of failing, fear of what other people thought of her and all those fears originated from fear of her father.

She was tired of the *F* word.

She didn't want to live life alone, which was why she'd decided that for Christmas she was giving herself a new gift.

Courage.

She didn't want to look back on her life in fifty years time and wonder about the things she might have done had she been braver. She didn't want to feel regret. During a happy Thanksgiving spent with Daniel and his soon-to-be wife, Molly, she'd distilled her fear list to a challenge a day.

Challenge Harriet.

She was going on a quest to find the confidence that eluded her and if she couldn't find it then she'd fake it.

For the month between Thanksgiving and Christmas, she would do one thing every day that scared her, or at least made her uncomfortable. It had to be something that made her think *I don't want to do that*.

For one month, she would make a point of doing the opposite of what she would usually do.

A month of putting herself through her own kind of hell.

She was going to emerge from the challenge a new,

improved version of herself. Stronger. Bolder. More confident. More…everything.

Which was why she was now hanging out of a bathroom window being supported by her new best friend, Natalie. Luckily for her, the restaurant wasn't on the roof terrace.

"Take your shoes off," Natalie advised. "I'll drop them down to you."

"They'll impale me or knock me unconscious. It might be safer to keep them on my feet, Natalie." There were days when she questioned the benefits of being sensible, but right now she wasn't sure if it stopped her having fun or if it kept her alive.

"Call me Nat. If I'm helping you escape, we might as well drop the formalities. And you can't keep those shoes on your feet. You'll injure yourself when you land. And give me your purse."

Harriet clung to it. This was New York City. She would no more hand her purse to a stranger than she would walk naked through Central Park. It went against every instinct she had. She was the type of person who looked twice before she crossed the road, who checked the lock on her door before she went to sleep. She wasn't a risk taker.

Which was exactly why she should do it.

Forcing down the side of her that wanted to clutch the purse to her chest and never let it go, she thrust it at Nat. "Take it. And drop it down to me." She eased one leg out of the window, ignoring the voice of anxiety that rang loud in her head. *What if she didn't? What if she ran off with it? Used all her credit cards? Stole her identity?*

If Nat wanted to steal her identity, she was welcome to it. She was more than ready to be someone else. Particularly after the evening she'd just had.

Being herself wasn't working out so well.

Through the open window she could hear the roar of traffic, the cacophony of horns, the squealing of brakes, the background rumble that was New York City. Harriet had lived here all her life. She knew virtually every street and every building. Manhattan was as familiar to her as her own living room, if considerably larger.

Nat took her shoes from her. "Try not to rip your coat. Great coat, by the way. Love the color, Harriet."

"The coat is new. I bought it especially for this date because I had high hopes. Which proves that an optimistic nature can be a disadvantage."

"I think it's lovely to be optimistic. Optimists are like fairy lights. They brighten everything around them. Are you really a twin? That's very cool."

Today's challenge had been *Don't be reserved with strangers*. She was fine when she got to know someone, but often she didn't even make it past those first excruciatingly awkward stages. She was determined to change that.

Given that she and Natalie had met precisely thirty minutes earlier when she'd served her a delicious-looking shrimp salad, she was satisfied she'd made at least some progress. She hadn't clammed up or responded in monosyllables as she frequently did with people she didn't know. Most important of all she hadn't stammered, which she took as evidence that she'd finally learned to control the speech fluency issues that had blighted her life until her twenties. It had been years since she'd stumbled her way through a sentence, and even stressful situations didn't seem to trigger it, so there was no excuse for being so cautious with strangers.

All in all, a good result. And part of that was down to the support of her sister.

"It is cool being a twin. Very cool."

Nat gave a wistful sigh. "She's your best friend, right? You share everything? Confidences. Shoes…"

"Most things." The truth was that, until recently, she'd been the one to do most of the sharing. Fliss found it hard to open up, even to Harriet, but lately she'd been trying hard to change.

And Harriet was trying to change, too. She'd told her twin she didn't need protecting, and now she had to prove it to herself.

Being a twin had many advantages, but one of the disadvantages was that it made you lazy. Or maybe *complacent* would be a better word. She'd never had to worry too much about navigating the stormy waters of the friendship pool because her best friend had always been right there by her side. Whatever life had thrown at them, and it had thrown plenty, she and Fliss had been a unit. Other people had good friendships but nothing, *nothing*, came close to the wonder of having a twin.

When it came to sisters, she'd won the lottery.

Nat tucked Harriet's purse under her arm. "So you share an apartment?"

"We did. Not anymore." Harriet wondered how it was some people could talk and talk without stopping. How long before the man sitting inside the restaurant came looking for her? "She's living in the Hamptons now." Not a million miles away, but it might as well have been a million miles. "She fell in love."

"Great for her, I guess, but you must miss her like crazy."

That was an understatement.

The impact on Harriet had been huge, and her emotions were conflicted. She was thrilled to see her twin so happy but, for the first time in her life, she was now living alone. Waking up alone. Doing everything alone.

At first it had felt strange and a little scary, like the first time you rode a bike without training wheels. It also made her feel a little vulnerable, like going out for a walk in a blizzard and realizing you'd left your coat behind.

But this was now the reality of her life.

She woke in the mornings to silence instead of Fliss's off-key singing. She missed her sister's energy, her fierce loyalty, her dependability. She even missed tripping over her shoes, which had been habitually strewn across the floor.

Most of all she missed the easy camaraderie of being with someone who knew you. Someone you trusted implicitly.

A lump formed in her throat. "I should go before he comes looking for me. I cannot believe I'm climbing out of a window to get away from a man I only met thirty minutes ago. This is not the kind of thing I do."

Neither was online dating, which was why she'd forced herself to try it.

This was her third date, and the other two had been almost as bad.

The first man had reminded her of her father. He'd been loud, opinionated and in love with the sound of his own voice. Overwhelmed, Harriet had retreated into herself, but in this instance it hadn't mattered because it had been clear he had no interest in her opinions. The second man had taken her to an expensive restaurant and then disappeared after dessert, leaving her with a check big enough to ensure she would always remember him, and as for the third—well, he was currently sitting at the table in the window, waiting for her to return from the bathroom so they could fall in love and live happily ever after. And in his case "ever after" wasn't likely to be long because despite his claim that he was in his prime, it was clear he was already long past retirement age.

She would have called time on the date and walked out of the front door if she hadn't had a feeling he would follow her. Something about him made her feel uneasy. And anyway, climbing out of the window of a ladies' room was definitely something she would never do.

In terms of Challenge Harriet, it had been a successful evening.

In terms of romance, not so much.

Right now, dying surrounded by dogs and cats was looking like the better option.

"Go." Nat opened the window wider and her expression brightened. "It's snowing! We're going to have a white Christmas."

Snowing?

Harriet stared at the lazy swirl of snowflakes. "It's not Christmas for another month."

"But it's going to be a white Christmas. I feel it. There is nowhere more magical than New York in the snow. I love the holidays, don't you?"

Harriet opened her mouth and closed it again. Normally her answer would have been yes. She adored the holidays and the emphasis on family, even if hers was restricted to siblings. But this year she'd decided she was going to spend Christmas without them. And that was going to be the biggest challenge of all. She had the best part of a month of practice to build up to the big one.

"I really should be going."

"You should. I don't want your body to be discovered frozen to the sidewalk. Go. And don't fall in the Dumpster."

"Falling into the Dumpster would be a step up from everything else that has happened this evening." Harriet glanced down. It wasn't far and anyway, how much further could she fall? She felt as if she'd already hit rock bottom. "Maybe I should go back and explain that he wasn't what I was expecting. Then I could walk out the front door and not risk walking home with a twisted ankle and food wrappers stuck to my new coat."

"No." Nat shook her head. "Don't even think about it. The guy is creepy. I've told you, you're the third woman he's brought here this week. And there's something not quite right about the way he looked at you. As if you were going to be dessert."

She'd thought the same thing.

Her instincts had been shrieking at her, but part of Challenge Harriet was learning to ignore her instincts.

"It seems rude."

"This is New York. You have to be street smart. I'm going to keep him distracted until you're a safe distance away." Nat glanced toward the door, as if she was afraid the man might burst in at any moment. "I couldn't believe it when he started calling you babycheeks. I have to ask this, but why did you agree to meet him? What was it about him that attracted you? You're the third gorgeous woman he's brought here this week. Does he have some special quality? What made you agree to choose him?"

"I didn't choose him. I chose the guy in his online dating profile. I suspect he may have reality issues." She thought back to the moment he'd sat down opposite her. He had so obviously *not* been the person in his profile that she'd smiled politely and told him she was waiting for someone.

Instead of apologizing and moving on, he'd sat down in the chair opposite her. "You must be Harriet? Dog lover, cake lover. I love an affectionate woman who knows her way round a kitchen. We're going to do just fine together."

That was the moment Harriet had known for sure she wasn't cut out for online dating.

Why, oh, why had she used her real name? Fliss would have made something up. Probably something outrageous.

Nat looked fascinated. "What did his dating profile say?"

"That he was in his thirties." She thought of the thick shock of white hair and the wrinkled brow. The yellowed teeth and the graying fuzz on his jaw. But the worst thing had been the way he'd leered at her.

"Thirty? He must be at least twice that. Or maybe he's like a dog where each year is seven years. That would make him—" she wrinkled her nose "—two hundred and ten in human years. Jeez, that's old."

"He was sixty-eight," Harriet said. "He told me he feels thirty inside. And his profile said that he works in investment, but when I questioned that he confessed that he's investing his pension."

Nat doubled over laughing, and Harriet shook her head.

She felt weary. And stupid.

"After three dates, I've lost my sense of humor. That's it. I'm done."

All she wanted was fun and a little human company. Was that too much to ask?

"You decided to give love a chance. Nothing wrong

with that. But someone like you shouldn't struggle to meet people. What's your job? Don't you meet anyone through work?"

"I'm a dog walker. I spend my day with handsome, four-legged animals. They are always who you think they are. Although having said that I do walk a terrier who thinks he's a Rottweiler. That does create some issues."

Maybe she should stick with dogs.

She'd proved to herself that she could do the whole online dating thing if she had to. She'd ticked it off her list. It was victory of a sort.

Nat opened the window wider. "Report him to the dating site so he doesn't put any more unsuspecting women in the position of having to jump out of the window. And look on the bright side. At least he didn't scam you out of your life savings." She checked the street. "You're clear."

"Nice meeting you, Nat." Harriet thrust a large note in her hand. Far more than she could afford, but she considered it money well spent. "Great service."

Natalie pushed the note back into Harriet's hand. "If a woman can't help another woman in trouble, where would we be? Come back soon."

Harriet felt a tug deep inside.

Friendship. That was perhaps the only *F* word she liked.

Feeling a flash of regret that she would never be going anywhere near this restaurant ever again because she genuinely liked Natalie, Harriet held her breath and dropped onto the sidewalk.

She felt her ankle twist and a sharp, agonizing pain shot up her leg.

"You okay?" Nat dropped her shoes and her purse and Harriet winced as they thudded into her lap. It seemed that the only thing she was taking away from this date was bruises.

"Never better."

Victory, she thought, was both painful and undignified.

The window above her closed and Harriet was immediately aware of two things. First, that putting weight on her ankle was agony. Second, that unless she wanted to hobble home in bare feet, she was going to have to put on the stilettos she'd borrowed from the pile of shoes Fliss had left behind.

Gingerly, she slid the shoe onto her foot and sucked in a breath as pain shot through her ankle.

For the first time in her life she used the *F* word to express something other than fear.

Another box ticked in project Challenge Harriet.

CHAPTER TWO

ACROSS TOWN IN the trauma suite of one of New York's most prestigious hospitals, Dr. Ethan Black and the rest of the trauma team smoothly and efficiently cut away the ripped, bloodied clothing of the unconscious man to expose the damage beneath. And the damage was plenty. Enough to test the skills of the team and ensure that the man on the trolley remember this night for the rest of his life.

As far as Ethan was concerned, motorcycles were one of the world's worst inventions. Certainly the worst mode of transport. Many of the patients brought in following motorcycle injuries were male, and a high proportion had multiple injuries. This man was no exception. He'd been wearing a helmet, but that hadn't prevented him from sustaining what looked like a severe head injury.

"Intubate him and get a line in—" He assessed the damage as he worked, issuing instructions.

The team was gathered round the trolley, finding coherence in something that to an outsider would have seemed like chaos. Each person had a role, and each person was clear about what that role was. Of all the places in the hospital it was here, in the emergency department, that the teamwork was the strongest.

"He lost control and hit an oncoming car.'

Screaming came from the corridor outside, followed

by a torrent of abuse delivered at a high enough pitch to shatter windows.

One of the residents winced. Ethan didn't react. There were days when he wondered if he'd actually become desensitized to other people's responses to crisis. Working in the emergency room brought you into contact with the most extreme of human emotions and distorted your view of both humanity and reality. His normal would be someone else's horror movie. He'd learned early in his career not to talk about his day in a social situation unless the people present were all medical. These days he was too busy to find himself in too many social situations. Between his clinical responsibilities as attending physician in the emergency room and his research interests, his day was full. The price he'd paid for that was an apartment he rarely saw and an ex-wife.

"Is someone caring for the woman on the end of that scream?"

"She's not the patient. She just saw her boyfriend knifed. He's in Trauma 2 with multiple facial lacerations."

"Someone show her to the waiting room. Calm her down." Ethan took a closer look at the man's leg, assessing the damage. "Whatever it takes to stop the screaming."

"We don't know how serious the injuries are."

"All the more reason to project calm. Reassure her that her boyfriend is in good hands and getting the best treatment."

It was a typical Saturday night. Maybe he should have trained as an ob-gyn, Ethan thought as he continued to assess the patient. Then he would have been there for the high point of people's lives instead of the low. He would have facilitated birth, instead of fighting to prevent death. He could have celebrated with patients. Instead his Saturday night was invariably spent surrounded by people at crisis point. The victims of traffic accidents, gunshot victims, stabbings, drug addicts looking for a fix—the list was endless and varied.

And the truth was he loved it.

He loved variety and challenge. As a Level 1 Trauma Unit, they had both in copious amounts.

They stabilized the patient sufficiently to send him for a CT scan. Ethan knew that until they had the results of that scan, they wouldn't be able to assess the extent of his head injury.

He also knew that it was difficult to predict what the scan would show. He'd had patients with minimal visible damage who turned out to have massive internal bleeding and others, like this man as it later turned out, who had a surprisingly minor internal bleed.

He paged the neurosurgeons and spoke to the man's girlfriend who had arrived in a panic, wearing a coat over her pajamas and terror in her eyes. In the emergency department everything was concentrated and intense, including emotions. He'd seen big guys who prided themselves on being tough break down and sob like a child. He'd seen people pray when they didn't believe in God.

He'd seen it all.

"Is he going to die?"

He handled the same question several times a day, and he was rarely in a position to give a definitive answer. "He is in good hands. We'll be able to give you more information when we see the results of the scan." He was kind and calm, reassuring her that whatever could be done was being done. He knew how important it was to know that the person you loved was receiving the very best care, so he took time to explain what was happening and to suggest she call someone to come and be with her.

When the man was finally handed over to the neurosurgical team, Ethan ripped off his gloves and washed his hands. He probably wouldn't see the patient again. The man was gone from his life, and he'd probably never know about the part Ethan had played in keeping him alive.

Later, he might check on his progress but more often than not he was too busy focusing on the next priority to come through the door to think about those who'd come and gone.

Susan, his colleague, nudged him out of the way and stripped off her gloves, too. "That was exciting. Are you ever tempted to take a job in primary care? You could live in a cute small town where you're caring for three generations of the same family. Grandma, grandpa, parents and a big bunch of grandkids. You'd spend your day telling them to give up smoking and lose weight. Probably never see a drop of blood."

"It was what my father did." And Ethan had never wanted that. His choices were the focus of lively argument whenever he was home. His grandfather kept telling him he was missing out by not following a family through from birth to death. Him arguing that he was the one who kept them alive so that they could go back to their families.

"All these months we've worked together and I never knew that about you." Susan scrubbed her hands. "So you come from two generations of doctors?"

They'd worked together for over a year but almost all their conversation had been about the present. The ER was like that. You lived in the moment in every sense.

"Three generations. My father and grandfather both worked in primary care. They had a practice in upstate New York." He'd sat, five years old, in the waiting room watching as a steady stream of people trooped through the door to speak to his dad. There had been times when he'd wondered if the only way to see his father was to get sick.

"Jeez, Black, I had no idea. So it's in the DNA." Susan yanked paper towel from the dispenser so vigorously she almost removed it from the wall. "Well, that explains it."

"That explains what?"

"Why you always act like you have something to prove."

Ethan frowned. Was that true? No. It certainly wasn't true. "I don't have anything to prove."

"You've got a lot to live up to." She gave him a sympathetic look. "Why didn't you join them? Doctors Black, Black and Black. That's one hell of a lot of Black right there. Don't tell me, you just love the warm fuzzy feelings that come from working in the emergency room." Through the door they heard the woman yell *fuck you* and exchanged a wry smile. "All those cute patients enveloping you with endless love and gratitude—"

"Gratitude? Wait—I think that did happen to me once a couple of years ago. Give me a moment while I cast my mind back."

He didn't feel as if he had to live up to anything.

Susan was wrong about that. He walked his own path, for his own reasons.

"You must have been hallucinating. Lack of sleep does that for you. So if the rare dose of gratitude isn't what does it for you, it must be the patients who curse you, throw up on your boots and tell you you're the worst doctor that ever graced God's earth and that they're going to sue the hell out of you. That works for you?"

The humor got them through days that were fraught with tension.

It sustained them through the darker shifts, through witnessing trauma that would leave the average man on the street in need of therapy.

Everyone in the trauma team found their own way of dealing with it.

They knew, as most people didn't, that a life could change in an instant. That there was no such thing as a secure future.

"I love that side of it. And then there's the constant buzz of working with adoring, respectful colleagues like you."

"You want adoring? Pick a different woman."

"I wish I could."

Susan patted his arm. "In fact I do adore you. Not because you're cute and built, although you are, but because you know what you're doing, and around here competence is as close as it gets to an aphrodisiac. And maybe that's driven by a desire to be better than your daddy or your granddaddy, but I love it all the same."

He shot her an incredulous look. "Are you hitting on me?"

"Hey, I want to be with a man who is good with his hands and who knows what he's doing. What's wrong with that?" Her eyes twinkled and he knew she was winding him up.

"We are still talking about work?"

"Sure. What else? I'm married to my job, same as

you. I promised myself to the ER in sickness and in health, for richer and for poorer and I can tell you that living in New York City, the emphasis is definitely on poorer. But don't worry—I wouldn't be able to stay awake long enough to have sex with you. When I leave this place I fall unconscious the moment I arrive home and I'm not waking up for anyone. Not even you, blue eyes. So if you're not here for the love and positive feedback, it has to be because you're an adrenaline junkie."

"Maybe I am." It was true that he enjoyed the fast pace, the unpredictability, the adrenaline rush that came with not knowing what would come through the doors next. Emergency medicine was often like a puzzle and he enjoyed the intellectual stimulation of figuring out where the pieces fit and what the picture was. He also enjoyed helping people, although these days the doctor-patient relationship had changed. Now it was all patient satisfaction scores and other metrics that appeared to have little to do with practicing good medicine. There were days when it was hard to stay in touch with the reasons he'd wanted to be a doctor in the first place.

Susan stuffed the towel into the bin. "Know what I love most? When someone comes in all bandaged up and you never know what you're going to find when you unwrap it. Man, I love the suspense. Will it be a cut the size of a pinhead or will the finger fall off?"

"You're ghoulish, Parker."

"I am. Are you telling me you don't like that part?"

"I like fixing people." He glanced up as one of the interns walked into the room. "Problems?"

"Where do you want me to start? There are around sixty of them currently waiting, most of them drunk.

We have a guy who fell off the table during his office party and hurt his back."

Ethan frowned. "It's not even December."

"They celebrate early. I don't think he needs an MRI but he's consulted Dr. Search Engine and is insisting on having one and if I don't arrange it he is going to sue me for every cent I'm worth. Do you think it would put him off if I tell him the size of my college loans?"

Susan waved a hand. "Ethan will handle it. He's great at steering people toward the right decision. And if that doesn't work he's good at playing bad cop."

Ethan raised an eyebrow. "Bad cop? Seriously?"

"Hey, it's a compliment. Not many patients get one past you."

Backache, headache, toothache—all commonly appeared in the department, along with demands for prescription pain meds. Most of the experienced staff could sense when they were being played, but for less experienced staff it was a constant challenge to maintain the right balance between compassion and suspicion.

Still pondering the "bad cop" label, Ethan walked to the door, but his progress toward the patient was interrupted by the arrival of another patient, this time a forty-year-old man who had suffered chest pains at work and a cardiac arrest in the ambulance. As a result, it was another thirty minutes before Ethan made it to the man with the back injury, by which time the atmosphere in the room was hostile.

"Finally!" The man stank of alcohol. "I've been waiting ages to see someone."

Alcohol and fear. They saw plenty of both in the emergency department. It was a toxic mix.

Ethan checked the records. "It says here that you

were seen within ten minutes of arriving in the department, Mr. Rice."

"By a nurse. That doesn't count. And then by an intern, and he knew less than I do."

"The nurse who saw you is experienced."

"You're the one in charge so it's you I want, but you took your sweet time."

"We had an emergency, Mr. Rice."

"You're saying I'm not an emergency? I was here first! What makes him more important than me?"

The fact that he'd been clinically dead on arrival?

"How can I help you, Mr. Rice?" He kept it calm, always calm, knowing that in an already tense environment a situation could escalate with supersonic speed. The one thing they didn't need in the department was a bigger dose of tension.

"I want a fucking MRI," the man slurred. "And I want it now, not in ten years' time. Do it, or I'll sue you."

It was an all too familiar scenario. Patients who had looked up their symptoms on the internet and were convinced they knew not only the diagnosis but every investigation that should be performed. There was nothing worse than an amateur who thought he was an expert.

And the threats and the abuse were just two of the reasons emergency department staff had a high burnout rate. You had to learn to handle it, or it would wear you down like the ocean wore away at rocks until they crumbled.

In the crazy period between Thanksgiving and Christmas, it was only going to get worse.

Anyone who thought it was the season of goodwill should have spent a day working with Ethan. His head was throbbing.

If he'd been one of his patients, he would have demanded a CAT scan.

"Dr. Black?" One of the residents hovered in the doorway, and Ethan gave him a quick nod, indicating he'd be there as soon as he could.

As attending physician, everyone looked to him for answers. Residents, interns, ancillary staff, nurses, pharmacists, patients. He was expected to know it all.

Right now all he knew was that he wanted to get home. It had been a long, miserable shift and that didn't seem likely to change anytime soon.

He examined the man thoroughly and explained calmly and clearly why an MRI wasn't necessary.

That went down as well as he'd thought it would.

Some doctors ran the tests because at least then the patient left happy. Ethan refused to do that.

As he listened to a tirade describing him as inhuman, incompetent and a disgrace to the medical profession, he switched off. Switching off his emotions was the easy part for him now. Switching it back on again—well, that was more of a challenge, a fact borne out by his disastrous relationship record.

He let the abuse flow over him, but didn't budge in his decision. He'd decided a long time before that he wasn't going to let his decision making be ruled by bullying or patient satisfaction scores. He did what was best for his patients, and that didn't include subjecting them to unnecessary testing or drugs that would have no impact or, worse, a negative impact on their condition.

"Dr. Black?" Tony Roberts, one of the most senior pediatricians in the hospital was standing in the doorway. "I need your help urgently."

Ethan issued instructions to the resident caring for the patient and excused himself.

"What's the problem, Tony? You have an emergency?"

"I do." Tony looked serious. "Tell me, do you believe in Santa Claus?"

"Excuse me?" Ethan gave him an incredulous look and then laughed. "If Santa existed, he'd probably threaten me for pointing out that not only should he lose a few pounds for the good of his health, but that if he intends to ride in a horse-drawn vehicle at an altitude in excess of thirty thousand feet he should probably be wearing a safety helmet. Or at least leathers."

"Santa in leather? Mmm, me likey," Susan murmured as she passed on her way to speak to the triage nurse.

Tony grinned. "Just the cynical answer I expected from you, Black, which is why I'm here. I am going to give you an opportunity you never thought would come your way."

"A year's sabbatical in Hawaii on full pay?"

"Better. I'm going to change your life." Tony slapped him on the shoulder, and Ethan wondered if he should point out that after a shift in the ER it wouldn't take much to knock him flat.

"If I don't get to the next patient fast, my life will be changed. I'll be fighting a lawsuit. Can we make this quick, Tony?"

"You know Santa visits the children's ward every Christmas?"

"I didn't, but I do now. That's great. I'm sure the kids love it." It was a world far removed from the one he inhabited.

"They do. Santa is—" Tony glanced around and lowered his voice. "Santa is actually Rob Baxter, one of the pediatricians."

"No kidding. And I thought he was real." Ethan signed a request that an intern thrust under his nose. "That's the last of my illusions shattered. You have broken my heart. I might have to go home and lie down."

"Forget it." Susan was passing again, this time in the other direction. "No one lies down in this place. Unless they're dead. When you're dead, you get to lie down and only after we've tried to resuscitate you."

Tony watched her go. "Is she always like this?"

"Yes. Comedy is all part of the service. Laughter cures all ills, hadn't you heard? What did you want, Tony? I thought you said it was an emergency."

"It is. Rob Baxter ruptured his Achilles running in Central Park. He's going to be off his feet until after Christmas. This is close to a crisis for the pediatric department, but even more of a crisis because he is Santa and we don't have a backup."

"Why are you telling me this? You want me to take a look at his Achilles? Ask Viola. She's a brilliant surgeon."

"I don't need a surgeon. I need a backup Santa."

Ethan looked at him blankly. "I don't know any Santas."

"Santas are made, not born." Tony lowered his voice. "We want you to be Santa this year. Will you do it?"

"Me?" Ethan wondered if he'd misheard. "I'm not a pediatrician."

Tony leaned closer. "You may not know this, but Santa doesn't actually have to operate or make any clinical decisions. He smiles and hands out presents."

"Sounds like my average working day," Ethan said, "only here they want you to hand out MRIs and prescription pain meds. Gift wrapped Vicodin is this year's must-have."

"You are cynical and jaded."

"I'm a realist, which is precisely why I'm not qualified to deal with wide-eyed children who still believe in Santa."

"Which is exactly why you should do it. It will remind you of all the reasons you went into medicine in the first place. Your heart will melt, Dr. Scrooge."

"He doesn't have a heart," Susan muttered, eavesdropping shamelessly.

Ethan glanced at her in exasperation. "Don't you have patients to see? Lives to save?"

"Just hanging around to hear your answer, boss. If you're going from Scrooge to Santa, I need to know about it. In fact, I want to be there to watch. I'd work Christmas just to see it."

"You're already working Christmas. And I'm not qualified to be Santa. Why would you think I'd agree to this?"

Tony looked at him thoughtfully. "You get to make a child's day. It doesn't get any better than that. Think about it. I'll call you in a week or so. It's an easy and rewarding job." He strode out of the department, leaving Ethan staring after him.

"Dr. Scrooge," Susan said. "How cute is that?"

"Not cute at all." Surely Tony couldn't be serious? He was the last person in the world who should play Santa with wide-eyed believing children.

He noticed one of the interns hovering. "Problems?"

"Young woman with an ankle injury. Badly swollen and bruised. I'm not sure whether to x-ray or not. Dr. Marshall is busy or I would have asked him."

"Is she on the hunt for Vicodin?"

"I think she's genuine."

Because Ethan knew the young doctor didn't have the experience to know if someone was genuine or not, he followed him through the department. Vicodin was an effective painkiller. It was also a commonly used recreational drug, and he'd ceased to be surprised at the lengths some people would go to get a prescription. He didn't want anyone dispensing strong painkillers to someone who was simply hoping to get high from Vicodin.

His first thought when he saw her was that she was out of place among the rainbow of humanity that decorated the halls of the emergency room on a Saturday night. Her hair was long, and the color of creamy buttermilk. Her features were delicate and her mouth was a curve of glossy pink. She was wearing one shoe with a heel so high it could have doubled as a weapon. The other she held in her hand.

Her ankle was already turning blue.

How did women expect to wear heels like that and not damage themselves? That shoe was an accident waiting to happen. And although she seemed normal enough, he knew better than to let appearances dull his radar for trouble. A few years before, a student had presented with toothache, which had turned out to be a way to get pain meds. She'd overdosed a few days later and been brought in to the emergency department.

Ethan had been present for her second visit, although not her first. It was a lesson he'd never forgotten.

"Miss Knight? I'm Dr. Black. Can you tell me what happened?"

It must have been a great party, he thought as he examined the ankle.

"I twisted it. I'm sorry to bother you when you're so busy." She sounded more than a little embarrassed, which made a change from the two patients he'd seen immediately before her who had taken his care as their God-given right.

He wondered what she was doing here on her own on a Saturday night. She was all dressed up, so he doubted she'd spent the evening on her own.

He guessed she was mid- to late-twenties. Thirty possibly, although she had one of those faces that was difficult to put an age to. With makeup she could look a little older. Without, she could pass as a college student. Her eyes were blue and her gaze warm and friendly, which made a refreshing change.

Generally speaking, he didn't see a lot of warm and friendly during his working day.

"How did you twist it?' Understanding the mechanism of the injury was one of the most helpful ways of piecing together a picture of the injury. "Dancing?'

"No. Not dancing. I wasn't wearing shoes when I twisted it.'

He watched in fascination as her cheeks reddened.

It had been a while since he'd seen anyone blush.

"So how did you do it?" Realizing she might think he was after details for his own entertainment, he clarified, "The more details you give me, the easier it is for me to assess the injury."

"I jumped out of a window. It wasn't far to the ground but I landed awkwardly and my ankle turned."

She'd jumped out of a window?

"You're a bit of a risk taker?"

She gave a wry smile. "My idea of risk is reading

my Kindle in the bath so no, I don't think I'd describe myself as a risk taker."

Ethan's senses were back on alert. Instead of thinking possible addict, or potential adrenaline junkie, he was thinking possible abuse victim. "So why did you jump out of a window?" He softened his voice, trying to convey with his voice and actions that he could be trusted.

"I needed to get away from someone." She must have seen something change in his expression because she shook her head quickly. "I can see what you're thinking, but I wasn't being threatened. It really was an accident."

"Jumping out of a window isn't usually an accident." Unless she was intoxicated, but he didn't smell alcohol and she seemed perfectly composed. More composed than most of the people around her. The ER on a Saturday night wasn't a pretty sight. "Why not leave by the front door?"

Her gaze slid from his. "It's a long story."

And one she obviously didn't intend to share.

Ethan thought through his options. They saw plenty of domestic abuse incidents in the ER, and they had a duty to offer a place of safety and whatever support was needed. But he'd also learned that not everyone wanted to be helped. That it was a process. "Miss Knight—"

"Seriously, you don't need to worry. I was on a date, if you must know, and it wasn't going well. My mistake."

"You jumped out of the window to get away from your date?"

She stared at a point beyond his shoulder. "He wasn't exactly the way his profile described him."

"You'd never met him before?" And now he was thinking trafficking. And maybe he'd been wrong about her age and she was closer to twenty than thirty.

He checked the form and saw from her date of birth that his first guess had been the correct one. She was twenty-nine.

"I hadn't met him before. It was online dating if you must know, and it didn't go quite how I thought it would. Oh, this is so embarrassing." She rubbed her fingers over her forehead. "He lied on his profile, and I didn't even realize people did that. Which makes me stupid, I know. And naive. And yes, maybe it also makes me a risk taker, even if I'm an unintentional risk taker. And I'm horribly bad at it."

He was still focused on her first words. "Lied?"

"He used a photo from thirty years ago and claimed to be all kinds of things he wasn't." She squared her shoulders. "I found him a little creepy. I had a bad feeling about the whole thing so I decided to make an exit where he couldn't see me. I didn't want him to follow me home. You don't need to hear this, do you?" She leaned down to rub her ankle and her hair slid forward, obscuring her features.

For a moment he stared at it, that curtain of shiny gold.

He breathed in a waft of her perfume. Floral. Subtle. So subtle he wondered if what he was smelling was her shampoo.

He never became emotionally involved with his patients. These days he didn't become emotionally involved in anything much, but for some reason he felt a spurt of anger toward the nameless guy who had lied to this woman.

"Why the window?" He dragged his gaze from her hair and focused on her ankle, examining it carefully.

"Why not go out through the front door? Or even the kitchen or the rear entrance?"

"The kitchen was in sight of our table. I was worried he'd follow me. And to be honest I wasn't thinking about much except getting away. Pathetic, I know. Is it broken?"

"It doesn't seem to be." Ethan straightened. The injury was real enough. Her hurt was real enough, and he suspected it extended a whole lot further than a bruised ankle. "I don't think you need an X-ray, but if it gets worse you should come back or contact your primary care provider."

He waited for her to argue with him about the need for an X-ray, but she simply nodded.

"Good. Thank you."

It was such an unusual response he almost repeated himself to check she'd heard him correctly. "I don't think an X-ray is necessary."

"I understand. I probably shouldn't have wasted your time, but I didn't want to make it worse by doing something I shouldn't. I'm grateful to you, and I'm relieved it isn't broken."

She was accepting his professional judgment just like that?

No arguing? No cursing? No questioning him or threatening to sue him?

"You can use whatever pain meds you have in your cabinet at home."

This was the point where a large proportion of his patients demanded something only available on prescription.

Or maybe he really was turning into a cynic.

Maybe he needed a vacation.

He had one coming, the week before Christmas. A week in a luxury cabin in Vermont.

He met up every year with family and friends and this year he needed the break more than ever. He loved his job but the relentlessness and the pressure took its toll.

"I don't need pain meds. I wanted to check it isn't broken, that's all. I walk a lot in my job." She gave him a sweet smile that fused his brain.

In his time in the ER he'd dealt with panic, hysteria, abuse and shock. He was comfortable with all those emotional reactions. He even understood them.

He had no idea how to respond to a smile like hers.

She struggled to her feet, and he had to stop himself from reaching out to help her.

"What's your job?" The question had clinical relevance. Nothing to do with the fact that he wanted to know more about her.

"I run a dog-walking business. I need to be able to get around and I don't want to make it worse."

A dog-walking business.

He looked at the freckles that dusted her nose.

He could imagine her walking dogs. And believing in Santa.

"If dog walking is your livelihood, you might want to steer clear of stilettos in the future."

"Yes, it was a stupid idea. A whim. I've been trying to do things I don't normally do, and—" She broke off and shook her head. "You don't need to hear this. You're busy and I'm taking up your time. Thank you for everything."

This one patient had thanked him more in the past five minutes than he'd been thanked in the past five weeks from all his other patients combined.

Not only that, but she hadn't questioned his clinical judgment.

Ethan, who was never surprised by a patient, was surprised.

And intrigued.

He wanted to ask why she'd been trying to do things she wouldn't normally do. Why she'd chosen to wear stilettos. *Why she'd had dinner with a man she'd never met before.*

Instead, he kept it professional. He talked to her about rest, ice, compression and elevation, the whole time feeling guilty that he'd doubted her.

He wondered when, exactly, he'd started being so suspicious of human nature.

He definitely needed a vacation.

Turn your love of reading into rewards you'll love with
Harlequin My Rewards

**Join for FREE today at
www.HarlequinMyRewards.com**

Earn **FREE BOOKS** of your choice.

Experience **EXCLUSIVE OFFERS** and contests.

Enjoy **BOOK RECOMMENDATIONS**
selected just for you.

PLUS! Sign up now
and get **500** points
right away!

Earn
FREE
REWARDS
Join
Today!
HarlequinMyRewards.com

MYR16R

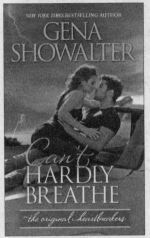

Get 2 Free Books,
Plus 2 Free Gifts –
just for trying the Reader Service!

STRS17R

Praise for Sarah Morgan's acclaimed series

From Manhattan with Love

"Snappy dialogue [and] well-developed characters mix with sweet romantic tension."
—*Publishers Weekly* on *Sleepless in Manhattan*

"Morgan's latest is a sensational chick-lit romance— a beautiful love letter to New York City."
—*RT Book Reviews* on *Sleepless in Manhattan* (Top Pick)

"Morgan's breezy dialogue will keep readers turning the red-hot pages and wishing they could sit down with this trio of women and the men who capture their hearts."
—*Booklist* on *Sleepless in Manhattan*

"Morgan's novel delivers the classic sweep-you-off-your-feet romantic experience."
—*Publishers Weekly* on *Sunset in Central Park*

"Morgan's magical series finale hooks readers from page one."
—*RT Book Reviews* on *Miracle on 5th Avenue* (Top Pick)

Puffin Island

"Morgan begins a new series with a sweet, sexy and emotionally layered story.... Touching, sensual and warmly inviting."
—*Kirkus Reviews* on *First Time in Forever*

"A delightful small-town romance, which is a little sweet and a lot sexy."
—*Booklist* on *First Time in Forever*

The O'Neil Brothers

"Uplifting, sexy and warm, Sarah Morgan's O'Neil Brothers series is perfection."
—Jill Shalvis, *New York Times* bestselling author

"This touching Christmas tale will draw tears of sorrow and joy, remaining a reader favorite for years to come."
—*Publishers Weekly* on *Sleigh Bells in the Snow* (starred review)

"Sharp humor, snappy dialogue, and memorable characters."
—*Library Journal* on *Maybe This Christmas*

**Also available from
Sarah Morgan
and HQN Books**

From Manhattan with Love

*Sleepless in Manhattan
Sunset in Central Park
Miracle on 5th Avenue
New York, Actually*

Puffin Island

*First Time in Forever
Some Kind of Wonderful
One Enchanted Moment*

The O'Neil Brothers

*Sleigh Bells in the Snow
Suddenly Last Summer
Maybe This Christmas*